FIVE GO TO DEMON'S ROCKS
FIVE HAVE A MYSTERY TO SOLVE
FIVE ARE TOGETHER AGAIN

Enid Blyton

The Famous Five

FIVE GO TO DEMON'S ROCKS
FIVE HAVE A MYSTERY TO SOLVE
FIVE ARE TOGETHER AGAIN

Hodder
Children's
Books

a division of Hodder Headline Limited

This collection published in 2005
by Hodder Children's Books
For sale in the Indian Sub-continent only.

Five Go To Demon's Rocks first published in Great Britain in 1961
Five Have A Mystery To Solve first published in Great Britain in 1963
Five Are Together Again first published in Great Britain in 1962

For further information on Enid Blyton please contact
www.blyton.com

4 6 8 10 9 7 5 3

A Catalogue record for this book is available from the
British Library.

ISBN 0 340 91088 7

Typeset by Hewer Text Ltd, Edinburgh
Printed and bound in India by
Gopsons Papers Ltd., Noida

Hodder Children's Books
a division of Hodder Headline Limited
338 Euston Road
London NW1 3BH

FIVE GO TO DEMON'S ROCKS

FIVE GO TO DEMON'S ROCKS

[1]

Three visitors arrive

'Fanny!' shouted Uncle Quentin, running up the stairs with a letter in his hand. 'FANNY! Where are you?'

'Here, dear, here, helping Joanna with the dusting,' said Aunt Fanny, appearing out of a bedroom. 'Don't shout like that. I'm not deaf, you know. What's the matter?'

'I've a letter here from that old friend of mine, Professor Hayling,' said Uncle Quentin. 'You remember him, don't you?'

'Do you mean the man who came here to stay a few years ago, and kept forgetting to come in for meals?' said Aunt Fanny, flicking some dust off her husband's coat.

'Fanny, don't flick at me like that,' said Uncle Quentin crossly. 'Anyone would think I was covered in dust. Listen – he's coming to stay *today* for a week – instead of next week.'

Aunt Fanny stared at her husband in horror. 'But he *can't* do that!' she said. 'George is coming home today – and her three cousins with her, to stay. You know that!'

'Oh – I'd forgotten,' said Uncle Quentin. 'Well, ring up and tell George to stay where she is – we can't have them while Professor Hayling is here. I shall want to be quite undisturbed – he and I have to confer about some new invention of his. Don't look like that, my dear – this may be very, very important.'

'Well, it's important to the Five that *their* plans shouldn't be spoilt,' said Aunt Fanny. 'After all, George only went to stay with Dick, Julian and Anne because you had some urgent papers to write, and you didn't want to be disturbed – and you *knew* today was the day they were due home. Quentin, you must ring up your professor friend and say he can't come.'

'Very well, my dear, very well,' said Uncle

Quentin. 'But he won't like it. He won't like it at all!' He went off to his study to use the telephone, and Aunt Fanny hurried up the stairs to get ready the rooms for the four cousins.

'Anne can sleep with George as usual,' she said to Joanna. 'And the two boys can sleep in the guest room.'

'It will be nice to have all the Five back again,' said Joanna, pushing the vacuum cleaner up and down the landing. 'I miss them – and you should see the cakes I made yesterday – two whole tins full!'

'You're too good to those children, Joanna,' said Aunt Fanny. 'No wonder they're so fond of you. Now, we'll – oh dear – there's my husband calling me again. All right, dear, I'm coming, I'm coming!'

She ran downstairs to the hall, and into the study. Uncle Quentin was standing there, holding the telephone receiver. 'What shall I do?' he almost shouted. 'Professor Hayling has left and is already on his way here. I can't stop him coming. And he's bringing his son with him, so there are two of them.'

'His *son*! Well, really!' said Aunt Fanny. 'There isn't room for them here, with the four cousins as well, Quentin. You know that.'

'Well, ring up George and tell *her* not to come back for a week, but to stay with her cousins,' said Uncle Quentin, crossly. 'There's no reason why they should ALL come here.'

'But, Quentin, you *know* perfectly well that George's aunt and uncle are shutting up the house today, and going on a cruise somewhere,' said Aunt Fanny. 'Oh dear, oh dear! Well, I'll ring up George, and try to stop them all coming!'

So once more the telephone was used, and Aunt Fanny tried anxiously to get in touch with George. For a long time nobody answered, and then at last a voice came. 'Hallo – who's there?'

'Mrs Kirrin here – may I speak to George, please?'

'Oh – I'm sorry – they've already left, on their bicycles,' said the voice. 'And the house is empty except for me. I'm a neighbour come in to lock everything up. I'm so sorry I can't get George for you.'

'Oh – thank you. Never mind!' said Aunt Fanny, and put back the receiver. She gave a heavy sigh. NOW what was to be done? Professor Hayling and his son were on their way to Kirrin Cottage – and so were the Five – and none of them could be stopped. What a household it would be!

'Quentin,' she said, going into the study where her husband was tidying up enormous piles of papers. 'Quentin, listen – George and all the others are on their way here. And HOW I am going to put everyone up, I do not know. It looks as if somebody will have to sleep in Timmy's kennel, and I've a good mind to make a bed up for *you* in the coal-house!'

'I'm busy,' said Uncle Quentin, hardly listening. 'I've all these papers to get in order before

Professor Hayling comes. And by the way, my dear, will you PLEASE tell the children to be quiet while the professor is here – he's rather short-tempered, and—'

'Quentin, *I'm* beginning to feel rather short-tempered too,' said Aunt Fanny. 'And if—' She stopped very suddenly and gazed through the study window in horror. Then she pointed her finger at it. 'Look! What's that at the window?'

Her husband turned and stared in amazement. 'It looks like a *monkey*!' he said. 'Where on earth did it come from?'

A voice called down the stairs. It was Joanna. 'There's a car at the door – I think it's your visitors – a man and a boy!'

Aunt Fanny was still staring in astonishment at the monkey, who was now scratching at the windowpane, chattering in a funny little prattle. He pressed his nose to the glass, just like a child.

'DON'T tell me that your friend owns a monkey – and has brought *him* to stay too!' groaned poor Aunt Fanny. She jumped as a loud bang came from the front door, and went to open it.

Yes – there stood Professor Hayling, the man who had so often forgotten to come in for meals when he had stayed at Kirrin Cottage years before. And by him was a boy of about nine, with a face a little like that of the monkey now on his shoulder!

The professor strode in, calling to the taxi driver behind. 'Bring the luggage in please. Hallo, Mrs Kirrin – nice to see you again. Where's your husband? My word, I've some interesting news to tell him. Ah, Quentin, there you are! Got your papers all ready for me?'

'My dear old friend!' said Uncle Quentin, shaking hands warmly. 'Fine to see you! So glad you could come.'

'This is Tinker, my son,' said Professor Hayling, clapping the boy on the back, and almost knocking him over. 'I always forget what his real name is – we call him Tinker because he's always tinkering with cars – mad on them, you know! Shake hands, Tinker. Where's Mischief?'

Poor Aunt Fanny hadn't been able to get in a word. The professor was now in the hall, still talking. The monkey leapt off the boy's shoulder, and was on the hallstand, swinging on a hat-peg.

'Really, it's like a circus!' thought poor Aunt Fanny. 'And the rooms not prepared yet – and what about lunch? Oh my goodness – and all the cousins coming as well. What *is* that monkey doing now? Making faces at himself in the hall mirror!'

Somehow or other the visitors were pushed into the living room, and they sat down. Uncle Quentin was so anxious to discuss some mighty problems with the professor that he actually fetched a great sheaf of papers and immediately spread them over the table.

'*Not* in here, dear – in your study please,' said Aunt Fanny, firmly. 'Joanna! Will you help me take the bags up to the guest room? And we can make up a bed there on the couch for the little boy. There won't be room anywhere else.'

'What about the monkey?' asked Joanna, eyeing it warily. 'Is he to have a bed too?'

'He sleeps with me,' said Tinker, in an astonishingly loud voice, and suddenly leapt up the stairs, making a most extraordinary purring noise as he went. Aunt Fanny stared after him in amazement.

'Is he in pain, or something?' she said.

'No, no – he's just being a car,' said his father. 'I told you he was mad about cars. He can't help pretending to be one now and again.'

'I'm a car, a Jaguar car!' yelled Tinker, from the top of the stairs. 'Can't you hear my engine? R-R-R-R-R-R-R! Hey, Mischief, come and have a ride!'

The little monkey scampered up the stairs and leapt on to the boy's shoulder, chattering in its funny little voice. The Jaguar car then apparently made a tour of all the bedrooms, occasionally giving a very loud honk.

'Does your boy always behave like that?' asked Uncle Quentin, amazed. 'How do you manage to do any work?'

'Oh, I have a soundproof workroom in my garden,' said the professor. 'I hope your work-room is soundproof, too?'

'No, it isn't,' said poor Uncle Quentin, still hearing the 'car' upstairs. What a boy! How could anyone bear him for more than two minutes? And to think he had come to STAY!

He shut the study door after the professor – but no door could shut out the sound of the small boy honking upstairs!

Poor Aunt Fanny was eyeing all the luggage brought in. Why hadn't the professor gone to a hotel? What was life going to be like, with the Five here, and the professor, and a small boy who apparently thought he was some kind of car all the time. To say nothing of a monkey called Mischief! And WHERE were they all going to sleep?

[2]

A little excitement

George and her three cousins were already on their way back to Kirrin. They cycled along the lanes with Timmy, George's dog, loping easily beside them.

'Won't it be fun to be at Kirrin Cottage again!' said Anne. 'It's so lovely to look out of a window and see Kirrin Bay, blue as the sky! I vote we go over to the island for a picnic!'

'You'll like to have your own kennel again, won't you, Timmy?' said George, and Timmy gave her ankle a quick lick, and barked.

'It's always so peaceful at Kirrin Cottage,' said Dick. 'And your mother's so kind and jolly, George. I hope we shan't upset Uncle Quentin with our talk and fun.'

'I don't *think* Father has any very important

work on hand,' said George. 'Anyway, he'll only have you for a week – it's a pity that professor friend of his is coming in a week's time, or you could have stayed longer.'

'Well, a week is quite a nice long time,' said Julian. 'Hallo – there's our first glimpse of Kirrin Bay, look – as blue as ever!'

They were all glad to see the little blue bay, and to catch sight of Kirrin Island lying there peacefully in the sun. 'You're lucky, George, to have an island all of your own,' said Anne. 'One that is really and truly yours!'

'Yes, I *am* lucky!' said George. 'I was never so pleased in all my life as the day Mother gave it to me. It's belonged to our family for years, of course – and now it's mine! We'll go over there tomorrow!'

At last they came to the end of their journey. 'I can see the chimneys of Kirrin Cottage!' said Julian, standing up on the pedals of his bicycle. 'And the kitchen fire is going – I can see smoke. I hope dinner's cooking!'

'I can smell it!' said Dick, sniffing. 'I think it's sausages.'

'Idiot!' said the other three together, and laughed. They rode up to the back gate, and leapt off their bicycles. They put them into the shed, and George gave a shout!

'Mother! We're *home*! Where are you?'

She had hardly finished yelling when Anne suddenly clutched her arm.

'George – what's that? Look! Peeping out of the window there!'

They all looked – and George shouted in astonishment: 'It's a monkey! A MONKEY! No, Timmy. No – come back! TIMMY!'

But Timmy too had seen the quaint little face peering out of the window, and had shot off to investigate. Was it a small dog? Or a strange sort of cat? Anyway, whatever it was, he was going to chase it away! He barked at the top of his voice as he galloped indoors, and almost knocked over a small boy there. The monkey, terrified, at once leapt on to the picture-rail that ran round the room.

'You leave my monkey alone, you big bully you!' cried a furious voice; and through the open door George saw a small boy give Timmy a sharp smack. She raced indoors, and gave the small boy a smack as sharp as the one he had given Timmy! Then she glared at him angrily.

'What are you doing here? How DARE you hit my dog? It's a good thing he didn't eat you up. And what's that creature doing up there?'

The little monkey was terrified. It sat clinging to the picture-rail, trembling, making a piteous chattering noise. Julian came in just as Joanna arrived from upstairs.

'What's all this?' she said. 'You'll have your father racing out of his study in a minute, George. Stop barking at the little monkey, Timmy, for goodness' sake! And stop crying, Tinker, and take your monkey away before Timmy eats him.'

'I'm NOT crying,' said Tinker fiercely, rubbing his eyes. 'Come here, Mischief. I won't let that dog hurt you! I'll – I'll . . .'

'You take your monkey away,' said Julian gently, thinking that the small boy was very brave to imagine he could fight old Timmy. 'Run along.'

Tinker made a clicking sound and the monkey dropped at once on to his shoulder, and nuzzled there. It put its tiny arms round the boy's neck, and made a little choking noise.

'Oh – poor little mite – it's crying!' said Anne. 'I didn't know monkeys could cry. Timmy, don't frighten it again, please don't. You mustn't bully tiny things.'

'Timmy never bullies anything!' said George at once, frowning at Anne. 'But after all, what do you expect him to do when he comes home and finds a strange boy *and* a monkey here. Who are you, boy?'

'I shan't tell you,' said Tinker, and marched out of the room, the monkey still whimpering into his neck.

'Joanna – who on earth is he?' asked Dick. 'And what is he doing here?'

'I thought you wouldn't like it,' said Joanna. 'It's that professor friend of your father's, George – the one who was coming to stay next week. He telephoned this morning to say he was coming *this* week instead – and bringing his boy as well! He didn't say anything about a monkey, though!'

'Are they *staying* here?' said George, in horror. 'How *can* Mother let them – she *knew* we were all coming today! How *mean* of her, how—'

'Be quiet, George,' said Julian. 'Let Joanna go on.'

'Well, they arrived before anything could be done to stop them,' said Joanna. 'And now your father is shut up in his study with Professor Hayling – the boy's father – and your mother and I are at our wits' end to know where to put you all. The boy and his father – and I suppose the monkey too – are sharing the guest room.'

'But that's where Julian and Dick were going to sleep!' said George, losing her temper again. 'I'll go and tell Mother that boy can't stay, I'll—'

'Don't be silly, George,' said Julian. 'We'll manage somehow. We can't go back home because our house will be all shut up now.'

'You could sleep up in the loft,' said Joanna, sounding rather doubtful. 'But it's very dusty and terribly draughty. I could put a couple of mattresses up there for you.'

'All right,' said Julian. 'We'll make do up in the loft. Thanks, Joanna. Where's Aunt Fanny? Does she mind all this?'

'Well – she's a bit rushed,' said Joanna. 'But you know what your aunt is – always so kind, never thinks of herself. That Professor Hayling! Just walked into the house as if he owned it, bringing luggage and that most peculiar little boy – and a *monkey*! Though the monkey seems a nice enough little thing. It came and watched me wash up, and bless me if it didn't try to dry the plates for me!'

The kitchen door swung open and George's mother came in. 'Hallo, dears!' she said smiling. 'I thought I heard Timmy barking. Dear Timmy – wait till you see the monkey!'

'He's seen him already,' said George, scowling. 'Mother, how *could* you take people in when you knew we were coming home today?'

'That's enough, George,' said Julian, who saw how worried his aunt looked. 'Aunt Fanny, we won't be ANY trouble! We'll keep out of the house as much as we can, we'll do the shopping for you, we'll go across to Kirrin Island and keep out of your way, we'll . . .'

'You're kind, Julian,' said his aunt, and smiled at him. 'Things *will* be rather difficult – especially as Professor Hayling never can remember to come to meals on time, and you know what your uncle is! He could forget breakfast, dinner and supper for a whole year, and then wonder why he felt hungry!'

That made everyone laugh. Julian slipped his arm round his aunt and gave her a hug. 'We'll sleep in the loft,' he said, 'and enjoy it, too. We will help with the housework and we'll do any odd jobs too. You've no idea how fine I look with an apron round my waist, and a broom in my hand!'

Even George smiled at the idea of Julian wearing an apron. Then Timmy went suddenly to the half-open door and barked. He could smell that monkey again. He heard a high chattering noise, and pushed the door open at once. What! Was that monkey calling him rude names?

He saw the little creature sitting on the top of the rail at the foot of the stairs. It saw Timmy, and danced up and down, sounding as if it were laughing. Timmy raced to the rail and leapt up, barking fiercely.

The study door flew open and out marched not one angry professor, but two!

'WHAT'S ALL THIS NOISE? CAN'T WE HAVE A MOMENT'S PEACE?'

'Oh *dear*!' said Aunt Fanny, foreseeing this

kind of thing happening twenty times a day, now that Timmy and the others were here. She shushed the two angry men.

'Now, now – Timmy just isn't used to the monkey yet. Go back, please, and shut the door. I'll see you aren't disturbed again!'

'woof-woof!' shouted Timmy, using his very loudest bark, and Professor Hayling shot back into the study at top speed!

'Any more rudeness from Timmy and I'll have him sent away!' roared Uncle Quentin, and he too disappeared.

'well!' said George, her face red with anger. 'What does he mean by *that*, Mother? If Timmy goes, I go too! Oh, *look* at that monkey – he's sitting on top of the grandfather clock now! *He* ought to be sent away, horrid little mischievous thing – not old Timmy!'

[3]

Mischief, Tinker – and Timmy!

Julian and Dick set to work to take a couple of old mattresses up to the loft, and some rugs and a couple of cushions for pillows. It *was* rather draughty! But what else was to be done? It was still too cold to sleep outside in a tent.

George was very sulky. 'That scowl will *grow* on your face, George, if you aren't careful,' said Dick. 'Cheer up, for goodness' sake. It's worse for your mother than it is for any of us. She's going to be very busy this week.'

She certainly was! Meals for nine people, five of them very hungry children, were not easy to provide. Joanna did an enormous amount of cooking, the four children helped with the housework and cycled off to Kirrin village in the mornings to do the shopping.

'Why can't that boy Tinker help?' demanded George, on the second day they were at home. 'What on earth does he think he's doing now? Look at him out in the garden rushing all round, making a frightful noise. Tinker, shut up! You'll disturb your father and mine.'

'You shut up yourself!' called back Tinker, rudely. 'Can't you see I'm a Mercedes car, with a very powerful engine? And see how well it stops when I put on the brakes – no jerk at all! And hear the horn – marvellous!'

He gave a remarkably good imitation of a powerful car horn. At once the study window shot up and two very angry men shouted together:

'TINKER! What do you think you're doing, making that noise? You've been told to be QUIET!'

Tinker began to explain about the Mercedes, but as this didn't seem to satisfy either of the angry men, he offered to be a little Mini. 'You see, it goes like this,' said Tinker, beginning to move off, making a low purring noise, 'and it—'

But the window was slammed shut, so the little Mini drove itself into the kitchen, and said it was very hungry, could it have a bun?

'I don't feed cars,' said Joanna. 'I have no petrol. Go away.'

The Mini purred out of the kitchen on its two legs, and went to look for passengers. Mischief the monkey scampered up, and ran up Tinker's body to his shoulder.

'You're my passenger,' said Tinker, and Mischief held on to his hair as he drove all round the garden at top speed, honking every now and again, but very quietly indeed.

'He's a funny child,' said Joanna to Aunt Fanny, when she came into the kitchen. 'Not bad really – him and his cars! I've never seen a child so mad on them in my life! One of these days he'll turn into one!'

It began to rain next day and Tinker couldn't go out. He nearly drove everyone mad, rushing about all over the house hooting, and purring like a car engine.

'Now look,' Joanna said to him, when, for the twentieth time, he drove himself all round her kitchen. 'I don't care if you're a Mini, or a Ford Fiesta, or even a Rolls – you just keep out of my kitchen! It's a funny thing to think that a fine car like a Rolls can steal a bun out of my tin – it ought to be ashamed of itself!'

'Well, if I can't get petrol, I've got to get *something* to run on, haven't I?' demanded Tinker. 'Look at Mischief – *he's* helping himself to apples in the larder, but you don't say anything to him!'

'Oh, lands sakes, is that creature in the larder again?' cried poor Joanna, rushing across the kitchen. 'Who left it open, I'd like to know?'

'Timmy did,' said Tinker.

'You little liar!' said Joanna as she shooed Mischief out of the larder. 'Timmy would never do a thing like that. He's as honest as the day, not like that little thief of a monkey of yours!'

'Don't you like him?' said Tinker, sorrowfully. 'He likes *you*.'

Joanna glanced across at the tiny monkey. He sat huddled in a corner, his arms over his face, looking very small and sad. One small brown eye peeped out at Joanna.

'You're a humbug, you are!' said Joanna. 'Looking as if you're the unhappiest monkey in the world, when all the time you're thinking what mischief to do next. Here – come and get this biscuit, you rascal – and don't you dare to go near Timmy this morning. He's very very angry with you.'

'What did Mischief do to Timmy?' asked Tinker, surprised.

'He went to Timmy's dish and stole one of the bones there,' said Joanna. 'Timmy growled like a roll of thunder! I really thought he would bite off the monkey's tail. My word, you should have seen Mischief skedaddle!'

Mischief had now crept up cautiously to Joanna, eyeing the biscuit she held. He had had one or two slaps from her for stealing, and he was rather wary of her quick right hand.

'Here you are – take the biscuit, for goodness' sake,' said Joanna. 'And don't look such a little misery, or I might suddenly find myself giving you another biscuit. Hallo – where's he gone?'

The monkey had snatched the biscuit with one of his tiny paws, and had scampered away to the door. It was shut, so Tinker opened it for him. At once Timmy came in. He had been lying outside the door, sniffing the good smell of soup cooking on the stove.

Mischief leapt to the top of a chair back and made a strange little whinnying sound – rather apologetic and sad. Timmy stood still and pricked up his ears. He understood animal language very well!

Mischief still held the biscuit. He leapt down to the seat of the chair – and then, to Joanna's enormous surprise, he held out the biscuit to Timmy! He chattered in a very small voice, and Timmy listened gravely. Then the big dog took the biscuit gently, threw it into the air, chewed it once, and swallowed it!

'Well, did you ever see anything like *that* before!' said Joanna, marvelling. 'For all the world as if Mischief was apologising to Timmy for stealing his bone – and offering him his biscuit to make up! Well, whatever will George say when she hears!'

Timmy licked his lips to see if any biscuit crumbs were left, and then put his big head forward, and gave the monkey a sudden lick on the tip of his funny little nose.

'Timmy's saying thank you!' cried Tinker, in delight. 'Now they'll be friends – you see if they won't!'

Joanna was astonished and pleased. Well, well – to think of that monkey being clever enough to present Timmy with a biscuit that he very much wanted to eat himself! He wasn't a bad little thing! She went upstairs to find George and tell her.

But George didn't believe her. 'Timmy would never take a biscuit from that silly little monkey!' she said. 'Never! You made all that up, Joanna, just because you're getting fond of Mischief. You wait till he runs off with your toasting-fork again!'

All the same, George went down with Joanna, curious to see if the two animals *were* becoming friendly – and she saw a very strange sight indeed!

Mischief was on Timmy's back, and Timmy was solemnly trotting round the kitchen, giving him a ride! The monkey was chattering in delight, and Tinker was shouting in glee.

'Go faster, Tim, go faster! You're a very fine horse! You'd easily win the Derby! Go on, gallop!'

'I don't want Timmy to give rides to the monkey,' said George. 'Stop it, Timmy! You look silly.'

The monkey suddenly leaned forward and hugged Timmy round the neck. Then he slid off and looked at George as if to say, 'All right! I won't make your dog look silly!'

Timmy knew that George was cross and he went to lie down on the rug. At once Mischief came sidling across to him, and settled himself between Timmy's big front paws, cuddling there without fear. Timmy bent his big head and licked him very gently.

Tears came suddenly to Joanna's eyes. That Timmy! He was just about the nicest dog in the whole world. 'See that!' she said to George. 'Big-hearted and kind that dog of yours is! Don't you scold him now for being great enough to make friends with a little creature who stole his bone!'

'I'm not *going* to scold him!' said George, astonished and proud. 'He's a marvel – the best dog in the world! Aren't you, Timmy darling?'

And she went over to Timmy and stroked his big soft head. He whined lovingly and licked her, looking up as if to say, 'Well, everything's all right now – we're *all* friends!'

Tinker had been watching from a corner of the kitchen, saying nothing. He was rather afraid of George and her quick temper. He was delighted when he saw her go over and pat Timmy, without even disturbing the monkey. In his joy he began to honk like a lorry, and startled everyone so much that they yelled at him:

'Stop it, Tinker!'

'Be quiet, you little nuisance!'

'Woof!' That was from Timmy.

'You'll have Mr Kirrin in here if you honk like that,' said Joanna. 'Can't you be something quiet for a change – a bicycle, for instance?'

Tinker thought that was quite a good idea. He ran round the kitchen and out into the hall, making a hissing noise like the sound of a bicycle's wheels on the road. Then he decided to make a noise like a bicycle bell, and produced a very loud ringing noise indeed! It was so like the ringing of a bell that Aunt Fanny ran out of the living room, thinking there was someone at the front door!

Then the study door flew open and out came Uncle Quentin and Tinker's father. Poor Tinker was caught, and his father shook him so hard that two pencils shot out of his pocket and rolled over the floor.

Tinker began to yell – and *how* he could yell! George came out of the kitchen to see what was happening, and Dick, Julian and Anne raced down the stairs. Joanna rushed out into the hall, too, and almost sent Uncle Quentin flying.

Then George did a very silly thing. She began to laugh – and when George laughed properly, her laugh was wonderful to hear! But neither Uncle Quentin nor Professor Hayling thought it wonderful – they merely thought it rude! George was laughing at *them* – and that wouldn't do at all!

'This is absolutely the last straw!' shouted Uncle Quentin, his face red with rage. 'First this boy ringing bells all over the place – and George encouraging him by laughing! I won't have it! Don't you know that very very important work is going on here, in Kirrin Cottage – work that may bring great benefits to the world! Fanny, send these children away somewhere. I won't have them in the house, disturbing us when we are doing such important work. Do you hear? SEND THEM AWAY! And that's my LAST word!'

And he and the professor stalked back to the study and banged the door. WELL! Now what was to be done?

[4]

Tinker has a wonderful idea

Aunt Fanny had appeared during the row, and sighed when she heard her husband shouting. Oh, dear, dear – these scientists who liked to do wonderful things for the world – and yet often made their own families unhappy! She smiled at George's angry face, and took her arm.

'Come into the living room, dear, and bring the others with you. We'll have to decide what can be done. Your father really *is* doing wonderful work, you know – and I must say that Tinker and Mischief and Timmy don't help very much! All right, all right, George – I know it isn't Timmy's fault – but he does have a very loud bark, you know!'

She took the five children and Timmy into the living room. The monkey, scared at the shouting, had gone into hiding and was nowhere to be seen. Aunt Fanny called to Joanna.

'Joanna – come and help us to discuss what's to be done. This kind of thing can't go on.'

They all sat down, looking rather solemn. Timmy flopped down under the table, and put his nose on his paws. Where was that little monkey who had given him his biscuit?

The discussion began. George spoke first, most indignantly.

'Mother, this is our *home*. Why do we have to go away just because Father wants this scientist friend to stay with him? I have to do holiday homework, and I don't make a row every time Father bangs a door when I'm studying. But if I so much as—'

'That will do, George,' said her mother. 'You ought to understand your father better than you seem to. You are both exactly the same – impatient, short-tempered, bangers-of-doors, and yet both so kind, too! Now – let's see if we can find a way out.'

'I only wish we could stay at *my* home,' said Julian, feeling awkward. 'But it's all shut up, now that my parents have gone away.'

'Can't we take tents over to Kirrin Island?' said George. 'Yes, Mother, yes – I know what you're going to say – it's only the beginning of April, and it's far too cold and all the rest of it, and—'

'The forecast for the weather is very bad,' said her mother. 'Rain, rain, nothing but rain. You can't possibly go and camp in the pouring rain – and row to and fro, getting drenched each day – I'd have you all in bed with bronchitis before three days had gone – and *then* what should we do!'

'All right, Mother – have *you* any good suggestions?' said George, still cross.

'Hey – what's that monkey doing?' said Dick, suddenly. 'Stop him!'

'He's only poking the fire,' said Tinker. 'He thinks it's cold in here.'

'Well, what next!' said Joanna and took the

poker firmly from the monkey's little paw. 'Do you want to set the house on fire, you – you little . . .'

'Monkey!' finished Dick, with a grin. 'I must say that Mischief is always up to mischief! Can't keep your eye off him for a moment!'

'Well, now – if we can't go to Kirrin Island, or back home, or stay here – where *can* we go?' said Julian, looking serious. 'Hotels are too expensive – and which of our friends would like to have five of us to stay, plus a wicked little monkey and a big dog with an enormous appetite?'

There was a silence. What a problem! Then suddenly Tinker spoke up.

'*I* know where we could go – and we'd jolly well have some fun, too!' he said.

'Oh – and where is this wonderful place?' asked George disbelievingly.

'Well – I was thinking of my lighthouse,' said Tinker, most surprisingly. And then, as no one said anything, but merely stared at him in astonishment, he nodded at them. 'I said my *light-house* – don't you know what a lighthouse is?'

'Don't be silly, please,' said Dick. 'This is no time for jokes.'

'It's *not* a joke,' said Tinker, indignantly. 'It's perfectly true. You ask my father.'

'But, Tinker dear – you can't possibly *own* a lighthouse,' said Aunt Fanny, smiling.

'Well, I do,' said Tinker, quite fiercely. 'You see, my father had some very special work to do, that couldn't be done on land – so he bought an old empty lighthouse, and did his work there. I went to stay with him – my, it was grand there, with the wind and the waves crashing about all the time.'

'But – surely he didn't *give* it to you, did he?' said Julian, disbelievingly.

'Yes, he did. Why shouldn't he, if I wanted it badly?' demanded Tinker. '*He* didn't want it any more, and nobody would buy it – and I wanted it terribly, so he gave it to me on my last birthday. And it's mine, I tell you.'

'Well, I'm blessed!' said Julian. 'Here's old George owning an island given to her by her mother – and Tinker owning a lighthouse given to him by his father! I wish my parents would present me with a volcano, or something really thrilling!'

George's eyes shone as she looked at the surprising Tinker. 'A lighthouse – of your very own! Where is it?'

'About twenty miles along this coast to the west,' said Tinker. 'It's not an awfully *big* one, you know – but it's smashing! The old lamp is still there, but it's not used now.'

'Why not?' asked Dick.

'Well, because a big new lighthouse was built farther along the coast, in a better position for warning ships,' explained Tinker. 'That's how it was this old one was put up for sale. It was fine for my father to work in. Nobody ever disturbed him there – though he did get very angry with the seagulls sometimes. He said they mewed like great cats all the time, and made him feel he ought to put out milk for them.'

This made everyone burst into loud laughter, and Tinker sat beaming round proudly. How clever he must be to make these children laugh like that – yes, and even Joanna and Aunt Fanny too! He broke into their laughter by banging on the table.

'You do believe me now, don't you?' he said. 'It's quite true that the lighthouse is mine. You ask my father. Do let's all go and stay in it till our two fathers have finished their work. We could take Timmy and Mischief too – there's plenty of room.'

This proposal was so astonishing that no one answered for a few moments. Then George gave him a friendly dig in the chest.

'*I'll* come! Fancy living in a *lighthouse*! I bet the girls at school won't believe *that*!'

'Aunt Fanny! May we go?' said Anne, her eyes shining too.

'Well – I don't know,' said her aunt. 'It really

is a most extraordinary idea. I shall have to discuss it with your uncle, and with Tinker's father too.'

'My father will say yes, I know he will!' said Tinker. 'We left some stores there – and some blankets – I *say*, wouldn't it be grand to run a lighthouse ourselves!'

The idea certainly appealed to all the Five – even Timmy thumped his tail on the floor as if he had understood every word. He probably had – he never missed anything that was going on!

'I've a map that shows where my lighthouse is,' said Tinker, scrabbling in one of his pockets. 'It's rather crumpled and dirty because I've looked at it so often. Look – here's a map of the coastline – and just there, built on rocks – is my lighthouse. It's marked by a round dot, look!'

Everyone pored over the grubby map. Nobody had the least doubt but that this was the answer to all their problems! Dick stared at the excited Tinker. How lucky he was to own a *lighthouse*! Dick had never before met a lighthouse owner – and to think it should be this funny little Tinker!

'The rocks that the lighthouse is built on used to wreck many ships,' said Tinker. 'Wreckers used to work along that coast, you know – they would shine a light as if to guide ships along the coast, and make them go on the rocks. Crash! They'd be broken to pieces, and everyone drowned – and the wreckers would wait till the ship was washed up on the shore, and then take everything they could from her.'

'The wicked wretches!' said Dick, horrified.

'There's a Wreckers' Cave there, too, where the wreckers stored the things they stole from the wrecked ships,' said Tinker. 'I haven't been very far into it – I'm too scared to. They do say there's an old wrecker or two there still.'

'Oh, nonsense!' said Aunt Fanny, laughing. 'That's probably just a tale to keep children away from dangerous caves and rocks. Well, dears – I really don't see any reason why you shouldn't go to Tinker's lighthouse, if his father agrees.'

'Mother! THANK YOU!' cried George, and gave her mother a hug that made her gasp. 'I *say* – living in an old *lighthouse* – it's too good to be true! I shall take my binoculars and keep watch for ships!'

'Well, Julian had better take his record-player as well,' said Aunt Fanny. 'If it's stormy weather, it may be a bit duller than you think, cooped up in a lonely lighthouse!'

'It will be MARVELLOUS!' cried Tinker, and he suddenly became a racing car, tearing round the room at top speed, making a most extra-ordinary noise. Timmy barked and Mischief began to chatter loudly.

'Shush!' said Aunt Fanny. 'You'll make your father cross, Tinker, and that will be the end of your fine idea. Switch your engine off, please, and sit down quietly! I'll talk to your father as soon as I can!'

[5]

Tinker's lighthouse

Aunt Fanny thought that she might as well go immediately to the study, and see if her husband and Professor Hayling could talk about the children going away to this lighthouse of Tinker's. Could it really be true? She knocked discreetly at the closed door.

She could hear voices inside the room, but nobody called 'come in'. She knocked again.

'What is it NOW?' shouted Uncle Quentin. 'If it's you, George, go away and keep away. And if it's Tinker, tell him to go to the garage and park himself there. I suppose it's he who has been making all that row this morning!'

Aunt Fanny smiled to herself. Well, well – if all scientists were like her husband and Professor

Hayling, it was a wonder they were ever calm enough to get any work done!

She went away. Perhaps she could bring up the subject of the lighthouse at dinner-time. What a relief it would be to have a peaceful house for a few days!

She went into the kitchen to find Joanna. The monkey was there, helping her! He had slipped away from Tinker and gone to see if there were any titbits about. Joanna was talking away to him as she rolled out pastry.

'See, I roll it like this – and like that – and I pick off a tiny bit for you!' And she gave Mischief a snippet for himself. He was very pleased, and leapt on Joanna's shoulder. He lifted a piece of her hair and whispered in her ear. Joanna pretended to understand.

'Yes, Mischief. If you're good I'll give you another titbit in a minute. Now get off my shoulder, and stop whispering. It tickles!'

'Well, Joanna – I never thought to see you rolling pastry with a monkey on your shoulder!' said Aunt Fanny. 'Joanna, what do you think about this lighthouse idea? I haven't been able to get into the study yet! My husband thought I was Tinker, and told me to go and park myself in the garage!'

'And a very good idea too,' said Joanna, rolling her pastry vigorously. 'Isn't that Tinker out in the hall now – sounds like a car of some sort! Well, I'd say that if the lighthouse is habitable, why shouldn't the Five go there, with Tinker and the monkey? They'd enjoy themselves all right, and Timmy would look after them. Sort of thing that they love – rushing off to a lighthouse! Ugh! Nasty lonely place, with waves crashing round and a wind fit to blow your head off!'

'Yes, but do you think they'd be all right all alone there, Joanna?' said Aunt Fanny.

'Well, Julian and Dick are old enough to look after the others – though I must say I wouldn't like the job of being in charge of that Tinker,' said Joanna. 'All I hope is that he doesn't imagine he's an aeroplane all of a sudden, and take off from the top of the lighthouse!'

Aunt Fanny laughed. 'Don't say that to *him*!' she said. 'His idea of being a car is bad enough. Well, Joanna, I feel very mean sending George and the others away immediately they come here – but with two excitable scientists in the house, I don't see that there's anything else to do. Look out for that monkey – he's found your bag of raisins!'

'Oh, you little mischief!' said Joanna, and made a grab at the monkey. He shot off to the top of a cupboard with the bag of raisins firmly held in one paw. He made a tiny chattering noise, as if he were scolding Joanna.

'You come down with those raisins!' said Joanna, advancing to the cupboard. 'Else I'll tie you to a chair with that long tail of yours. You little monkey!'

Mischief said something in his funny little voice that sounded rather cheeky. Then he put his paw into the bag and took out a raisin. But he didn't eat it – he threw it straight at Joanna!

It hit her on the cheek, and she stared at Mischief in astonishment.

'What! You'd pelt me with my own raisins! Well, that I will NOT have!' She went to the sink and filled a cup with water, while Mischief pelted both her and Aunt Fanny with raisin after raisin! He danced about on the top of the cupboard, screeching loudly in glee!

A bowl on the top of the cupboard fell off as the monkey danced about, and crashed to the ground. The noise scared him, and, with a flying leap, he shot off the cupboard and landed on the top of the half-open door. He pelted the two women from there, making the most extraordinary noises.

The study door was flung open, and out came Uncle Quentin, followed by the professor. 'What was that crash? What's happening here? How *can* we w—'

It was most unfortunate that Joanna should have thrown the cup of water at Mischief at that moment. He sat there on the top of the door – and the water fell all over him, splashed over the top of the door – and down on to Uncle Quentin's head as he pushed the door open!

Joanna was horrified. She disappeared into the scullery at once, not knowing whether to laugh or to make her apologies.

Uncle Quentin was astounded to find himself dripping wet. He stared angrily up at Mischief, absolutely certain that it was the monkey who had emptied the water over him.

By this time the Five had come out of the living room, wondering what the noise was. 'It's old Mischief,' said Tinker. 'Throwing water, I should think!'

'Well, actually, *I* threw the water,' began Joanna apologetically, peeping out of the scullery, 'because—'

'YOU threw it?' said Uncle Quentin, amazed. 'What *is* happening in this house? Things have come to a pretty pass if *you* start flinging water at people, Joanna. You ought to be ashamed of yourself! Are you mad?'

'Listen, Quentin,' said his wife. 'Nobody's mad at present, but pretty soon we all shall be, if this sort of thing goes on! Quentin, are you LISTENING? I've something important to say to you – and to you too, Professor.'

The professor remembered his manners. 'Please go on,' he said politely, and then flinched as a raisin hit him squarely on the head. Mischief had found one on the floor, and had taken a pot shot at the professor. Dick looked at the monkey admiringly – he really was a very good shot!

'What's that little idiot of a monkey throwing!' said Uncle Quentin, fiercely, and knew at once when a raisin hit him smartly on the nose. 'Get rid of him! Put him in the dustbin! Why have I to put up with monkeys that throw things and boys that chug about the house like cars gone mad? I tell you Fanny, I will NOT have it!'

Aunt Fanny looked at him very sternly. 'Listen Quentin, I have something to say. LISTEN!

Tinker says his father gave him a lighthouse for his own, and he suggests that he and all the others should leave here and go and stay in the lighthouse. Quentin, are you listening?'

'A lighthouse! Are you mad? What, that little monkey of a boy says he owns a *lighthouse*? And you believed him?' said Uncle Quentin amazed.

'Tinker's quite right, as it happens,' said Professor Hayling. 'I bought a lighthouse to work in when I wanted to get right away from everywhere and concentrate – and when I'd finished, I couldn't sell it – so as Tinker pestered me for it, I gave it to him. But not to *live* in!'

'A *lighthouse* to work in!' said Uncle Quentin, thinking what a truly marvellous idea this was. 'I'll buy it from you! I'll—'

'No, Quentin, you won't do anything of the sort,' said his wife, firmly. 'Will you PLEASE listen to me, both of you. Professor Hayling, is the lighthouse fit for these five to stay in – and if so, they want to know if they can go there until you two have finished your work here. They're a nuisance to you – and to be quite honest, you're a nuisance to *them*!'

'Fanny!' said her husband, astonished and angry.

'Father, listen. We'll all get out of your way as soon as possible, if you'll say we can go to Tinker's lighthouse,' said George, planting herself firmly in front of her father. 'Say one word – "YES" – that's all we want.'

'YES!' shouted Uncle Quentin, suddenly tired of all the argument, and longing to get back to his papers with the professor. 'YES! Go to the lighthouse – go to the Tower of London – go and live at the Zoo, if you like! The monkeys will welcome that mischievous little creature, sitting grinning up there on the cupboard! But go SOMEWHERE!'

'Oh, thank you, Father!' said George, joyfully.

'We'll go off to the lighthouse as soon as we can. HURRAY! THREE CH—'

But before she could continue, the study door shut with a bang behind the two exasperated men. George bent down, took Timmy's two front legs, and proceeded to dance all round the living room with him, shouting 'HURRAY! THREE CHEERS!' over and over again.

Aunt Fanny sat down suddenly in a chair, and began to laugh. Joanna laughed too. 'If we don't laugh, we shall cry!' she said. 'What a hullabaloo! Well, it's a good thing they'll soon be off. That loft is much too draughty for the boys, you know. Look at poor Julian – he's got such a stiff neck he can hardly turn it this morning.'

'Who cares?' said Julian. 'We'll soon be off again together, all the Five – and two more to keep us company. It will be quite an adventure!'

'An adventure?' said Tinker, surprised. 'But you can't have adventures in a lighthouse – it's out on the rocks, all by itself, as lonely as can be! There aren't any adventures to be found *there*!'

Ah – you wait and see, Tinker! You don't know the Five! If there's any adventure about, they're bound to be right in the middle of it!

[6]

Making plans

It was very exciting making plans to go to the lighthouse. Tinker told them all about it, time and time again. 'It's very tall, and there's an iron stairway – a spiral one – going from the bottom up to the top. And at the top is a little room for the lamp that used to flash to warn ships away.'

'It sounds smashing,' said George. 'What about Timmy, though? Can he climb up a spiral stairway?'

'Well, he can live down at the bottom, can't he, if it's too difficult for him to climb up?' said Tinker. 'Mischief can climb it easily – he simply *races* up!'

'If Timmy has to live at the bottom, I shall live there with him,' said George.

'Why not wait and see the lighthouse before

you arrange the sleeping places?' said Julian, giving her a friendly punch. 'Now first we must find out exactly where it is – and the way to get there. It's a pity Tinker can't turn into a *real* car – he could run us there in no time!'

Tinker at once imagined himself to be a large van, taking the Five and all their luggage along the road. He raced round the room, making his usual car noise, and hooting so loudly that he made everyone jump. Julian caught him as he raced round the table and sat him down firmly.

'Any more of that and we leave you behind,' he said. 'Now – where's that map of yours – let's have a look at it – and then we'll get Aunt Fanny's big map of the coast, and track down the road to your lighthouse.'

Soon Tinker and the Five were studying a large-scale map of the coast, Mischief sitting on Dick's shoulder and tickling his neck.

'See – that's the way to go,' said Julian. 'It really wouldn't be far by sea – look, round the coast here, cut across this bay, round the headland – and just there are the rocks on which the old lighthouse stands. But by road it's a very long way.'

'Better go by car, though,' said Dick. 'We've a good bit of luggage to take – not only our clothes, but crockery and things like that. And food.'

'There are still some stores there,' said Tinker, eagerly. 'Dad left some when we went away from the lighthouse.'

'They'll probably have gone bad,' said Julian.

'Well – don't take too much,' said Tinker. 'It's a pretty rough way over the rocks to the lighthouse – there isn't a road that runs right up to it, you know. We shall have to carry everything ourselves, once we get to the place. We can always get fresh food if we want it – the village isn't all that far away – but there are some days when you can't even leave the lighthouse! You see the waves splash house-high over the rocks when there's a rough wind. We'd have to get across by boat if the tide's in – the rocks are covered then!'

'This sounds too exciting for words!' said Dick, his eyes shining. 'What do *you* think about it, Anne? You haven't said a word!'

'Well – I do feel just a *bit* scared!' said Anne. 'It sounds so lonely. I do hope no ships will be wrecked on those awful rocks while *we're* there!'

'Tinker said there was a fine new lighthouse farther along the coast,' said Julian. 'Its light will keep every ship away from that wicked stretch of rocks. Look, Anne, you *would* like to come, wouldn't you? If not, Aunt Fanny wouldn't mind just *you* staying here – you're a little mouse, you wouldn't bother Uncle Quentin or the professor at all!'

'I shouldn't DREAM of not coming with you,' said Anne, indignantly. 'Julian – you don't think there are still wreckers about do you? I should hate that.'

'They belong to years gone by,' said Julian. 'Cheer up, Anne – this is just a little visit we're going to pay to Tinker's seaside house! He is kindly taking in visitors this spring!'

'Well, let's get on with our plans,' said Dick. 'We go there by car – er, *what* was that you just said, Tinker?'

'I said I'll drive you, if you like,' said Tinker. 'I could dr—'

'You haven't a driving licence, so don't talk nonsense,' said George, crossly.

'I know I haven't – but all the same I *can* drive!' said Tinker. 'I've driven my father's car round and round our garden, see? And—'

'Oh, do shut up,' said Dick. 'You and your pretend cars! Julian, when shall we go to his lighthouse?'

'Well, why not tomorrow morning?' said Julian. 'I'm sure everyone would be glad if we left as soon as possible! It's hard on Aunt Fanny and Joanna to have so many here. We'll see about a car and someone to drive us, and then we'll pack and make our getaway!'

'Hurray,' said George in delight, and pounded on the table, making Mischief leap up to the top of a bookcase in fright. 'Oh, sorry, Mischief – did I scare you? Timmy tell him I'm sorry, I didn't mean it. He probably under-stands your doggy language.'

Timmy looked up at Mischief, gave two little whines and a comforting wuff. Mischief lis-tened with his head on one side, and then leapt down, landing neatly on Timmy's back.

'Thanks for giving him my message, Tim,' said George, and everyone laughed. Good old Timmy! He wagged his long tail and put his head on George's knee, looking up at her beseechingly.

'All right old thing – I understand your language, whether you talk with your voice or your eyes,' said George, patting him. 'You want a walk, don't you?'

'Woof!' said Timmy joyfully, and tore to the door.

'Let's walk down to the garage and see if they have a car or a van to hire out to us,' said Julian. 'We'll have to have a driver too, because someone has to take back the car. Come on, Timmy-dog!'

They all set off to the garage in the village. The rain held off for a while, and the sun came out, making Kirrin Bay sparkle and shine.

'I wish we could have gone to stay on my island,' said George. 'But it really is too damp to camp out. Anyway, a lighthouse will be nice for a change!'

The man at the garage listened to Julian's tale of wanting a car to go to the lighthouse. 'It's the old lighthouse at Demon's Rocks, not the new one at High Cliffs,' he said. 'We're going to stay there.'

'Stay at a *lighthouse*!' said the man. 'This isn't a joke is it?'

'No. It happens to belong to one of us,' said Julian. 'We have a few things to take there, of course, and we hoped you'd have a taxi tomorrow for us. We'd let you know somehow when we are ready to come back from the lighthouse, and you can send the same car for us then.'

'Right,' said the man. 'And you're staying at Kirrin Cottage now, you say? Oh – your uncle is Mr Kirrin? Well, I know Master George here, of course – but I wasn't certain who *you* were. Some funny people order cars, you know!'

George was pleased to be called *Master* George. It was nice to be thought a boy. She dug her hands deep down in the pockets of her jeans.

'We'd better take a few rugs and cushions,' said Julian. 'And some sweaters and wind-cheaters. I can't imagine it's very warm in the lighthouse.'

'There's an oil-heater there,' said Tinker. 'I think it was for the lighthouse lamp when it was in use. We can use that for warmth, if we're cold.'

'What sort of stores did you and your father leave there?' asked Dick. 'We'd better order some foodstuffs at the grocer's – and some ginger-beer or something – and take it all in the car.'

'Well – there's plenty of tinned food, I think,' said Tinker, trying to remember. 'We left it there in case my father wanted to come back at any time and work again in peace and quiet.'

'Hm. It's a pity he didn't fix up with Uncle Quentin to have him there with him,' said Julian. 'Then everyone would have been happy!'

They went to the grocer's and Anne tried her best to order what she thought they would need, outside of tinned food. 'Sugar – butter – eggs – oh dear – help me, George. How much shall I order?'

'Don't forget we *can* go shopping in Demon's Rocks village,' said Tinker. 'Only it's a bit of a nuisance if there's windy weather – the path over the rocks isn't very safe then. We might have to stay in the lighthouse for a day or two without leaving it. Even a boat might be too risky.'

'It sounds thrilling!' said George, picturing them all marooned by fierce storms, waiting to be rescued from peril and starvation! 'Get some biscuits, Anne. And bars of chocolate. And lots of ginger-beer. And a big bottle of lemonade. And a—'

'Wait a minute – do you know who's paying for all this?' said Julian. '*I* am. So don't ruin me completely!' He took out his wallet. 'Here's ten pounds,' he said. 'That's all I can spare at present! Dick can buy the next lot of food we want!'

'Well, I've plenty of money too,' said Tinker, taking out a handful from his pocket.

'You would have!' said George. 'I suppose your father just hands out money whenever you ask him. He's so vague he wouldn't know if he paid you three times a day!'

'Well, *yours* seems pretty vague too,' said Tinker, smartly. 'He poured the coffee over his porridge this morning, instead of the milk. I saw him. And what's more, he ate it without even *noticing* it was coffee!'

'That's enough,' said Julian. 'We don't tell

tales about our parents in public. Tinker, don't you want to take anything for Mischief to eat while we're in the lighthouse? George has bought biscuits for Timmy, and we're going to lay in a supply of bones, too.'

'I'll buy Mischief's food myself, thank you,' said Tinker, not very pleased at being ticked off by Julian. He gave an order for a packet of raisins, a packet of currants, a pound of apple rings and some oranges. Mischief eyed all these with very great *pleasure*.

'Paws off!' said George, sharply, as the little monkey slyly slid his paw into the bag of biscuits put ready for Timmy. Mischief jumped on to Tinker's shoulder and hid his face in his tiny paws, as if he were ashamed!

'We'll just buy some more fruit,' said Julian, 'and then I think we'll have enough. We'll take it all round to the garage, and put it in the car ready to take away tomorrow.'

'Tomorrow!' said George, her eyes shining. 'Oh, I hope it comes soon. I can't *wait* for it!'

[7]
Off at last!

It was very exciting that evening to talk about the next day – the taxi coming to fetch them – the drive round the coast to Demon's Rocks – exploring the lighthouse – looking out over the endless sea, and watching the great waves coming in to pound on the rocks!

'What *I'm* looking forward to is our first night there,' said George. 'All alone, high up in that old lighthouse! Nothing but wind and waves around! Snuggling down in our rugs, and waking up to hear the wind and waves again.'

'And the gulls,' put in Tinker. 'They cry all the time. You can watch them from the lighthouse top. I wish I had wings like a gull – spread out wide – sitting on the wind as they glide!'

'Sitting on the wind – yes, that's exactly what they do!' said Anne. 'I just wish their cry didn't sound so mournful though.'

Aunt Fanny was half-inclined not to let the children go after all! The weather forecast was bad, and she pictured them sitting half-frozen, and perhaps very scared, in the old deserted lighthouse. But no sooner did she begin to wonder out loud if she ought to let them go than the children raised their voices in indignant chorus!

'But we've ordered the TAXI!'

'And heaps of food! And Joanna has packed up a big tin of all kinds of things. She even baked a special cake for us!'

'*Mother*! How *could* you think of saying no when you've already said yes!'

'All right, all right, dears!' said Aunt Fanny. 'I wouldn't really stop you going. But do send me a card or two, will you? That's if there's anywhere to post one!'

'Oh, there's a tiny post office in the village,'

said Tinker. 'We'll send a card every day. Then you'll know we're all right.'

'Very well – but if a card doesn't come I'll be very worried,' said Aunt Fanny. 'So please do keep your word! You won't forget your anoraks will you – and your rubber boots, and . . .?'

'Mother! I feel as if you're going to mention *umbrellas* next!' said George. 'But honestly, we'd be blown out to sea if we put an umbrella up on Demon's Rocks. Tinker says there's always a gale blowing round the coast there.'

'You can think of us playing snap with our packs of cards, and having a fine time in the lighthouse while storms rage round and howl like demons!' said Dick. 'We'll be sitting snug in our rugs, with ginger-beer beside us, and chocolate biscuits all round—'

'Woof,' said Timmy, at once, pricking his ears up at words he knew so well.

'Ha – you think you're going to feed on chocolate biscuits, do you, Tim?' said Dick, ruffling the dog's hairy head. 'And please don't interrupt the conversation. It's not good manners.'

'Woof,' said Timmy apologetically, and licked Dick's nose.

'I think you'd all better go to bed early to-night,' said Aunt Fanny. 'You've still some packing to do tomorrow – and you say you've ordered the taxi for half past nine.'

'We'll be down to breakfast at eight o'clock sharp,' said Julian. 'I bet the professor won't be down till about eleven, and forget all about his bacon and eggs! Tinker, does your father *ever* have a really hot meal? I mean – it seems to me he either forgets them altogether, or wanders in hours late, and then doesn't know if he's having breakfast, dinner, or supper!'

'Well, I can always eat up everything that's there, if I think he's forgotten to come,' said Tinker, sensibly. 'Mischief helps too. You'd be surprised how fond Mischief is of fat bacon.'

'I'm not a *bit* surprised at anything Mischief does,' said Julian. 'I'm just wondering how we are going to put up with his tricks when we're all cooped up in the lighthouse together! We can't send him out into the garden then, to work off some of his high spirits. Aunt Fanny, do you know he took my pencil this morning and scribbled monkey words all over my wallpaper? It's a good thing I can't read monkey language for I'm sure he wasn't scribbling anything polite!'

'You're not to say things like that about Mischief,' said Tinker, offended. 'He's very good-mannered for a monkey. You should see *some* monkeys I know!'

'I'd rather not, thanks,' said Julian.

Tinker was cross. He picked up Mischief and went out of the room. Soon there was the noise of a car out in the hall – one that needed repairing by the sound of it!

'R-r-r-r-RRRRRR-r-r-r-r, OOOOOOPH, Rrrrrrr, PARP!' Aunt Fanny rushed to the door. 'You *know* you've been told not to be a car out in the hall. Come back before your father hears you,

Tinker. My goodness me, this house will be an entirely different place, once it is rid of all the cars that have driven about in it since you came!'

'I was only being a tractor,' said Tinker, surprised. 'I always feel as if I *must* go and be a car when people are horrid to me or Mischief.'

'Oh, be your age!' said George.

'I shall go up to bed,' said Tinker, offended again.

'Well, that's not a bad idea, seeing that you have to be punctual tomorrow morning,' said Aunt Fanny. 'Good night, then, Tinker dear. Good night, Mischief.'

Tinker found himself gently propelled to the door. He went up the stairs, grumbling, Mischief on his shoulder. But he soon stopped frowning as he undressed and thought of the next day. Off to the lighthouse – HIS lighthouse! Ha, that would make George and the others sit up. He snuggled down in bed with Mischief nestling beside him, one little paw down the front of Tinker's pyjama jacket.

Next morning George awoke first. She sat up, afraid that the weather forecast might be right, and that it would be pouring with rain. No – it was wrong for once – the sun shone down and she could not hear the sound of the sea – that meant that there was not much wind to blow up big waves that pounded on the shore.

She awoke Anne. 'Lighthouse day!' she said. 'Buck up – it's half past seven.'

They were all down very punctually to breakfast – except Professor Hayling! As usual he did not appear until breakfast was over, and then he sauntered in at the front door!

'Oh – you *are* up then,' said Aunt Fanny, 'I thought you were still asleep in bed.'

'No – Tinker woke me up at some very early hour,' complained the professor. 'Or else it was the monkey – I really don't know. They both look alike to me in the early morning.'

Uncle Quentin was already down, but hadn't come into breakfast. He was in his study as usual. 'George – go and fetch your father,' said Aunt Fanny. 'His breakfast will soon be inedible.'

George went to the study door and knocked. 'Father! Don't you want your breakfast?'

'I've had it!' said a surprised voice. 'Very nice – couple of boiled eggs.'

'Father! That was your *yesterday's* breakfast!' said George, impatiently. 'It's bacon and *fried* eggs today. You've forgotten as usual. Do come. We're leaving for the lighthouse soon.'

'Lighthouse – what lighthouse?' said Uncle Quentin, in tones of great astonishment. But he had no answer. George had gone back to the dining room, not knowing whether to laugh or frown. Really! Father was so forgetful that he would forget where he lived next!

There was great excitement after breakfast. Rugs – coats – night clothes, the warmest that could be found – tins of cakes and mince-pies packed by Joanna – sandwiches to eat on the way – books – games – as George said, anyone would think they were going away for a month!

'The car's late!' said Dick, impatiently. 'Or else my watch is fast.'

'Here it comes!' said Anne, excited. 'Oh, Aunt Fanny, I wish you were coming too! We're going to have such fun! Where's Mischief – oh, there he is! And Timmy – Timmy, we're going to live in a lighthouse! You don't even know what that is, do you?'

The car came up to the front gate of Kirrin Cottage, and the driver blew his horn, making Uncle Quentin almost jump out of his skin. He turned on poor Tinker at once. 'Was that *you* up to your silly tricks of pretending to be a car, and hooting again? Own up, now!'

'No, it wasn't, on my honour it wasn't,' said Tinker indignantly, hopping out of the way of what looked as if it might be a very powerful slap. 'See – it's that car!'

'I'll just ask the driver what he means by driving up here and hooting fit to scare us all!' said Uncle Quentin indignantly. 'What's he come here for, anyway?'

'FATHER! It's the TAXI that's come to take us to the LIGHTHOUSE!' said George, not knowing whether to laugh or be cross.

'Ah yes,' said Uncle Quentin. 'Why didn't you tell me before? Well, good-bye, good-bye! Have a good time, and don't forget to dry yourselves well after a swim.'

They piled into the car, and the man put their luggage into the big boot. He stared as Timmy and Mischief leapt in. 'Sure you've all got enough room?' he said. 'What a carful!'

Then to the accompaniment of a loud R-r-r-r-r-RRR from the car's engine, and an equally loud one from the delighted Tinker, the car turned and drove away down the sandy lane.

'We're off,' said George, in a happy voice. 'Off all by ourselves again. It's the thing I like best of all. Do you like it too, Tim?'

'woof!' said Timmy, agreeing heartily, and lay down with his head on George's foot. Ah – now for a lovely holiday with George. Timmy didn't mind where he went – even to the end of the world – so long as he was with George!

There's the lighthouse!

Once they were out on the main road, Tinker began to talk to the driver, asking him questions about all kinds of cars. The others listened, amused.

'Well, I don't think much of the new cars,' said Tinker. 'All gadgets!'

'Some of the new gadgets are very good,' said the driver, amused with the cocky little boy, and he touched a little lever beside him. At once the window next to Tinker went down smoothly, with a curious low moan. Tinker was extremely startled.

'Oh, don't open that window,' said Anne, as a rough wind swooped in. 'For goodness sake shut it, Tinker.'

Tinker shut it and began to talk about cars

again. Once more the driver touched the lever beside him, and once more Tinker's window slid mournfully down, and a cold draught came in.

'TINKER! Don't mess about with the windows,' ordered Julian.

'I never touched the thing,' said Tinker, eyeing the window with suspicion. It suddenly shut itself, sliding upwards very smoothly. Tinker began to feel uncomfortable. He watched the window closely, afraid that it might play tricks again. The others, knowing perfectly well that the driver could open and shut any of the windows automatically from his own seat, nudged one another, and giggled. 'That shut up poor old Tinker!' murmured Dick.

It had. Not another word about new cars or old came from Tinker during the whole drive! It was a very pleasant one, mostly round the coast, and very little inland. The views were magnificent.

'That dog of yours seems to like the views,'

said the driver. 'His head has been out of the window all the time.'

'Well – I always thought it was because he liked the fresh air,' said George. 'Timmy, is it because you enjoy the views?'

'Woof,' said Timmy, and withdrew his head to give George a lick. He also gave the little monkey a lick. Poor Mischief didn't much like the motion of the car. He sat very still indeed, afraid that he might be sick. The car purred along, sounding just like Tinker's usual imitation!

They stopped for an early lunch, and ate their sandwiches hungrily, sitting on a cliff. The driver had brought his own, and once Mischief had discovered that half the man's sandwiches were made of tomato, he sat on his knee in a very friendly manner, sharing his sandwiches in delight.

'We'll be there in about ten minutes,' said the man. 'Where are you staying at Demon's Rocks? The garage didn't tell me.'

'At the lighthouse,' said Julian. 'Do you know it?'

'Yes – but people don't *stay* there!' said the driver, thinking that Julian was pulling his leg. 'What hotel are you going to – or are you staying with friends?'

'No. We really *are* going to the lighthouse,' said Tinker. 'It's mine. My very own.'

'Well – you've certainly got a place with a fine view!' said the driver. 'I was born at Demon's Rocks. My old great-grandad is still in the same cottage where I was born. My word – the stories he used to tell me of that old lighthouse – and how the wreckers got into it one night and grabbed the keeper there, and doused the light, so that a great ship might go on the rocks.'

'How horrible – and *did* it get wrecked?' asked Dick.

'Yes. Smashed to bits,' said the driver. 'Ab-so-lutely – smashed – to bits! And then they waited for the tide to wash up the wreckage.

You ought to look up my old great-grandad, and get him to tell you his tales. He might even show you the Wreckers' Cave . . .'

'Oh – we heard about that,' said George. 'Is it really true – *can* we see it? And is there someone in there still?'

'No – no, all the old wreckers are gone long ago,' said the driver. 'As soon as the new lighthouse was built, the wreckers' day was done. It's so powerful, you see. Its beams can be seen even in the fiercest storm. The beam from the lighthouse you're going to wasn't very good – but it saved a good many ships, all the same!'

'What's your great-grandad's name?' asked George, making up her mind to look him up as soon as she could. 'Where does he live?'

'Ask for Jeremiah Boogle,' said the driver, carefully skirting a herd of cows. 'You'll find him sitting somewhere on the quay, smoking a long pipe, and scowling at anyone that comes near him. But he likes children, so don't you be afraid of his scowl. He'll tell you a few tales, will my old great-grandad! Well, bless us all, if there isn't *another* herd of cows coming round the corner.'

'Hoot at them,' said Tinker.

'Ever heard the rhyme about the cow that jumped over the moon, boy?' said the driver. 'Well, someone hooted when it came by, see? And that's what it did – jumped over the moon! No good driver hoots at cows. It scares them silly, and they jump like hares. Look – see that cliff round the curve of the coast there? Well, that's the first bit of Demon's Rocks. We'll soon be there now.'

'Why is it called that?' asked George.

'Well, the rocks there are so wicked that it was reckoned they could only have been put there by some kind of savage demon,' said the driver. 'Some are just below the water so that they catch the keel of a boat and rip it. Others stick up sharp as sharks' teeth – and there's a great ledge of rocks where a boat can be pounded to bits by the waves. Ah, they're Demon's Rocks all right!'

'When shall we see the lighthouse?' asked Tinker. 'We ought to see it soon.'

'Wait till another bit of the coast comes in sight as soon as we get to the top of this hill,' said the driver. 'And just tell that monkey of yours to take his paw out of my coat pocket. I've no more tomatoes there!'

'Behave yourself, Mischief,' said Tinker, so sternly that the little creature hid its face in its paws and whimpered.

'Little humbug!' said George. 'There's not a *tear* in his eye! Oh look – is *that* the lighthouse?'

'Yes. That's it,' said the driver. 'You get a good view of it now, from this hill. Fine one, isn't it, for an old one? Ah, they could build well in those days. That one's made of stone. It's wave-swept so it has to be fairly tall, or the shining of the lamp would have been hidden by the spray falling on the windows.'

'Where did the lighthouse keeper live?' asked Dick.

'Oh, there's a cosy enough room just under the lamp-room,' said the driver. 'My grandad took me up there once. I never saw such a view of a stormy sea in my life!'

'My father lived there all one summer,' boasted Tinker. 'I was with him most of the time. It was grand.'

'Why did your father want to live in a lighthouse?' asked the driver, curiously. 'Was he hiding, or something?'

'Of course not. He's a scientist, and he said he wanted peace and quiet, with no telephones ringing, and no one coming to see him,' said Tinker.

'And do you mean to say he had peace and quiet with *you* there?' said the driver teasingly. 'Well, well!'

'It's not so quiet there really,' said Tinker. 'The waves make such a noise, and so does the wind. But my father didn't really notice those.

He only notices things like bells ringing, or people talking, or somebody knocking at the door. Things like that drive him mad. He loved the lighthouse.'

'Well – I hope you enjoy yourselves there,' said the driver. 'It's not my cup of tea – hearing nothing but waves and gulls crying. Better you than me!'

They descended the other side of the hill and the lighthouse was no longer to be seen. 'Soon be there now,' said Tinker. 'Mischief, will you like to be at the lighthouse again? How quickly you could go up the spiral staircase and down – do you remember?'

The car swept down almost to the edge of the sea. The lighthouse was now plainly to be seen, a good way out from the shore. A small boat bobbed at a stone jetty, and Tinker pointed it out with a scream of joy. 'That's the boat we had – the one that took us to and from the lighthouse when the tide was in! It's called *Bob-About*, and it does bob about too.'

'Is it yours?' asked George, rather jealously.

'Well, it was sold with the lighthouse, so I suppose it is,' said Tinker. 'Anyway, it's the one we'll use when we can't wade over the rocks.'

'Well, see you don't get storm-bound in the lighthouse,' said the driver, bringing the car to a stop. 'The sea between Demon's Rocks and the jetty will be too rough for that little boat, in stormy weather.'

'I can manage boats all right,' said George. 'I've had one since I was small.'

'Yes. You're pretty good with them, that I do know,' said the driver. 'Well – here we are. Are you going to go straight to the lighthouse – in that boat? Shall I help you carry your things to it?'

'Well, thanks,' said Julian, and between them they carried everything to the little boat. An old man sat nearby, and he touched his cap to them. 'Message came through from Kirrin to say I was to get the old boat out for you,' he said. 'Which of you's Master Hayling?'

'I am,' said Tinker. 'And that's *my* boat, and *that's* my lighthouse! Come on, everyone – let's row to the lighthouse – come on! I can hardly wait to get there!'

[9]

Inside the lighthouse!

The five children jumped down into the boat, which was certainly acting up to its name of *Bob-About*! Timmy leapt in after George, but Mischief the monkey cried in terror when Tinker took him into the bobbing boat and sat down, holding him firmly.

'It's all right, Mischief,' said Tinker. 'Don't you remember this little boat of mine? You never did like going in a boat, though, did you?'

There were two pairs of oars. Julian took one pair, and George was going to take the other, when Dick quietly took them himself, grinning at George's angry face.

'Sorry – there's a good old swell on the sea, and we've to row through some pretty good waves. I'm just a *bit* stronger than you, George!'

'I row *just* as well as you do,' said George. The boat gave a great roll to one side just then, and she just managed to save one of their suitcases from toppling overboard.

'Well saved!' said Julian. 'And only just in time too! What a swell there is just here!'

'Are you going to row right over the rocks?' asked Anne peering down into the water. 'They are covered by the water now – we shan't scrape the bottom of the boat at all.'

'These are the rocks that we can walk over when the tide's out,' said Tinker. 'Lovely pools there are in them, too! I used to wallow in a nice warm one that was so well-heated by the sun that I wished I had a cold tap to turn on when the water felt too hot!'

Anne chuckled. 'I wish it was warm enough to swim now,' she said. 'My word – look down and see what horrible rocks there are, just beneath the boat!'

'Yes – I bet they ripped up many a poor ship in the old days,' said Julian. 'No wonder they called them Demon's Rocks! It's a bit of a pull over them, isn't it, Dick?'

'Let *me* have a turn,' said George, grabbing at one of Dick's oars.

'Nothing doing,' said Dick, with a grin. 'You just look after those bags, old thing!'

'Is it a very *old* lighthouse?' asked Anne, as they swung over the hidden rocks, and the lighthouse came nearer and nearer. 'It *looks* old!'

'Yes, it is,' said Tinker. 'It's an odd little lighthouse, really – built by a rich man years and years ago. His daughter was drowned in a ship that was wrecked on these rocks – so he built a lighthouse, partly as a memorial to the girl, and partly to prevent other shipwrecks.'

Anne gazed at it. It was sturdily built and seemed very tall to her. Its base was firmly embedded in the rocks below it. Dick thought that the foundations must go very deep down into the rocks, to hold the lighthouse firmly in the great gales that must blow in bad weather.

A gallery, rather like a verandah, ran round the top, just below the windows through which the lighthouse lamp once shone. What a view there would be from that gallery, thought Anne.

They came near to the lighthouse, which had stone steps running from the rocks up to a doorway built some way above the crashing waves.

'Will the door be locked?' asked Dick, suddenly. 'I wouldn't want to row all this way and then find we can't get into the place!'

'Of course the door will be locked,' said Tinker. 'Anyone got the key?'

'Oh, don't be a donkey!' said Julian, resting his oars, and glaring at Tinker. 'Do you mean to say we can't get in, after all this?'

'It's all right!' said Tinker, grinning at Julian's dismayed face. 'I just wanted to pull your leg. Here's the key! It's *my* lighthouse, you see, so Dad gave me the key, and I always carry it about with me. It's very precious.'

It was an extremely large key, and George

marvelled that Tinker could keep it in his pocket. He flourished it at them, grinning again. 'I'm looking forward to unlocking *my* lighthouse with *my* key!' he said. 'I bet *you* wish you had a lighthouse of your own, George.'

'Well, yes, I do,' said George, gazing up at the towering lighthouse, now so near to them.

'You'd better be a bit careful now,' said Tinker to the boys. 'Wait till a big wave swells up, then ride over it, and make for that rock over there – the one standing out of the water. There's a calm bit beyond it, for some reason, and you can row up to the steps quite safely. Look out for a stone post there, and chuck the rope round it, George. You're in a better position than I am for that.'

It was all done much more easily than the Five hoped. The boat swung into a stretch of fairly calm water, and the two boys rowed hard for the steps. George neatly threw the loop of rope over the post – and there they were, at the foot of the lighthouse, with only a few rocks to climb over to reach the steps. These rocks were not under water, and one by one the children and Timmy jumped out, and stared up at the lighthouse. It seemed much bigger now that they were just at the bottom!

'I'll unlock the door,' said Tinker, proudly, and climbed up the steep stone steps. 'Look at the enormous great stones that my lighthouse is made of. No wonder it has stood so long!'

He thrust the great key into the lock of the stout wooden door, and tried to turn it. He struggled for a minute, and then turned to the others with a scared face. 'I can't open the door!' he said. '*Now* what do we do?'

'I'll have a try,' said Julian. 'It's probably stuck.' He took hold of the key, gave it a strong twist – and opened the door! Everyone was most relieved. Julian pushed the others in out of the wind and the spray, and shut the door firmly.

'Well – here we are!' he said. 'Isn't it dark! Good thing I brought a torch!'

He shone the torch round, but all that was to be seen was a steep iron staircase spiralling up the middle of the lighthouse!

'The staircase goes right up to the top, to the lamp-room,' explained Tinker. 'It passes through a few rooms on the way. I'll show you. Hang on to the railing of the staircase, you may feel giddy going up round and round so steeply.'

Tinker proudly led the way up the steep little staircase, that went round and round and round! They came to a hole through which the stairway passed into a little dark room. 'One of the storerooms,' said Tinker, and flashed his torch round. 'See – there are tins of food that I told you my father and I left here. Now we go on up to the oil-room – that's not very big.'

'What's the oil-room?' asked Anne.

'Oh it was just where tins of paraffin oil used to be kept – the oil they used for the light at the top of the lighthouse. The old lamp had to burn oil, you see – there wasn't electricity in those days. Look – here's the oil-room.'

The oil-room had a very low ceiling, no window, and was packed with old tins. It had a nasty smell, and Anne held her nose with her fingers.

'I don't like this room,' she said. 'It has a horrid smell and a horrid *feel* about it! Let's go on up the staircase.'

The next room had one of the few little windows in the lighthouse, and as the sun came through it, it was much lighter and more cheerful.

'This was where my father and I slept,' said Tinker. 'Look, we forgot to take that old mattress away with us. What a bit of luck! We can use it!'

Up the spiral staircase they went once more, and this time they came to a room with a higher ceiling than the others, and a good window, though small. The sun came through this one too, and it looked quite homely! It had a table, and three chairs, and a box. It also had an old desk, and a little paraffin stove for boiling water or frying food.

'There's my old frying-pan!' said Tinker. 'We'll find that jolly useful. And a kettle – and a saucepan. And we left spoons and forks and knives behind, though not enough for all five of us, I'm afraid. And there's crockery too – though not as much as there ought to be. I broke rather a lot. But there are some tin cups and plates – I used just to wipe them clean with a cloth. Water's precious in a lighthouse you know.'

'Where is the water tank?' asked George. 'We'll have to have some water.'

'My father arranged a catch-tank on the west side of the lighthouse,' said Tinker, proudly. 'It catches rainwater, and runs into a pipe that goes through one of the windows and fills a little tank over a sink. I forgot to show you that. There's a tap to turn the water on and off. My father's very clever you know – and a thing like that is as simple as ABC. He didn't want to have to fetch water every day for washing in! Gosh, we did have fun here!'

'Well, it looks as if you'll have some *more* fun!' said Dick. 'You've plenty of company this time! You must have been jolly lonely before.'

'Oh, well – I had Mischief,' said Tinker, and when he heard his name, the little monkey came scampering over to him, and leapt into the boy's arms, cuddling into him lovingly.

'And what's the next room in this marvellous little lighthouse?' asked Julian.

'There's only one more – and that's the lamp-room. I'll show you that – it used to be the most important room in the place – but now it's lonely – never used – quite forgotten! Come and see!' And up the last spiral of the stairway went Tinker. How very, very proud he was of his lighthouse!

[10]

Settling in

Once more they all climbed up the spiral stair-way, Timmy rather slowly, for he found the winding stairs difficult. Mischief shot up in front of them, almost as if *he* were the owner of the lighthouse, and was showing off his home!

The lamp-room was a high room with big windows all round it. It was very bright, for the sun shone steadily into it. The view was magnificent!

Anne gave a shout of wonder. The lighthouse was so high that the children could see for miles and miles over the heaving dark blue sea. They went all round the lamp-room, looking in every direction.

'Look! There's a door here!' cried Dick.

'Does it open on to that little balcony, or gallery, or whatever it is that runs all round this room?'

'Yes. The gallery goes completely round the lamp-room,' said Tinker. 'You should see it sometimes when the weather's rough, and the gulls go seeking somewhere out of the storm. They perch on that gallery by the dozen! But you can't go out there except in calm weather – you might be blown right off! You've no idea what it's like when there's a storm. Honestly, one night when my father and I were here I thought I felt the lighthouse rocking!'

'This is about the most exciting place I've ever stayed in,' said Anne, her eyes shining. 'Tinker, I think you are the luckiest boy in the world!'

'Do you really?' said Tinker, pleased. He gave Anne a little pat. 'I hoped you'd like it. Mischief loves it – don't you, Mischief?'

Mischief was up on top of the great lamp. He chattered down to Timmy as if he were telling him all about it. Timmy listened, his ears cocked, his head on one side.

'He looks just as if he understood that monkey-gabble!' said George. 'Tinker – this lamp is never lit now, is it?'

'No, never,' said Tinker. 'I told you there is a fine new lighthouse a bit farther down the coast. It has a terrific lamp – run by electricity. We shall see its beams sweeping the sea at night.'

'Why don't people build lighthouses and live in them?' wondered George, as she gazed out over the wide blue sea.

'Anyone feeling hungry?' asked Tinker, rubbing his tummy. 'I feel jolly empty. Oh gosh – we haven't taken the things out of my boat! Come on – let's carry them all indoors, and have a meal. What's the time? Past four o'clock! No wonder I feel empty. Come on, Mischief – to work! You can carry some of the things in too.'

They ran down the spiral stairway, through

room after room, and came to the great door. 'I suppose it had to be built as thickly and strongly as possible, because of the sea dashing against it in storms,' said Julian, pulling it open. The wind rushed in and almost knocked him over! They pushed their way out, and climbed back over the rocks to where they had left the boat. It was bobbing gently up and down in the little stretch of calm water.

'Hallo, *Bob-About*!' said Tinker. 'Did you think we were never coming? Got all our goods safely? Good little boat!'

'Idiot!' said Dick, grinning. 'Come on, Ju – I'll take half the heavy things, you take the rest. The girls and Tinker can manage the smaller things. Hey, Mischief, what do you think you're doing?'

Mischief had picked up a parcel or two, and was bounding off with them. 'It's all right! He's used to helping!' shouted Tinker. 'He often goes shopping with me, and carries bags and things. Let him help, he likes it.'

The monkey certainly was very useful. He scampered to and fro with all kinds of little things, and chattered happily. Timmy stood staring at him, his tail down, wishing he could use his paws as nimbly as Mischief could. George gave him a loving pat.

'It's all right, Timmy, darling. Here – take this basket.'

Timmy took the basket in his mouth by the handle and leapt happily up the steps of the lighthouse. He might not be able to pick up the little things that Mischief so easily managed – but at least he could carry baskets!

'We'll leave the boat bobbing up and down,' said Tinker. 'It will be quite all right there, tied to the post, unless the sea gets terribly rough – then we'll have to pull it halfway up the steps.'

'Let's have our meal and unpack before we arrange our things,' said Anne. 'I really do feel very hungry now. What sort of a meal shall we have? I feel as if I want something more than a tea-time meal!'

'That's the worst of living in a lighthouse,' said Tinker, quite seriously. 'You're awfully hungry nearly all the time. I used to have five or six meals a day when I stayed here with my father.'

'Sounds all right to *me*,' said Dick, with a grin. 'Let's have a "tea-sup" meal, shall we? A mixture of tea and supper! Tea-sup!'

Some of the things were put into the bed-room and some into the living room. Soon Tinker popped a saucepan of water on the stove to boil. Because of the rainy weather, the little rain catch-tank had provided plenty of water for the small inside tank set over the sink, which was most conveniently put in the living room. When Tinker turned on the tap, out came clear rainwater!

'Magic!' said Anne, delighted. 'I feel as if I'm in a dream!'

Eggs were put into the saucepan, and were soon boiled. 'Exactly three minutes and a half,' said Anne, ladling out each one with a spoon.

'TWO eggs each! At this rate we shall have to go shopping every day!' George, you cut some bread-and-butter. The bread's in that bag – but goodness knows where the butter is. I know we bought some.'

'What about having a few of Joanna's famous mince-pies too?' said Dick, taking the lid off a big square tin. 'Whew! Dozens! And cherry buns as well! And home-made macaroons – Joanna's speciality! I *say* what a meal!'

'What shall we have to drink?' said Julian. 'Ginger-beer? Lemonade? Or shall we make some tea?'

Everyone voted for ginger-beer. It was a very pleasant and cheery meal that the Five had in the old lighthouse, with Mischief and Tinker. The gulls called outside, the wind gave the lighthouse an occasional buffet, and the sound of the sea was mixed with all the other noises – lovely! Anne hugged her knees as she waited for her ginger-beer. To think they were going to stay here for days and days. All by themselves.

When the meal was over, Anne and George washed up in the little sink. 'Oh don't wash up – just give the things a quick wipe-over!' said Tinker. 'Like this!'

'Oh *no*!' said Anne. 'That's just like a boy! You'd better leave this side of things to me. I *like* doing jobs like this, see?'

'Just like a girl!' said Tinker, with a grin.

'No, it isn't,' said George. 'I hate doing them, and *I'm* a girl – though I wish I wasn't!'

'Never mind – you *look* like a boy, and you're often as *rude* as a boy, and you haven't an awful lot of manners,' said Tinker, quite thinking that he was comforting George.

'I've more manners than *you*,' said George, and stalked off in a huff to look out of the windows. But nobody could be in a huff for long, with that wonderful view – sea for miles and miles, tipped here and there with white breakers. George gave a sigh of pleasure. She forgot that she was annoyed with Tinker, and turned to him with a smile.

'If I could own this view, I'd feel I was the richest person in all the world!' she said. 'You're very lucky, Tinker.'

'Am I?' said Tinker, thinking it over. 'Well, you can have half the view, if you like. I don't want it all.'

Julian laughed, and clapped the boy on the back. 'We'll all share it, while we're here!' he said. 'Come on – let's unpack and arrange everything. Girls, you had better sleep here in this living room – and we three boys will sleep down in the bedroom. That all right by you, Tinker?'

'Fine – so long as you don't mind Mischief sleeping with us,' said Tinker. 'Anyway I expect Timmy will sleep with the girls.'

'Woof,' said Timmy, agreeing. He was certainly not going to sleep anywhere without George!

They all had fun unpacking, and putting the things in the different places. 'Storeroom for that,' Julian said, 'and living room for this and this – and bedroom for these rugs – though these two had better go to the living room, because the girls will sleep there.'

'Cards for the living room,' said Dick, handing them to Anne. 'And books. And papers. Gosh, we mustn't forget to send a card each day to Aunt Fanny. We promised we would.'

'Well, she'll know we arrived safely today because the taxi driver will be sure to send a message to her,' said George. 'But tomorrow we'll go down to the village and buy a stock of postcards – and we'll send one every single day. I know Mother will worry if we don't.'

'All mothers are worriers,' said Dick. 'It's a nuisance – but on the other hand it's one of the nice things about them. Now then – what about a game of cards?'

And there they all are in the lighthouse, playing cards with shouts and laughter, Timmy and Mischief watching. You do have fun together, Five, don't you?

[11]

Jeremiah Boogle

When it began to get dark, Tinker left the card table, and fetched an old-fashioned oil-lamp. He shook it.

'It's still got some oil in,' he said. 'Good. I'll light it, then we can see properly.'

'What a pity we can't light the great oil-lamp at the top of the lighthouse,' said George. 'That must have been the lighthouse keeper's great moment – lighting up the lamp to warn ships away. I wonder who first thought of a lighthouse – someone whose folk sailed, and might be wrecked on rocks, I suppose?'

'One of the first great lighthouses was built ages ago on an island called Pharos at the mouth of the Nile, not far from the great port of Alexandria,' said Julian.

'What was it built of – stone, like this one?' asked Tinker.

'No. It was built of white marble,' said Julian. 'I thought of it today when we went up the spiral staircase here – because the Pharos lighthouse had one too – much, much bigger than ours.'

'What was their lamp like?' asked Tinker.

'I don't know if it had a *lamp*,' said Julian. 'It's said that an enormous fire was built each night on the top of the lighthouse, whose flames could be seen by ships a hundred miles away!'

'Goodness – it must have been a pretty high lighthouse, then, this Pharos!' said Dick.

'Well, it was supposed to be about 180 metres high!' said Julian.

'Whew! I wonder the wind didn't blow it down!' said Dick. 'Let's go and see it one day – if it's still there.'

'Idiot!' said Julian. 'It's gone long since. After all, it was built over twenty-two hundred years ago! An earthquake came along one day and

the magnificent lighthouse was shaken to bits –
completely destroyed!'

There was a shocked silence. Everyone looked
round at the walls of the lighthouse they were in.
An earthquake! What a catastrophe that would
be for even a *little* lighthouse!

'Cheer up, Anne!' said Julian, with a laugh.
'*We're* not likely to be visited by an earthquake
tonight! That old lighthouse on Pharos Island
was one of the Seven Wonders of the Ancient
World. No – *don't* ask me the others – I'm
getting too sleepy to remember!'

'I wish we could light the lamp in *this* lighthouse,' said Anne. 'It can't like being a *blind*
lighthouse, after shining brightly for so many
years. *Could* the lamp be lit, Tinker, or is it
broken now?'

'Anne – if you think we're going to scramble
round that lamp-room and light the lamp just
because you feel sorry about it, you're mistaken,' said Dick, firmly. 'Anyway, it's sure to be
out of order after all these years.'

'I don't see why it should be,' objected Tinker. 'The lamp's never been interfered with.'

'Look – are we going to go on with our game, or are we not?' said Julian. 'I may as well remind you that I have won practically every game so far! Unless someone else wins a game soon I shall consider that I'm playing with a bunch of nitwits!'

That was quite enough to make everyone pick up their cards, and see if they couldn't possibly beat Julian!

'We'll jolly well play till you're well and truly beaten!' said Dick.

But no – nobody could beat Julian that night. Luck went his way all the time. At the end of the fifth game Anne yawned loudly.

'Oh, sorry!' she said. 'Don't think I'm bored. That yawn came too suddenly for me to stop it!'

'Well, I feel decidedly yawny too,' said Dick. 'What about a snack of something – and then we'll go to bed. We had such an enormous tea-sup that I feel I can't manage another *meal* – but a chocolate biscuit or two would be quite welcome.'

'Woof!' said Timmy at once, agreeing heartily, and Mischief said something in his little chattering voice, and tugged at Tinker's sleeve.

'I'll bring you a snack or two,' said Anne, getting up. She soon came back with a tray on which she had put lemonade, large slices of Joanna's new cake, and a chocolate biscuit for everyone, including Timmy and Mischief.

They ate with enjoyment, feeling lazy and comfortable. 'And now to bed!' said Julian. 'Girls, do you want any help with your mattress or rugs or anything?'

'No, thanks,' said Anne. 'Do you boys want to wash, and clean your teeth at the sink here? Because if so, do it now.'

Before a quarter of an hour had gone, everyone was bedded down comfortably. The three boys curled up in rugs in the bedroom below, with Mischief cuddled into Tinker's neck. The two girls and Timmy lay on a mattress, with a blanket over them. Timmy lay beside George, occasionally licking her ear with his big tongue.

'*Dear* Timmy!' said George, sleepily. 'I love you – but do please keep your tongue to yourself!'

And soon they were all asleep, boys, girls, and animals too. Outside, the sea sighed and splashed and swirled, and the wind cried like the daytime gulls. But all was peace and quiet inside the old lighthouse. Not even Mischief the monkey stirred in his sleep.

It was fun to wake up in the morning, and hear the gulls screaming round; fun to have breakfast of eggs and bread and butter, and apples to crunch afterwards – fun to plan what to do that day.

'I vote we do a bit of shopping and buy some more eggs, and fresh bread, and a bottle or two of creamy milk,' said Anne.

'And we might try and find the taxi driver's great-grandad, and ask him a few things about the lighthouse, and the wreckers that came in the old days,' said Dick.

'Yes – and he might show us the Wreckers' Cave!' said Julian. 'I'd like to see that! Let's buck up with whatever jobs there are to do, and we'll go over the rocks to the jetty. The tide should be out, so we ought to be able to walk over.'

'Well, we *must* be back before the tide comes in, then,' said Tinker. 'Because if we leave the boat tied up here by the lighthouse, we shan't be able to get back once the sea sweeps over the rocks and cuts us off!'

'Right,' said Julian. 'Be ready as soon as you can.'

Everyone was ready very quickly, and the little party set off over the rocks that at low tide lay between the lighthouse and the shore. Wicked rocks they were too – with sharp edges and points that would hole a ship at once!

Soon the children were on the little stone jetty. 'What was the name of old Great-Grandad?' said Dick frowning.

'Jeremiah Boogle,' said Anne. 'And he smokes a long pipe, and scowls at people.'

'Well – he *should* be easy to find!' said Julian. 'Come along. He's probably somewhere on the quay.'

'There he is!' said George, spotting an old man with a long pipe in his mouth. 'That's Jeremiah, I'm sure!'

Yes, there he was, sitting with his legs stretched out in front of him, an old, old man, smoking a very long pipe! He had a fine beard, a yachting cap askew on his head, and such enormous shaggy eyebrows that it was difficult to see his eyes beneath them!

The Five went up to him, with Timmy trotting behind, and Mischief on Tinker's shoulder. The old man spotted Mischief at once.

'Well, well – a monkey!' he said. 'Many's the little monkey I've brought home from my voyages.' He snapped his fingers and made a curious noise in his throat. Mischief stared at him, listening. Then he leapt from Tinker's shoulder on to the old man's, and rubbed his head against the old sailor's hairy ear.

'Mischief!' said Tinker, amazed. 'Look at that, George. He never goes to a stranger!'

'Well, maybe I knew his great-grandfather!' said the old sailor, laughing, and scratching Mischief's neck. 'All monkeys like me – and I like them!'

'Er – are you Mr Jeremiah Boogle?' asked Julian.

'Jeremiah Boogle, that's me,' said the old fellow, and touched his cap. 'How do you know my name?'

'Well, Jackson, the taxi driver, told us he was your great-grandson,' said Julian. 'You see we're staying at the old lighthouse – and Jackson said you could tell us a few things about it – its history, you know. And about the wreckers that lived here before the lighthouse was built.'

'Oh, I can tell you tales all right!' said Jeremiah, puffing out a cloud of smoke, and making Mischief cough. 'That's more than that

silly young great-grandson of mine can! He
don't know nothing, nothing at all – except
about cars. Well, who wants cars, nasty, smelly,
noisy things? Pah! That young George Jackson
is a ninny!'

'He's not. He's the cleverest mechanic in the
place!' said George, at once. 'There's not a
thing he doesn't know about cars!'

'CARS! There now, what did I say – nasty,
noisy, smelly, things!' said Jackson's great-
grandad, with a snort.

'Well, look – we don't want to talk about
cars,' said Julian. 'You tell us about the old
days – the wreckers and all that!'

'Ah – the old days!' said Great-Grandad.
'Well, I knew some wreckers myself, once –
there was One-Ear Bill, now . . .' And then old
Jeremiah told a story that the Five could hardly
believe!

[12]

Jeremiah's tale

'Now when I was a boy,' began the old man, 'a boy not much older than this here youngster,' and he poked Tinker with his horny forefinger, 'there wasn't a lighthouse out there – but there were always those wicked rocks! And many's the time in a stormy season when ships have been caught by their teeth, a-glittering there, waiting. You know what they're called, don't you?'

'Yes. Demon's Rocks,' said Tinker.

'Well, up on that high cliff there, lived a wicked old man,' said Jeremiah. 'And he had a son as bad as himself, and a nephew too. The Three Wreckers, they was called, and I'll tell you how they came by their name.'

'Did you know them?' asked Dick.

'That I did! And if I was hidden behind a bush when they came marching by, I'd send a stone skedaddling after them!' said the old man. 'Mean and cruel and wicked they were. And everyone was scared of them, right down afraid! There was One-Ear, the old man. They say his left ear was chewed off by a monkey, but do I blame that monkey? No, I do not, not more than I'd blame *your* monkey for chewing off the ear of somebody else I know – but I won't mention no names, he might hear me.'

The old fellow looked over his shoulder as if the man he was thinking of might be about.

'Well – there was One-Ear, the old man – and there was Nosey, the son – and Bart, his nephew – and not a pin to choose between them for meanness. There was only one thing they was after – and that was money! And a mighty wicked way they chose to get it.' The old man stopped and spat in disgust on the pavement.

'Pah! I'll tell you how they got rich, oh yes, I'll tell you. And I'll tell you what happened to them in the end too. Be a lesson to you and to everyone! Well now, you see that high cliff away down the coast there – the one with the flag-post and the flag a-waving in the wind?'

'Yes,' said everyone, looking at the waving flag.

'Now ships mustn't hug the coast beyond that point!' said Great-Grandad. 'If they do, they'll be forced inland by the current, and thrown on those rocks down there – Demon's Rocks. And that's the end of them. No ship has ever been able to escape the sharp teeth of those wicked rocks, once she's caught in that current. Well now, to stop the ships going near to the cliff in those days, they flew a flag in the day-time – and lit a lamp up there at night. And both said as plain as could be "BEWARE! KEEP OUT! DANGER".

'Of course, all sailors knew the flag and the lamp too, and many a one blessed them, and took their ships out to sea, away from Demon's

Rocks. But that didn't suit old One-Ear Bill. *He* didn't mind a wreck or two! He'd be down on the beach picking up what he could, if a ship came smashing down on the rocks. And would he save a single soul – not he! There were some people who said he was the Demon of Demon's Rocks himself!'

'What a wicked old man!' said Anne, horrified.

'Aye, you're right, missie,' said the old fellow. 'Well, the wrecks didn't come often enough for him and Nosey and Bart. So they put their ugly heads together and thought up as wicked a plan as any man could think of!'

'What was it?' said Tinker, his eyes almost falling out of his head.

'Well, on a stormy night he put out the lamp shining brightly on the far cliff, and he and Nosey carried it to that bit of cliff over there, see?' and the old man pointed to a jutting-out piece nearby. 'And you know what's just below *that* cliff, don't you – all round the lighthouse!'

'Rocks! Sharp, horrible rocks – the Demon's Rocks!' said George, horrified.

'Do you mean to say that One-Ear Bill and the others deliberately shone the lamp there on stormy nights, to guide ships straight on to the rocks?' said Julian.

'Aye, that's exactly what I mean,' said Jeremiah Boogle. 'And what's more I met old One-Ear Bill myself one dark night when the storms were on – and what was he carrying between himself and Nosey – the lamp! They'd doused the light, of course, but I'd my own little lantern with me, and I saw the lamp plain enough. Aye, that I did! And when they saw me, they set Bart on to me, to push me over the cliff, so I wouldn't tell on them. But I got away, and I DID tell on 'em! Ho, yes, I told all right. And One-Ear Bill went to prison, and serve him right, the wicked man. But he didn't care – and why should he? He was rich! RICH!'

'But how was he rich?' asked Dick.

'Well, young man, the ships that came sailing

round this coast in those days came from far-off countries, and many of them carried treasure,' said Jeremiah. 'And One-Ear Bill stole so much gold and silver and pearls and other things from the wrecks, that he knew he wouldn't need to do another day's work when he came out of prison. A rich man he would be – he wouldn't even need to wreck a ship again!'

'But why weren't the stolen goods taken from him?' said Julian.

'He'd hidden them!' said the old man. 'Ah, he'd hidden them well, too. Not even Nosey his son, nor Bart his nephew, knew where he'd put them. They were sure he'd got everything hidden in one of the caves in the cliff – but search as they might, they never found the treasure! They went to prison too, but they came out long before old One-Ear Bill was due out – and how they hunted for the gold and silver, and all that One-Ear had hidden away!'

'Did One-Ear Bill get it when he came out of prison?' asked Dick, thinking this was a much more exciting story than he had ever read in a book – and a true one too!

'No. No, he didn't get it,' said Jeremiah, puffing out a cloud of smoke. 'And glad I am to say that. He died in prison, the wicked old man.'

'Well then – what happened to the treasure from the wrecked ships?' asked George. 'Who found it?'

'No one,' said the old man. 'No one at all! It's still there, hidden wherever that old rascal put it. His secret went with him. Bart looked for it, and Nosey too – ho, I've seen 'em in those caves day after day, and with a lamp night after night. But they never found even a pearl necklace. Ho – that was a good joke, that was! They're dead and gone now – but there're relatives of theirs still living in Demon's Rocks, who could do with a bit of that treasure – poor as church mice they are, with two children as skinny as ever you'd see!'

'Doesn't anyone even have an *idea* where the

loot from the wrecked ships is?' asked Julian. 'What about the cave we've been hearing about – the Wreckers' Cave?'

'Oh aye – we've a Wreckers' Cave, all right,' said the old man, knocking out his pipe. 'And I reckon about five thousand people have been in it, scouting round, looking into holes and corners hoping to find what Bart and Nosey never did find! Or maybe ten thousand, who knows? I don't mind telling you, I've been there meself – but not a smell of a little gold coin did I ever see! I'll take you there myself some day if you like. But mind – don't you hope to find anything. It's my belief that One-Ear Bill never did hide his treasure there – he just said it was there to fool Nosey and Bart!'

'We'd love to go and see the cave,' said Dick, and George nodded her head in delight. 'Not to hunt for treasure, of course – it's pretty obvious it's not there now – maybe somebody *did* find it, and took it away secretly!'

'Maybe,' said Jeremiah. 'All right, young

man – you come and tell me when you're ready. I'm sitting here most days. And if you've any nice sweets you don't have any use for, think of me, see?'

'We'll go and buy you some straightaway,' said Julian. He couldn't help laughing. 'What kind do you like?'

'Oh, you tell Tom the sweetshop owner it's for old Jeremiah Boogle – he'll give you what I like,' said the old man. 'And mind now – don't you go snooping round them old caves by yourselves – you might get lost. It's a proper laby – laby . . .'

'Labyrinth,' said Julian, smiling. 'Right – we'll be careful.'

The Five went off, Timmy glad to be on the move again. He couldn't understand the old man's story of course, and he wondered why George hadn't taken him for his usual after-breakfast walk. He gave a little whine, and she patted his big head.

'Sorry, Timmy!' she said. 'That old man told

such an interesting story that I quite forgot you were longing for a walk. We'll go for one now.'

'Let's call in at the sweetshop first, shall we?' said Julian. 'That old chap deserves an extra something for his tale. Goodness knows how much was true – but he certainly told it well!'

'Of *course* it was true!' said George. 'Why ever should he tell lies?'

'Well – he might have, to get some sweets, you know!' said Julian, smiling. 'I don't blame him! It's a jolly good story – but please don't think there's any treasure still hidden somewhere, George. It's no use believing that.'

'Well, I do believe it!' said George, defiantly. 'I think he was telling the truth, sweets or no sweets. Don't you, Tinker?'

'Oh *yes*,' said Tinker. 'You wait till you see the caves round about here! Hoo – there might be any *amount* of treasure there, and no one would ever know! I did hunt round a bit myself – but those caves are scary, and when I coughed once, my cough came echoing back to me a hundred times and I was so scared I ran for my life – and fell splash into a pool!'

Everyone laughed. 'Let's buck up and do our shopping,' said Dick. 'And then what about going for a good long walk?'

'Well, *I* don't want to carry eggs and bread and milk for miles,' said George. 'I say a walk first – and then we'll come back, have ice-creams, do our shopping – and go back to the lighthouse.'

'Right!' said Julian. 'Come on, Timmy. We're off for a WALK – a WALK! Ha, that's the word to set your tail wagging, isn't it? Look at it, Mischief. Don't you wish you could wag *your* tail like that!'

A pleasant morning – and a shock!

'Where shall we go for our walk?' said George, as they wandered through the village. 'Oh look – there's a tiny little shop with "Tom's Sweetshop" written over the door. Let's get the sweets while we remember.'

So in went Julian, and rapped on the counter. A very small man, like a hobgoblin, appeared out of a dark corner.

'I want some sweets for Jeremiah Boogle, please,' said Julian. 'I think you know the kind he wants.'

'I do that!' said Tom, scrabbling about on a shelf. 'The amount that old Jeremiah has eaten since I've been here would keep an army going for years. There you are, young man!'

'He tells a fine story,' said Julian, putting down the money for the sweets.

Tom laughed. 'He's been going on about Bart and Nosey and all them old folks, I suppose,' he said. 'He's a funny one, is old Jeremiah. Never forgets a thing, even if it happened eighty or more years ago! Never forgives, either. There're two folk in this village that he spits at when he passes by them. Naughty old man, he is.'

'What have they done to earn his spite?' asked Dick, in surprise.

'Well, they're some kin of his old enemy, One-Ear Bill,' said Tom. 'I reckon he told you about him all right, didn't he?'

'Yes, he did,' said Julian. 'But all that business about the wrecking happened years and years ago! Surely Jeremiah doesn't vent his anger on any descendants of the wicked One-Ear Bill.'

'Oh, but he *does*!' said Tom. 'You see, these two fellows he spits at have the job of showing people round the caves here – especially the Wreckers' Cave – and I reckon old Jeremiah still broods about One-Ear's hidden treasure, and is scared in case these two chaps ever find it. Find it! It's nearly seventy years since all that happened. Why, that lighthouse over there was built over sixty years ago – after that wrecking business went on. No one will come across any treasure now!'

'But surely they *might*,' said George. 'It depends where it was hidden. If it was in some dry, watertight place, it should still be all right. After all, gold and silver don't decay, do they? Wherever it was hidden, it must still be there!'

'That's what all you visitors say!' said Tom. 'And that's what Ebenezer and Jacob say – they're the two chaps who show people round the caves. But they only say that to make a bit of a thrill for the visitors, you know. Same as old Jeremiah does. Takes them in properly! Well – you believe what you like, youngsters – but you won't find any treasure! I reckon the sea took that years ago! Good day to you! I'll give Jeremiah the sweets when he calls in.'

'Well,' said Dick, as soon as they were outside the shop, 'this is all very interesting! I think probably old Tom's right. The reason why the treasure was never found is because it was probably hidden where the sea managed to get at it – in some water-hole, or somewhere like that.'

'I still believe it's somewhere safe,' said George. 'So does Tinker.'

'Oh well . . . I should think probably Timmy believes it as well,' said Dick. 'He has a childlike mind too!'

Dick at once received a hard punch on the back from George. He laughed. 'All right! We'll give you a chance to hunt for the treasure, won't we, Ju? We'll visit the Wreckers' Cave as soon as we can. Let's go up on the cliffs for our walk, and see if we can spot where the first old lamp used to be, that warned ships to swing out to sea, and avoid Demon's Rocks.'

It was a lovely walk along the cliffs. The celandines and tiny dog violets were out, and clumps of pale yellow primroses were everywhere. The breeze blew strongly, and Mischief held tightly to Tinker's right ear, afraid of being blown off his shoulder. Timmy enjoyed himself thoroughly, bounding along, tail flourishing happily, sniffing at everything.

They came to the flag-post set high on the cliff, its great red flag waving vigorously in the breeze. A notice-board was beside it. George read it.

'This flag warns ships off Demon's Rocks by day. By night the great lighthouse at High Cliffs, farther along the coast, gives warning. In the old days a lamp shone from this spot to give the ships warning, and later a small lighthouse was built out on Demon's Rocks. It is still in existence, but is no longer in use.'

'Ha – they're wrong there!' said Tinker, pointing to the last sentence. '*We're* using it!

I'll alter the notice!' and Tinker actually took a pencil to scratch out the last six words!

Julian took it from him. 'Don't be silly. You can't mess about with public notices. Don't say you're one of the idiots who like to scribble all over the place!'

Tinker held out his hand for the pencil. 'All right. It was just that I thought it wanted correcting. I'm *not* the kind of idiot who scribbles on walls or public notices.'

'Right,' said Julian. 'Tinker, can we see Demon's Rocks – the rocks themselves, I mean, with our lighthouse – from these cliffs?'

'No,' said Tinker. 'The cliff swings away to the left, look, and the Demon's Rocks are away right round the corner, if you see what I mean – so no ship should follow the coastline here, but should keep well out at sea, or it'd be on the rocks. You can see quite well that if the wreckers took the lamp from its warning place here, and put it much farther back, along the way we've come, the ships would swing too far inland, and find themselves wrecked!'

'I think *I* should have hated old One-Ear Bill as much as old Jeremiah does,' said George, imagining the beautiful ships being ground to pieces all those years ago – just because of a greedy man who liked the pickings from wrecks!

'Well, we'd better go back,' said Julian, looking at his watch. 'We've some shopping to do, remember! Better buck up too – it looks like rain all of a sudden!'

He was right. It was pouring by the time they reached the village! They crowded into a little shop that said 'Morning Coffee' and ordered a cup each, and buns. The buns were so nice that they bought some to take back to the lighthouse with them. Then Anne remembered postcards.

'We *must* buy some,' she said, 'and send one off today. Better get some now, and write one and post it while we're here.'

Dick slipped out of the coffee shop and

returned with a packet of very gaudily coloured cards. 'Some of them show the lighthouse,' he said. 'We'll send one of those – and you choose a card to send to your father too, Tinker.'

'It would be a waste,' said Tinker. 'He wouldn't even bother to read it.'

'Well, send one to your mother,' said Anne.

'I haven't one,' said Tinker. 'She's dead. She died when I was born. That's why my father and I always go about together.'

'I'm very, very sorry, Tinker,' said Anne, shocked. The others were sorry too. No wonder Tinker was so wild. No mother to teach him anything! Poor Tinker! Anne felt as if she wanted to buy him every bun in the shop!

'Have another bun, Tinker,' she said. 'Or an ice-cream. I'll pay. Mischief can have one too.'

'We're *all* going to have another bun each, *and* an ice-cream,' said Julian. 'Timmy and Mischief too. Then we'll do our shopping and go home – home to the lighthouse. That sounds grand, doesn't it!'

They wrote three cards – one to Uncle Quentin and Aunt Fanny – one to Joanna – and one to the professor. 'Now they'll know we are safe and happy!' said Anne, sticking on the stamps.

The rain had stopped, so they went to do their shopping – fresh bread, more butter and eggs, two bottles of milk, some fruit and a few other things. Then off they went down to the little jetty.

'Tide will soon turn,' said Julian, as they jumped down from the jetty to the rocky little beach. 'Come on – we'll just have time to walk over the rocks to the lighthouse. PLEASE don't drop the eggs, Tinker!'

They made their way over the rocks, jumping over little pools here and there and avoiding the slimy strands of seaweed that in places covered the rocks. The lighthouse seemed very tall as they came up to it.

'It's *tiny* compared to the great new one away at High Cliffs,' said Tinker. 'You ought to go over that! The revolving lamp at the top is magnificent! Its light is so powerful that ships can see it for miles!'

'Well, this little lighthouse looks nice enough to me at the moment,' said Dick, climbing up the stone steps to the strong wooden door. 'Hallo! Look – two bottles of milk on the top step! Don't tell me the milkman's been!'

'He used to call when my father and I were here,' said Tinker. 'Only when the tide was out in the morning though, because he hasn't a boat. I suppose he heard *we* were all staying here, and came to see if we wanted milk – and left two bottles when he found we were out. He probably yelled through the letter-box and when we didn't answer he just left the milk, on chance.'

'Sensible fellow!' said Dick. 'Get out your key, Tinker, and unlock the door.'

'I don't remember locking it behind us when we went out this morning,' said Tinker, frantically feeling in all his pockets. 'I must have left it in the lock on the inside of the door. Let's see now – we locked the door last night, and left the key in the lock. So I *must* have unlocked it this morning for us all to get out.'

'That's right – but after you unlocked it you ran straight down the steps with George, and the rest of us followed,' said Julian. 'Anne was last. Did *you* lock the door after you, Anne?'

'No. I never thought of it!' said Anne. 'I just shut the door with a bang and raced after you all! So the key must still be on the other side of the door!'

'Well, if we push the door, it should open!' said Julian, with a grin. 'And the key will be on the inside, waiting for us! Let's go in!'

He pushed hard, for the door shut very tightly – and sure enough, it swung open. Julian put his hand round to the inside lock to feel for the key.

It wasn't there! Julian looked at the others, frowning.

'*Someone's been here* – and found the door unlocked – taken the key – and probably plenty of other things as well!' he said. 'We'd better go and look. Come on!'

'Wait – there's something on the doormat,' said Dick, picking up a letter. 'The postman has visited the lighthouse too – here's a letter forwarded from Kirrin – so at least *two* people came while we were out! But surely neither of them would take the key – or anything else either!'

'Well – we'll soon see!' said Julian, grimly, and up the first bend of the spiral stairway he went, at top speed!

[14]

The old, old map

Julian and Dick went into each room of the lighthouse, racing up the spiral stairway from one to the other. Why, oh why, hadn't they watched to see that Tinker locked the door and took the key!

Yes – a few things *had* been taken!

'My rug!' said George. 'That's gone!'

'And my purse,' said Anne. 'I left it here on the table. That's been taken, too!'

'So has my little travelling clock,' groaned Julian. 'Why did I bring it? I could have used my watch!'

There were a few other things gone, all small. 'Horrible fellow, whoever he is, to creep into the lighthouse while we were out and take our things!' said Anne, almost crying. 'Who would come here – they would surely be seen from the quay, wouldn't they?'

'Yes – you're right there,' said Julian. 'Though probably the thief slipped in when it was pouring with rain, and the quay was deserted! I think we'll have to tell the police, you know. Let's have our dinner, and then I'll take the boat and slip across to the village. The tide will be in then, and I shan't be able to walk over the rocks. Blow that thief! I was looking forward to a nice quiet read this afternoon!'

After their meal, Julian took the boat and rowed across to the jetty. He went straight to the police station, where a stolid-looking policeman listened to him, and wrote slowly in a book.

'Have you any idea who the thief might be?' asked the policeman. 'Or if anyone came to the lighthouse while you were out?'

'Well, two people seem to have come,' said Julian. 'The milkman, because we were surprised to find milk bottles on the step. And the postman. There was a letter for us on the mat inside the door. I don't know of anyone else.'

'Well, as far as I can tell you, both Willy the Milkman, and Postie are as honest as the day,' said the policeman, scratching his chin with his pencil. 'There may have been a third visitor – one who didn't leave milk or a letter! I'll see if anyone was on the quay this morning, who saw the thief going over the Demon's Rocks. Er – do you suspect anyone?'

'Good gracious, no!' said Julian. 'I don't know anyone here – unless you can count Jeremiah Boogle, or Tom the sweetshop owner!'

'No. No, I think we can rule both of them out,' said the policeman, smiling. 'Well, I'll do what I can, and let you know if I hear of anything. Good-afternoon, and by the way, as you can't lock that lighthouse door now, and it's plain there are thieves about, I shouldn't leave the lighthouse empty, see?'

'Yes. Yes, I'd already thought of that,' said Julian. 'I can jam the door all right with something when we're *in* the lighthouse – but I can't do that when we're out.'

'Well – it looks as if we're in for a wet spell,' said the policeman. 'So maybe it won't be much hardship to keep indoors. I hope you're comfortable in the lighthouse – seems a funny place to stay, really.'

'Oh we're *very* comfortable, Constable,' said Julian, smiling. 'Why not pay us a call sometime, and see us?'

'Thanks,' said the policeman, and took Julian to the door.

The constable was right in forecasting a wet spell. It poured all that afternoon, and the little company in the lighthouse whiled away the time playing cards. Julian and Dick had managed to find a heavy piece of wood in the storeroom to jam the door from the inside. They all felt much safer when they knew that had been done!

Now no one could get in without making a terrific noise!

'I'm stiff,' said George, at last. 'I want to stretch my legs. I've a good mind to run up and down the stairway half a dozen times.'

'Well, go on, then,' said Dick. 'Nobody's stopping you!'

'How far down does the lighthouse go, Tinker?' asked George. 'We always scoot up the first bit of the spiral stairway and never think about the lighthouse foundations deep down in the rock. *Are* they deep down?'

'Oh, they are,' said Tinker, looking up from his book. 'My father told me that when the lighthouse was built, they drilled right down into the rock for a long way – made a kind of shaft. And he said that under these rocks there are all kinds of queer holes and tunnels – the drill kept shooting downwards when it came to a sudden space.'

'*Really?*' said Dick, interested. 'I hadn't thought of what would have to be done to make a high lighthouse safe from the gales and storms. It would *have* to have deep foundations, of course!'

'My father found an old map somewhere,' said Tinker. 'A sort of plan made when the lighthouse was first built.'

'Like architects draw when they plan how to build a house?' said Anne.

'Something like that,' said Tinker. 'I can't remember much about it. I know it showed all the rooms in the lighthouse, connected by the spiral stairway – and it showed the big lamp-room at the top – and at the bottom of the map the foundation shaft was drawn.'

'Can you go down the shaft?' asked Dick. 'Is there a ladder, or anything?'

'I don't know,' said Tinker. 'I've never been down there. I never thought about it!'

'Do you know where the old map is – the one made by the architect who drew up plans for the lighthouse builder to follow?' said Julian. 'Where did your father put it?'

'Oh, I expect he threw it away,' said Tinker. 'Wait a minute though – it may be in the lamp-room! I remember him taking it up there, because it had a drawing of how the lamp worked.'

'Well, I'd rather like to go and see if I can find it,' said Julian, interested. 'Come up with me, Tinker. Thank goodness you don't keep turning into some sort of car now – you must be growing up!'

So the two of them went up the spiral stairway to the lamp-room at the very top of the tower. Again Julian marvelled at the magnificent views all around. The rain had stopped for a time, and the sea, swept by strong winds, was a swirling tumult of angry waters.

Tinker scrabbled about in a little dark space under the lamp. He at last brought up a roll of something white and waved it at Julian. 'Here's the map. I thought it would be in the lamp-room.'

Julian took it down to the others, and they

spread it out. It showed the plan of the lighthouse, and was very clearly and beautifully drawn.

'How is it that architects draw so marvellously?' said George. 'Are they architects because they can do this kind of thing so well – or do they draw beautifully because they are architects?'

'A bit of both, probably,' said Julian, bending over the finely drawn plan. 'Ah – here are the foundations, look – my goodness, they do go down a long way into the rock!'

'Great tall buildings like this *always* have deep, strong foundations,' said Dick. 'Last term at school we studied how—'

'Let's not talk of school,' said Anne. 'It's already looming in the distance! Tinker – can anyone get down into this foundation place?'

'I told you – I don't know,' said Tinker. 'Anyway I should think it would be a horrible place down there – dark and smelly, and narrow, and . . .'

'Let's go and see,' said George, getting up. 'I'm so bored at the moment that if I don't do something, I'll fall asleep for a hundred years.'

'Idiot,' said Dick. 'Still – quite a good idea of yours. We'd have a bit of peace and quiet while you were sleeping! Oooooch – don't jab me like that, George!'

'Come on,' said George. 'Let's trot down and find out what's down the shaft.'

Anne didn't want to go down the shaft, but the others ran down the stairway, Timmy too, and soon came to the bottom, opposite the entrance door of the lighthouse.

Tinker showed them a large, round trap-door in the floor there. 'If we open that, we'll be looking down into the foundation shaft,' he said.

So they pulled up the large, round, wooden trap-door, and gazed downwards. They could see nothing at all except darkness! 'Where's my torch?' said Julian. 'I'll fetch it!'

Soon his torch was lighting up the round

shaft, and they saw an iron ladder going down it on one side. Julian climbed down a few steps and examined the walls of the shaft.

'They're cement!' he called. 'And they must be enormously thick, I should think. I'm going on down.'

So down he went, and down, marvelling at the sturdy cement lining of the enormous shaft. He wondered why it had not been filled in. Perhaps a hollow cement-lined shaft was stronger than a filled-in one? He didn't know.

He came almost to the bottom – but he didn't go down the last steps of the iron ladder. A peculiar noise came from below him! A gurgling, choking noise! What in the world could it be?

He shone his torch down to see – and then stared in amazement! There was water at the bottom of the shaft, water that swirled and moved around, making a strange, hollow, gurgling noise. Where did it come from?

As he watched it, it disappeared – then it

came back again! He shone his torch here and there to find out how the water made its way into the shaft.

'There must be a tunnel or a passage of some sort down there, that the sea can enter,' he thought. 'It's high tide now – so the water is swirling in. I wonder – now I *wonder* – if it's free of water when the tide is out! And if so where does that tunnel, or whatever it is, lead to? Or is it always under water? I'll go back and tell the others – and have another look at that old map!'

He climbed back, glad to be out of the smelly darkness of the old shaft. The others were at the top, looking down rather anxiously.

'Here he is!' said George. 'See anything interesting, Julian?'

'I did, rather,' said Julian, climbing out of the shaft. 'Got that old map with you? I want to look at something, if so.'

'Come upstairs, then,' said Dick. 'We can see better there. What was down there, Ju?'

'Wait till we're up in the living room,' said Julian. He took the map from Tinker as soon as he arrived there, and sat down to look at it. He ran his finger down the shaft to the bottom, and then jabbed at a round mark drawn there.

'See that? That's a hole at the bottom of the shaft, through which sea-water comes in. It's high tide now, so the water is seeping into the shaft – but it's not very deep. At low tide there wouldn't be a single drop coming in. Wouldn't I love to know where that water-tunnel went to – up to the surface of the rocks? Through them to somewhere a good way off? Or what?'

'An undersea tunnel!' said George, her eyes bright. 'Why don't we explore it sometime when the tide is out?'

'Well – we'd have to be pretty certain we wouldn't suddenly be drowned!' said Julian, rolling up the map. 'Very interesting, isn't it? I suppose the hole was left in case the constant push of water there, when the tide was in, might undermine the foundations. Better to have the

shaft half-full of water than eaten away by
constant tides!'

'Well,' began Anne, and then suddenly
stopped in fright. A very loud voice came up
the stairway, and made everyone jump violently.

'ANYONE AT HOME? HEY, ANYONE AT HOME?'

[15]

Jacob is in trouble

'Who's that shouting like that?' said Anne, fearfully. 'It can't be the robber, can it?'

'Of course not,' said Julian, and went to the door of the living room. He yelled down the stairway:

'Who is it? What do you want?'

'It's the police!' shouted back the enormous voice.

'Oh. Come on up, then,' said Julian, relieved. Footsteps could be heard coming up the iron stairway, accompanied by loud puffs and pants. Then a policeman's helmet appeared, followed by his shoulders and the rest of him. Soon he was standing in the living room, beaming round at the surprised company, panting with the effort of climbing so many stairs.

'How did you get in?' asked George. 'We jammed the door shut from the inside.'

'Well, I managed to unjam it, miss,' said the policeman, mopping his forehead, and smiling. He was the same policeman that Julian had seen that afternoon. 'Not much protection that, really. You ought to get a new key made.'

'How did you get over here – the tide's in,' said Julian. 'You couldn't have walked over Demon's Rocks.'

'No. I got Jem Hardy's boat,' said the policeman. 'By the way, my name's Sharp – Police Constable Sharp.'

'A very good name for a policeman,' said Julian, with a cheerful grin. 'Well, have you caught the thief who took our key, and the other things?'

'No. But I've a pretty good idea who it is,' said Sharp. 'I couldn't find anyone who'd been sitting on the quay during the time you were away from the lighthouse, but I did by chance find a lady whose windows look down on the jetty, and she happened to see someone standing about there. She said he went over the rocks to the lighthouse.'

'Who was it? The milkman, the postman?' asked Dick.

'Oh no, I told your friend they were good fellows,' said the constable, looking quite shocked. 'It was er – well, a man who's a bit of a bad lot.'

'Who's that?' asked Julian, suddenly afraid it might be old Jeremiah. *Could* he be a bad lot – he had sounded such a good fellow!

'Well, it's no one you know,' said Sharp. 'It's one of a family with rather a bad name – a man called Jacob – Jacob Loomer. He comes of a family that used to do a bit of wrecking, and—'

'Wrecking! Old Jeremiah was telling us of long-ago wreckers!' said Dick. 'One was called Nosey – and another was called Bart – relations of a well-known wrecker called One-Ear – er, One-Ear . . .'

'Bill,' said Sharp. 'Ah, yes – One-Ear Bill. He lived a long time ago, when old Jeremiah was a young man. This here Jacob, the one that was seen going into your lighthouse today, would be his great-great-great-grandson, I reckon – something like that. Living image of old One-Ear Bill, according to Jeremiah. There's a bad strain in that family – can't seem to get it out!'

'Well – you say it was Jacob who came into the lighthouse? Why can't we have him arrested then?' said Julian. 'And make him give up the key he took – and the other things?'

'Well, if you'll come along with me and identify your things, maybe I can do something about it,' said the constable. 'But he may have hidden them all by now – though he's that free-handed I wouldn't be surprised if he hasn't *given* them all away. A bit of a fool, Jacob is, as well as a rogue. Ah – he'd have liked the job of wrecking ships, he would – right up his street.'

'I'll come with you now,' said Julian. 'The others don't need to, do they?'

'Oh no – you'll do,' said the policeman, and he and Julian went down the spiral stairway to the entrance. The others heard the door bang, and looked at one another.

'Well! To think that a great-great-great-grandson of that horrid old One-Ear Bill is still living in the same place that the old wrecker himself did!' said Dick. '*And* he's a rogue too. History repeating itself?'

'We *must* go and see the Wreckers' Cave tomorrow, if we can,' said George. 'Jeremiah Boogle said he would show it to us.'

'So long as there isn't an old, old wrecker hiding there!' said Anne. 'Older than Jeremiah Boogle – with a beard down to his feet – a sort of Old Man of the Sea – with a horrid gurgling voice, and eyes like a fish!'

'*Really*, Anne!' said George astonished. 'I'll be scared to go into caves if you say things like that!'

'I wonder how Julian's getting on,' said Tinker. 'Mischief, stop jigging up and down – you make me feel out of breath!'

Julian was at Jacob's house, and there, sure enough, were the things he had stolen – the rug, the clock and Anne's purse – empty now!'

'And what about the key?' demanded the constable. 'Come on now, you took the key out of the door of the lighthouse, we know you did. Give it here, Jacob.'

'I didn't take it,' said Jacob, sullenly.

'I'll have to take you in, you know, Jacob,' said the constable. 'You'll be searched at the police station. Better give up the key now.'

'Search me all you like!' said Jacob. 'You won't find that key on me. I tell you. I didn't take it. What would I want that key for?'

'For the same reason that you usually want keys for,' said the constable. 'For breaking in and stealing. All right, Jacob. If you won't let this young gentleman have his key, I'll have you searched at the police station. Come along with me.'

But alas, no key was found on the surly

Jacob, and the constable shrugged his shoulders and raised his eyebrows at Julian.

'If you take my advice, I'd get a different lock put on your door. Jacob's got your key somewhere. He'll be at the lighthouse again as soon as he sees you all go out.'

'Bah!' said Jacob, rudely. 'You and your keys. I tell you I didn't take it. There wasn't a key there . . .'

'Come along with me, Jacob,' said the constable. He turned to Julian. 'Well, that's all. We'll have his house searched. The odds are that he's hidden the key somewhere. He's an artful dodger, this one!'

Julian went back to the lighthouse, rather worried. It might take a few days, in a little place like this, to have a new lock put in. In the meantime they would either have to keep themselves prisoners in the lighthouse – or leave a front door that anyone could open!

The others listened excitedly to his tale, when he went back. They were glad to have the rug, the clock and the purse again – though Anne was sad that all her money was gone.

'We'll have to get a new lock and key,' said Julian. 'After all, this lighthouse has only been *lent* to us, and it's our responsibility to look after it and all it contains. It's a good thing it was only *our* things that were taken – not Professor Hayling's!'

'It's getting rather late,' said Anne, jumping up. 'We haven't had our tea yet! I'll get it. Anyone feel like buns with butter and jam?'

Everyone did, and soon Anne produced a large plate of delicious-looking buns. They talked as they drank their tea, and ate the buns.

'I vote we go and find Jeremiah Boogle tomorrow, and see if he's heard of the robbery, and if he has anything interesting to say about it,' said George.

'And also we really must get him to show us the Wreckers' Cave,' said Julian. 'By the way, what were the names of the two men who have the job of showing the visitors round the caves? I'm pretty sure one was Jacob!'

'You're right – it was – and the other man was called Ebenezer!' said Dick. 'Well – let's hope Jacob is locked up, or out of the way somewhere when we go to see the caves. We shall get some black looks from him, if not!'

'Well, we can give him some back!' said George, putting on a terrific scowl, and making Timmy give a sudden whine. She patted him. 'It's all right, Timmy – that scowl wasn't for you!'

'We'd better go to the caves tomorrow morning when the tide will be more or less out,' said Julian. 'And I'd better see if I can find a locksmith here who can give us a new lock and key quickly!'

'Why not slip out now?' said Dick. 'I'll come with you for a bit of fresh air. Want to come, girls?'

'No, I'd like to finish my book,' said Anne, and George said the same. Tinker was playing with Mischief, and he didn't want to come either.

'Well, you and the lighthouse will be safe with Timmy and Mischief to look after you!' said Julian, and down the stairway he went, with Dick close behind him.

The locksmith promised to come and look at the door in the next day or two. 'Can't leave my shop just now,' he said. 'Nobody to see to it! It'll take me a few days to do the job for you, I'm afraid.'

'Oh, blow!' said Julian. 'We've already had a thief in the lighthouse! We don't like to go out and leave it empty now!'

They rowed back to the lighthouse, shut and jammed the door as best they could, and went up to the girls. Timmy gave them an uproarious welcome, and Mischief took a flying leap from a chair back on to Dick's shoulder.

'No lock or key for a few days,' said Dick, sitting down and tickling the delighted little monkey. 'I did want to go and see the caves

tomorrow – especially the famous Wreckers'
one – but we can't possibly leave the lighthouse
empty.'

'Woof,' said Timmy at once.

'He says, why not leave *him* behind, and let
him guard it,' said George, solemnly, and Timmy at once said, 'Woof', again.

They all laughed. Dick patted Timmy, and
ruffled the fur behind his ears. 'Dear old Tim –
all right, *you* guard the lighthouse – you shall
have a Very Special Bone for a reward!'

'That's settled then. We leave Timmy here on
guard, and we all go off to the caves,' said
Julian. 'Well, one of the brothers who show
visitors round will be missing tomorrow, I fear
– Jacob will *not* be there!'

'I bet we'll get some scowls from the other
brother – what's his name now – Ebenezer?'
said Anne. 'We'll have to be careful that we
don't get pushed into a deep pool of water!'

'Dear me, yes,' said Julian. 'One never
knows! We'll certainly be on our guard!'

[16]

Down in the caves

Next morning George awoke with a jump. Timmy was pushing her gently with his nose. 'What is it, Tim?' said George. Timmy gave a bark, and ran to where the spiral stairway led downwards.

'Go down and tell the boys what it is you want,' said George, sleepily. So down the stairway went Timmy, and into the room where the boys were sleeping. He trotted in and nudged Julian with his nose, but Julian was so fast asleep that he didn't stir.

Timmy pawed at him, and Julian awoke with a jump. He sat up. 'Oh, it's you, Tim – what on earth do you want? Is anything wrong with the girls?'

'Woof,' said Timmy, and ran to the spiral stairway. He disappeared down it, barking.

'Blow! He's heard someone!' said Julian, yawning. 'Well, if it's Ebenezer or Jacob – no, it can't be Jacob, of course – I'll tell him what I think of people who steal!'

He unjammed the door of the lighthouse and opened it. On the step stood two milk bottles! 'Well, really, Timmy, fancy waking me because the milkman came!' said Julian, taking in the bottles. 'Good old milkman – I wonder if he had to come by boat – the sea's pretty high this morning – but I suppose he *could* just about have waded over the rocks!'

At breakfast the children remembered that they meant to see the caves that morning. They had a very fine meal of fried bacon, bought the day before, and eggs, with buttered toast and marmalade to follow. Anne had made some good hot coffee, and they all enjoyed themselves immensely. Mischief made himself a real nuisance by putting a paw deep in the marmalade jar and then, when smacked, running all over the place leaving sticky marmaladey marks everywhere!

'We'd better all take a wet rag with us as we go about the room,' said Anne, in disgust. 'He's run over the table and desk and everything. BAD Mischief! I do so hate feeling sticky.'

Mischief was sad to feel himself in disgrace, and leapt on to Tinker's shoulder, putting his sticky paws lovingly round the boy's neck. 'That's right!' said Tinker, 'rub all your stickiness off on *me*, you little monkey!'

'We'll wash up in the sink, and you boys can tidy up the rooms,' said Anne. 'Then we'll all go out. It's a lovely day.'

'Looks a bit stormy to me,' said Dick. 'What do *you* say, Tim?'

Tim agreed. He thumped his tail vigorously on the floor, making Mischief pounce on it in joy. Anne gathered up the crockery and took it to the sink.

In an hour or so they were ready to go out. 'Let's write a card to Aunt Fanny before we leave,' said Anne. 'Then *that* will be done. We won't say a word about the things that were stolen, though. She might feel upset, and tell us to go back! And *then* what would Uncle Quentin and Professor Hayling say?'

'I bet they're having a wonderful time, arguing all day long, working out figures, and studying papers!' said Julian. 'And I'm pretty certain that Aunt Fanny will have to call them to a meal at least twenty times before they arrive at the table!'

Anne wrote the postcard and put on a stamp. 'Now I'm ready,' she said, standing up. Timmy ran to the top of the stairs, glad that everyone seemed to be on the move at last. He did so love a walk.

'Darling Timmy,' said George, 'I'm afraid you'll have to be left behind to guard the lighthouse! You see, we haven't a key – and we can't jam the door from outside. So please, Timmy dear, stay behind – on guard. You know what *that* means, don't you? ON GUARD!'

Timmy's tail went right down. He gave a small whine. He did so hate being left out of anything – especially a walk. He pawed gently at George as if to say, 'Do please change your mind.'

'On guard, Timmy, now,' said George. 'The lighthouse is in your charge. Don't let ANYONE *in*. You'd better lie on the mat just inside the entrance.'

Timmy ran slowly down behind Julian and the others, looking very mournful indeed. 'Now lie there,' said George, and gave him a pat on the head. 'We'll take you out again soon, and then one of *us* will stay to guard the lighthouse – but this time we *all* want to go out. ON GUARD!'

Timmy lay down on the mat, and put his head on his paws, his brown eyes looking up at George. 'Dear old faithful,' she said ruffling the hair on his head. 'We won't be very long!'

They slammed the door and went down the lighthouse steps. The tide was still out far enough for them to be able to wade over the rocks to the jetty. 'We must be back before it's well in,' said Julian. 'Or we'll have to stay ashore till it's out again. Our boat is tied to the lighthouse post, remember!'

They went for a stroll along the quay and who should be there, sitting on a stone seat, but old Jeremiah Boogle, smoking his long pipe, staring solemnly out to sea.

'Good-morning, Jeremiah,' said Dick, politely. 'I hope we bought the right kind of sweets for you from Tom.'

'Oh aye,' said Jeremiah, puffing out very strong-smelling smoke. 'Hallo, little monkey – so you've come to my shoulder again, have you? Well, what's the news from Monkey Lane?'

The others laughed as Mischief at once poured out a stream of monkey chatter into the old man's ear. 'We thought we would go and see the caves today,' said Julian. 'Especially the old Wreckers' Cave.'

'Now don't you let that Ebenezer take you round!' said the old man, at once. 'You won't

find Jacob there – oho – I know what's happened to *him*. And serve him right. Never could
keep his fingers to himself, that one! Ebenezer's
as bad. He could steal the buttons off your coat,
and you'd never know! Now look – what about
me showing you the caves? I know them inside
out, and I can show you things that that rat of
an Ebenezer doesn't even know of.'

'Well – we'd certainly much rather *you* took
us, and not Ebenezer,' said Julian. 'Ebenezer
may be feeling rather angry because we told the
police about his brother stealing things. We'll
give you some more sweets if *you'll* guide us
round.'

'Well, let's go now,' said Jeremiah, getting up
very spryly. 'This way!'

And off they went, Mischief too – the little
monkey did Jeremiah the honour of sitting on
his shoulder all the way down the village street.
The old man was delighted to see how everyone
stared and laughed.

He took them round the foot of some very

high cliffs. They came to a rocky beach farther along, and walked over it. 'There's the entrance,' said the old man, pointing to a large hole in the cliff nearby. 'That's the way to the caves. Got a torch?'

'Yes – we brought one each,' said Julian, patting his pocket. 'Do we have to pay to go in?'

'No. People give Ebenezer a tip – a couple of pounds or so – if he shows them round – or Jacob, when he's there,' said Jeremiah. '*I'll* deal with Ebby, though. Don't you waste your money on that scoundrel!'

The hole in the cliff led to the first cave, which was a big one. Lighted lanterns hung here and there, but gave very little light.

'Mind your step, now,' warned Jeremiah. 'It's really slippery in places. This way – through this old arch.'

It was cold and damp in the cave, and the children had to go carefully, and avoid the puddles left by the sea. Then suddenly Jeremiah turned a corner and went in a completely different direction! Down and down and down they went!

'Hey – we're going towards the *sea* now surely?' said Julian, in surprise. 'Do the caves go *under* the sea, then? Not away back into the cliff?'

'That's right,' said Jeremiah. 'This is a real rocky coast – and the way we're taking leads down a tunnel under the rocks, and then into the caves deep underground. See the rocky roof over our heads – well, if you listen, you can hear the sea now, mumbling and grumbling over it – that roof is the bed of the sea!'

That was a very strange thought indeed, and rather alarming! Anne gazed fearfully up at the rocky roof overhead, and shone her torch on it, half-expecting to see a few cracks leaking salt water from the sea rolling over the rocky roof! But no – there was a little moisture shining on it, and that was all.

'Are we soon coming to the Wreckers' Cave?'

asked George. 'Mischief, stop making those noises. There's nothing to be scared of!'

Mischief didn't like this cold, dark, strange walk underground, and had begun to make harsh, frightened noises, and then suddenly gave a loud scared screech.

'Don't! You made me jump!' said Anne. 'Goodness – listen to the monkey's screech echoing all along the tunnel and back! Sounds like a hundred monkeys chattering at once! *Our* voices echo too!'

Mischief was most alarmed to hear the enormous amount of screeches and chattering noises that now filled the tunnel. He began to cry almost like a baby, and clung to Tinker as if he would never let him go.

'I expect he thinks this place is absolutely full of screeching monkeys,' said Anne, sorry for the terrified little creature. 'It's only the echo, Mischief.'

'He'll soon get used to it,' said Tinker, hugging the monkey close to him.

'You want to hear the echo just round the next bend of the tunnel!' said Jeremiah, stroking the little monkey, and very foolishly gave an enormous yell just as they got there!

The yell came back ten times as loud, and the tunnel seemed suddenly full of shouts tumbling over one another. Everyone jumped violently, and Mischief leapt high in the air in terror. He sprang to the ground, and scampered away at top speed, wailing in his little monkey voice. He tore down the tunnel, tail in air, and disappeared round the corner. Tinker was very upset.

'Mischief! Come back!' he yelled. 'You'll get lost!'

And along came the echo at once. 'Get lost, get lost, get lost – lost – lost!'

'Don't you worry about your monkey,' said Jeremiah, comfortingly. 'I've had a score of monkeys in my time – and they always come back!'

'Well, I'll jolly well stay down here till Mischief *does* come back!' said Tinker, in rather a shaky voice.

They came out into a cave. This too was lit by lanterns, though very poorly. They had all heard the murmur of voices as they came to it, and wondered who was there.

Three other visitors were in the cave, sight-seeing, like the children. A big burly fellow was with them, with jet-black hair, deep-set dark eyes, and a surly mouth – so like Jacob that Julian guessed at once that he was the brother, Ebenezer.

As soon as Ebenezer set eyes on Jeremiah, he roared in fury.

'You get out! This is *my* job – you get out. *I'll* show the caves to those youngsters!'

And with that such a battle of words followed that the Five were almost deafened, especially as the echo repeated everything very loudly indeed! The three visitors fled away up the tunnel, fearing a fight. Anne was very frightened, and clung to Julian.

Ebenezer came shouting up to old Jeremiah, his hand raised. 'Haven't I told you more than a hundred times to keep out of these caves? Haven't I told you I'M the one to show folks around – and Jacob too?'

'Don't listen to him!' said Jeremiah, turning his back on the angry man. 'He's nothing but a big-mouth, same as his brother Jacob!'

'Look out!' yelled Julian, as the angry Ebenezer rushed at Jeremiah, his fist raised to strike him. 'LOOK OUT!'

Mischief again –
and a surprise!

Jeremiah saw the angry man coming at him, and very neatly side-stepped. Ebenezer couldn't stop, stepped heavily on a strand of very slippery seaweed – and went sprawling into a corner!

'Ho!' said Jeremiah, delighted. 'Very nice, Ebenezer! Get up, and run at me again!'

'He'd better not,' said Julian, in his most grown-up voice. 'I shall report him to the police if he does – and that will make a pair of them in two days. Jacob got into trouble yesterday – and now it will be Ebenezer.'

Ebenezer got up, scowling, and glared at Jeremiah, who grinned back in delight. 'Coming at me again, Ebby?' he said. 'It's grand fun to hit an old man, isn't it?'

But Ebenezer was very much afraid that Julian would do what he had threatened, and report him to the police. He rubbed his shoulder where it had struck a piece of rock, and debated what to do.

'Come along,' said Jeremiah, to the five watching children. 'I'll take you down to the Wreckers' Cave. Ebby can come too, if he can behave himself. But maybe he'd like to run away home, and get his shoulder looked to!'

That was enough for Ebby! He was determined to follow the little company, and make rude remarks all the time. So he tailed them, and shouted at them from a safe distance. How they wished they had Timmy with them! He would have made short work of the rude Ebenezer!

'Don't take any notice of him,' said Julian. 'Lead on, Jeremiah. My word, isn't it dark in this tunnel! Good thing we all brought good torches!'

The tunnel came to an end at last and opened out into an extraordinary cave. The roof was unexpectedly high, and the irregular sides were ridged with shelves of rocks. On the shelves were dirty old boxes, a crate or two and some sacks.

'What in the world are those?' asked Dick, shining his torch on them.

'Well young sir, they're just what they look like – ordinary boxes and sacks,' said Jeremiah. 'Put there by Ebenezer and Jacob to fool people! They tells everybody they're what the old wreckers got out of ships they wrecked, years ago! Hoo-hoo-hoo! Anybody that believes those lies *deserves* to be fooled. They're all from Ebby's backyard. Seen them lying there myself! Hoo-hoo-hoo!'

His hoo-hooing laugh echoed round the cave, and Ebenezer made an angry growling noise rather like a dog.

'*I'm* not going to fool these kids,' said Jeremiah. 'You and your sacks and boxes! I know where the old things are, the real old things – oh yes I do!'

'They're no better than the sacks and boxes there, wherever they are!' said Ebby, in a growling voice. 'You're lying, old Jeremiah – you don't know nothing!'

'Take us on farther,' said Dick. 'There must be more caves. I think this is exciting. Is this really where the old wreckers hid the things they salvaged from the wrecks they caused – or just a tale?'

'Oh, this is their cave, that's true enough. Dressed up a bit by Ebby there!' said Jeremiah. 'But *I* know the caves farther on. Ebby doesn't! He's too scared to go farther under the sea. Aren't you, Ebby?'

Ebby said something that sounded rude. Julian turned to Jeremiah eagerly. 'Oh, do take us farther – if it isn't dangerous!'

'Well, *I'm* going farther on, anyway,' said Tinker suddenly. 'Mischief hasn't come back – so he must be lost – and *I'm* going to find him!'

Julian saw that Tinker was quite determined. 'Right,' he said. 'We'll come with you. Jeremiah, lead the way! But it's not *really* danger-ous, is it? I mean – we don't want to find the sea sweeping through these caves, right up to where we are!'

'Tide's not on the turn yet,' said Jeremiah. 'We're all right for a while. When it comes in, it swirls up this passage here – but it stops at the Wreckers' Cave – that's just too high for it, see? The tunnel runs downwards fast now. It goes right under your lighthouse. Have you seen it down at the bottom of the shaft?'

'Good gracious, yes!' said Julian, remember-ing. 'I went down it – and the sea was swirling in and out at openings in the bottom of the shaft. Do you mean to say that the sea that rises in the shaft at high tide comes racing up into these tunnels too?'

'Aye, that it does,' said Jeremiah. 'You can get from here to the lighthouse under the rocky

seabed right to that foundation shaft. But nobody dares! Tide comes in so quickly, you
might get caught and drowned!'

Ebby at once shouted something rude again –
it sounded as if he was telling Jeremiah to go
and get drowned too!

'Do let's go on farther,' said Dick. 'Come on,
Jeremiah.'

So Jeremiah led them farther on under the
rocky bed of the sea. It was strange and rather
frightening to hear the constant noise of the
water racing over the roof of the winding
tunnel. Their torches lit up slimy walls, and
rocky shelves and hollows.

'You know – this would have been a very
good place to hide treasure,' said Julian, glan-
cing up at a dark hollow in the roof of the
tunnel. 'Though I don't know how anyone
would set about looking for it – there are
hundreds of nooks and crannies – and isn't it
cold in this tunnel!'

'Well, the sun's rays never penetrate down

here,' said Dick. 'My word, the sea sounds pretty loud now!'

'I wish we could find Mischief,' said Anne to George. 'Look at poor Tinker. He's crying. He's pretending not to, but I could see the tears rolling down his cheeks last time I flashed my torch on him.'

They stopped to look at something – a strange jelly-like thing, like an enormous sea anemone. Ebby caught them up, and bumped into Dick. He rounded on Ebby at once.

'Keep off! Follow us if you like, but don't come so near. We don't like you!'

Ebby took no notice but kept as close behind everyone as he possibly could, and Dick realised that he was probably feeling very scared! Then, as they rounded another corner of the tunnel, and saw yet another cave, Tinker gave a yell that echoed everywhere.

'MISCHIEF! LOOK! THERE HE IS! MISCHIEF!'

And sure enough, there was the little monkey, crouched under a small shelf of rock, shivering in fright. He wouldn't even go running to Tinker. Tinker had to pick him up and hug him.

'Mischief! Poor Mischief – were you very frightened?' he said. 'You're trembling all over! You shouldn't have run away! You might have been lost for ever!'

Mischief had something clutched in his tiny paw. He chattered to Tinker, and put his furry little arms round his neck. As he did so, he opened one paw – and something fell out and rolled over the rocky floor.

'What have you dropped, Mischief?' said Dick, and shone his torch down on to the floor of the cave. Something was glittering there – something round and yellow! Everyone stared, and a shock of excitement went through Julian, who was nearest. 'A gold coin!' he cried, and picked it up. 'As bright as when it was minted. Mischief, where did you get it from? Look, Dick, look George – it's gold all right!'

Immediately everyone was full of the greatest excitement, one thought only in their heads.

The treasure! Mischief must have found the treasure! It was an old coin – very old. Where *could* Mischief have found it?

'Oh, let's go farther on and see!' cried Dick. 'Jeremiah, it *must* be the treasure! Mischief will lead us to it!'

But Mischief would do nothing of the sort. He was NOT going to lose himself again. He was going to sit on Tinker's shoulders, with an arm safely round the boy's neck! He hadn't liked being lost, all by himself in the dark.

Jeremiah would not go any farther, either. He shook his head. 'No – not today. Tide will soon be sweeping up these tunnels – faster than we can walk. Better turn back now, in case we're caught. Many's the visitor that's had to run for his life, when the tide came up all of a sudden!'

George's sharp ears caught the sound of a 'swoosh-swoosh'! Somewhere the tide had crept in! 'Come on!' she said. 'We'd better do what Jeremiah says. The sea's coming up the tunnel now as well as over it – and soon it will be sweeping up the beach too, and in at the cliff passages. We'll be caught in the middle, and have to stay here for ages!'

'No need for alarm, missy,' said old Jeremiah. 'There's a bit of time yet. Halloo – where's Ebenezer gone?'

'Blow – he must have heard us talking about Mischief's gold piece,' said George. 'I forgot all about him! Now he knows that Mischief has found a gold coin, he'll feel sure that the treasure *may* be somewhere down here – and he'll look for it as soon as ever he can! WHY didn't we keep quiet about it?'

'I forgot he was standing near us,' groaned Dick. 'Well I suppose the whole of Demon's Rocks village will know by now that a monkey has found the treasure – and hordes of sightseers will swarm down here, hoping to find it. It must have been put in a pretty dry place,

surely, for that coin to be so bright and un-
tarnished.'

'Buck up – we'd better go back as quickly as
possible,' said Julian. 'Look at old Jeremiah –
he's too thrilled for words! He's planning to
find the treasure himself at the earliest possible
moment!'

'Well, I vote we have a shot at it ourselves
tomorrow,' said Dick, excitement welling up in
him at the thought. 'Good old Mischief! You're
better than any detective!'

Then away up the tunnels they went, making
all kinds of plans. WHAT an excitement!

[18]

Back in the lighthouse – and an exciting talk!

Old Jeremiah was as excited as the others, but he said very little. He was angry to think that Ebenezer should have been there to see the find. He didn't trust that Ebby – nor that Jacob either! They'd be ferreting after that treasure as sure as nuts were nuts, and monkeys were monkeys! Ha – wouldn't they like to know where it was! He stumped on, up the old tunnels, thinking hard, and at last they came out into the welcome daylight again!

'Here, Jeremiah – buy yourself some more sweets,' said Julian, putting some money into the old man's hand. 'And don't count too much on that treasure! I expect it's just an odd coin that Mischief found in a dry corner somewhere!'

'Thank you!' said the old man. 'I don't want the treasure myself – I'm just hoping that Ebby and Jacob don't find it. They'll be hunting all the time for it now!'

They were glad to be out in the open again. The sun had gone now, and the wind had whipped up. It was raining hard.

'I say – we'd better buck up, else we shan't be able to walk back to the lighthouse over the rocks!' said Julian, worried. But fortunately the wind was against the tide and they just had time to wade over to the lighthouse steps.

'There's our little boat bobbing about,' said Tinker. 'And listen – I can hear old Timmy barking! He's heard us coming!'

So he had. He had been lying on the door-mat, his ears glued to the crack under the door, listening. Nobody had come near the light-house and not a sound did old Timmy hear but the wind and the sea, and a few gulls gliding by.

'We're back, Timmy!' yelled George, and she

pushed at the door. It opened, and Timmy leapt out, almost knocking her over. Mischief sprang on to the dog's back, and chattered at him without stopping.

'He's telling him about the gold coin he found,' said Tinker, with a laugh. 'Oh, I WISH you'd been with us, Timmy. It was grand!'

'It feels as if we've been away for ages,' said George. 'But it wasn't very late after all – unless my watch is slow! I'm hungry. Let's have something to eat and talk about everything – and what we're going to do!'

So, over biscuits and sandwiches and coffee, they talked and talked. 'We must get down to the caves again as soon as possible!' said George. 'I'm absolutely certain that Jacob and Ebby will be down there, hunting for coins, as soon as the tide's out again.'

'Well, we can't do anything today, that's certain,' said Dick. 'For one thing the tide's in now – and for another thing it's blowing up for a storm. Just *listen* to the wind!'

Timmy was sitting as close to George as he possibly could. He hadn't liked her going out without him. She sat with her arm round him, eating her biscuits, occasionally giving him half of one. Tinker was doing the same with Mischief!

The children talked and talked. Where could Mischief have found that coin? Was it one on its own, that the sea had swept into the tunnel? Or was it part of a whole lot of coins? Had it come from an iron-bound box whose wooden sides had rotted away? They talked endlessly, their eyes bright, the round gold coin on the table in front of them.

'I suppose it would be treasure trove if we found it?' said Dick. 'I mean – it would be so old that it would belong to the Crown, and not to anyone in particular.'

'I expect we'd be allowed to keep a few coins ourselves,' said George. 'If only we could go straight away now and hunt in that tunnel! I feel as if I can't wait!'

'Woof,' said Timmy, agreeing though he really hadn't much idea of what they were talking about!

'I say – LISTEN to the sea crashing over the rocks between us and the jetty!' said Julian, startled at the sudden booming. 'The wind must be working up to a gale!'

'Well, bad weather's been forecast for some time,' said Dick gloomily. 'Blow! It'll be jolly difficult rowing to and fro in that little *Bob-About* boat. I doubt if we'd be able to walk across the rocks, even at low tide, with a big sea running before the wind.'

'Oh, don't be so gloomy!' said Anne.

'Well, do you want us to be prisoners here in the lighthouse?' demanded Dick.

'It wouldn't matter – there's plenty of food,' said Anne.

'No there isn't! Remember there are five of us – and Timmy and Mischief as well,' said Dick.

'Shut up, Dick,' said Julian. 'You're scaring Anne and Tinker. This storm will soon blow over – we'll be able to pop out and do some shopping tomorrow.'

But the storm grew fiercer, and the sky became so dark that Anne lit the lamps. Rain slashed against the lighthouse, and the wind made a loud howling noise that made Timmy growl deep down in his throat.

Anne went to look out of the window. She felt frightened when she saw the great waves that came surging over the rocks below. Some of them broke on the rocks, and the spray flew so high that it spattered the window out of which she was looking! She drew back in alarm.

'Do you know what hit the window then? It was spray from a great wave!'

'Whew!' said Julian, and went to the window himself. What a wonderful sight! The sea was grey now, not blue, and it raced along towards the shore, great waves curling over into white manes, spray flying. Out to sea there were angry waves too, topped with white, which turned into spray as the strong wind caught them. Only a few gulls were out, screaming in excitement, allowing the wind to take them along on their great white wings.

'Well, I certainly wouldn't mind being a gull today,' said Dick. 'It must be a wonderful feeling to ride on a storm – no wonder they are screaming in joy!'

'Ee-oo, Ee-oo, EE-OOO, EE-OOOOO!' cried the gulls, sounding like cats mewing in hunger.

'I'm sorry for the ships out in this,' said Julian. 'Goodness – think of the sailing ships in the olden days, caught on this rocky coast in a wind like this – it's almost a hurricane!'

'And think of that wicked old One-Ear Bill, gloating when he saw a ship sailing nearer and nearer the rocks!' said George. 'And even taking the warning lamp out of its place on the cliff, and bringing it near here to make sure that any ship out that night would make straight for the rocks – CRASH!'

'Don't,' said Anne. 'I hate to think of things like that.'

'Let's have a game,' said Julian. 'Where are the cards? Move that lamp a bit closer to the table, Dick. It's getting so jolly dark. Now no more talk of wrecks! Think of something cheerful – tea-sup, for instance – the treasure – and . . .'

'You know, I think it would be quite easy to find the treasure,' said Dick, bringing the lamp close to the table. 'Mischief is a very clever little thing. I'm sure he would remember where he found that coin, and lead us straight to the place.'

'It might have been just an odd coin, dropped by the man who hid the hoard,' said Anne.

'It might – but wherever it was found I think we can safely say that the main hoard wouldn't be very far away,' said Dick.

'Well, if we do go hunting we'll have to go when the tide is well out,' said Julian. 'I don't really fancy scrabbling about in those caves and tunnels under the rocky seabed, when I know that somehow or other when the tide is coming in the water gets *under* the seabed, as well as on it.'

Dick sat frowning, thinking out something. 'Ju,' he said at last, 'you remember the direction we went in, as soon as we were underground this morning? We went leftish all the way, didn't we?'

'Yes, we did,' said Tinker, at once. 'I had my little compass with me – look – it clips to my wristwatch – and we went sharp west all the time.'

'Towards the lighthouse, that would be,' said Julian, and drew a quick plan. 'See – here's the lighthouse, say – and just here is the entrance into the cliff, where we first went – here's the path we took, curving right back to the sea again, under the rocky beach here it goes – and that's a cave, see, then more tunnel, and caves – the way always curving sharply to the left . . .'

'A bit farther on and we'd have been almost

under the lighthouse!' said Dick, in amazement.

'That's right,' said Julian. 'And maybe in the old days, before this lighthouse was built, and ships were sent crashing on the rocks on which it now stands, there was a tunnel down from those lighthouse rocks that joined up with the tunnel we were in this morning – so that the wreckers would find it very easy to stow away anything valuable they found in a wrecked ship, without being seen!'

'Whew! You mean they waited till the ship smashed up, then waded over the rocks, as we do, took what they could find, and disappeared down a tunnel there to hide it!'

'And came out the other end!' said Anne.

George stared at Julian, and her eyes were bright.

'Maybe the tunnel is *still* somewhere in these rocks!' she said. 'Somewhere down at the edge of them, because we know the sea gets into the tunnel. Julian, let's look for it tomorrow. I think you're right. There *may* be a hole in the rocks here somewhere, that drops down into the tunnel we were in.'

Nobody wanted to play a game after that! They felt much too excited. They studied Julian's plan again and again, glad that Tinker's little compass had shown him so clearly that morning that the undersea passages had led due west to the lighthouse rocks.

'Do you suppose that everyone has forgotten the old hole?' said Dick. 'Nobody has told us anything about it, not even Jeremiah. Do you think it may have been blocked up?'

Julian frowned, thinking hard.

'Well, yes – it may have been,' he said. 'It *is* odd that Jeremiah didn't say anything about it. Anyway we'll have a good hunt tomorrow.'

'And if we find it, we'll drop down and hunt for the treasure!' said Tinker, his eyes shining. 'WHAT a shock for Ebenezer and Jacob if we find it first!'

[19]

A nasty shock!

The storm blew itself out that evening, and next day was much calmer. The sky still looked angry, and rain fell now and again, but it was possible to get out of the lighthouse door in the morning, and go down the steps on to the rocks.

'Shall we go shopping first – or look for the hole?' said Julian.

'Look for the hole,' said Dick, promptly. 'The wind is still pretty strong, and the storm might blow up again – just look at that angry sky! We wouldn't be able to mess about round the edge of the rocks if the sea gets any rougher.'

They spread out and went cautiously over the great rocks on which the lighthouse was built. At low tide the rocks stood well up, out of the sea. The lighthouse was built on the highest part, and seemed to tower over the searchers as they clambered here and there, seeking for any hole that looked as if it might lead down into some tunnel below.

'Here's a hole!' called Anne, suddenly, and they all clambered over to her in excitement, Timmy too.

Julian looked down to where Anne was pointing. 'Yes – it does look a likely one,' he said. 'Big enough to take a man, too. I'll climb down and see.'

He slid down the hole, holding on to projecting pieces of rock as he went. The others watched, thrilled. Timmy barked. He didn't like to see Julian disappearing like this!

But before Julian quite disappeared, he shouted again; 'I'm afraid it's no good! It's come to a sudden end! I'm standing on firm rock, and though I've felt all round with my feet, there's no opening anywhere. It's a dead end!'

What a disappointment! 'Blow!' said Dick, lying down on the rocks and putting his arm down the hole to help Julian to climb up again. 'I had high hopes then! Julian – here's my hand. Do you want any help?'

'Thanks – it is a bit difficult!' said Julian. He climbed up with difficulty, and squeezed out of the hole thankfully. 'I wouldn't like to get *wedged* in here!' he said. 'Especially with the tide coming in!'

'It's beginning to pour with rain again!' said Anne. 'Shall we go shopping now – or wait a bit?'

'Oh, let's wait,' said George. 'I'm cold and wet now. Let's go into the lighthouse and make some hot coffee. WHAT a disappointment! Never mind – we can always go down the tunnels we were in yesterday and search around – maybe Mischief will show us where he found the gold coin!'

They all went into the lighthouse, and once more Julian jammed the door. 'I wish that locksmith would come,' he said. 'If we go down into the caves, we'll have to leave old Timmy behind on guard – and it is such a shame!'

'Woof,' said Timmy, heartily agreeing. They all went upstairs and Anne began to make the coffee. As they were sitting drinking it, Timmy suddenly sprang to his feet with a most blood-curdling growl. Everyone jumped, and Anne spilt her coffee.

'Timmy! What's up?' said George, in alarm. Timmy was standing with his nose towards the closed door of the room, his hackles rising up on his neck. He looked truly fierce!

'What on *earth* is the matter, Tim?' said Julian, going to the door. 'There can't be any-one on the stairway – the entrance door's jammed!'

Timmy raced out of the door as soon as Julian opened it and tore down the spiral stair-way at such a speed that he fell, and rolled to the bottom. George gave a terrified scream. 'Timmy! Have you hurt yourself?'

But Timmy leapt to his feet at once, and ran to the entrance door, growling so ferociously that Anne felt really frightened. Julian ran down and went to the door. It was still well and truly jammed.

'Timmy! Maybe it's just the poor milkman, come with some milk again,' he said, and un-jammed the door. He took hold of the handle to open it.

It wouldn't open! Julian pulled and tugged, but it was of no use. The door simply would NOT open!

By this time everyone was down beside him. 'Let *me* try,' said Dick. 'The door must just have stuck.'

No – he couldn't open it either! Julian looked gravely round at everyone. 'I'm afraid – very much afraid – that SOMEBODY has locked us in!' he said.

There was a horrified silence. Then George cried out in anger. 'Locked us in! How dare they! Who's done this?'

'Well – I think we can guess,' said Julian. 'It was whoever came and stole our key the other day!'

'Ebenezer – no, Jacob!' cried Dick. 'One of the two, anyway. How DARE they? What are we going to do? We can't get out. Why have they done this – this – silly – *wicked* thing?'

'I'm afraid it's because they think we might go looking for the treasure – and find it,' said Julian, his face grave, 'We felt sure that Mischief might remember where he had found the gold coin – and lead us there – and I'm pretty sure they think the same. So this is their way of making sure *they* have time to find the treasure, before we do!'

'They're wicked, they're wicked!' cried George, taking hold of the handle of the door, and pulling it violently. 'We're prisoners!'

'Don't pull the handle off, old thing,' said Julian. 'That wouldn't help at all. Let's go upstairs and talk about it. We'll have to think of some way out of this unexpected difficulty.'

They went soberly upstairs again, and sat down in the living room. Yes – they were certainly prisoners!

'What are we going to do?' said Dick. 'We are in a real fix, Julian.'

'Yes. You're right,' said Julian, looking worried. 'We can't get out of the lighthouse, that's certain. On the other hand – how can we get help? No telephone. Shouting would never be heard. Can't use our boat. No one would ever know we are prisoners – they've seen us going in and out of the lighthouse, and if we suddenly don't appear any more they'll simply think we have gone home, and that the lighthouse is empty again!'

'We shall die of starvation!' said Anne, scared.

'Oh no – I expect we shall think of something,' said Dick, seeing that Anne was really frightened. 'All the same, it's a puzzle. We can't get *out* – and no one can get *in*! Whoever locked that door has certainly taken the key away with him.'

They talked and they talked, and finally they felt hungry, so they had a meal – though they felt that they ought to eat sparingly, in case their food ran short too quickly.

'And I feel so hungry,' complained George. 'I *keep* feeling hungry here.'

'That's what I told you. Living in a lighthouse somehow makes you feel hungry all the time!' said Tinker.

'We'll try and catch the milkman tomorrow morning,' said Julian, suddenly. 'Let's see, now – we could write a note, and push it under the door, so that he would see it tomorrow when he comes. We could put HELP – WE ARE LOCKED IN.'

'It would blow away,' said George. 'You know it would.'

'We could pin it down our side – and then it wouldn't,' said Anne. 'Half of it would still stick out under the door.'

'Well, it's worth trying,' said Dick, and immediately wrote out the note on a large sheet of

paper. He shot downstairs to pin it to the mat –
and shoved half the paper underneath so that it
stuck out on the other side of the door.

He ran back upstairs. 'I don't for a moment
think that the milkman will come across the
rocks in this weather,' he said. 'They'll be almost impassable. Still we'll hope for the best.'

There didn't seem anything else to do. The
evening came early, for the sky was dark again,
and the wind once more got up, and howled
dismally. Even the gulls decided that it was no
longer a good idea to glide to and fro.

They played games that evening, and tried to
laugh and make jokes. But secretly everyone
was worried. Suppose that the stormy weather
went on and on, and nobody guessed they were
locked in the lighthouse, and the milkman
didn't bring any milk, and didn't see the note
– and they ate all their food and . . .

'Cheer up, everyone,' said Julian, seeing the
dismal looks around the table. 'We've been in
worse fixes than this.'

'Well, *I* don't think we have!' said Anne. 'I just can't see ANY way out of this one!'

There was rather a long silence during which Timmy sighed heavily, as if he too was worrying! Only the monkey seemed cheerful, and went head-over-heels at top speed round the room, sitting up for laughs at the end. But nobody laughed. Nobody even seemed to notice him. Mischief felt very sad, and crept over to Timmy for comfort.

'There is one idea that *might* be a good one,' said Julian, at last. 'It's been running round in my head for a while – and I'm not sure whether it's possible or not. Anyway, it's one we might try tomorrow, if help doesn't come.'

'What?' asked everyone at once, and Timmy lifted his head and whined, as if he too quite understood.

'Well, do you remember that I went down that foundation shaft?' said Julian, 'and saw the water swirling at the bottom? Now – do you suppose it's at all possible that that shaft was bored down through a *natural* hole – and the lighthouse builders chose to put the foundation shaft there because there was a ready-made shaft they could use? – a fine hole going right down through the rock! And they made the hole into a cement-lined shaft, strong and ever-lasting, so that the lighthouse would never be at the mercy of the waves and wind – but would stand firm, whatever happened?'

This was a new idea to everyone, and it took a little while to sink in. Then Dick smacked the table top and made them all jump.

'Julian! You've got it! Yes – that strong cement-lined shaft runs down a *natural* hole – and that hole must be the one we've been looking for! The one that connects up with the tunnels we were in yesterday! No wonder we couldn't find it when we hunted all over the rocks! The shaft-makers used it!'

There was silence again. Everyone was taking this in, even Tinker. Julian looked round the table and smiled. 'Have you all jumped to it?'

he said. 'If that *is* the hole we were looking for – what about one of us going down that iron ladder again to the bottom – and finding out if it *does* lead into the tunnel we were in yesterday?'

'And walking through it, and up the passage and coming out through the cliff entrance we used yesterday!' said George. 'Julian! What an absolutely wonderful idea! We could escape that way! What a shock for Ebby and Jacob! We'll do it somehow – we'll DO it!'

[20]

Down the shaft
and into the tunnel

It was a most exciting idea to think that the iron ladder in the great cement-lined shaft might possibly lead to the tunnel they had been into yesterday. Julian had seen water swirling at the bottom, when the tide was in – possibly if they went down it when the tide was going out, there would be no danger of being trapped!

The storm was very fitful now – sometimes it came back again, and then the wind blew so hard that it seemed as if the buffeted lighthouse must fall! Rain fell in torrents that night, and during the dark early hours of the morning, when the tide was in, great waves pounded over the rocks, sending spray almost over the top of the lighthouse. Julian awoke and looked out of the bedroom window in awe.

'I hope there's no ship out anywhere near here tonight,' he said, and then gave a sudden exclamation. 'What's that – something swept right across the sky!'

'It's the beam from the new lighthouse at High Cliffs, said Dick. 'I saw it last night. It must have a very powerful beam, mustn't it, to show even on a night like this?'

They watched for a little while, and then Julian yawned.

'Let's try to go to sleep,' he said. 'We thought we were going away for a nice little holiday – and BANG – we're in the middle of something again!'

'Well, let's hope that we come out of it all right,' said Dick, settling down in his rugs once more. 'I must say that I feel a bit cut off from civilisation at the moment. 'Night, Julian.'

In the morning the storm was still about, and the wind was terrific. Julian ran down to the entrance door to see if the milkman could possibly have come – and had seen their message for help.

But no – the paper was still half on their side, flapping on the mat. Obviously the milkman hadn't dared to cross the rocks that morning, either on foot or by boat!

Dick had looked out of the window to make sure that their boat was still safely moored to the post – and to his surprise and distress, it was no longer there! Tinker was very upset.

'Where's my little boat gone? Has somebody stolen it?'

'Maybe – or possibly the storm broke the mooring rope, and the boat was smashed to pieces on the rocks,' said Julian. 'Anyway, it's gone. Poor old Tinker. What a shame!'

Tinker was very sad, and Mischief tried to comfort him, doing all sorts of silly tricks to make him laugh. But Tinker wouldn't laugh. He really was right down in the dumps.

They had rather a sparse breakfast, and were

very silent. Anne cleared away and washed up, and then Julian called them all together.

'Well, now we must decide about this descent down the shaft to what we hope will be the tunnel we were in,' he said. 'I am going down myself.'

'Toss for it!' said Dick, at once. 'There's no reason why *I* shouldn't go, is there? Or what about us both going, in case one gets into trouble, and needs help?'

'Not a bad idea,' said Julian. 'Except that there won't be anyone to look after the girls and Tinker.'

'woof!' said Timmy, indignantly, standing up at once. Julian laughed and patted him.

'It's all right, Timmy. I just wanted to see if you thought *you* could guard them well. All right – Dick and I will go down the shaft. The sooner the better. We simply must go while the tide is out. What about now, Dick?'

Solemnly they all went down the spiral stairway to the entrance door, where the trap was that opened on to the great shaft. Julian pulled up the lid and gazed down into blackness. He shone his torch down, but he could not see the bottom. 'Well – here goes,' he said, and lowered himself down into the shaft, his feet seeking the rungs of the iron ladder. 'Keep cheerful, girls. We'll get through the tunnels and passages, and to the entrance in the cliff – and fetch help for you in no time at all!'

'Julian, please take care,' said Anne, in a shaky voice. 'Please, please do take care!'

Down went Julian, his torch now held between his teeth. After him went Dick. The girls shone their own torches down the shaft, but soon the boys were so far down that they could not be seen. Only their voices came up now and again, sounding very hollow and peculiar.

'We're at the bottom!' shouted Julian, at last. 'It's rock, and there's no water at present! We've a clear way to follow! I crawled out of the hole at the bottom, and there's some kind of tunnel there all right. We're off now –

crawling out, and into the tunnel. Cheer up, all of you! See you soon!' And then the peculiar hollow voice stopped, and the girls and Tinker heard nothing more. Timmy began to whine. He couldn't understand these strange goings-on at all!

Julian and Dick were feeling pleased with themselves. It hadn't been very difficult to squeeze out of the arches at the bottom of the shaft. Now they were in a dark narrow tunnel, whose roof sometimes came down so low that they had to bend double. It smelt damp and seaweedy, but there seemed to be plenty of air. In fact at times quite a little breeze seemed to flow round them.

'I shall be glad when we come into a tunnel we recognise!' said Julian, at last. 'We surely must be near where we were yesterday. Hallo, what's this? Dick – look, Dick!'

Dick looked to where Julian's torch was shining and gave a shout. 'A gold coin – another one! We must be near where old Mischief ran off to. Look – there's another – and another. Where on earth did they come from?'

The boys shone their torches all around, and saw at last where the coins had fallen from. Above their heads was a dark hole, running up into the rock. As they shone their torches on it, a gold coin slid out and dropped down to join the others.

'*This* is where Mischief found the coin!' cried Dick. 'Julian there must be a box or something up there which is rotting away, and letting out the money it contains bit by bit.'

'Whoever would have guessed at such a hiding place!' said Julian, marvelling as he shone his torch above his head. 'There's absolutely nothing to be seen except that dark hole – no box, nothing. It must have been pushed right into a recess at the side of the hole, by someone who knew a good hiding place was there.'

'Give me a leg-up so that I can put in my hand and feel,' said Dick. 'Buck up – this is too exciting for words!'

Julian gave him a leg-up, and Dick put his head and shoulders into the hole. He felt to one side – nothing – felt to the other side, and his hand came across something hard and cold – an iron band perhaps? He ran his hand over it and touched something soft and crumbly – old, old wood rotting away, maybe – possibly a wooden chest – only held together by the iron bands. He scrabbled about and Julian gave a sudden shout.

'Hey – you've showered me with money! Whew – I never saw so many gold coins in my life!'

'Julian – I think there's more than one box or chest up there,' said Dick, jumping down, and looking at the big heap of shining coins at his feet. 'There may be a fortune there! Talk about treasure trove! Look – let's not disturb anything else up that hole. No one knows about it except ourselves. Better gather up these coins though, just in *case* that awful Ebby takes it into his head to come down this way!'

So they filled their pockets with the coins and then made their way onwards again. To their joy they soon recognised one of the tunnels they had been in before. 'Plain sailing now,' said Dick joyfully. 'We'll soon be out, and then we'll get the locksmith to pick the lock of the lighthouse, so that we can get in.'

'Sh!' said Julian, suddenly. 'I think I can hear something.' They listened, but went on again, thinking that Julian was mistaken.

But he wasn't! As they turned a dark corner that led into a cave, someone leapt at them! Julian went down to the ground at once, and Dick followed. He just had time to see that Ebenezer was there with someone else – Jacob perhaps?

As Dick fell, gold coins spilled out of his pocket. Ebenezer gave a cry and bent down to them at once. Julian tried to take his chance and slip by him – but the other man caught him and sent him spinning backwards. 'Where did you find that money? You tell us or you'll be sorry!'

shouted Ebenezer, and the echo came back at once, 'Sorry – sorry – sorry!'

'Run, Dick!' panted Julian. 'It's our only chance!' He gave Ebenezer a terrific shove, which sent him into the other man – yes, it *was* Jacob, who must somehow have escaped from police custody – and then he and Dick were off at once, running as fast as they could, back along the way they had come. 'You come here!' yelled Ebenezer, and they heard him pounding after them.

'Hurry!' panted Dick. 'If only we can get to the shaft, we're all right.'

But alas, they took the wrong turning, and soon found themselves in a cave they had never seen before. Ebenezer and Jacob blundered past without seeing them. 'Better stay here a while,' said Julian. 'Let them get a good way off.'

So they stayed still and quiet, and then at last ventured out of their hiding place and tried to find their way back to the right path.

'You know – if we get lost down here, we're

done for!' said Julian. 'And once the tide flows in, we shall be in a pretty poor way! Somehow we've got to get out through the cliff way or back to the shaft. Hang on to me, Dick. We mustn't get separated, whatever happens!'

They stumbled on, not really knowing whether they were going in the right direction or not. They seemed to go through endless tunnels and caves – what a labyrinth there was in that great stratum of rocks! Then they heard voices!

'That's Ebby's voice – and Jacob's too,' whispered Julian. 'They're coming this way. Hide here, and keep still!'

So they hid quietly, and listened to Ebby and Jacob. 'Those boys have *got* to come back here,' said Ebby. 'We'll wait. Don't make a sound!'

'We'll have to make a dash for it, and hope for the best!' whispered Julian. 'Come on! We'll be caught by the tide soon if we're not quick!'

They both made a sudden rush, and passed

the surprised Ebby and Jacob at a run. Then down the tunnel beyond them they went as fast they could, bumping their arms and legs and heads against the rocky walls, but holding their torches steadily in front of them. On they went and on – and behind them, breathing heavily, came Ebby and Jacob.

'I think this must be a bad dream!' panted Dick. 'JULIAN! JULIAN! look – there's water coming along this tunnel! The tide's coming in!'

'Come *on*,' said Julian. 'I feel as if the shaft isn't far away now. I seem to know this tunnel – and this cave. Come *on*, Dick, we haven't a minute to spare! We've GOT to get to the ladder!'

'Look! There's the shaft!' yelled Dick at last. 'Come on – we shall just about be able to squeeze under the arch at the bottom! Hurry, Julian – the water's up to our ankles now!'

They reached the shaft and squeezed under the small archway that let the water run through from side to side over the rocky bottom of the shaft. They began to mount the ladder, and then stopped to hear if there were any sounds from Ebby or Jacob.

They heard yells. 'EBBY! COME BACK! Tide's flowing in!' and then they heard Ebby's angry voice.

'I'm coming! They've gone farther down – and they won't like it! They'll be drowned before they get much farther!'

Dick grinned. 'Come on, Ju – up we go! I can see the light through the trap-door at the top. The girls have left it open, bless them.'

And soon the two boys were clambering out of the trap-door, with Timmy barking madly and licking their necks, the girls and Tinker too excited for words!

'What happened? Didn't you get out of the tunnel to find help for us? Were those men there? What *happened*?'

'Plenty!' said Julian. 'But unfortunately we didn't get past Ebby and Jacob, who were lying in wait for us. So we're *still* stuck in this lighthouse, with nobody to help us. BUT . . .'

'But what?' asked George, shaking his arm. 'Julian, you look excited. What's happened?'

'We found the treasure!' said Julian. 'Come on – we'll tell you all about it!' And he led the way up the spiral stairway, with Tinker and the excited girls close behind.

Soon the boys were telling their story, and George and Anne and Tinker listened and exclaimed and danced about, and were altogether marvellous listeners to a marvellous tale.

'It MUST have been the treasure – in an iron-bound chest – oh, Ju, weren't you excited when the coins poured out?'

'Yes. It was certainly a very fine moment,' said Julian. 'Mischief, stop pulling my hair. Wow! It's been an exciting morning! What about a drink of lemonade – and by the way, what's the weather been like? We couldn't see a thing down below!'

'Oh, it's *awful* again, Julian!' said Anne. 'There's another storm coming – look at those scurrying black clouds.'

'It does look bad,' said Julian, his excitement leaving him, as he saw clearly that another big storm was blowing up. 'We certainly shouldn't be able to get out of here today, even if we could get out of the door!'

'Julian, Tinker found his father's old pocket radio in a cupboard,' said Anne. 'And it still works. We listened to the weather report, and it gave an important warning to all ships at sea or by the coast. It said they must run to safety as soon as they could.'

'Well, I'm blessed if I know what to do for the best,' said Julian, looking out of the window. 'How in the world are we to let people know we're here, marooned in the lighthouse? We'll simply *have* to think of something!'

But that was easier said than done! How did one get help when there was no way to get help? How did one escape out of a locked lighthouse when there was no key?

[21]

A wonderful idea

'I'm thirsty,' said Tinker. 'I'll get some lemon-ade.'

'Well, go slow with it, then,' said Dick. 'You don't know how long we may be locked up here – and we haven't endless food and drink!'

Tinker looked alarmed. 'Might we be locked up here for weeks and weeks?' he said.

'If people thought we had left the lighthouse and gone back home because of the bad weather, we might easily be here for some time,' said Julian, soberly. 'Nobody would bother about us – they'd think we were safe at home.'

'But Mother would soon feel worried if she didn't hear from us,' said George. 'We said we'd send her a card each day, you know – and if she doesn't have one for a day or two, she

would be sure to get worried, and send someone over here.'

'Hurrah for mothers!' said Dick, relieved.
'All the same – I don't fancy a week or so here
with hardly anything to eat. We'll have plenty
of one thing though – and that's rainwater!'

'There must be *some* way out of this,' said
Julian who had been sitting silent, frowning at
his thoughts. 'Can't we get a message out *somehow*? Are there any flags here, Tinker, that we
could wave out of the window?'

'No,' said Tinker. 'I've never seen any. What
about a white tablecloth? We've one of those.'

'Yes. That would do,' said Julian. 'Fetch it,
Tinker.'

Tinker pulled it off the table and gave it to
Julian. Julian went to the window and looked
through the glass, which was misted with spray.
'I don't expect anyone will notice a tablecloth
being shaken out of this window,' he said. 'But
I'll try it. My word – the window's hard to
open. It seems to have stuck.'

He opened it at last, and immediately an enormous gust of wind came in, and everything went flying – papers, books, carpets – chairs fell over, and poor Mischief was blown from one side of the lighthouse room to the other. Timmy barked in fright and tried to catch the flying papers as they went by his nose. The tablecloth disappeared at once!

Julian managed to close the window again after a terrific effort, and once more the room became peaceful. 'Whew!' said Julian. 'I didn't guess there was such a gale outside. I should think that tablecloth is about five miles away by now! The gulls will get a surprise when it comes flapping along in the sky.'

George couldn't help laughing at that, frightened though she was. 'Oh, Julian – it was a jolly good thing you didn't fly off with the tablecloth! My WORD, what a gale! I wonder the lighthouse stands it.'

'Well, we do feel a buffet now and again,' said Dick. 'There – did you feel that? It was either a wave bumping into the rocks or spray forced against us – I distinctly felt the lighthouse shake a little.'

'Rubbish!' said Julian, seeing Anne's scared face. 'Don't make silly jokes like that.'

'You're quite *sure* that the lighthouse can't be blown down?' said Anne, in a small voice.

'Dear Anne, use your commonsense,' said Julian. 'Would it have stood for all these years if it hadn't been strong enough to stand against storms far worse than this?'

'Mischief is feeling frightened too,' said Tinker. 'He's gone and hidden, look.'

'Well, long may he stay there,' said Julian. 'At least, he's not trying to open the biscuit tin, or delve into the bag of sweets! I should just like to know how many of our sweets he has eaten up to now!'

WHOOOOOOOOOSH!

That was an extra big gale of wind that buffeted the lighthouse, and made Timmy stand up and growl. Rain pattered against the window, sounding as if someone was throwing pebbles.

Julian was very worried. It really did look as if the stormy weather was going on and on. It might quite well continue for a few days, and their food certainly would not last long. There were still some tins left, and they had plenty of water, of course – the rain saw to that – but somehow they were all always so *hungry*!

'Cheer up, Julian,' said George. 'You do look grim.'

'I feel it,' said Julian. 'I cannot for the life of me think of any way to escape from here, or even to get help. We've no way of signalling . . .'

'Pity the lighthouse lamp is no longer going,' said Tinker. 'That would have been a fine signal.'

To Tinker's enormous surprise Julian suddenly gave a shout, leapt up, came over to Tinker, and gave him such a clap on the back that the surprised boy almost fell off his chair!

'W-w-what's the matter?' stammered Tinker, rubbing his shoulder.

'Don't you *see* – perhaps we can set the old lamp going, and make it shine out as it used to do – not to warn ships, of course – but to make people realise that we are prisoners in the light-house!' said Julian, jubilantly. 'Tinker – do you know if it's *possible* to light the lamp?'

'I think so,' said Tinker. 'My father showed me how it worked, and I think I remember. Oh – and there's a bell that can be struck, too!'

'Better and better!' said Julian. 'Where is the bell?'

'It was dismantled and put away,' said Tinker. 'It used to hang in that sort of verandah place that runs outside, round the lamp-room – there's a big hook for it there.'

'Oh – it hung in that outside gallery, did it?' said Julian. 'Well – that means that one of us would have to go out there in the wind and hang it up – not too good! There must be a ninety-mile-an-hour gale up there. Anyway, let's get the bell and have a look at it.'

The great bell was down in the storeroom, covered up. It was made of brass, and once had had a hammer that struck it at intervals, worked by some simple machinery. But the machinery was in pieces – no good at all!

'We'll take the bell upstairs,' said Julian. 'Gosh, it's heavy as lead. Dick, I'll want your help.'

Between them the two boys carried the heavy bell up to the living room, and Tinker brought up the old hammer that used to strike it. Julian and Dick held up the bell by its loop of iron. 'Hit it with the hammer, Tinker,' said Julian. 'See if it still sounds loudly.'

Tinker struck it hard with the hammer – and at once a great deep clang filled the room from side to side, making Timmy jump almost out of his skin. He and Mischief left the room at top speed and fell down the spiral stairway to-gether. All the others jumped too, and stared at one another in awe. The sound of the bell went booming round and round the room, filling their ears so that they had to shake their heads to try and get rid of the sound. Julian at last clasped the rim of the bell with both his hands and the sound died away.

'What a WONDERFUL bell!' he said, in awe. 'Look how old it is, too – see, it says, "Cast in 1896"! If only we could get it hung up in its place on the gallery, the sound of it would go right to the village and beyond! I wonder how many ships heard it in the old days, booming out every now and again as the hammer struck it.'

Tinker raised the hammer again, but Dick stopped him. 'No – you saw how scared Timmy and Mischief were. They'll probably jump through a window, glass and all, if we sound the bell again!'

'We'll wait till we think the wind has died down a bit, and then try to hang the bell,' said Julian. 'Now let's look at the lamp. Will it want oil, Tinker?'

'It may do – though I think there's some still in it, left when the lighthouse was closed down,' said Tinker. 'But there is plenty down in the storeroom.'

'Good,' said Julian, feeling decidedly more cheerful. 'Now – if the gale dies down at all, we'll try to hang the bell. We can strike that as soon as it's hung, and not wait till we light the lamp.'

But the gale seemed to get worse, and Julian really did wonder if the old lighthouse would stand up to it! Should he take everyone down to the storeroom? Just in case? 'I will if the gale gets worse,' he thought. Though if the lighthouse should fall, there wouldn't be much chance for us, whatever part of it we're in!

They went up to the lamp-room in the afternoon and looked at the great old lamp. Tinker explained how it worked. 'It used to go round and round mechanically,' he said, 'and there were screens here – and here – that shut out the light in places as it went round – so that the light seemed to go on and off, if any ship was watching it – it seemed to *flash*, you see, instead of to shine steadily. Ships noticed it more quickly then.'

The screens were broken in pieces. There was still some oil in the lamp, but Julian added more. The wick seemed perfectly good. Now, if only they could light the lamp, and keep it going, someone would be sure to see it, and wonder about it!

Julian felt in his pocket for matches. As the lamp-room was enclosed in glass, it was easy to keep the match alight. He touched the oily wick with it – and, hey-presto, the lamp was lit!

It was a very big lamp, and, close to, the light was quite blinding. Dick crowed with delight. 'We've done it! Old lighthouse, you're going to shine once more tonight! You're alive again!'

'Now to hang the bell,' said Julian, and he cautiously opened the door leading on to the gallery outside, having waited until the wind died down for a moment. He and Dick lifted the bell up to the hook there and slipped the iron loop over it. It hung there, swinging, and Julian lifted the hammer – but at that moment a great gust took him and he staggered, almost falling over the railing!

Dick caught him just in time, and, with George's help, dragged him into the lamp-room. They were all very white-faced! 'That was a narrow escape,' said George, her hands shaking and her body trembling. 'We'll have to be careful if we go out on the gallery again! Perhaps we had better rely only on the lamp.'

'I vote we all go down and have some hot tea,' said Julian, thankful for his escape. His legs felt shaky as he went down the stairs. He was most surprised! Julian was seldom scared, and it was peculiar to have legs that suddenly gave at the knees!

However, everyone soon recovered when they were drinking hot tea and eating ginger biscuits. 'I wish it was dark so that we could see how bright the light is from the lamp when it shines,' said Dick. 'It will be dark very quickly today.'

It was! So dark that the light streaming from the old lamp at the top of the lighthouse was brilliant! It cut a shining path through the night, gleaming yellow.

And through the roar of the sea went a great clanging, as Julian, with Dick holding on to him, struck the old bell hanging in the gallery.

'Listen!' said George, her hand on Timmy's collar. 'Listen! BOOM! BOO-OOO-OOM! BOOOOM! Tim, that bell must feel happy to-night – it's found its voice again!'

BOOOOOOOOOM! Has anyone heard that old bell on this stormy night? Has anyone seen the light from the old, old lamp?

BOOOOOOOOOOM!!!

[22]
The end of the adventure

Down in the village of Demon's Rocks that night, people drew their curtains, made up their fires, and sat down in their armchairs. They were thankful not to be out in the wind and the rain.

Old Jeremiah Boogle was lighting his pipe, sitting by his own roaring fire, when he heard a sound that made him drop the flaring match, and listen in amazement.

BOOOOOOM! BOOOOOOM!

'A bell! A bell I've not heard for nearly forty years!' said old Jeremiah, standing up, hardly able to believe his ears. 'No – it *can't* be the lighthouse bell. That's been gone for many a day!'

BOOOOOOM!

Jeremiah went to his window and pulled aside the old curtain. He stared out – and could not believe his eyes! He gave a yell. 'MILLIE! Where's that grand-daughter of mine? MILLIE!'

'What is it, Grandad, now?' said a plump little woman, bustling in.

'Look, Millie – am I seeing right – isn't that the lighthouse lamp shining there?' said Jeremiah.

'Well – there's a bright light shining out there high above Demon's Rocks,' said Millie. 'But I never in *my* life saw the lighthouse lamp shining out before! And what's that booming noise, Grandfather – like a wonderful great bell?'

'That's the old bell in the lighthouse!' said Jeremiah. 'I couldn't mistake that! Many's the time I heard it booming out to warn ships off Demon's Rocks in the old days. Millie, it can't be! It doesn't hang there any more. And the light doesn't shine any more. What's happening?'

'I don't know, Grandad,' said Millie, scared.

'There isn't anyone in the lighthouse, far as *I* know!'

Old Jeremiah smacked his hand down on the windowsill, knocking over a plant pot. '*There are* folk there – three boys and two girls, and a monkey too – and a dog as well!'

'Well, there now!' said Millie. 'And what would they be there for? Did *they* set the lamp going and sound that bell? BOOOOM – there it goes again – enough to wake all the babies in Demon's Rocks village!'

Millie was right. It did wake all the babies, and the children – and amazed every man and woman in the place, including Ebenezer and Jacob. They had leapt to their feet when they had heard the bell, and were astounded to see the great light shining out steadily in the night.

They heard people hurrying by their cottage, on their way to Demon's Rocks jetty. They heard Jeremiah's big voice booming out too. 'It's those children up there in the lighthouse, banging that bell, and setting that light shining.

Something's wrong! It's help they're needing, folks! Something's wrong!'

Ebenezer and Jacob knew quite well what was wrong! The children were locked in the lighthouse and couldn't get out! They might be ill or hurt – or starving – but they couldn't get out to fetch help. And now the whole village was aroused, and when the morning came, a boat would bob out on the great waves and find out what had happened!

Ebby and Jacob disappeared that night! It wasn't Constable Sharp they feared – it was the people of the village! They slipped away in the dark and the rain, and were gone. But you'll be caught, Ebby, you'll be caught, Jacob! And no one will be sorry for you. No one at all!

When daylight came, there were many people on the jetty, ready to go across to the lighthouse. The wind was so rough that great waves still rolled over the rocks on which the lighthouse stood. Soon a boat was launched, and Jeremiah, Constable Sharp and the village doctor went across, the boat careering from side to side like a mad thing, as the waves caught it.

They went up the steps to the lighthouse and banged at the door – and from the other side came Julian's glad voice, 'You'll have to break down the door. Ebby and Jacob locked us in and took the key. We can't get out, and we're running short of food!'

'Right. Stand back,' shouted Jeremiah. 'Constable and I are going to break in!'

Jeremiah was old but he was still hefty, and Constable Sharp was heftier still. The lock suddenly splintered under their enormous shoves, and the door flew wide open! Jeremiah and the policeman shot inside and bumped into Julian and the rest, sending them flying. Timmy barked in astonishment and Mischief fled up the stairway!

Soon they were all in the living room, and Julian was pouring out his story. Anne made tea and handed round steaming cups. Jeremiah listened open-mouthed, and the policeman busily took notes. The doctor, glad that no one was ill or hurt, sipped his tea and listened, too.

'We didn't know *how* to get out when we were locked in,' said Julian, coming to the end of his long story. 'So in the end we lit the old lamp, and hung up the old bell, and struck it with the hammer. I could hardly stand in the gallery, though, there was such a wind! I struck it for half an hour, and then my brother here went on till he felt too cold. The lamp didn't burn all night – it went out early this morning.'

'But both bell and light did their job well, son,' said Jeremiah, looking twenty years younger, he was so excited. 'Ah, to think that old lamp shone again, and that old bell sounded – I thought I must be dreaming!'

'We'll be after that Ebenezer and Jacob,' said the policeman, shutting his notebook. 'And it seems to me you'd all better go home. This weather's going on for a bit – and there's nothing to keep you here, is there?'

'Well,' said Julian, 'actually there *is* something to keep us here. You know the old wreckers' lost treasure you told us about, Jeremiah? Well – we've found it!'

Jeremiah was so astounded that he couldn't say a word! He goggled at Julian, and opened and shut his mouth like a fish. Julian took some golden coins out of his pocket and showed them to the policeman and the doctor, and to Jeremiah.

'There you are!' he said. 'We know where there are thousands of these – they are in iron-bound boxes and chests down in one of the tunnels in the rock. What do you think of that? We can't leave here till we've given the treasure into the hands of the police! It belongs to the Crown, doesn't it?'

'Yes, it does,' said Constable Sharp, gazing at the bright gold coins. 'But you'll get a fine reward – all of you will! Where's this treasure? I'd better get it straightaway.'

'Well – you have to go down the foundation shaft of the lighthouse,' said Julian, gravely, but with a twinkle in his eye, 'and crawl under the archway at the bottom, and then make your way down the tunnel – but be careful the sea doesn't catch you – and then when you come to . . .'

The policeman stopped scribbling down what Julian was saying, and looked startled. Julian laughed.

'It's all right – Dick and I will fetch it ourselves today, and give it to you, complete with every single gold coin,' he said. 'We don't *need* to go down the shaft – there's another way in – the way *you* took us, Jeremiah. We'll go this morning, for a last excitement. And then – home! Perhaps you would kindly telephone Kirrin Garage for a car to fetch us at twelve o'clock, Constable?'

'Oh *good*!' said Anne. 'An adventure is always exciting but I've really had enough at the moment! This was such a bad-weather one!

Oh, Constable, look out – that monkey has pulled out your whistle!'

So he had – and what is more he blew it – PHEEEEEEEEEE! Jeremiah almost jumped out of his skin, and Mischief received a slap that almost made *him* jump out of his skin too!

'Good-bye, Jeremiah,' said Julian. 'It's been fine meeting you – and thanks for coming to rescue us. We'll see you again some day. Come along, Constable – we'll go and find the treasure with you now.'

'I don't think I'll come,' said Anne, who really didn't like dark, smelly tunnels and caves. 'I'll do the packing.'

'Timmy and I will help you,' said George, who knew that Anne wouldn't like to be left alone in the lighthouse.

The boys went off with Jeremiah, the doctor and Constable Sharp, rowing over the rocks to the jetty. The doctor and Jeremiah said good-bye at the jetty, and the three boys and Mischief took Constable Sharp to find the treasure. They had to push their way through quite a crowd of people who had collected on the quay, anxious to know why the light had shone out from the lighthouse in the night, and why the bell had sounded.

'Make way, please,' said the policeman, politely. 'Everything is all right. These children were locked in the lighthouse and couldn't get out. Make way, please. There is no need for any excitement!'

'No – that's all over now – isn't it, Ju?' said Dick. 'Whew – it was just a bit *too* exciting at times! I shall be quite glad to be at Kirrin Cottage again, with peace and quiet all around us.'

'You've forgotten that Uncle Quentin and his friend will still be there,' said Julian, with a grin. 'There'll be plenty going on while they're around! I'm afraid they won't be at all pleased to see us back!'

Oh yes, they will, Julian – especially when they hear the exciting story you have to tell!

You'll have some fun showing round a gold coin or two. Timmy is to have one hung on his collar, as a reward for guarding you so well – how proud he will be!

Well, good-bye to you all! Good-bye, Julian and Dick, and a good journey home! Good-bye, Anne and George – and Tinker too, and Mischief, you funny little monkey!

And good-bye, dear old Timmy, best of friends. How we wish we had a dog like you! See you all again some day!

FIVE HAVE A MYSTERY TO SOLVE

FIVE HAVE A MYSTERY TO SOLVE

[1]

Easter holidays

'The nicest word in the English language is holidays!' said Dick, helping himself to a large spoonful of marmalade. 'Pass the toast, Anne. Mother, do you feel downhearted to have us all tearing about the place again?'

'Of course not,' said his mother. 'The only thing that *really* worries me when holidays come, is Food – Food with a capital F. We never seem to have enough in the house when all three of you are back. And by the way – does anyone know what has happened to the sausages that were in the larder?'

'Sausages – sausages – let me think!' said Julian, frowning. Anne gave a sudden giggle. She knew quite well what had happened.

'Well, Mother – you said we could get our own meal last night, as you were out,' said

Julian. 'So we poked about and decided on sausages.'

'Yes, but Julian – two *whole* packets of sausages!' said his mother. 'I know Georgina came over to spend the evening – but even so . . .!'

'She brought *Timmy*,' said Anne. '*He* rather likes sausages too, Mother.'

'Well, that's the last time I leave the larder door unlocked, when I go out!' said her mother. 'Fancy cooking those lovely pork sausages for a *dog* – especially Timmy, with his enormous appetite! Really, Anne! I meant to have them for our lunch today.'

'Well – we rather thought we'd go and spend the day at Kirrin, with George and Timmy,' said Dick. 'That's if you don't want us for anything, Mother.'

'I *do* want you,' said his mother. 'Mrs Layman is coming to tea, and she said she wants to see you about something.'

The three groaned, and Dick protested at once. 'Oh *Mother* – the first day of the holidays

– and we have to be in for tea! It's too bad – a glorious spring day like this, too!'

'Oh – we'll be in for tea all right,' said Julian, giving Dick a sharp little kick under the table, as he saw his mother's disappointed face. 'Mrs Layman's a nice old thing – she's been so kind since we moved near to Kirrin.'

'And she gave me a present last birthday,' said Anne. 'Do you think we could ask George over too – with Timmy? George will be awfully disappointed if we aren't with her the first day of the hols.'

'Yes, of course you can,' said her mother. 'Go and ring her up now, and arrange it. And don't forget to put our old Tibby-cat in the shed, with a saucer of milk. She's scared stiff of Timmy – he's so enormous. And please, all of you, TRY to look clean at tea-time.'

'*I'll* see to Dick and Anne,' said Julian, with a grin. 'I must remember to find their overalls!'

'I'm going to phone George now, this very minute,' said Anne, getting up from the table. 'Do you mind, Mother? I've finished – and I'd

like to catch George before she takes Tim for a
walk, or does some shopping for Aunt Fanny.'

'Uncle Quentin will be glad to be rid of
George, even for a meal,' said Dick. 'He fell
over her lacrosse stick yesterday, and wanted to
know why she left her *fishing* net about! George
didn't know what he was talking about!'

'Poor old Georgina,' said his mother. 'It's a pity
that both she and her father have exactly the same
hot tempers. Her mother must find it difficult to
keep the peace! Ah – here's Anne back again. Did
you get George on the phone, dear?'

'Yes. She's thrilled,' said Anne. 'She says it's
just as well we're not going to spend the day
with her, because Uncle Quentin has lost some
papers he was working on, and he's turning the
house upside-down. George said she will probably be mad as a hatter by the time she arrives
this afternoon! Uncle Quentin even made Aunt
Fanny turn out her knitting bag to see if the
papers were there!'

'Dear old Quentin,' said her mother. 'Such a
truly brilliant scientist – remembers every book

he's ever read – every paper he's ever written –
and has the finest brain I know – and yet loses
some valuable paper or other almost every week!'

'He loses something else every day of the
week too,' said Dick, with a grin. 'His temper!
Poor old George – she's always in some sort of
trouble!'

'Well, anyway, she's jolly glad to be coming
over here!' said Anne. 'She's biking over, with
Timmy. She'll be here for lunch. Is that all right,
Mother?'

'Of course!' said her mother. 'Now – seeing
that you had today's dinner for last night's
supper, you'd better do a little shopping for
me. What shall we have?'

'SAUSAGES!' said everyone, at once.

'I should have thought you were quite literally *fed up* with sausages, after last night's
feast,' said their mother, laughing. 'All right –
sausages. But Timmy can have a bone – a nice
meaty bone. I am NOT going to buy any more
sausages for him, that's quite certain.'

'And shall we get some nice cakes for tea as

Mrs Layman is coming?' said Anne. 'Or are you going to make some, Mother?'

'I'll make a few buns,' said her mother. 'And you can choose whatever else you like – so long as you don't buy up the shop!'

The three went off shopping, cycling along the lane to the village. It was truly a lovely spring day. The celandines were golden in the ditches, and daisies were scattered everywhere. Dick burst into song as they went, and the cows in the nearby fields lifted their heads in surprise as Dick's loud voice swept round them.

Anne laughed. It was good to be with her brothers again. She missed them very much when she was at school. And now they would have almost a whole month together with their cousin George too. She was suddenly over-whelmed with joy, and lifted up her voice and joined Dick in his singing. Her brothers looked at her with affection and amusement.

'Good old Anne,' said Dick. 'You're such a quiet little mouse, it's nice to hear you singing so loudly.'

'I am NOT a quiet little mouse!' said Anne, surprised and rather hurt. 'Whatever makes you say that? You just wait – you may get a surprise one day!'

'Yes – we may!' said Julian. 'But I doubt it. A mouse can't suddenly turn into a tiger! Anyway, one tiger's enough. *George* is the tiger of our family – my word, she can put out her claws all right – and roar – and rant and rave!'

Everyone laughed at the picture of George as a tiger. Dick wobbled as he laughed and his front wheel touched Anne's back wheel. She turned round fiercely.

'LOOK OUT, IDIOT! You nearly had me over! Can't you see where you're going? Be sensible, can't you?'

'Hey, Anne – whatever's the matter?' said Julian, amazed to hear his gentle little sister lashing out so suddenly.

Anne laughed. 'It's all right. I was just being a tiger for a moment – putting out my claws! I thought Dick and you might like to see them!'

'Well, well!' said Dick, riding beside her, 'I've

never heard you yell like that before. Surprising – but quite pleasing! What about you showing old George your claws sometime when she gets out of hand?'

'Stop teasing,' said Anne. 'Here's the butcher's. For goodness' sake go and get the sausages, and be sensible. I'll go and buy the cakes.'

The baker's shop was full of new-made buns and cakes, and smelt deliciously of home-made bread. Anne enjoyed herself choosing a vast selection. 'After all,' she thought, 'there will be eight of us – counting Timmy – and if we're all hungry, cakes soon disappear.'

The boys were very pleased to see all the paper bags.

'Looks like a good tea today,' said Dick. 'I hope the old lady – what's her name now? – Layman – who's coming to tea today, has a good appetite. I wonder what she's going to tell us about.'

'Did you buy a nice meaty bone for Timmy?' asked Anne. 'He'll like that for his tea.'

'We bought such a beauty that I'm pretty

sure Mother will say it's good enough to make soup from,' said Dick, with a grin. 'So I'll keep it in my saddle-bag till he comes. Dear old Tim. He deserves a jolly good bone. Best dog I ever knew!'

'He's been on a lot of adventures with us,' said Anne, bicycling beside the boys, as the road was empty. 'And he seemed to enjoy them all.'

'Yes. So did we!' said Dick. 'Well – who knows? An adventure may be lying in wait for us these hols too! I seem to smell one in the air!'

'You don't!' said Anne. 'You're just making that up. *I'd* like a bit of peace after a hectic term at school. I worked really hard this last term.'

'Well – you were top of your form, and captain of games – so you deserve to have the kind of holiday you like,' said Julian, proud of his young sister. 'And so you shall! Adventures are OUT! Do you hear that, Dick? We keep absolutely clear of them. So that's that!'

'Is it, Ju?' said Anne, laughing. 'Well – we'll see!'

[2]

A visitor to tea

George and Timmy were waiting for Julian,
Dick and Anne when they arrived home. Timmy was standing in the road, ears pricked, long
tail waving. He went quite mad when he saw
their bicycles rounding the corner, and galloped
towards them at top speed, barking madly,
much to the horror of a baker's boy with a
large basket.

The boy disappeared into the nearest garden
at top speed, yelling 'Mad dog, mad dog!'
Timmy tore past, and forced the three to dis-
mount, for they were afraid of knocking him
over.

'*Dear* Timmy!' said Anne, patting the excited
dog. 'Do put your tongue in – I'm sure it will
fall out some day!'

Timmy ran to each of them in turn, woofing

in delight, licking everyone, and altogether behaving as if he hadn't seen them for a year!

'Now that's enough, old boy,' said Dick, pushing him away, and trying to mount his bicycle once more. 'After all, we did see you yesterday. Where's George?'

George had heard Timmy barking, and had now run out into the road too. The three cycled up to her, and she grinned happily at them.

'Hallo! You've been shopping, I see. Shut up barking, Timmy, you talk too much. Sorry you couldn't come over to Kirrin Cottage – but I'm jolly glad you asked me to come to *you* – my father still hasn't found the papers he's lost, and honestly, our place is like a madhouse – cupboards being turned out, even the kitchen store-cupboard – and I left poor Mother up in the loft, looking there – though *why* Father should think they might be there, I don't know!'

'Poor old George – I can see your father tearing his hair, and shouting, and all the time he's probably put the papers into the waste-paper basket by mistake!' said Dick, with a chuckle.

'Gracious – we never *thought* of that!' said George. 'I'd better phone Mother at once, and tell her to look. Bright idea of yours, Dick.'

'Well, you go and phone, and we'll put our bikes away,' said Julian. 'Take your nose away from that bag of sausages, Timmy. You're in disgrace over sausages, let me tell you. You're suspected of eating too many last night!'

'He did eat rather a lot,' said George. 'I took my eye off him, and he wolfed quite a few. Hey, who's this Mrs Layman who's coming to tea? Have we *got* to stay in and have tea with her? I hoped we might be going off for a picnic this afternoon.'

''Fraid not,' said Dick, 'Mrs Layman is apparently coming to talk to *us* about something. So we have to be in – with clean hands, nice manners, and everything. So behave yourself, George!'

George gave him a friendly punch. 'That's unfair,' said Dick. 'You know I can't punch you back. My word, you should have seen Anne this morning, George – yelled at me like a tiger howling, and showed her teeth, and —'

'Don't be an idiot, Dick,' said Anne. 'He called me a mouse, George – he said we had *one* tiger – you – and that was enough in the family. So I went for him – put out my claws for a moment, and gave him such a surprise. I rather liked it!'

'Good old Anne!' said George, amused. 'But you're not really cut out to be a tiger, and rage and roar, you know.'

'I could be, if I had to,' said Anne, obstinately. 'One of these days I'll surprise you all. You just wait!'

'All right. We will,' said Julian, putting his arm round his sister. 'Come on, now – we'd better get indoors before Timmy gets some of the cakes out of the bags. Stop licking that bag, Tim – you'll make a hole in it.'

'He can smell the cherry buns inside,' said Anne. 'Shall I give him one?'

'NO!' said Julian. 'Cherry buns are wasted on him, you know that. Don't you remember how he chews the bun apart and spits out the cherries?'

'Woof,' said Timmy, exactly as if he agreed. He went to sniff at the bag with his bone inside.

'That's your dinner, Tim,' said Anne. 'Plenty of meat on it, too. Look, there's Mother at the window, beckoning. I expect she wants the sausages. NO, Timmy – the sausages are NOT for you. Get down! Good gracious, I never in my life knew such a hungry dog. Anybody would think you starved him, George.'

'Well, they'd think wrong, then,' said George. 'Timmy, come to heel.'

Timmy came, still looking round longingly at the various bags that the others were now taking from their saddle-bags.

They all went indoors, and deposited the goods on the kitchen table. Doris, the lady who helped their mother in the holidays, opened the bags and looked inside, keeping a sharp eye on Timmy.

'Better take that dog of yours out of my kitchen,' she said. 'Funny how sausages always disappear when he's around. Get down, now – take your paws off my clean table!'

Timmy trotted out of the kitchen. He thought it was a pity that cooks didn't like him. He liked *them* very much indeed – they always smelt so deliciously of cooking, and there were always so many titbits around which he longed for, but was seldom offered. Ah well – he'd trot into the kitchen again when Doris had gone upstairs for something! He might perhaps find a few bits and pieces on the floor then!

'Hallo, Georgina dear!' said her aunt, coming into the kitchen, Timmy following her in delight. 'Timmy, go out of the kitchen. I don't trust you within a mile of sausages. Go on – shoo!'

Timmy 'shooed'. He liked Anne's mother, but knew that when she said 'Shoo!' she meant it. He lay down on a rug in the living room, with a heavy sigh, wondering how long it would be before he had that lovely meaty bone. He put his head on his paws, and kept his ears pricked for George. He thought it most unfair that George shouldn't be shooed out of the kitchen too.

'Now, for goodness' sake keep out of my way while I cook the lunch,' said Doris to the children milling round her kitchen. 'And shut the door, please. I don't want that great hungry dog sniffing round me all the time, making out he's starving, when he's as fat as butter!'

'He's NOT!' said George, indignantly. 'Timmy has never been fat in his life. He's not that kind of dog. He's *never* greedy!'

'Well, he must be the first dog ever born that wasn't greedy,' said Doris. 'Can't trust any of them! There was that pug-dog of Mrs Lane's – crunched up lumps of sugar whenever it could reach a sugar bowl – and that fat poodle next door – came and knocked over the cream that the milkman left outside the back door – *deliberately* knocked it over, mark you – and then licked up every drop. Ha – his mistress tried to make out he didn't like cream – but you should have seen his nose – covered in cream up to his eyes!'

Timmy looked in at the kitchen door, his nose in the air, for all the world as if he were deeply offended at Doris's remarks. Julian laughed. 'You've wounded his pride, Doris!' he said.

'I'll wound him somewhere else, too, if he comes sniffing round me when I'm cooking,' said Doris. That made George give one of her scowls, but the others couldn't help laughing!

The morning went very pleasantly. The Five went down to the beach and walked round the high cliffs, enjoying the stiff breeze that blew in their faces. Timmy raced after every seagull that dared to sit on the smooth sand, annoyed that each one rose up lazily on great wings as soon as he almost reached it.

They were all hungry for their dinner, and not one single morsel was left when they had finished! Doris had made a tremendous steamed pudding, with lashings of treacle, which was, as usual, a huge success.

'Wish I had a tongue like Timmy's and could lick up the lovely treacle left on the bottom of the dish,' said George. 'Such a waste!'

'You certainly won't be able to eat any tea,

I'm sure of that!' said her aunt. But, of course, she was wrong. When tea-time came they all felt quite ready for it, and were most impatient when Mrs Layman was late!

The tea looked lovely, laid on a big table covered with a white lace cloth. The children sat and looked at it longingly. When would Mrs Layman arrive?

'I begin to feel I'm not going to like Mrs Layman,' said George, at last. 'I can't *bear* looking at those cream cakes when I'm hungry.'

The front door bell rang. Hurrah! Then in came a cheerful, smiling old lady nodding to everyone, very pleased to see such a nice little party waiting for her.

'Here's Mrs Layman, children,' said Julian's mother. 'Sit down, Mrs Layman. We're delighted to have you.'

'Well, I've come to ask the children something,' said Mrs Layman. 'But we'll have tea first, and then I'll say what I've come to say. My, my – what a wonderful tea! I'm glad I feel hungry!'

Everyone else was hungry too, and soon the bread and butter, the sandwiches, the buns, the cakes and everything else disappeared. Timmy sat quietly by George, who slipped him a titbit now and again when no one was looking. Mrs Layman chatted away. She was a most interesting person, and the children liked her very much.

'Well now,' she said, when tea was finished, 'I'm sure you must be wanting to know why I asked to come to tea today. I wanted to ask your mother, Julian, if there was any chance of you three . . . and this other boy here, what's his name – George! . . . would you like to help me out of a difficulty?'

Nobody pointed out that George was a girl, not a boy, and that George was short for Georgina. George, as usual, was pleased to be taken for a boy. They all looked at Mrs Layman, listening to her with interest.

'It's like this,' she said. 'I've a dear little house up on the hills, overlooking the harbour – and I've a grandson staying with me there –

Wilfrid. Well, I have to go to look after a cousin of mine, who's ill – and Wilfrid can't bear to be left alone. I just wondered if your mother would allow you children to share the little house with Wilfrid, and, well keep him company. He feels a bit scared being on his own. There's a nice woman there, who comes in to cook and clean – but poor Wilfrid's really scared of being in such a lonely place, high up on the hill.'

'You mean that lovely little house with the wonderful view?' said Julian's mother.

'Yes. It's rather *primitive* in some ways – no water laid on, only just a well to use – and no electricity or gas – just candles, or an oil-lamp. Maybe it sounds too old-fashioned for words – but honestly the view makes up for it! Perhaps the children would like to come over and see it, before they decide?' Mrs Layman looked earnestly round at everyone, and nobody knew quite what to say.

'Well – we'll *certainly* come and see it,' said Julian's mother. 'And if the children feel like it, well, they can stay there. They do like being on their own, of course.'

'Yes,' said Julian. 'We'll come and see it, Mrs Layman. Mother's going to be busy with a bazaar soon – she'll be glad to get us out of the way – and, of course, we *do* like being on our own!'

Mrs Layman looked extremely pleased. 'To-morrow, then?' she said. 'About ten o'clock. You'll love the view. Wonderful, wonderful! You can see right over the great harbour, and for miles around. Well – I must be going now. I'll tell Wilfrid you children may be keeping him company. He's *such* a nice lad – so helpful. You'll love him.'

Julian had his doubts about the nice, helpful Wilfrid. He even wondered if Mrs Layman wanted to get away from Wilfrid, and leave him to himself! No – that was too silly. Anyway, they'd soon see what the place was like, tomorrow.

'It *would* be fun to be on our own again,' said George, when Mrs Layman had gone. 'I don't expect this Wilfrid would be any bother. He's probably just a silly kid, scared of being left alone – though apparently there *is* a woman there! Well – we'll go tomorrow! Maybe the view will make up for dear Wilfrid!'

[3]

The cottage on the hill – and Wilfrid

Next day the children prepared to go and see the cottage belonging to Mrs Layman. 'You coming too, Mother?' asked Julian. 'We'd like your advice!'

'Well no, dear,' said his mother. 'I've rather a lot to do – there's a meeting on at the village hall, and I promised to go to it.'

'You're full of good works, Mother,' said Julian, giving her a hug. 'All right, we'll go by ourselves. I daresay we shall know at once whether we'd like to stay in the cottage – or not. Also, we MUST know what this Wilfrid is like! It's a quarter to ten, and George is already here, with Timmy. I'll call the others and we'll get our bikes.'

Soon the four were on their bicycles, with

Timmy, as usual, running alongside, his long tongue out, his eyes bright and happy. This was Timmy's idea of perfect happiness – to be with the four children all day long!

They went along a road that ran on the top of a hill. They swung round a corner – and there, spread far below them, was a great sea vista that included a wonderful harbour, filled with big and little ships. The sea was as blue as the Mediterranean, quite breathtaking. Anne jumped off her bicycle at once.

'I must just feast my eyes on all this before I go any further!' she said. 'What a panorama! What miles of sea and sky!'

She put her bicycle against a gate and then climbed over and stood by herself, gazing down at the view. Dick joined her.

Then suddenly a voice shouted loudly, 'FORE! FORE!' A small white thing came whizzing through the air and landed just by Anne's foot. She jumped in surprise.

'It's a golf ball,' said Dick. 'No, don't pick it up. Whoever's playing with it has to come and hit it from exactly where it fell. Good thing you weren't hit, Anne. I didn't realise that this gate led on to a golf course!'

'We ought to have a walk over it,' said Anne. 'Just look at those gorsebushes over there, absolutely flaming with yellow blossom – and all the tiny flowers springing up everywhere – speedwell and coltsfoot and daisies and celandines – beautiful. And what a view!'

'Yes – and if Mrs Layman's cottage has a view anything like this, I'd certainly like to stay there!' said Dick. 'Think of getting out of bed in the morning and seeing this enormous view out of the window – the harbour – the sea beyond – the hills all round – the great spread of sky . . .'

'You ought to be a poet, Dick!' said Anne, in surprise. The golfers came up at that moment, and the children stood aside and watched one of them address the ball, and then strike it easily and strongly. The ball soared through the air, and landed far away on a smooth green fairway.

'Good shot!' said the man's partner, and the two sauntered off together.

'Funny game, really,' said Anne. 'Just hitting a ball all round the course.'

'Wish I had some clubs!' said Dick. 'I'm sure I could hit some smashing shots!'

'Well, if that cottage is anywhere near the golf course perhaps you could pay to have a lesson,' said Anne. 'I bet you could hit a ball as far as that man!'

The others were now yelling for them to come back, so they went to fetch their bicycles. Soon they were all riding along the road again. 'We have to look for a small white gate, with "Hill Cottage" painted on it,' said George. 'On the hillside facing the sea.'

'There it is!' cried Anne. 'We'll pile our bicycles together against the hedge, and go in at the gate.'

They left their bicycles in a heap and went through the gate. Not far to their left stood a funny old cottage, its back to them, its front looking down the steep hill that ran towards the great harbour and the sea beyond.

'It's like a cottage out of an old fairy-tale,'

said Anne. 'Funny little chimneys, rather crooked walls, a thatched roof, all uneven – and what tiny windows!'

They walked down a little winding path that led to the cottage. They soon came to a well, and leaned over it to see the water deep down. 'So that's the water we'd have to drink!' said Anne, wrinkling up her nose. 'And we'd have to let down the bucket by winding this handle – and down it would go on the rope! Do you suppose the water is pure?'

'Well, seeing that people must have drunk it for years on end – the ones living in that cottage, anyway – I should imagine it's all right!' said Julian. 'Come on – let's find the front door of the cottage – if it has one!'

It had a wooden door, hung rather crooked, with an old brass knocker. It faced down the hill, and was flanked on each side by small windows. Two other small windows were above. Julian looked at them. The bedrooms would be very small, he thought – would there *really* be room for them all?

He knocked at the door. Nobody came to open it. He knocked again, and then looked for a bell, but there wasn't one.

'See if the door is unlocked,' said Anne. So Julian turned the handle – and at once the door gave under his hand! It opened straight into a room that looked like a kitchen-living room.

Julian gave a shout. 'Anyone at home?'

There was no answer. 'Well – as this is obviously the cottage we were meant to see, we'd better go in,' said Julian and in they all went.

It was old, very old. The carved wooden furniture was old too. Ancient oil-lamps stood on two tables in the room, and in a recess there was an oil-stove with a saucepan on top. A narrow, crooked stairway made of wood curved up to the floor above. Julian went up, and found himself in a long, darkish room, its roof thatched with reed and held up by black beams.

'This place must be hundreds of years old!' he called down to the others. 'I don't think it's big enough for us four and the others too – Wilfrid and the helper.'

Just as he finished calling down the stairs, the front door was flung open and someone came in.

'What are you doing here?' he shouted. 'This is *my* cottage!'

Julian went quickly down the stairs, and there, facing them all, stood a boy of about ten, a scowl on his brown face.

'Er – are you Wilfrid, by any chance?' asked Dick, politely.

'Yes, I am. And who are you? And where's my grandmother? She'll soon chuck you out!' said the boy.

'Is your grandmother Mrs Layman?' asked Julian. 'If so, she asked us to come and see her cottage, and decide if we'd like to keep you company. She said she had to go away and look after a sick relative.'

'Well, I don't want you!' said the boy. 'So clear off. I'm all right here alone. My grandmother's a nuisance, always fussing around.'

'I thought there was a lady who looks after you too,' said Julian. 'Where is she?'

'She only comes in the morning, and I sent her off,' said Wilfrid. 'She left me some food. I want to be alone. I don't want *you*. So clear off.'

'Don't be an idiot, Wilfrid,' said Julian. 'You can't live all alone here. You're just a kid.'

'I shan't be living all alone. I've plenty of friends,' said Wilfrid, defiantly.

'You CAN'T have plenty of friends here in this lonely place, with only the hills and sky around you,' said Dick.

'Well, I *have*!' said Wilfrid. 'And here's one – so look out!' And, to the horror of the two girls, he put his hand into his pocket, and brought out a snake!

Anne screamed, and tried to hide behind Julian. Wilfrid saw her fright and came towards her, holding the snake by its middle, so that it swayed to and fro, its bright little eyes gleaming.

'Don't be scared, Anne,' said Julian. 'It's only

a harmless grass-snake. Put the creature back into your pocket, Wilfrid, and don't play the fool. If that snake is the only friend you have, you'll be pretty lonely here by yourself!'

'I've *plenty* of friends, I tell you!' shouted Wilfrid, stuffing the snake back into his pocket. 'I'll hit you if you don't believe me.'

'Oh no, you won't,' said Dick. 'Just show us your other friends. If they're kids like you, it's just too bad!'

'Kids? I don't make friends with *kids*!' said Wilfrid, scornfully. '*I'll* show you I'm speaking the truth. Come out here on the hillside, and see some of my other friends.'

They all trooped out of the little cottage, on to the hillside, amazed at this fierce, strange boy. When they were in the open, they saw that he had eyes as bright blue as the speedwell in the grass, and hair almost as yellow as the celandines.

'Sit down and keep quiet,' he ordered. 'Over there, by that bush. And don't move a finger. I'll soon make you believe in my friends! How dare you come here, doubting my word!'

They all sat down obediently beside the gorsebush, puzzled and rather amused. The boy sat down too, and drew something out of his pocket. What was it? George tried to see, but it was half-hidden in his right hand.

He put it to his mouth, and began to whistle. It was a soft, weird whistle that grew loud and then died away again. There was no tune, no melody, just a kind of beautiful dirge that pulled at the heart. 'Sad,' thought Anne, 'such a sad little tune – if you could *call* it a tune!'

Something stirred a little way down the hill – and then to everyone's astonishment, an animal appeared – a hare! Its great ears stood upright, its big eyes stared straight at the boy with the curious little pipe. Then the hare lolloped right up to Wilfrid – and began to dance! Soon another came, but this one only watched. The first one then seemed to go mad, and leapt about wildly, utterly unafraid.

The tune changed a little – and a rabbit

appeared. Then another and another. One came to Wilfrid's feet and sniffed at them, its whiskers quivering. Then it lay down against the boy's foot.

A bird flew down – a beautiful magpie! It stood nearby, watching the hare, fascinated. It took no notice of the children at all. They all held their breath, amazed and delighted.

And then Timmy gave a little growl, deep down in his throat. He didn't really mean to, but he just couldn't help it! At once the hares, the rabbits and the magpie fled, the magpie squawking in fright.

Wilfrid faced round at once, his eyes blazing. He lifted his hand to strike Timmy – but George caught his fist at once.

'Let go!' yelled Wilfrid. 'That dog scared my friends! I'll get a stick and whip him. He's the worst dog in the world, he's—'

And then something strange happened. Timmy came gently over to Wilfrid, lay down, and put his head on the angry boy's knee, looking up at him lovingly. The boy, his hand still raised to strike, lowered it, and fondled Timmy's head, making a curious crooning noise.

'Timmy! Come here!' ordered George, amazed and angry. To think that *her* dog, her very *own* dog, should go to a boy who had been about to strike him! Timmy stood up, gave Wilfrid a lick, and went to George.

The boy watched him, and then spoke to them all. 'You *can* come and stay in my cottage,' he said, 'if you'll bring that dog too. There aren't many dogs like him – he's a *wonderful* dog. I'd like him for one of my friends.'

Then, without another word, Wilfrid sprang up and ran away down the hill, leaving four most astonished people – and a dog who whined dismally because the boy had gone. Well, well, Timmy – there must indeed be something about that boy, if you stand looking after him as if you had lost one of your very best friends!

[4]
Settling in

The Five stared after Wilfrid in silence. Timmy wagged his tail and whined. He wanted the boy to come back.

'Well, thank you, Timmy, old thing,' said Anne, patting the big dog on the head. 'We certainly wouldn't have had this lovely little cottage, with its incredible view, if you hadn't made friends with Wilfrid. What a funny boy he is!'

'Rather peculiar, I think!' said George, still amazed at the way that Timmy had gone to Wilfrid, when the boy had been about to strike him. 'I'm not sure that I like him!'

'Don't be silly, George,' said Dick, who had been very much impressed by the boy's handling of the hares, the rabbits and the magpie. 'That boy must have a wonderful love for animals. They would never come to him as they did, if they didn't trust him absolutely. Anyone who loves animals as he does must be all right.'

'I bet I could make them come to *me* if I had that pipe,' said George, making up her mind to borrow it if she could.

Anne went back into the cottage. She was delighted with it. 'It must be very, very old,' she thought. 'It stands dreaming here all day long, full of memories of the people who have lived here and loved it. And how they must all have loved this view – miles and miles of heather, great stretches of sea – and the biggest, highest widest sky I've ever seen. It's a happy place. Even the clouds seem happy – they're scurrying along, so white against the blue!'

She explored the cottage thoroughly. She decided that the room above, under the thatch, should be for the three boys. There were two mattresses – one small, one larger. 'The little one for Wilfrid – the big one for Dick and Julian,' she thought. 'And George and I can sleep down in the living room, with Tim on guard. I wonder if there are any rugs we could sleep on. Ah – wait a bit – this couch is a pull-out bed – just right for us two girls! Good!'

Anne enjoyed herself thoroughly. This was the kind of problem she liked – fixing up this and that for the others! She found a little larder, facing north. It had a few tins in it, and a jug of milk, slightly sour. It also had two loaves of extremely stale bread, and a tin of rather hard cakes.

'Mrs Layman doesn't seem to be a very good housekeeper for herself and Wilfrid,' thought Anne, seriously. 'We'll have to go down to the village and put in a stock of decent food. I might get a small ham – the boys would like that. Goodness – this *is* going to be fun!'

Julian came to the door to see what she was doing. When he saw her happy, serious face, he chuckled. 'Acting "mother" to us, as usual?' he said. 'Deciding who's going to sleep where, and which of us is to do the shopping, and which the washing-up? Dear old Anne – what should we do without you when we go off on our own?'

'I love it,' said Anne, happily. 'Julian, we need another rug or two, and a pillow, and some food. And . . .'

'Well, we'll have to go back home and collect a few clothes and other things,' said Julian. 'We can shop on the way back, and get whatever we want. I wonder if that woman that Mrs Layman spoke about will be coming in to help?'

'Well – Wilfrid said he sent her off,' said Anne. 'And I think perhaps as the cottage is so small, it might be better if we managed it ourselves. I think I could do a bit of cooking on that oil-stove in the corner – and anyway we can pretty well live on cold stuff, you know – ham and salad and cheese and fruit. It would be easy enough for any of us to pop down to the village on our bikes, to fetch anything we needed.'

'Listen!' said Julian, cocking his head to one side. 'Is that somebody calling us?'

Yes – it was. When Julian went outside, he saw Mrs Layman at the gate that led on to the hillside where the cottage stood. He went over to her.

'We LOVE the cottage!' he said. 'And if it's all right, we'd like to move in today. We can easily pop home and bring back anything we want. It's a glorious old place, isn't it – and the view must be the finest anywhere!'

'Well, that harbour is the second biggest stretch of water in the whole world,' said Mrs Layman. 'The only stretch that is any bigger is Sydney harbour – so you have something to feast your eyes on, Julian!'

'You bet!' said Julian. 'It's amazing – and so *very* blue! I only wish I could paint – but I can't. At least, not very well!'

'What about Wilfrid?' said Mrs Layman, anxiously. 'Is he behaving himself? He's – well – he's rather a *difficult* boy at times. And he can be very rude. He hasn't any brothers to rub off his awkward corners, you see.'

'Oh, don't you worry about Wilfrid!' said Julian, cheerfully. 'He'll have to toe the line, and do as he's told. We all do our bit when we're away together. He's a wonder with animals, isn't he?'

'Well – yes, I suppose he *is*!' said Mrs Layman. 'Though I can't say I like pet snakes, or pet beetles, and owls that come and hoot down the chimney at night to find out if Wilfrid will go out and hoot back at them!'

Julian laughed. 'We shan't mind that,' he said. 'And he's managed to get over what might have been our biggest difficulty – he has made friends with our dog, Timmy. In fact, he informed us that if Timmy stayed, we could *all* stay – but *only* if Timmy stayed!'

Mrs Layman laughed. 'That's so like Wilfrid,' she said. 'He's an odd boy. Don't stand any nonsense from him!'

'We shan't,' said Julian, cheerfully. 'I'm surprised he wants to stay on with us, actually. I should have thought he would rather go home than be with a lot of strangers.'

'He can't go home,' said Mrs Layman. 'His sister has measles, and his mother doesn't want Wilfrid to catch it. So you'll have to put up with him, I fear.'

'And he'll have to put up with us!' said Julian. 'Thanks very much for letting us have the cottage, Mrs Layman. We'll take great care of everything.'

'I know you will,' said the old lady. 'Well, good-bye, Julian. Have a good time. I'll get back to my car now. Give Wilfrid my love. I hope he doesn't fill the cottage with animals of all kinds!'

'We shan't mind if he does!' said Julian, and waited politely until Mrs Layman had disappeared and he could hear the noise of a car starting up.

He went back to the cottage and stood outside, looking down at the amazing view. The harbour was full of boats, big and little. A steamer went busily along, making for a great seaside town far away on the other side.

Anne came to join Julian. 'Glorious, isn't it?' she said. 'We're so very high up here that it seems as if we can see half the world at our feet. Is that an island in the middle of the harbour,

Ju?'

'Yes – and a well-wooded one too!' said Julian.
'I wonder what it's called – and who lives there. I
can't see a single house there, can you?'

Dick called to Anne. 'Anne! George and I are
going to fetch our bikes and ride down to the
village. Give us your shopping list, will you?
Julian, is there anything special you want us to
pack for you at home, and bring back, besides
your night things and a change of clothes?'

'Yes – don't go off yet!' called Julian, hurrying into the cottage. 'I've made a list somewhere. I think I'd better go with you. There will
be food and other things to bring back – unless
Mother would bring everything up by car this
afternoon.'

'Yes – that's a good idea,' said Dick. 'We'll
go to Kirrin Cottage first and get George's
things – and then home to get ours. I'll leave
all the shopping with Mother, and all our
luggage, so that she can pop up here in the
car with it. She'll love the view!'

'I'll stay behind and tidy up the cottage, and

find out how the stove works,' said Anne, happily. 'I'll have everything neat and tidy by the time Mother comes this afternoon, Dick. Oh, here's Julian with the list. Why don't you go off on your bike with George and Dick, Julian? I'll be quite happy here messing about.'

'Yes, I'm going to,' said Julian, putting his list into his pocket. 'Look after yourself, Anne! We'll take Timmy with us, to give him a run.'

Off went the three, Timmy loping behind, very glad of the run. Anne waited till they were out of sight, then went happily back to the cottage. She was almost there when she heard someone calling her. She turned and saw a fresh-faced woman waving.

'I'm Sally!' she called. 'Do you want any help with the cooking and cleaning? Wilfrid told me not to come any more, but if you want me, I will.'

'Oh, I think we can manage, Sally,' said Anne. 'There's so many of us now, we can all do the jobs. Did you sleep here?'

'Oh no!' said Sally, coming up. 'I just came in

to help, and then went back home. You tell me if you want me any time, and I'll gladly come. Where's that monkey of a Wilfrid? He spoke to me very rudely this morning the little devil! I'll tell his grandmother of him – not that that's much good! He just laughs at her! Don't you stand any nonsense from him!'

'I won't,' said Anne, smiling. 'Where do you live, in case we *do* want you?'

'Just the other side of the road, in the small wood there,' said Sally. 'You'll see my tiny cottage when you go by the wood on your bikes.'

She disappeared up the hill and across the road there. Anne went back happily to her household tasks. She cleaned out the little larder, and then found a pail and went to the well. She hung the pail on the hook at the end of the rope, and then worked the old handle that let the pail down to the water, swinging on the rope. Splash! It was soon full, and Anne wound it up again. The water looked crystal clear, and was as cold as ice – but all the same Anne wondered if she ought to boil it.

Someone came quietly behind her – and jumped at her with a loud howl! Anne dropped the pail of water, and gave a scream. Then she saw it was Wilfrid, dancing round her, grinning.

'Idiot!' she said. 'Now you just go and get me some more water.'

'Where's that big dog?' demanded Wilfrid, looking all round. 'I can't see him. You can't any of you stay here unless you have that dog. I like him. He's a wonderful dog.'

'He's gone down to the village with the others,' said Anne. 'Now will you please pick up that pail and get more water?'

'No, I won't,' said Wilfrid. 'I'm not your servant! Get it yourself!'

'Very well, I will. But I'll tell George, who owns Timmy, how rude you are – and you may be *quite* sure that Timmy won't be friends with you,' said Anne, picking up the pail.

'I'll get the water, I'll get the water!' shouted Wilfrid, and snatched the pail. 'Don't you dare to tell George or Timmy tales of me. Don't you dare!'

And off he went to the well and filled the pail. Well! What a time they were all going to have with such a very peculiar boy! Anne didn't like him at all!

[5]

Wilfrid is most annoying – and Anne is most surprising!

Wilfred brought back the pail to Anne, and dumped it down. 'Like to see my pet beetles?' he said.

'No thank you,' said Anne. 'I don't like beetles very much.'

'Well, you ought to!' said Wilfrid. 'I've two very beautiful ones. You can hold them if you like. The tiny feet feel very funny when they walk all over your hand.'

'I don't *mind* beetles, but I don't want them walking over my hand,' said poor Anne, who really was a bit afraid of what she called 'creepy-crawly' things. 'Do get out of my way, Wilfrid. If you had any manners, you'd carry that pail indoors for me.'

'I *haven't* any manners,' said Wilfrid. 'Everybody tells me that. Anyway, I don't want to carry your pail if you don't want to see my beetles.'

'Oh, go away!' said Anne, exasperated, picking up the pail herself. Wilfrid went to a little thick bush and sat down by it. He put his face almost on the grass, and looked under the bush. Anne felt uncomfortable. Was he going to call his beetles out? She couldn't help putting down her pail, and standing still to watch.

No beetles came out from under the bush – but something else did. A very large, awkward-looking toad came crawling out, and sat there, looking up at Wilfrid with the greatest friendliness. Anne was amazed. How did Wilfrid know the toad was there? And why in the world should it come out to see *him*? She stood and stared – and shivered, because she really did *not* like toads. 'I know they have beautiful eyes, and are intelligent, and eat all kinds of harmful insects, but I just can't go near one!' she thought. 'Oh goodness – Wilfrid's tickling its back – and it's scratching where he's tickled – just like *we* would!'

'Come and say how-do-you-do to my pet toad,' called Wilfrid. 'I'll carry your pail for you then.'

Anne picked up her pail in a hurry, afraid that Wilfrid might whistle up a few snakes next. What a boy! How she wished the others would come back! Why, Wilfrid might own a boa constrictor – or have a small crocodile some-where – or . . . but no, she was being silly! If *only* the others would come back!

To her horror the toad crawled right on to Wilfrid's hands, and looked up at him out of its really beautiful eyes. That was too much for Anne. She fled into the cottage, spilling half the water as she went.

'I wish I was like George,' she thought. 'She wouldn't really mind that toad. I'm silly. I ought to try and like *all* creatures. Oh my goodness, look at that enormous spider in the corner of the sink! It's sitting there, looking at me out of its eight eyes!' 'Wilfrid, Wilfrid – PLEASE come and get this spider out of the sink for me!'

Wilfrid sauntered in, fortunately without the toad. He held his hand out to the spider and made a curious clicking, ticking noise. The spider perked up at once, waved two curious little antennae about, and crawled across the sink to Wilfrid's hand. Anne shuddered. She simply couldn't help it! She shut her eyes and when she opened them, the spider had gone and so had Wilfrid.

'I suppose he's now teaching it to dance, or something,' she thought, trying to make herself smile. 'I can't *think* how insects and animals and birds like him. I simply can't *bear* him. If *I* were a rabbit or a bird or beetle, I'd run miles away from him. What's this curious attraction he has for creatures of all kinds?'

Wilfrid had completely disappeared, and Anne thankfully went on with her little jobs. 'I'll tidy up the loft where the boys will sleep,' she thought. 'I'll wash this living room floor. I'll make a list of the things in the larder. I'll clean that dirty window over there. I'll . . . good gracious, what's that noise?'

It was the sound of magpies chattering noisily – a harsh but pleasant noise. Anne peered out of the little cottage window. Well, what a sight! There stood Wilfrid in front of the window, a magpie on each outstretched hand – and one on the top of his head! It stood there, chattering loudly, and then turned round and round, getting its feet mixed up in the boy's thick hair.

'Come out here and I'll tell one of my magpies to sit on your head too!' shouted Wilfrid. 'It's such a nice feeling. Or would you like a young rabbit to cuddle? I can call one for you with my little pipe!'

'I don't *want* a magpie on my head,' said Anne, desperately. 'For goodness' sake get a nice little baby rabbit. I'd like that.'

Wilfrid jerked the magpies off his hands and shook his head violently so that the third one flew up, squawking cheerfully. He then sat down and pulled out his funny little whistle-pipe, as Anne called it. She watched, fascinated, as the strange little dirge-like tune came to her ears. She found her feet walking to the door. Good gracious – could there be some peculiar kind of magic in that pipe that made *her* go to Wilfrid, just as the other creatures did?

She stopped at the door, just as a baby rabbit came lolloping round a tall clump of grass. It was the funniest, roundest, dearest little thing, with a tiny bobtail and big ears.

It went straight to Wilfrid and nestled against him. The boy stroked it and murmured to it. Then he called to Anne softly.

'Well – here's the baby rabbit you asked for. Like to come and stroke it?'

Anne went softly over the grass, expecting the rabbit to bolt at once. Wilfrid continued to fondle it, and the little thing looked at him with big, unwinking eyes. Anne bent down to stroke it – but immediately it leapt in fright and fled into the grass.

'Oh *dear* – why did it do that?' said Anne, disappointed. 'It was quite all right with *you*! Wilfrid, how do you get all these creatures to come to you?'

'Shan't tell you,' said Wilfrid, getting up. 'Is there anything to eat in the cottage? I'm hungry.'

He pushed Anne aside and went into the cottage. He opened the larder door, and took down a tin. There was a cake inside and he cut off a huge piece. He didn't offer Anne any.

'Couldn't you have cut *me* a piece too?' said Anne. 'You really are a rude boy!'

'I *like* being rude,' said Wilfrid, munching his cake. 'Especially to people who come to my cottage when I don't want them.'

'Oh, don't be so *silly*!' said Anne, exasperated. 'It *isn't* your cottage – it belongs to your grandmother. She told us so. Anyway, you said we could stay if Timmy stayed too.'

'I'll soon make Timmy *my* dog,' said Wilfrid, taking another bite. 'You'll see! Soon he won't want that girl George any more – and he'll follow at my heels all day and night. *You'll* see!'

Anne laughed scornfully. Timmy following at this boy's heels? That could never happen! Timmy loved George with all his doggy heart.

He would never desert her for Wilfrid, no matter how much he whistled on pipes, or put on his special croony voice. Anne was absolutely certain of that!

'If you laugh at me, I'll call up my grass-snake *and* my adder!' said Wilfrid, fiercely. 'Then you'll run for miles!'

'Oh no I won't!' said Anne, hurrying into the cottage. 'Just watch *yourself* run!' She picked up the pail of water, went out with it, and threw it all over the astonished Wilfrid! Somebody else was *most* astonished too – and that was Julian, who had arrived back before the others, anxious not to leave Anne alone in the cottage for too long.

He came just in time to see Anne drenching Wilfrid, and stared in the utmost amazement. *Anne* behaving like that? Anne looking really *fierce* – quiet, peaceful Anne! What in the world had happened?

'Anne!' he called. 'What's the matter? What's Wilfrid been doing?'

'Oh – *Julian*!' said Anne, glad to see him, but

horrified that he had come just then. Wilfrid was drenched from head to foot. He stood there, gasping, taken aback, bewildered. Why, Anne had seemed such a *quiet*, frightened little thing – scared even of a spider!

'That girl!' said Wilfrid, half-choking, shaking the water off himself. 'That bad, wicked girl! She's like a tiger! She sprang at me, and threw the water all over me! I won't let her stay in my cottage!'

The boy was so angry, so wet, so taken aback, that Julian had to laugh! He roared in delight, and clapped Anne on the back. 'The mouse has turned into a tiger! Well, you said you might one day, Anne – and you haven't lost much time! Let me see if you've grown claws!'

He took Anne's hands and pretended to examine her nails. Anne was half-laughing, half-crying now, and pulled her hand away. 'Oh Julian, I shouldn't have soaked Wilfrid – but he was so IRRITATING I lost my temper, and—'

'All right, all right – it's quite a good thing to

do sometimes,' said Julian. 'And I bet young Wilfrid deserved all he got. I only hope the water was icy cold! Have you a change of clothes here, Wilfrid? Go and get into them, then.'

The boy stood there, dripping wet, and made no effort to obey. Julian spoke again. 'You heard what I said, Wilfrid. Jump to it! Go and change!'

The boy looked so wet and miserable that Anne felt suddenly sorry for what she had done. She ran to him and felt his wet shoulders. 'Oh, I'm *sorry*!' she said. 'Truly I am. I don't know *why* I turned into a tiger so suddenly!'

Wilfrid gave a little half-laugh, half-sob. 'I'm sorry too,' he mumbled. 'You're nice – and your nose is like that baby rabbit's – it's – it's a bit woffly!'

He ran into the cottage and slammed the door. 'Let him be for a while,' said Julian, seeing that Anne made a move to go after him. 'This will do him good. Nothing like having a pail of cold water flung over you to make you see things as they really are! He was really touched when you said you were sorry. *He's* probably never apologised to anyone in his life!'

'*Is* my nose like a rabbit's?' said Anne, worried.

'Well, yes – just a bit,' said Julian, giving his sister an affectionate pat. 'But a rabbit's nose is very nice, you know – very nice indeed. I don't think you'll have much trouble with Wilfrid after this little episode. He didn't know that you had the heart of a tiger, as well as a nose like a rabbit's!'

Wilfrid came out of the cottage in about ten minutes, dressed in dry clothes, carrying his wet ones in a bundle. 'I'll hang those out on the bushes for you, to dry in the sun,' said Anne, and took them from him, smiling. He suddenly smiled back.

'Thanks,' he said. 'I don't know how they got so wet! Must have been *pouring* with rain!'

Julian chuckled and smacked him gently on the back. 'Rain can do an awful lot of good at times!' he said. 'Well, Anne, we've brought you back a whole lot of goods for your larder. Here come the others. We'll carry everything in for you – with Wilfrid's help too!'

[6]

Lucas – and his tale

It was fun storing all the shopping away. Anne enjoyed it more than anyone, for she really was a most domesticated little person.

'A real home-maker!' said Dick, appreciatively, when he saw how neat and comfortable she had made the loft, where the three boys were to sleep. 'Just about room for the three of us, plus all the baggage in the corner! And how good the larder looks!'

Anne looked at her well-stocked larder, and smiled. Now she could give her little 'family' really nice meals. All those tins! She read the names on them. Fruit salad. Tinned pears. Tinned peaches. Sardines. Ham. Tuna. A new cake in that round tin, big enough to last for at least three days. Biscuits. Chocolate wafers – good old Julian

– he knew how much she loved those – and
George did, too!

Anne felt very happy as she arranged all her
goods. She no longer felt guilty at drenching
poor Wilfrid. Indeed she couldn't help feeling a
little thrill when she remembered how she had
suddenly turned into a tiger for a minute or
two! It was fun to be a tiger for once. 'I might
even be one again, if the chance arose,' thought
Anne. 'How surprised Wilfrid was – and Julian
too. Oh dear – poor Wilfrid. Still, he's much
nicer now.'

And indeed he was! He was most polite to
both the girls, and, as Dick said, he didn't
'throw his weight about' nearly so much. They
all settled down very well together in the little
cottage.

They had most of their meals out of doors,
sitting on the warm grass. It was rather a
squeeze indoors, for the cottage really was very
small. Anne enjoyed herself preparing the
meals, with sometimes a little help from George
– and the boys carried everything out. Wilfrid

did his share, and was pleased when he had a clap on the back from Julian.

It was glorious sitting out in the sun, high up on their hill. They could look down on the harbour, watch the yachts and the busy little boats, and enjoy the wonderful views all around.

George was very curious about the island that lay in the middle of the harbour. 'What's it called?' she asked Wilfrid. But he didn't know. He did know, however, that there was a strange story about it. 'It belonged to a rich but lonely old man,' he said. 'He lived in a big house in the very middle of the wood. The island was given to his family by a king – James the Second, I think. This old man was the very, very last one of his family. People kept wanting to buy his island, and he had some kind of watchmen to keep people from landing on it. These watch-men were pretty fierce – they had guns.'

'Gosh – did they shoot people who tried to land, then?' asked Dick.

'Well – they just shot to frighten them off, not to hurt them, I suppose,' said Wilfrid. 'Anyway, a lot of sightseers had an awful fright when they tried to land. BANG-BANG! Shooting all round them! My granny told me that someone she knew, who had a lot of money, wanted to buy part of the island – and *he* had his hat shot right off when his boat tried to land!'

'Is there anyone there now?' asked Julian. 'I suppose the old fellow is dead? Has he a son or anyone to follow him?'

'I don't think so,' said Wilfrid. 'But I don't know an awful lot about it. I'll tell you who does, though – one of the groundsmen on the golf course, called Lucas. He was once one of the watchmen who kept visitors away from the island.'

'It might be rather interesting to talk to him,' said Dick. 'I'd rather like to walk over the golf course, too. My father plays a good game of golf, and I know something about it.'

'Well, let's go now,' said George. 'Timmy is longing for a good long walk, even though he ran all the way down to the village and back yesterday! Walk, Timmy? Walk?'

'Woof-woof,' said Timmy, and leapt up at once. Walk? Of *course* he was ready for a walk! He leapt all round George, pretending to pounce at her feet. Wilfrid tried to catch hold of him, but couldn't. 'I wish you were *my* dog,' he told Timmy. 'I'd never let you out of my sight.'

Timmy ran up to him then, and gave him a loving lick. It was astonishing how he seemed to like Wilfrid. Nobody could understand it. As George said, 'Timmy is usually so particular about making friends! Still, Wilfrid *is* nicer than he was!'

The Five, with Wilfrid too, went up the hill, crossed over the road that ran along the top, and climbed over a stile. They found themselves on one of the fairways of the golf course not far from a green, in which stood a pole with a bright red flag waving at the top.

Wilfrid knew very little about the game of golf, but the others had watched their parents play many a time. 'Look out – someone's going to pitch his ball on this green,' said Julian, and they stood by the hedge to watch the man play his ball. He struck it beautifully with his club, and the ball rose, and fell right on to the green. It rolled very close to the hole in which the flag-pole stood.

Timmy ran forward a few steps, as he always did when a ball rolled near him. Then he remembered that this was golf, and he must never, never touch a ball on the fairway or on the green.

The players passed, and went on with their game. Then they disappeared, to play off another tee.

'Well, let's see if we can find Lucas now,' said Wilfrid, crossing the fairway to where he could get a good look over the course. 'You'll like him. There's not much he doesn't know about the animals and birds here. *I* think he's a wonderful man!'

Wilfrid stood on the slope of a hill and looked all round. 'There he is!' he said, pointing to where a man was trimming up a ditch. 'See? Down there. He's using his billhook to make things tidy.'

They went down the hill towards the ditch at the bottom. 'I bet there's an awful lot of balls in that ditch,' said Wilfrid. 'Hey, Lucas! How are you?'

'Morning, young man,' said the groundsman, turning towards them. His face was as brown as a well-ripened nut, and his arms and shoulders were even browner. He wore no shirt or vest, and his dark, deep-set eyes twinkled as they took in the five children and the dog.

He held out a brown hand to Timmy, who licked it gravely, wagging his tail. Then Timmy smelt Lucas all over and finally lay down with his head on the man's feet.

'Ha!' said Lucas to Timmy, and gave a loud, hearty laugh. 'Think I'm going to stand here all morning, do you? Well, I'm not. I've got work to do, old dog, so get up! You're a right good-un, you are, lying on my foot so I can't move a step! Want me to stop and have a rest, don't you?'

'Lucas, we came to ask you something,' said Wilfrid. 'About the island in the harbour.

What's its name – and does anyone live there now?'

'We can see it from that little cottage almost at the top of the hill on the other side of the road,' said Dick. 'It looks awfully quiet and lonely.'

'And so it is,' said Lucas, sitting down on the bank of the ditch. Timmy at once sat up beside him, sniffing him with pleasure. He put his arm round the dog, and began to talk, his bright eyes going from one to another of the children. He was so friendly, and so completely natural, that the children felt he was an old, old friend. They sat down too, sniffing the smell of the gorse bushes nearby. 'They smell like coconut,' thought Anne. 'Yes – just like coconut!'

'Well, now,' said Lucas, 'that island's always been a mystery place. It's called Wailing Island by some folks because the wind makes a right strange wailing noise round some of its high cliffs. And others call it Whispering Island because it's full of trees that whisper in the strong winds that always blow across it. But

most of us call it Keep-Away Island – and that's
the best name of all, for there's never been any
welcome there, what with the dark cliffs, the
cruel rocks, and the dense woods.'

Lucas paused, and looked at the listening
faces around him. He was a born storyteller,
and knew it. How often Wilfrid had listened to
his tales of the birds and animals he met during
his work on the course! Lucas was one of the
few people that the boy admired and loved.

'Do go on, Lucas!' said Wilfrid, touching the
man's bare, warm arm. 'Tell us about the old
man who lived on the island years ago.'

'I'm telling the story my own way,' said
Lucas, with great dignity. 'Be patient now, or
I'll start my ditching again. Sit like this dog, see
– he doesn't even twitch a muscle, good dog
that he is. Well now, about this old man. He
was so afraid of being robbed that he built
himself a great castle right in the middle of the
thick woods. Cut down about a hundred trees
to make room for it, so the story goes, and
brought every single stick and stone from the

mainland. Did you see the old quarry on this here golf course, as you came along to me?'

'Yes, we did,' said Julian, remembering. 'I felt sorry for anyone who sent a golf ball there!'

'Well, out of that quarry came the great stones that the old man used for his castle,' said Lucas. ''Tis said that big, flat-bottomed boats had to be made to ferry the stones across to the island – and to this day the road through this golf course is the one made by horses dragging the great stones down to the water's edge.'

'Were you alive then?' said Wilfrid.

'Bless you, boy, no, of course not,' said Lucas, with a great chuckle of a laugh. 'Long before my time, that was. Well, the stone house – or castle, whatever you like to call it – was built. And the old man brought to it all kinds of treasures – beautiful statues, some of gold, it was said, but I don't believe that. There are many strange tales I've heard of what that rich old man took over to Whispering Island – a great bed made of pure gold, and set with precious stones – a necklace of rubies as big as pigeons' eggs – a wonderful sword with a jewelled handle, worth a king's fortune – and other things I can't remember.'

He paused and looked round. Julian asked him a quick question. 'What happened to all these things?'

'Well now, he fell foul of the king of the land, and one morning, what did he see landing on the shores of his island but ships of all kinds,' said Lucas, enjoying the rapt attention of his audience. 'A lot of them were sunk by the wicked rocks but enough men were left to storm the strange stone castle in the wood, and they killed the old man and all his servants.'

'Did they find the treasures the old fellow had collected?' asked Dick.

'Not one thing!' said Lucas. 'Not one thing. Some say it was all a tale – the old man never did bring any wonders there – and some say they're still there, on Whispering Island. I think it's all a yarn – but a good yarn at that!'

'Who owns the island now?' asked Dick.

'Well, an old fellow and his wife went to live there – maybe they paid rent to the Crown for it, maybe they bought it – but they didn't care for anything except for the birds and the animals there,' said Lucas, picking up his curved billhook again, and hacking lightly at some briars. 'They wouldn't allow anybody there, and it was they who kept the gamekeepers with guns to frighten away sightseers. They wanted peace and quiet for themselves, and for all the wildlife on the island – and a fine idea too. Many a time when I was there with the other keepers – three of us there were – many a time I've had rabbits gambolling over my feet, and snakes gliding by me – and the birds as tame as canaries.'

'I'd *love* to go there,' said Wilfrid, his eyes shining. 'I'd have a good time with all the wild creatures! Can anyone go there now?'

'No,' said Lucas, getting up. 'Not a soul has lived in the old stone castle since the old man and his wife fell ill and died. The place is empty.

The island belongs to a great-nephew of the old couple now, but he never goes there. Just keeps a couple of men on the island to frighten off visitors – pretty fierce they are, so I've been told. Well, there you are, that's the story of Whispering Island – not very pleasant – a bit grim and ugly. It belongs to the birds and the beasts now, and good luck to them!'

'Thank you for telling us the story,' said Anne, and the old countryman smiled down at her, his eyes wrinkling, and his brown hand patting her cheek.

'I'll be off to my hedging and ditching again,' he said, 'and I'll feel the sun warm on my bare back, and hear the birds singing to me from the bushes. That's happiness enough for anyone – and it's a pity that more folks don't know it!'

Up on the golf course

The children walked round the golf course together, after talking to old Lucas. 'We must keep out of the way of anyone playing,' said Dick, 'or we might get hit on the head with a ball! Hey, Timmy, what are you doing in the bracken?'

Timmy came out with something in his mouth. He dropped it at George's feet. It was a golf ball, fairly new. George picked it up. 'What do we do with this?' she said. 'There's no golfer near us. It must be a lost ball.'

'Well, all balls lost on golf courses should be taken in to the pro,' said Julian. 'By right they belong to him if found on the course.'

'What's a pro?' asked Anne.

'A professional golfer – a man who's very, very good at the game, and is in charge of a golf course,' explained Julian. 'Hey look! Here comes old Tim again with *another* ball. Timmy, we ought to hire you out to golfers who keep losing their balls – you'd save them no end of trouble!'

Timmy was pleased to be patted and praised. He set off into the rough again at once, sniffing here and there.

'Anyone would think that golf balls smelt like rabbits or something, the way Timmy sniffs them out!' said Anne, as Timmy ran up with yet another ball. 'Golfers must be jolly careless, losing so many balls!'

They went on round the course, which was set with great stretches of gorse, full of brilliant blossom. A baby rabbit fled from the bracken as Timmy nosed there for balls. Timmy chased it, and the frightened little creature dodged this way and that, trying to escape. 'Let it go, Tim, let it go!' yelled George, but Timmy was much too excited to pay any attention.

Wilfrid suddenly bent down as the rabbit raced near him, and gave a curious low whistle. The rabbit swerved, came straight towards him, and leapt into his arms, lying there trembling. Timmy jumped up to it at once, but George dragged him away.

'NO, Timmy. Sorry, but NO, you can't have the little thing. Down! DOWN, I say!'

Timmy gave George a disgusted look. He was very cross with George. Rabbits were meant to be chased, weren't they? Why did George have to spoil his fun?

George stared at Wilfrid. The rabbit was still nestling in his arms, and he was making a curious noise to it. The tiny thing was trembling from head to tail. Everyone watched it, glad that it was safe. They were all silent, astonished at the way that Wilfrid had rescued the little creature. How had the rabbit known that Wilfrid's arms were ready to save it?

He took it to the bracken, dropped it gently, and watched it race like lightning to the nearest burrow. Then he turned and patted Timmy, who stood silently by, watching.

'Sorry, Tim,' he said. 'It's so little, and you're so big!'

'Woof,' said Tim, exactly as if he understood,

and he gave Wilfrid's hand a quick lick. Then he pranced round the boy, barking, as if he wanted a game, and Wilfrid raced off with him at top speed.

The others followed, impressed once again by Wilfrid's uncanny way with animals. He was such a horrid little boy in some ways – so rude, so mannerless, so selfish – then how was it that animals liked him so much? George frowned. She thought it was all wrong that animals should love Wilfrid and go to him – why, even Timmy was all over him! If she wasn't careful he would spend more time with Wilfrid than with her! That would never do!

Timmy found five more balls, and soon Julian's pockets were heavy with them. They made their way to the small clubhouse in the distance, meaning to give in the balls. It was set in a little dip, and looked friendly and welcoming. They all went in at the door, and Julian walked over to the pro, who was checking some scorecards. He emptied his pockets of balls and grinned. 'A present from our dog!' he said.

'My word – did he find all those?' said the

pro, pleased. 'Not bad ones, either. I'll stand you all some lemonade or orangeade – which will you have?'

They all had orangeade, and the pro sent a packet of biscuits to Timmy, who was waiting patiently outside. He was delighted!

'We're staying in that little cottage up on the hillside,' said Dick. 'Do you know it?'

''Course I do!' said the pro. 'My grand-mother lived there once upon a time. You've a wonderful view there, haven't you? One of the finest in the world, I reckon! You can see Whispering Island from there, too. Ought to be called Mystery Island! It's said that folks have gone there and never come back!'

'What happened to them?' asked Anne.

'Oh well – maybe it's all a tale!' said the pro. 'There's supposed to be priceless things there, packed away somewhere – and collectors from all over the world have come here, and tried to get over to that island – not to steal, you understand, but just to see if they could find anything worthwhile and buy it for museums –

or maybe for their own collections. It's said there are statues in the wood, white as snow – but that I never did believe!'

'And didn't the collectors ever come back?' asked Julian.

'It's said that a lot of them didn't,' said the pro, 'but that may all be silly tales. But I do know that two men came down here from some museum in London, and hired a boat to go across. They took a white flag with them so that the two keepers wouldn't shoot them – and after that nobody heard a word about them. They just disappeared!'

'Well – what could have happened to them?' asked Julian.

'Nobody knows,' said the pro. 'Their boat was found miles out to sea, drifting – and empty. So the police reckoned a mist came down, they lost direction, and ended by drifting way out to sea.'

'But did they jump out of their boat, and try to swim back – and get drowned?' asked Dick. 'Or did a passing steamer or yacht save them?'

'They weren't picked up, that's certain,' said the pro. 'Else they'd have arrived safely back at their homes, sometime or other. But they didn't. No – I reckon the poor fellows were drowned. Of course, maybe they were shot by the keepers, when they tried to land, and their boat was set adrift!'

'Didn't the police do anything?' asked Julian, puzzled.

'Oh, yes – they went across to the island in the coastguard patrol boat,' said the pro. 'But the keepers swore they'd seen nobody arriving, and that they were the only people on the place. The police landed and searched everywhere, and they found nothing except the great white castle-like house in the woods and hundreds of wild animals, so tame that they'd sit and watch you as you walked by.'

'All very mysterious,' said Julian, getting up. 'Well, thanks for the welcome orangeade, and for your information! We'd already heard a bit from a groundsman of yours – Lucas – a real old countryman, and a born storyteller!'

'Ah, Lucas – yes, he knows that island well,' said the pro. 'He was once one of the keepers, I believe! Well – come and see me again some time – thanks for the balls. It isn't everyone who's honest enough to come and give them in when they find them!'

They all said good-bye and went out. Timmy pranced along in joy. Sitting down outside the clubhouse didn't suit him at all!

'Did you enjoy your biscuits, Tim?' asked George, and he ran up and gave her hand a quick lick. What a question! He *always* enjoyed biscuits! He ran off into the bracken and began to nose about there again, hunting for balls.

The others went to walk up the hill, talking about the island. 'I wonder what really *did* happen to those two collector men who were never heard of again,' said Anne. 'Funny that their boat was found adrift and empty.'

'They must have been drowned, of course,' said Dick. 'I wonder if anything *is* left of the old treasures that were once taken there. No – there wouldn't be – the police would have made a very thorough search!'

'I wish *we* could go to the island!' said George. 'I don't expect the keepers would shoot at *us*, would they? They might even let us on, to make change for them – they must be so bored with only themselves to talk to.'

'That's *very* wishful thinking, George,' said Julian. 'We are CERTAINLY not going near the island, so put that right out of your head.'

'Well – I knew it was impossible, really,' said George. 'But wouldn't it be a *grand* adventure if we managed to get on the mysterious Whispering Island and explore it without the keepers knowing!'

'Not such a grand adventure if we were all peppered with shot from the keepers' guns!' said Dick. 'Anyway, we wouldn't find anything of interest – the treasures must have been removed long ago. The only possible things of interest would be the very tame wild creatures there! Wilfrid would go mad with joy – wouldn't you, Wilfrid?'

'I'd like it very much,' said the boy, his eyes shining. 'What's more, I might hire a boat myself and row round the island to see if I could spot any animals there.'

'You'll do nothing of the sort!' said Julian, at once. 'So don't try any silly tricks, see?'

'I shan't promise! said Wilfrid, irritatingly. 'You just never know!'

'Oh yes, I do know! You're just trying to sound big!' said Julian. 'Come along quickly, everyone – it's past our dinner-time, and I'm ravenous! What's for lunch, Anne?'

'We'll open a tin of tuna,' said Anne, 'and there's plenty of bread left, and lettuce, which I left in water. And tomatoes. And heaps of fruit.'

'Sounds good!' said George. 'Dinner, Timmy, dinner!'

And, hearing that welcome word, Timmy shot up the steep hill at top speed, his tail waving joyously.

'Wish I was a dog and could tear up a hill like that!' said Anne, panting. 'Give me a push, Julian! I'll *never* get to the top!'

Mostly about Wilfrid

Timmy was waiting for the children at the top of the hill, his tail waving, his mouth open as he panted. He picked something up, as the children came, threw it into the air, and caught it.

'Another golf ball, Timmy?' said Dick, as Timmy threw the ball into the air again with a toss of his big head.

'No – it's too big for that,' said George. 'Drop it, Timmy. What have you found?'

Timmy dropped the ball at George's feet. It was bigger than a golf ball, and had a hole right through it. 'Oh, it's one of those balls that children throw up and try to catch on a stick,' said George. 'Somebody must have dropped it. All right, Tim, you can have it.'

'He won't swallow it, will he?' said Wilfrid, anxiously. 'It's not *awfully* big – and I once saw a dog swallow something by mistake, that he threw into the air to catch.'

'Timmy's *much* too sensible to swallow *any* ball,' said George. 'You needn't worry about *him*. Anyway, *I* can do any worrying necessary. He's *my* dog.'

'All right, all right, all right!' said Wilfrid. 'Miss High-and-Mighty can look after her own dog. Fine!'

George looked round at him furiously and he made a face at her. Then he whistled to Timmy – yes, he actually dared to whistle to him!

'Nobody whistles for my dog except me,' said George. 'And anyway, he won't come to *you*.'

But, to her surprise and horror, Timmy *did* go to Wilfrid, and pranced all round him, expecting a game. George called him sternly, and he looked at her in surprise. He began to trot over to her when Wilfrid whistled again, and obediently Timmy turned as if to go to him.

George caught hold of the dog's collar, and aimed a punch at the whistling boy. It missed him, and he danced round, laughing.

'Stop it now, you two,' said Julian, seeing George's look of fury. 'I said STOP IT! Wilfrid, go on ahead, and *keep* going. George, don't be an ass. He's only teasing you to make you lose your temper. Don't please him by losing it!'

George said nothing more, but her eyes blazed. 'Oh dear!' thought Anne, 'now we shan't have any peace! She won't forgive Wilfrid for making Timmy go to him! Blow Wilfrid – he really is a little pest at times.'

They were all very hungry for their lunch and very pleased with everything that Anne provided. Dick went into the little cottage to help her, because George insisted on keeping her hand on Timmy's collar all the time, in case Wilfrid should entice him to his side.

'He's making some of his peculiar noises now,' said Dick to Anne. 'Noises that animals can't seem to resist! I don't wonder that George has got Timmy tightly by the collar! I'm not a dog, but I find those little whiny noises Wilfrid is making very curious indeed, and I'd love to go nearer!'

'Well, I hope we're not going to have black looks from George from now on,' said Anne. 'Wilfrid's an awful little idiot at times, and MOST irritating – but he's not bad underneath, if you know what I mean.'

'Well, I don't really,' said Dick, cutting some tomatoes in half. 'I think he's a badly brought-up little pest – and if I were a dog, I'd bite him, not fawn on him! Have I cut up enough toma-toes, Anne?'

'Good gracious, yes!' said Anne. 'How ever many do you think we're going to eat – forty or fifty? Look, you open this tin for me, Dick. I hate opening tins. I nearly always cut myself.'

'Don't you ever open one again, then,' said Dick. 'I'm the official tin-opener from now on! Dear old Anne, whatever should we do without you? You take everything on your shoulders, and we just *let* you! We all ought to help you more.'

'No, don't,' said Anne, in alarm. 'I *like* doing things on my own. You lot would only break things or upset them. You're all so ham-handed when it comes to washing-up or setting out crockery, though I know you *mean* well.'

'So we are all ham-handed, are we?' said Dick, pretending to be offended. 'When have *I* ever broken anything, I'd like to know? I'm just as careful as you when I handle crockery!'

Alas for Dick! The glass he was holding suddenly slipped from his hand, fell to the floor, and broke! Anne looked at him and gave a sudden delighted giggle. 'Old ham-hand!' she said. 'Can't pick up a glass without dropping it! Look, take out this tray for me, and for goodness' sake don't drop *that*!'

They all had a delicious lunch, and ate practically everything. Wilfrid sat a little away from everyone, scattering crumbs around as he ate. Birds of all kinds were soon round him, even hopping on to his hands. A magpie flew down to his left shoulder. Wilfrid greeted it like an old friend. 'Hallo, Maggie Pie! How's the family? I hope Polly Pie has recovered from her cold. And is Peter Pie's bad leg better? And what about old Grandpa Pie – does he still chase you young ones?'

The magpie put its glossy head on one side and chattered back to him in bird language, which Wilfrid appeared to understand. He stroked the bird's gleaming breast, and fondled it lovingly. George deliberately didn't watch. She turned her back on Wilfrid and the magpie, and talked to Timmy. The others couldn't help being amused.

The magpie put an end to Wilfrid's conversation very suddenly. The boy was about to put half a tomato into his mouth when the bird bent down its head and snatched away the tomato with its powerful beak. Then it rose quickly into the air on its big wings, making a noise exactly as if it were laughing!

Everyone roared with laughter except the surprised Wilfrid. 'He's gone to take your tomato to Polly Pie, I should think,' said Anne, and that made everyone laugh again.

'I'll have another tomato now, please,' said Wilfrid.

'Sorry. You're unlucky. They're all gone,' said Dick.

It was lovely sitting up on the hillside, watching the boats in the harbour, and seeing the beautiful, white-sailed yachts bending to and fro in the strong wind that blew there. They could all see Whispering Island quite clearly, and noticed that no boats went anywhere near it. Clearly everyone knew that men might be there, watching for intruders.

'There might be badgers there,' said Wilfrid, suddenly. 'I've never been really *close* to a badger.'

'I shouldn't think anyone but you would *want* to be!' said George. 'Smelly things! There's one thing – you can't call one with your whistle-pipe – there aren't any here!'

'Wilfrid – get out your pipe and make the little rabbits come again,' said Anne, suddenly. 'While we're all sitting here quietly. Would they come?'

'Yes, I think so,' said Wilfrid, and felt in his pocket. He felt in another pocket, and looked worried. Then he stood up and patted himself all over, looking really distressed. He stared round at the others, anguish on his face.

'It's gone,' he said. 'I must have lost it! It's gone and I'll never have another one like it, never.'

'Oh, it *must* be in one of your pockets,' said Dick, touched by the look on the boy's face. 'Here, let *me* feel.'

But no – the pipe wasn't there. Wilfrid looked as if he were about to burst into tears. He began to hunt all round, and everyone helped him. No – not quite everyone. George didn't. Dick glanced at her, and frowned. George was *pleased* that the precious pipe was lost. How she must dislike poor Wilfrid! Well, he *was* dislikeable at times, no doubt about it – but he was so distressed now that surely nobody could help feeling sorry for him!

George got up and began to clear away the remains of the meal. She carried plates and glasses to the cottage, and after a while Anne followed her.

'I'm sorry for poor old Wilfrid, aren't you?' she said.

'No, I'm not,' said George, shortly. 'Serves him right! I hope he never finds his silly pipe. That will teach him not to try and get Timmy away from me!'

'Oh, don't be silly! He only does it for fun!' said Anne, shocked. 'Why do you take things so seriously, George? You know Timmy loves you better than anyone in the world and always will. He's your dog and nobody, nobody else's! Wilfrid's only teasing you when he tries to get Timmy to go to him.'

'Timmy goes, though,' said George, desperately. 'And he shouldn't. He *shouldn't.*'

'He can't help it, I think,' said Anne. 'Wilfrid has some peculiar attraction for animals – and that little whistle-pipe of his is like a magic call to them.'

'I'm *glad* it's gone!' said George. 'Glad, glad, glad!'

'Then I think you're silly and unkind,' said Anne, and walked off, knowing that she could do nothing with George in this mood. She worried a little as she went. Did George *know* where the pipe was? Had *she* found it – and hidden it – or destroyed it? No – no! George could be difficult and unkind at times, but she wasn't *mean*. And *what* a mean thing it would be, to destroy the beautiful little pipe with its magic trills!

Anne went back to the others, meaning to try and comfort Wilfrid – but he wasn't there. 'Where's he gone?' asked Anne.

'To look for his precious whistle-pipe,' said Dick. 'He's really heartbroken about it, I think. He says he's going to walk back the way we came from the golf course, and then he's going to walk everywhere there that we walked this morning, and hunt and hunt. He's even going down to the clubhouse to see if he dropped it there. He'll never find it!'

'Poor old Wilfrid!' said Anne, tender-hearted as ever. 'I wish he'd waited for me. I'd have gone with him. He's awfully upset, isn't he? Won't he be able to call the wild animals to him any more?'

'I've no idea,' said Dick. 'Er – I suppose old George doesn't know anything about it? Perhaps that's a mean thing to say – but George might have found it and kept it just for a joke.'

'No. No, I don't think she'd do that,' said Anne. 'It would be a *very* poor joke. Well – we'll just have to hope Wilfrid finds it. What are you going to do this afternoon? Sleep, by the look of you!'

'Yes – sleep out in the warm sun here, till three o'clock,' said Julian. 'Then I'm going for a walk – down to the harbour. I might even have a swim.'

'We'll all go,' said Dick, sleepily. 'Oh how lovely it is to feel lazy – and warm – and well-fed – and sleeeeeeepy! So long, everyone! I'm asleep!'

[9]

Off to Whispering Island

The two boys, and Anne and George, slept soundly in the sun until just past three o'clock. Then a large fly buzzed around Anne's head and awoke her. She sat up and looked at her watch.

'Gracious! It's ten past three!' she said, in surprise. 'Wake up, Julian! Dick, stir yourself! Don't you want to go and swim?'

Yawning loudly the two boys sat up and looked all round. George was still asleep. Wilfrid hadn't yet come back.

'Still hunting for his precious pipe, I suppose,' said Anne. 'Get up, you two boys. Dick, you're *not* to lie down, you'll only go to sleep again. Where are your swimming things? I'll get them. And does anyone know where our swimming towels are? We'll probably have to dress and undress with them round us!'

'They're up in our room, chucked into a corner,' said Dick, sleepily. 'Gosh, I *was* sound asleep. I really thought I was in my bed when I awoke!'

Anne went to fetch the swimming towels and the swimming things. She called back to the boys. 'I've got everything. Buck up, Julian, *don't* go to sleep again!'

'Right!' said Julian, sitting up and stretching himself. 'Oh, this sun – it's GLORIOUS!'

He poked Dick with his toe. 'Get up! We'll leave you behind if you snore again. George, good-bye – we're going!'

George sat up, yawning, and Timmy stood over her and licked her cheek. She patted him. 'All right, Timmy, I'm ready. It's so warm that I'm LONGING for a dip – and you'll love it too, Tim!'

Carrying their swimming things they made their way down the hill, and across a stretch of moorland to the edge of the sea, Timmy running joyously behind them. Beyond lay Whispering Island, a great tree-clad mass, and all around and about little boats plied, and yachts sailed in the wind, enjoying themselves in the great harbour which stretched far beyond the island to a big seaside town on the opposite coast.

The four went behind some rocks, and stripped off their clothes, emerging three minutes later in their scanty swimming things. Anne raced to the edge of the water, and let it lap over her toes. 'Lovely!' she said. 'It's not a bit cold! I *shall* enjoy my swim!'

'Woof!' said Timmy and plunged into the water. He loved the sea too, and was a fine swimmer! He waited for George to come in and then swam to her. She put her arms round his neck and let him drag her along with him. Dear Timmy! How strong he is, thought George.

They had a wonderful time in the water. Further out the waves were big and curled over like miniature waterfalls, sweeping the children along with them. They yelled in joy, and choked when the water splashed into their mouths. It was an ideal day for swiming.

When they came out, they lay on the sand in
the sun, Timmy beside George, keeping guard
as usual. It was really warm. George sat up and
looked longingly out to sea, where the wind
was whipping up the waves tremendously.

'Wish we had a boat!' she said. 'If we were
back home, I could get out my own boat, and
we could go out in the cool breeze and get dry.'

Julian pointed lazily to a big notice not far
off. It said 'BOATS FOR HIRE. ENQUIRE AT HUT.'

'Oh good!' said George. 'I'll go and enquire.
I'd *love* a good row!'

She slipped on her sandals, and went to the
hut to which the sign pointed. A boy of about
fifteen sat there, staring out to sea. He looked
round as George came along.

'Want a boat?' he said.

'Yes, please. How much?' asked George. 'For
four of us – and a dog.'

'Three pounds an hour,' said the boy. 'Or six
pounds a day. Or fifteen pounds a week. Better
to take it by the week if you're staying here. It
works out very cheap then.'

George went back to the boys and Anne. 'Shall we take the boat by the week?' she said. 'It'll cost fifteen pounds. We could do lots of rowing about, and it would be fun.'

'Right,' said Dick. 'Anyone got any money?'

'There's some in my pocket, but not enough, I'm afraid,' said Julian. 'I'll go and fix up the boat for us to have tomorrow – we'll take it for a whole week. I can easily bring the money with me in the morning.'

The boat boy was very obliging. 'You can have the boat today and onwards, if you like, you needn't wait till tomorrow,' he said. '*I* know you'll bring me the money all right! So, if you'd like to have it this afternoon, it's up to you. Choose which boat you like. They're all the same. If you want to take it out at night too and do some fishing, you can – but tie it up safe, won't you?'

'Of course,' said Julian, going to look at the boats. He beckoned to the others, and they all came over.

'Any boat we like, day *or* night!' said Julian.

'Which do you fancy? *Starfish – Splasho – Adventure – Seagull – Rock-a-bye*? They all look good, sound little boats to me!'

'I'd like *Adventure*, I think,' said George, thinking that that particular little boat looked sturdy, clean and sound. 'Nice name – and nice little boat!'

So *Adventure* it was! 'And a jolly good name for any boat of ours!' said Dick, pushing it down to the sea with Julian. 'Whooooosh! There she goes! Steady, my beauty – we want to get in! Chuck in all the clothes, George! We can dress when we feel cold.'

Soon they were all in the boat, bobbing about on the waves. Julian took the oars and pulled out to sea. Now they were in the full breeze – and a strong one it was too! 'I'm certainly not hot any more!' said George, pulling her swimming towel round her shoulders.

The tide was running out, and pulled the boat strongly out to sea. Whispering Island suddenly seemed very much nearer! 'Better look out!' said George, suddenly. 'We don't know if a keeper's on guard somewhere on the shore of the island. We're getting pretty near.'

But the outgoing tide swept the boat on and on towards the island, so that very soon they could see a sandy shore. Dick then took one oar, and Julian the other, and they tried to row against the tide and take the boat back into calm water.

It was no good. The tide was far too strong. Very soon the boat was quite near the shore of the island, and then an enormous wave flung them right up the sand and left the boat grounded as it went back again. It slid over to one side, and they all promptly fell out!

'Whew!' said Julian. 'What a tide! I'd no idea it ran so strongly, or I'd never have brought the boat out so far.'

'What shall we do!' said Anne, rather scared. She kept looking all round for a keeper with a gun. Suppose they got into real trouble through coming right on to the island?

'I think we'll have to say on the island till the tide turns, and we can row back on it,' said

Julian. 'I can't think why that boat boy didn't warn us about the tide. I suppose he thought we knew.'

They pulled the boat a little further up on the firm sand, took out their bundles of clothes and hid them under a bush. They walked up the beach towards a wood, thick with great trees. As they neared them, they heard a strange, mysterious sound.

'Whispering!' said George, stopping. 'The trees are *really* whispering. Listen! It's just as if they were talking to one another under their breath! No wonder it's called Whispering Island!'

'I don't like it much,' said Anne. 'It almost sounds as if they're saying nasty things about us!'

'Shooey, shooey, shooey, shooey!' said the trees, nodding towards one another as the wind shook them. 'Shooey, shooey!'

'JUST the noise of whispering!' said George. 'Well – what do we do now? We'll have to wait an hour or two till the tide turns again!'

'Shall we explore?' said Dick. 'After all, we've got Timmy with us. No one is likely to attack us if they see *him*!'

'They can shoot him, can't they, if they have guns?' said George. 'If he growled one of his terrifying growls, and ran at them showing his teeth, they'd be scared to bits and fire at him.'

'I think you're right,' said Julian, angry with himself for landing them all into what might be serious trouble. 'Keep your hand on Timmy's collar, George.'

'You know what I think?' said Dick suddenly. 'I think we ought to try and find the guards, and tell them the tide swept us on to the island quite by accident – we couldn't stop the boat surging on! We're not grown-ups, come to snoop around, so they're sure to believe us – and we'd be safe from any chasing or shooting then.'

They all looked at Julian. He nodded. 'Yes – good idea. Give ourselves up, and ask for help! After all, we hadn't any real intention of actually *landing* – the tide simply *threw* the boat into that sandy cove!'

So they walked up to the back of the cove and into the wood, whose whispering was very loud indeed, once they were actually among the trees. No one was to be seen. The wood was so thick that it was in parts quite difficult to clamber through. After about ten minutes' very hard walking and clambering, Julian came to a stop. He had seen something through the trees.

The others pressed behind him. Julian pointed in front, and the others saw what looked liked a great grey wall, made of stone.

'The old castle, I imagine!' Julian whispered, and at once the trees themselves seemed to whisper even more loudly! They all made their way to the wall, and walked alongside it. It was a very high wall indeed, and they could hardly *see* the top! They came to a corner and peeped round. A great courtyard lay there – quite empty.

'Better shout, I think,' said Dick, beginning to feel rather creepy, but before they could do that two enormous men suddenly came down a flight of great stone steps. They looked so fierce that Timmy couldn't help giving a blood-curdling growl. They stopped short at once and looked all round, startled.

'The noise came from over there,' said one of the men, pointing to his left – and, to the children's great relief, both swung off in the wrong direction!

'We'd better get back to the cove,' whispered Julian. 'I don't like the look of those men at all – they look proper thugs. Quiet as you can, now. George, don't let Timmy bark.'

They made their way back beside the stone wall, through the whispering trees, and there they were at the cove.

'We'd better row back as quickly as we can,' said Julian. 'I think something's wrong here. Those men looked like foreigners. They certainly weren't gamekeepers. I wish we hadn't come.'

'Ju – where's our boat?' said Dick in a shocked voice. 'It's gone. This can't be the right cove!'

The others stared round. Certainly there was

no boat! They *must* have come to the wrong cove.

'It looks the same cove to *me*,' said George. 'Except that the sea has come in a bit more. Do you think it took our boat away – gosh, look at that big wave sweeping right in – and sucking back!'

'My word, yes! Our boat could easily have been dragged out on a wave like that!' said Julian, very worried. 'Look out – here comes another!'

'It *is* the same cove!' said Anne, looking under a bush at the back. 'Here are our clothes, look! We hid them here!'

'Take them out quickly!' called Julian, as another big wave swept right in. 'What an idiot I am! We should have pulled our boat as far up as we could.'

'I'm cold now,' said Anne. 'I'm going to dress. It will be easier to carry a swimming costume than a heap of clothes!'

'Good idea!' said Dick, and they all promptly dressed, feeling warmer at once.

'We might as well leave our swimming things under the bush where we left our clothes,' said George. 'At least we'll know it's the same cove if we find them there!'

'The thing is – what are we going to do *now*?' said Julian, worried. 'No boat to get back in – and why on earth did we choose one called *Adventure*? We might have *known* something would happen!'

[10]

The Five are in a fix

Julian went to the mouth of the cove and looked out over the waves, hoping that he might see their boat bobbing somewhere. 'I could swim out to it if so,' he thought, 'and bring it in. No – there's not a sign of a boat! I could kick myself for being so careless!'

Dick came up, looking worried. 'I suppose it's too far to swim back to the mainland, isn't it?' he said. 'I could have a shot – and get another boat and come back for everyone.'

'No. Too far,' said Julian. 'The tide's too strong for any swimmer at the moment. We're certainly in a fix!'

'We can't signal, I suppose?' said Dick.

'What with?' asked Julian. 'You could wave a shirt for an hour and it wouldn't be seen from the mainland!'

'Well – we must think of *something*!' said Dick, exasperated. 'What about trying to find a boat *here*? Surely those men must have one to get to and fro.'

'Of course!' said Julian, clapping Dick on the back. 'Where are my brains? They seem to be going soft or something! We could snoop round and about tonight, to see if there's a boat anywhere. They may have two or three. They'd have to get food from the mainland at times.'

The two girls and Timmy came up then, and Timmy whined. 'He doesn't seem to like this island,' said George. 'I think he smells danger!'

'I bet he does!' said Dick, putting his hand on Timmy's firm head. 'I'm jolly glad he's with us. Can you girls think of any good ideas? We can't!'

'We could signal,' said George.

'No good. A signal from here couldn't be seen,' said Dick. 'We've already thought of that.'

'Well – if we lit a fire here on the beach

tonight, when the tide's out, surely *that* would be seen?' said Anne.

Dick and Julian looked at one another. 'Yes!' said Julian. 'If we lit it on a hilly bit it would be better still – on that cliff up there, for instance.'

'Wouldn't the guards see it?' asked Dick.

'We'd have to chance that,' said Julian. 'Yes – we could do that. Good idea, Anne. But we're going to get jolly hungry, aren't we? Anyone got anything to eat?'

'I've two bars of chocolate – a bit soft now though,' said George, digging into the pocket of her shorts.

'And I've some peppermints,' said Anne. 'What about you boys? You always take barley-sugars about with you, Dick – don't say you haven't any just when we could all do with them!'

'I've a new packet!' said Dick. 'Let's all have one now!' He pulled the packet from his pocket and handed it round. Soon they were all sucking barley-sugars. Timmy was given one too, but his was gone in a flash!

'Wasted on you, Tim, absolutely *wasted*!' said Anne. 'Crick, crack, swallow – that's all a barley-sugar means to you! Why can't dogs suck a sweet as we do! They never seem to suck *anything*. No, Timmy, don't go sniffing into Dick's pocket for another!'

Timmy was disappointed. He went snuffling round the cove, and then, scenting a rabbit smell, he followed it with his nose to the ground. The children didn't notice that he had disappeared but went on talking, trying to solve their very real difficulty.

No boat. No food. No way of getting help except by signalling in some way. *Not* very funny, thought Dick.

And then, very suddenly, a loud sound broke the silence – CRACK!

Everyone jumped up at once. 'That was a gunshot,' said Dick. 'The keepers! But what are they shooting at?'

'Where's Timmy?' cried George, looking all round. 'Tim, Tim, where are you TIM?'

Everyone's heart went cold. Timmy! No, the

shot couldn't have been meant for old Timmy!
Surely the keepers wouldn't shoot a *dog*!

George was nearly mad with dread. She
clutched at Dick, tears streaming down her
cheeks. 'Dick! It couldn't be Timmy, could
it? Oh Timmy, where are you? TIMMY! Come
to me!'

'Listen! Listen a minute, George!' said Dick,
as shouts came from the distance. 'I thought I
heard Tim whine then. Isn't that him coming
through the bushes?'

There was the noise of rustling as some
creature pressed through the last year's bracken
fronds – and then Timmy's head appeared, his
bright eyes looking for them.

'Oh Timmy, darling Timmy, I thought you'd
been shot!' cried George, hugging the big dog.
'*Did* they shoot at you? Are you hurt anywhere?'

'I bet I know why he was shot at,' said Dick.
'Look what he's got in his mouth – half a ham!
Drop it, you robber, you!'

Timmy stood there, the ham in his mouth,

wagging his tail joyously. He had felt hungry, and was sure the others did too – so he had gone hunting!

'Where did you get that, you bad dog?' said Julian. Timmy wished he could tell him. He would have said, 'Well, I went sniffing after a rabbit – and I came to a shed stored with tins of food – and one was open with this piece of ham inside, waiting for me. And here it is!'

He dropped the ham at George's feet. It smelt extremely good. 'Well, thanks, old fellow,' said Julian. 'We could do with some of that – though we'll have to pay for it when we meet the owner, whoever he is!'

'Julian – he *has* been shot at!' said George, in a trembling voice. 'Look – his tail's bleeding, and some fur is gone.'

'Oh, yes!' said Julian, examining Timmy's tail. 'Good gracious – those fellows mean business. I really think I'd better find them and tell them we're here, in case they take a pot-shot at us too!'

'Well, let's go *now* – all of us,' said Dick.

'They probably thought Timmy was a wolf or a fox or something, slinking through the trees. Poor old fellow!'

Timmy was not at all disturbed. He was so proud of finding and bringing back the ham that he even wagged his wounded tail!

'It's quite certain that no animals or birds will be tame and friendly on this island now,' said Anne. 'They'll have been scared stiff by the gamekeepers potting at this and that.'

'You're right,' said Julian. 'It rather makes me think that the fellows on the island are no longer merely gamekeepers, put in to preserve the wildlife, and to frighten sightseers away – but real, fierce guards of some kind. Like those two horrible men we saw in the courtyard!'

'Well, what *are* they guarding then?' said George.

'That's what I'd very much like to find out,' said Julian. 'And I think perhaps I'll snoop round a bit and see what I can discover. When it's getting dark, though, not now.'

'I wish we hadn't come,' said Anne. 'I wish

we were safe in our cottage with Wilfrid. I
wonder if he's found his whistle-pipe. Goodness, it seems *ages* since we hired that boat!'

'Can't we go quietly through the woods and
explore a bit?' asked George. 'Or walk round
the shore to see if there's a boat anywhere? I'm
getting bored, sitting here, talking.'

'Well – I suppose old Tim would give us
warning at once if he heard anyone near,' said
Julian, who was also longing to stretch his legs.
'We'll go in single file and make as little noise as
we can. Timmy can go ahead. He'll give us
instant warning if we come near any of the
keepers.'

They all stood up, and Timmy looked at
them, wagging his nicked tail. 'I'll look after
you,' said his two bright eyes. 'Don't be
afraid!'

They made their way carefully and quietly
through the whispering trees. 'Sh, sh, sh, shoo,
shooey,' said the leaves above their heads, as if
warning everyone to go as quietly as possible.
And then suddenly Timmy stopped and gave a

low, warning growl. They all stood still at once, listening.

They could hear nothing. They were in a dense part of the wood, and it was dark and sunless. What was Timmy growling at? He took a step forward, and growled softly again.

Julian went forward too, as silently as he could. He stopped suddenly and stared. What in the world was that strange figure, gleaming out of the shadows? His heart began to beat loudly. The figure stood there, silently, an arm outstretched as if pointing at something!

He thought it moved and he took a step backwards in fear. Was it a ghost or something? It was so very, very white and shone so strangely. The others, coming up behind, suddenly saw it too and stopped in fright. Timmy growled again, and all the hackles on his neck rose up. What was THIS?

Everyone stood absolutely still, and Anne gave a gulp. She took hold of Dick's arm, and he held it tightly against him. And then George gave a very small laugh. To everyone's horror she went forward, and touched the hand of the gleaming figure.

'How do you do?' she said. 'It is so nice to meet a well-mannered statue!'

Well! A statue! Only a *statue*! It had looked so real standing there, and yet so ghostly. Everyone heaved a sigh of relief, and Timmy ran forward and sniffed at the statue's flowing robes.

'Look around you,' said Julian. 'The wood's full of statues just here – and aren't they BEAU-TIFUL! I hope they don't suddenly come alive – they really look as if they might!'

A strange discovery

The children were astonished to see so many gleaming statues standing in the darkness of the wood. They wandered round them, and then came to a large shed. They peeped inside.

'Look here!' said Dick, excited. 'Long, deep boxes, strong as iron! And see what's in these two!'

They all came to look. In the first, packed in what looked like sawdust, was a beautifully carved statue of a boy. The next box seemed to be entirely full of sawdust, and Anne had to scrape quite a lot away to see if anything was packed there too.

'It's a little stone angel!' she said, scraping sawdust from a quaint little face, a small crown and the tips of small wings. 'Lovely! Why are these statues being packed away like this?'

'Use your brain!' said Dick. 'It's obvious that they're works of art – and are probably very old. They're being packed to send away in some boat or ship – to be transported somewhere where they'll fetch a lot of money – America, probably!'

'Did they come from the old castle, do you think?' asked George. 'It's quite near. I expect this shed belongs to it. But how was it that the police didn't find them in the castle when they searched? They must have gone there, and looked into every corner! And what about the statues in the wood outside – why haven't *they* been packed away?'

'Too big, probably,' said Julian. 'And too heavy. A small boat wouldn't be strong enough to take great things like that. But those little statues are quite perfect for transporting – they don't weigh as much as the big ones – and they aren't marked by the weather, through standing in rain, sun and snow! Not a mark on them!'

'You're right,' said Anne. 'I noticed that

those big ones outside were green here and
there, and some had bits knocked off them. I
wish we could get inside the castle and see the
things there!'

'The man at the golf club, the one we took
those lost balls to – *he* said something about
statues as white as snow, standing in this wood
– do you remember?' said Dick.

'Yes. They must have stood there for some
time,' said Julian. 'I don't feel they can be very
valuable, else they would be put carefully indoors, under cover. But these little beauties – I
guess they're worth a lot of money!'

'Who do you suppose packed them in here?'
said Anne.

'Maybe those big men we saw,' said Julian.
'Even small statues like these need someone
very strong indeed to carry them here to this
shed, and pack them like this. Then, of course,
they would have to be carried to some boat – or
ship – probably to a boat first and then rowed
out to a waiting ship. But I don't think those
guards are the men behind all this – someone

with a great knowledge of old things must be the ringleader. He probably heard the old legend of the island, came to have a look round, and made quite a lot of interesting discoveries!'

'*Where?*' asked George. 'In the castle?'

'Probably – though carefully hidden away!' said Julian. 'For all we know there may be scores of really valuable old treasures hidden there still. That sword with a jewelled handle, for instance! And the bed made of gold, and—'

'To think they might all be quite near us, somewhere on Whispering Island!' said Anne. 'Wouldn't I love to be able to say I'd slept on a bed of pure gold!'

'Well, I think you'd find it jolly hard,' said Dick.

Timmy suddenly gave a small whine, and licked George's hand. 'What is it?' she said. 'What do you want, Timmy?'

'Perhaps he's hungry,' said Anne.

'Thirsty, more likely!' said Julian. 'Look at his tongue hanging out!'

'Oh, *poor* Tim – you haven't had a drink for hours!' said George. 'Well – where on earth can we get you one? We'll have to look for a puddle, I'm afraid. Come on!'

They left the shed where the beautiful little statues were lying in their sawdust, and went out into the sunshine. Everywhere was dry, Julian felt worried.

'We shall *all* be thirsty soon!' he said. 'I wonder where we can get some water?'

'Would it be too dangerous to go near the castle and see if there's a tap anywhere?' asked George, ready to face almost anything to get her dog a drink!

'Yes, it would,' said Julian, in a very decided voice. 'We're not going near any of those men with guns. They might have been told to shoot on sight, and that wouldn't be very pleasant. We'd be peppered all over with shot!'

'Look – what's that round thing over there – like a little circular wall?' said Dick, pointing to something behind the shed where the statues lay in their boxes.

They all went over to it – and Anne guessed what it was at once! 'A well! An old well!' she said. 'Look, it has an old wooden beam over the top, with a pulley to wind and unwind a bucket. *Is* there a bucket – let's hope so! We can let it down to the water and fill it for Timmy then.'

Timmy put his paws on the rim of the wall and sniffed. Water! That was what he wanted more than anything. He began to whine.

'All right, Timmy – we'll send the bucket down,' said George. 'It's still on the hook! Julian, this handle's awfully stiff – can you turn it to let down the bucket?'

Julian tried with all his strength – and quite suddenly the rope loosened, and the bucket gave a sudden jerk and jump. Alas – it jumped right off the hook, and with a weird echoing, jangling sound, fell from the top to the bottom of the well – landing in the water with a terrific splash!

'Blow, blow, blow!' said Julian, and Timmy gave an anguished howl. He peered town at the lost bucket, now on its side in the water at the bottom of the well gradually filling itself.

'It'll probably sink below the water now,' said Julian with a groan. 'Is there a ladder down the well? – if so I could shin down and get the bucket.'

But there wasn't, though it looked as if there had been at some time, for here and there were staples in the brick side of the well wall.

'What can we do?' asked Anne. 'Can we possibly pull up the bucket?'

'No – I'm afraid we can't,' said Dick. 'But wait a minute – I could shin down the rope, couldn't I, and pick the bucket out of the water? And easily get up again, because George and Julian could turn the well handle, and pull me up that way!'

'Righto. Down you go then,' said Julian. 'The rope's good and strong, not frayed or rotten. We'll wind you and the bucket up all right!'

The boy sat on the side of the well wall, and reached out for the rope. He swung himself on to it, and swayed there a moment or two, looking down the long, dark hole below him, with the water at the bottom. Then down he went, hand-over-hand, just as he often did at school in the gym.

He came to the bottom, reached down, took hold of the bucket handle, and filled the bucket full. The water felt as cold as ice to his hand. 'All right. Pull me up!' he shouted, his voice sounding very hollow and strange as it rose up through the well walls.

Dick was heavy to pull up. Julian and George turned the handle valiantly, but it was slow work. Gradually Dick came up nearer and nearer to the top. When he was halfway they heard him give an exclamation, and call out something; but they couldn't make out what it was and went on winding the groaning rope, slowly but surely.

They reached down and took the bucket from Dick as soon as his head appeared at the top. Timmy fell on it with excited barks, and began to lap vigorously.

'Didn't you hear me yelling to you to stop when I was halfway up?' demanded Dick, still swinging on the rope. 'Don't let go that handle. Hang on to it for a minute.'

'What's the excitement?' asked Julian, in surprise. '*Why* did you yell to us? We couldn't make out what you said.'

Dick swung himself to one side, caught hold of the well top and hauled himself up, so that he could sit on the well wall. 'I shouted because I suddenly saw something quite peculiar as I came up the well,' he said. 'And I wanted to stop and see what it was!'

'Well – what *was* it?' asked Julian.

'I don't quite know. It looked awfully like a little door! An iron door,' said Dick. 'Hey, don't let Timmy drink all that water – he'll be ill. We'll let the pail down again in a minute and get some more for ourselves.'

'Go on about what you saw,' said George. 'How *could* there be a door in the side of a well going deep down into the earth?'

'Well, I tell you, there *was* one,' said Dick.

'Look, Timmy's gone and upset the pail now! Let's send it down on the pulley to be filled again, and I'll go down on the rope again too. But when I come up and you hear me shout "Stop" just stop winding, see?'

'Here's the bucket for the hook,' said Julian. 'I'll be careful not to jerk it off this time. Ready?'

Down went Dick and the bucket again – splash went the bucket and filled with water once more. Then up came Dick again, wound up by Julian and George as before. As soon as they heard him shout 'Stop', they stopped their winding and peered down.

They saw Dick peering hard at the side of the well wall, and pulling at it with his fingers. Then he shouted again. 'All right. Up we go!'

They hauled him up to the top, and he clambered off the rope, swung himself on to the well wall and sat there.

'Yes. It *is* some kind of opening in the well wall – it *is* a door – and it has a bolt this side to undo, but it was too stiff for my fingers. I'd have to go down and jiggle it about with my knife before I could loosen it.'

'A door in a well! But where on earth would it lead to?' said Julian, astonished.

'That's what we're going to find out!' grinned Dick, rather pleased with himself. 'Who would ever think of putting a door in the side of a well? *Some*body did – but WHY? Very cunning – and mysterious – and unguessable. I rather think I'll go straight down again and see if I can't open that door – and discover what it leads to!'

'Oh DO, Dick do!' said George. 'If you don't, *I* will!'

'Hang on to the rope. Down I go again!' said Dick. And down he went, much to Timmy's surprise. The others looked down anxiously. Could Dick open the well door? What would he find behind it? Quick, Dick, quick – everybody's waiting for you!

[12]

A great surprise –
and a shock for George

As soon as Dick shouted 'Stop', Julian and George hung on to the rope to stop it going down any further. Dick was swinging just opposite the strange door. He began to feel round it, and to jiggle it. It had no lock, apparently, but there was a bolt on his side. He tried to push back the bolt – and suddenly it came away from the door, and dropped down into the well. It had rusted so much that it could not even hold to the door, once it was handled!

The door felt loose, now the bolt was gone. Dick ran his hands round it, trying to loosen it further, and banged it with his fist. Rust fell off it, and Dick's hands were soon brown with the old, old rust.

He saw a little knob at the top of the door

and gave it a tug. Ah – the door felt looser now. He ran his knife all round the edges, scraping away all the rust he could find. Then he managed to get his strongest knife-blade in between the door edge and the well wall, and used it as a lever to force the door open.

It opened slowly and painfully, with creaks and groans. It was about fifty centimetres high and not quite so much wide. Dick pulled it back with difficulty and then peered through the hole.

He could see nothing at all but black darkness – how very disappointing! He fumbled in his pocket to see if he had a torch. Yes – good! He shone it through the little door, his hand trembling with excitement. What would he see?

His torch was small and not very powerful. The light fell first of all on a face with gleaming eyes, and Dick had such a shock that he almost fell down the well. The eyes seemed to glare up at him in a very threatening manner! He switched his torch to the right – and yet another face gleamed up to him. 'An odd face,' thought

Dick. 'Yellow as can be! YELLOW! YELLOW! I believe that face is made of gold!'

His hand trembling even more, he shone his torch here and there through the opening, catching first one yellow face in its light, and then another. The faces had yellow bodies too, and their eyes glinted very strangely.

'I believe – yes, I really do believe – that I've found the hiding place of the golden statues,' thought Dick. 'And those gleaming eyes must be precious jewels. I did have a shock when I saw them all looking at me! Whatever is this place they're in?'

'DICK! What can you see? Do tell us!' yelled Julian, and poor Dick almost fell off the rope when the shouts echoed round him. 'Pull me up!' he shouted. 'It's too extraordinary for words. Pull me up and I'll tell you!'

And before a minute had passed he was standing by the others, his eyes gleaming almost as brightly as the eyes of the golden statues, his words tumbling over one another.

'That door leads into the place where all the

treasures are hidden. The first thing I saw was a golden statue staring at me – brilliant eyes in a yellow face – a golden face, real gold! There are dozens of them. I don't think they liked me very much – they glared so! Thank goodness they didn't say a word – though I half expected them to. What a hiding place – right down under the earth!'

'There must be another entrance to it,' said Julian, thrilled to hear such extraordinary news. 'The well door must be a secret one. Statues couldn't be pushed through it. My word, what a find, Dick.'

'Let's all go down in turn and look through the door!' said George. 'I can't believe it. I think I must be dreaming it. Quick, let me go down!'

One by one they all went down on the rope and looked through the door. Anne came back rather scared. She had felt very strange when she had seen the silent statues looking at her. 'I know they're not *really* looking, it's only that their eyes gleam,' she said. 'But I kept expecting one or other to take a step forward and speak to me!'

'Well – the next thing to do is to climb through the door, and see exactly where the statues are underground,' said Julian. 'And find out the opening *they* were brought in by. There must be a door the other end of their room, through which they were brought. What a hiding place, though! No wonder the police could find nothing in the way of statues or other treasures.'

'We might find the golden sword there, with the jewelled handle!' said Anne. 'And the golden bed.'

She had hardly finished speaking when there came a loud noise from behind them. Timmy was barking his head off! Whatever was the matter?

'Sh!' said George, fiercely. 'You'll bring the guards here, you idiot! Stop it!'

Timmy stopped barking and whined instead. Then he ran off towards the wood, his tail waving happily. 'Who in the world is he going to meet?' said George, amazed. 'Someone he knows, by the look of his tail!'

The others all followed Timmy, who raced along towards the cove where they had landed – and lost their boat. And there, in the cove, was another boat! A small one, to be sure, but still a boat – and by it, fondling Timmy, was Wilfrid! Wilfrid! What an amazing thing!

'WILFRID! How did you get here – did you hire that boat? Did you come all by yourself? Did you . . .'

Wilfrid grinned round in delight, thrilled at the surprise he was giving everyone. Timmy licked him without stopping, and George didn't even seem to notice!

'Well,' he said, 'you didn't come back, so I guessed something was wrong – and when the boat boy told me you'd taken one of his boats and it had been reported tossing about, empty, on the water near the island, I guessed what had happened – I said, "Aha! they didn't make the boat fast when they got to the island – and now they're marooned there!" You were pretty mean to go without me – but I guessed you'd be pleased to see me if I borrowed a boat and came over!'

Anne was so pleased that she gave the boy a hug. 'Now we can go back whenever we want to,' she said.

'But we *don't* want to, at the moment,' said Dick. 'We've made some startling discoveries, Wilfrid – and I'm jolly pleased you'll be able to share in them! Er – what have you got in your pocket? Something keeps poking its head out at me.'

'Oh, that's only a baby hedgehog,' said Wilfrid, taking it out gently. 'It got trodden on – by a horse, I think – so I'm just caring for it for a day or two.' He put it back into his pocket. 'But go on – tell me what you've found. Not the lost treasures, surely?'

'Yes!' said Anne. 'We saw them when we went down a well near the castle.'

'Gracious – did somebody throw them into the water there?' said Wilfrid, amazed.

'No,' said Dick, and told him about the

curious door in the side of the well wall. Wilfrid's eyes nearly fell out of his head.

'I *am* glad I came!' he said. 'I nearly didn't. I
thought you wouldn't really want me – and I
knew George wouldn't be pleased, because of
Timmy. I can't help him coming round me –
and anyway he'd feel hurt if I pushed him off.'

Timmy came nosing round him at that moment, with his ball. He wanted Wilfrid to throw
it for him. But Wilfrid didn't notice the ball. He
just patted the soft head, and went on talking.

'The boat boy wasn't very pleased when he
heard that the boat you hired was loose on the
sea. He said you'd hired it for a week, and there
it was, back the same day, wet and empty! His
cousin brought it in. No damage done.'

'I'll make it up to him when I see him,' said
Julian. 'I haven't paid him for the hire of it
either, but he knows I will, when I get back. I
had no idea that the sea would throw up waves
here whose backwash would drag out an un-
moored boat.'

'You ought to have taken me with you,' said

Wilfrid, grinning. Timmy, tired of trying to make him throw his ball, went off to George, who was only too pleased to. She threw it into the air, and Timmy leapt up and caught it.

Then, very suddenly, he made a horrible noise and rolled over, kicking as if he were in great pain. 'What's the matter, Timmy?' cried George, and rushed to him. Wilfrid ran too. The dog was choking, and his eyes were almost starting out of his head.

'That ball's stuck in his throat!' cried Wilfrid. 'I knew it was dangerous! I told you it was! Cough it up, Timmy, cough it up. Oh, you poor, choking thing! Oh Timmy, Timmy!'

The boy was beside himself with fear that the dog would choke, as he had once seen another dog do, and as for George, she was wild with terror. Poor Timmy's eyes looked terrible as he choked and choked, trying to get the ball out of his throat.

'He'll choke to death,' cried Wilfrid. 'Julian, force his mouth open, and hold it. I must try to get out the ball. Quick!'

Timmy was growing weaker, and it was not too difficult to force his mouth wide open. Wilfrid could see the ball down the dog's throat – the ball with the hole in the middle. He put his small hand into the dog's big mouth, and forced his forefinger into the hole in the ball. His finger joint stuck there – Wilfrid gently drew back his hand – and the ball came too, on his finger! There it was, with his finger still stuck in the hole! Timmy began to breathe again, great panting breaths, while George stroked his head and cried for joy that he was all right.

'I shouldn't have given you that ball, I shouldn't!' she said. 'It was too small for a big dog like you – and you *will* throw them up in the air and catch them. Oh Timmy, Timmy, I'm very, very sorry. Timmy, are you all right?'

Wilfrid had gone off, but now came back with some water in the pail. He dipped his hand in it and let drops of water drip into the dog's mouth. Timmy swallowed it gratefully. His throat was sore, but the water was cool and soothing. George let Wilfrid do this without a word. She looked rather white and shaken. Why – Timmy might be dead by now if Wilfrid hadn't put his finger into that hole in the ball and drawn it out!

'Thank you, Wilfrid,' she said, in a low voice. 'You were very clever.'

'Thank goodness the ball had a hole through it,' said Wilfrid, and he put his arms round Timmy's neck. The dog licked him gratefully. Then he turned and licked George too.

'He says he belongs to both of us now,' said George. 'I'll share him with you. You saved his life.'

'Thanks,' said Wilfrid. 'I'd love to have just a *bit* of him – he's the nicest dog I know!'

[13]

A meal – a sleep –
and a disappearance

'I feel hungry again,' said George, who always had a very good appetite indeed. 'We've finished all that ham, haven't we? I *had* to give old Timmy some. What about a barley-sugar, Dick?'

'Two more left for each of us – just ten,' said Dick, counting. 'Sorry, Timmy, old thing – none for you this time. Have one, everybody. We'll have five left then!'

'Oh, I quite forget to tell you,' said Wilfrid, taking a barley-sugar. 'I brought some food in my boat! I didn't think you'd taken any, and I guessed you'd soon be jolly hungry!'

'You're a marvel, Wilfrid!' said Julian, wondering why he had ever disliked the boy. 'What have you brought?'

'Come and see,' said Wilfrid, and they all went over to the boat, Timmy walking as close to the boy as he could. Higgledy-piggledy in the boat was a pile of tins, a large loaf of bread, and some butter, looking rather soft.

'Oh good!' said Anne, in delight. 'But how in the world did you carry all this from the cottage to your boat? Look, everyone, Wilfrid has even brought some plates and spoons!'

'I put everything into a sack, and carried it over my shoulder,' said Wilfrid, enjoying everyone's delighted surprise. 'I fell over going down the hill to the shore and all the tins rolled out, and *shot* down the slope!'

Everyone laughed at the thought of tins rolling at top speed down the hill. Anne slipped her arm through Wilfrid's and gave it a squeeze.

'You did really well,' she said and Wilfrid beamed at her, astonished and pleased at everyone's warm friendliness. Timmy went up to the boat and began sniffing at the bread. Then he turned and barked as if to say 'Is there anything here for *me*?'

Wilfrid understood at once. 'Oh *yes*, Timmy!' he said. 'I brought a special tin of dogmeat for you – here you are – a large tin of Waggomeat!'

Timmy recognised the tin at once, and barked joyfully. He pawed Wilfrid as if to say 'Come on, then – open it! I'm hungry!'

'Anyone got a tin-opener?' said George. 'It would be too dreadful if we couldn't open the tins!'

'Gosh – I never even *thought* about that!' said Wilfrid. 'What an idiot I am!'

'It's all right. I've got a thing on my pocket-knife that's *supposed* to open tins,' said Dick, taking out a very large closed knife. 'I've never bothered to use it – so let's hope it *will* do the trick. Chuck me a tin, Wilfrid.'

Wilfrid threw him the tin of Waggomeat. With everyone watching very anxiously indeed, Dick opened a peculiar-looking tool in his knife, and jabbed the point into the top of the tin. It worked!

'First time I've ever used it,' said Dick, running the gadget round the tin top. 'Three cheers for the man who thought of including it in a knife!'

'Will Timmy be able to swallow yet?' asked George, anxiously. 'His throat must still be hurting him where that wooden ball choked him.'

'Oh, Timmy will be able to judge that for himself,' said Julian. 'If I know anything about him not even a sore throat will stop him from wolfing half that tin!'

Julian was right. As soon as Dick scraped out a third of the meat with his knife on to a flat stone nearby, Timmy was wolfing it in great gulps!

'Nothing much the matter with your throat now, Tim!' said Anne, patting him. 'Dear old Tim. Don't ever choke again. I simply couldn't bear it!'

'Let's have a meal ourselves now,' said George. 'We'll open more of those tins. We don't need to be stingy about them because we can leave in Wilfrid's boat at any time, and get back to the mainland.'

Soon they had opened a tin of tuna, two tins of fruit and a large tin of baked beans. They cut the big loaf into six pieces (one for Timmy, of course) and then sat down at the back of the cove to feast.

'Best meal I ever had in my life!' said Dick, enjoying himself. 'Tasty food – fresh air – sea nearby – sun on our heads – and friends sitting all round me!'

'Woof!' said Timmy, at once, and gave Dick a very wet lick.

'He says he couldn't agree more,' said Anne with a laugh.

'The sun's going down,' said George. 'What are we going to do? Go back to the mainland in Wilfrid's boat – or stay here for the night?'

'Stay here,' said Julian. 'Nobody knows we're here, and I want to snoop round a bit tonight, when those men can't see me. There's a lot of things that puzzle me. For instance, how on earth do they send away the things from here – such as those packed statues we saw? It must mean that a fairly big vessel comes along to collect them, I suppose. And I'd like to know how many men there are on the island – presumably the guards we saw, with guns – and the men who have found that underground cave, where everything was hidden. Then we'll go back, tell the police, and leave things to them!'

'Couldn't Wilfrid take the two girls back to the mainland then come back with the boat?' said Dick. 'I don't think we ought to let them run any risk.'

Before Julian could reply, George spoke quickly – and crossly. 'We're staying here – though Anne can go back if she wants to. But Timmy and I are staying with you boys, so that's that.'

'All right, all right, no need to shout!' said Dick, pretending to cover his ears. 'What about you, though, Anne? You're the youngest, and . . .'

'I'm staying,' said Anne. 'I'd be worried stiff all night if I left you on the island. And I certainly don't want to miss any excitement!'

'Right,' said Julian. 'We all stay then. Wilfrid, did you know that Timmy has his nose in the pocket where you keep your hedgehog?'

'Yes. They're just making friends,' said Wilfrid. 'Anyway, the hedgehog's only a baby – his quills won't prick Timmy's nose, they're still too soft. He's a dear little thing. I thought I'd call him Spiky.'

'Wuff,' said Timmy, quite agreeing. He was sitting between George and Wilfrid, very happy indeed, for both fondled him and patted him at the same time.

'I think I'll take a walk round the island,' Wilfrid announced suddenly. 'Timmy, like to come with me?'

Timmy got up at once, but George pulled him down. 'Don't be an idiot, Wilfrid,' she said. 'Timmy's been shot at once by the men here – and I'm not going to risk it again – besides, we don't want them to know we're here.'

'I'd be very careful,' persisted Wilfrid. 'I wouldn't let them spot me. They didn't spot me coming over in the boat.'

Julian sat up very suddenly. 'How do we know they didn't?' he said. 'I never thought of that! They might have a telescope – they might keep watch all the time – they might even have seen *us* in *our* boat! After all, they can't risk being spied on!'

'I don't *think* they could have seen us,' said Dick. 'They would have made a search.'

'I'm jolly sure they didn't see *me*,' boasted Wilfrid. 'They'd have been waiting for me on the shore, if they had.' He got up and looked all round. 'I think I'll go for my walk now,' he said.

'NO! You are DEFINITELY not to go for a walk, Wilfrid,' said Julian, and lay back in the sun again. It was sinking now, but still very bright. Dick began to think of the night, and how he and Julian would snoop round and find the way into that strange place underground where those golden statues stood silently in the darkness.

Then he fell asleep, and only awoke when Anne gave him a friendly punch. He sat up and began a long and leisurely conversation with his sister – and then Anne suddenly looked all round.

'Where's Wilfrid?' she said. They *all* sat up then, and looked startled. Wilfrid was nowhere to be seen!

'He must have slipped away without a sound! said Dick, angrily. 'The little idiot. He's been gone quite a long time! He'll get caught, as sure as can be. Good thing Timmy didn't go with him – he might have been caught too – and shot!'

George put her arms round Timmy in fear. 'Timmy would never go with Wilfrid if I wasn't there too,' she said. 'What a little fool he is! Those men will guess there's someone else on the island with Wilfrid, won't they? They might even *make* him tell all he knew – and where the boat is, and everything!'

'What shall we do?' said Anne. 'We'd better go after him.

'Timmy will track him for us,' said George, getting up. 'Come on, Tim. Find Wilfrid. Find that silly disobedient boy Wilfrid!'

Timmy understood at once. He put his nose to the ground, found Wilfrid's scent, and began to walk away. 'Not too fast, Timmy,' said George, and he at once slowed down. George looked round at the little place among the bushes where they had been sitting. 'Had we better take a tin or two with us?' she said.

'Yes. Good idea,' said Julian. 'You just never know!'

He and Dick took a couple of tins each, stuffed uncomfortably into their pockets. Stupid Wilfrid!

'He must have gone in this direction,' said Dick. 'I never spotted him slinking away, the little nuisance! I'm surprised Timmy didn't make a sound! Track him, Tim, track him!'

'Listen!' said Anne, suddenly, and she stopped. 'Listen!' They all listened – and didn't at all like what they heard. It was Wilfrid's voice, yelling in fright.

'Let me go! Let me go!'

And then a stern, loud and threatening voice

came. 'Who are you with? Where are they? You're not alone, we're certain of that!'

'Quick – we must hide!' said Julian, angry and worried. 'Dick, look about for a good place and I will too.'

'No good,' said Dick. 'They'll beat everywhere for us. Better climb trees.'

'Good idea!' said Julian. 'Anne, come with me. I'll give you a shove up. Hurry, everybody! Hurry!'

[14]

Wilfrid has an adventure on his own

'What about Timmy? He can't climb,' said George, fearfully. 'He might be shot.'

'Put him under a bush and tell him to sit, sit, sit!' said Julian, urgently. 'He knows perfectly well what that means. Go on, George, quick.'

George took Timmy by the collar and led him to a very thick bush. She pushed him under it. He turned himself round, poked his nose out of the leaves, and looked at her in surprise.

'Sit, Timmy! Sit, and keep quiet!' said George. 'Sit, sit, sit – and keep *quiet*. Understand?'

'Woof,' said Timmy, very quietly, and withdrew his nose so that nothing of him could be seen at all. He knew perfectly well what George meant. Clever old Timmy!

Dick was giving Anne a shove up a tree with drooping branches thick with leaves. 'Get as high as you can,' he said, in a low voice. 'And then stay put till you hear me call you. Don't be afraid. Old Timmy's down here to protect you!'

Anne gave him rather a small smile. She was not like George, fearless and always ready to rush into trouble. Anne was all for a peaceful life – but how could she have that if she was one of the Five!

The boys and George were now high up in trees, listening to the shouting going on. Apparently Wilfrid was not going to give away his friends – one up to him!

'How did you get here?' a man was shouting.

'In a boat,' said Wilfrid.

'Who was with you?' shouted another man.

'Nobody. I came alone,' said Wilfrid, perfectly truthfully. 'I wanted to visit the island. I'm an animal lover and I heard that all the wild creatures here were tame.'

'A likely story that!' sneered a man's voice. 'Huh! Animal lover!'

'All right then – look what I've got here in my pocket,' said Wilfrid, and apparently showed the man his baby hedgehog. 'He was trodden on by a horse – and I've been looking after him.'

'Very well – you can go back to your boat, and row away,' said the man. 'AT ONCE, mind. And don't look so scared. We shan't hurt you. We've business of our own here, and we don't want strangers round – not even silly little kids with hedgehogs in their pockets!'

Wilfrid took to his heels and fled. He felt lost now. He would never find the others – or the cove where his boat was. WHY had he disobeyed Julian? Had the others heard the men shouting at him? Which way should he go?

He had entirely lost his sense of direction and had no idea whether to go to the left or the right. He began to panic. Where could the others be? He *must* find them, he must! He ran through the trees, wishing that Timmy was with him. Then he stopped. Surely this was quite the wrong way? He turned and went in a different direction. No, this couldn't be right either, he didn't recognise a thing!

He thought he heard voices in the distance. He stood and listened. Could it be the others? If only George would tell Timmy to find him! But she wouldn't, in case he was shot at. *Was* that noise voices – or was it just the wind? Perhaps it was the others looking for him. Wilfrid rushed off towards the distant sound. But alas, it died down. It was only the wind!

The trees thinned out in bushes – and then Wilfrid suddenly saw the sea in the distance! Good! If he could get to it, he could walk round the shore till he came to his cove. He would know where he was then. He began to run towards the blue sea.

Through the bushes he went, and came out at last on to what seemed to be a very high cliff. Yes – there was the sea, below and beyond. If only he could scramble down the cliff he could bear to the right and at last come to his cove. He came to the edge of the cliff and looked down – and then he started back in fear. What was that noise – that awful, dreadful noise? It was like a giant wailing and wailing at the top of his voice, the wailing going up and down in the wind. Wilfrid found his knees were shaking. He simply didn't dare to go on. He sat down and tried to get his breath, putting his hands over his ears to keep out the horrible wailing.

And then he suddenly remembered something and heaved a sigh of heartfelt relief. 'Of course – these must be the Wailing Cliffs we were told about,' he thought thankfully. 'We heard about the Whispering Wood – and it *does* whisper – and the Wailing Cliffs – and they *do* wail! At least, it's really the wind, of course. But goodness, what a strange sound!'

He sat for a while longer, then, feeling much bolder, he went to the edge of the great cliff, and looked over. He stared down in surprise.

'There's somebody down there – three or four people! Mustn't let them see me – they must belong to the men on the island! What are they doing down there?'

He lay down and peered over. Four men

were there – but, as Wilfrid watched, they disappeared. Where had they gone? He craned over the cliff to see. 'There must be caves in the cliff, I suppose,' he said to himself. 'That's where they've gone! Gosh, I wish this wailing would stop. I shall start wailing myself in a minute!'

After some time voices came faintly up to him, as he lay watching, and he saw two men coming out on to the rocks below again. What were they carrying? A long, deep box – why, it looked exactly like one of the boxes in which the others had seen those beautiful little statues, packed in sawdust!

'So *that*'s how they get them away from here – take them down through some passage in the cliffs to a waiting boat. Where's the boat, though? I can't see one. Not arrived yet, perhaps.'

He watched with intense interest as the men carried out box after box and piled them on a great flat rock that abutted a stretch of fairly calm water.

'Big boxes – little ones – those men have been busy lately!' thought Wilfrid, wishing and wishing and wishing that the others were with him. 'I wonder what's in them. Not the bed of gold, that's certain. I bet it would be far too big to put into a boat. Have to be pulled to pieces first! Hallo – here comes another box – a small one this time. Wow, they'll soon need a steamer to take all these!'

Almost as he thought it, he saw a small steamer in the far distance! 'Well! There's the steamer, just as I said! I bet the boat will appear soon, and be loaded – and then chug off to the waiting steamer!'

But the steamer came no nearer, and no boats appeared. 'Waiting for the tide, I expect,' thought Wilfrid. 'What *will* the others say when I tell them all this! They won't believe me! And I bet they won't scold me for going off by my-self!'

He decided to go back and find the others and tell them what he had seen. He set off, trying to remember the way. Surely he must be near the place where he had left them? And then quite suddenly, someone leapt out from behind a tree and caught hold of him!

'Let me go, let me go!' shouted Wilfrid, in a panic. And then he gave a cry of relief as he suddenly saw Timmy running towards him.

'Timmy! Save me!'

But Timmy didn't coming running to save him. He stood there, looking up at him, rather puzzled, while poor Wilfrid went on struggling, really frightened!

Then Wilfrid heard a giggle. A GIGGLE? Who in the world could be giggling just then? He forced himself to look round – and saw Dick and Anne, doing their best not to laugh, and George holding her sides. His captor let go of him and began to laugh too. It was Julian!

'This is too bad! You gave me an awful fright,' said Wilfrid. 'I've already been captured once this afternoon. Whatever do you think you're doing?'

'Where have you been, Wilfrid?' said Julian,

rather sternly. 'I forbade you to go for a walk – and you went.'

'I know. I went off by myself – and a man caught me and scared me. Then I ran away and lost myself. I couldn't find any of you,' said poor Wilfrid. 'But I saw something very very interesting on that walk of mine!'

'What?' asked Julian, at once.

'Let's sit down, and I'll tell you,' said Wilfrid. 'I feel quite shaky. You really were beasts to jump on me like that.'

'Never mind, Wilfrid,' said Anne, feeling sorry for the boy, who really did look rather shaken. 'Now go on, tell us everything that happened.'

Wilfrid sat down. He was still trembling a little. Everything seemed to have happened at once. He began to tell the others about the Wailing Cliffs, and all he had seen.

They all listened with intense interest. 'So *that's* the other way to the underground treasure chamber – through a passage in the cliffs!' said Julian. 'I never thought of that! That is something to know! I vote we go and explore the cliffs ourselves, when there's nobody about.'

'Well, it had better be in the evening,' said Wilfrid. 'Just in case we were spotted climbing down the cliffs to find the passage – if there *is* one, and I think there must be! Those men might be on the watch, now they know there's someone on the island. I bet they guess I'm not the only one – even though I told them I came alone.'

'I vote we have something to eat,' said George. 'We can talk over everything then. It's ages since we had a meal. Let's go and open some more tins, and plan what we're going to do tonight. This is getting too exciting for words. Isn't it, Timmy?'

'Woof,' agreed Timmy. *Too* exciting, he thought. Yes – and dangerous, too. He'd keep close to George that evening, as close as ever he could! If she went into danger, Timmy would be close by her side!

[15]

Julian has an exciting plan

The five children talked and talked, as they opened more tins and had a most peculiar meal of ham spread with fruit salad and beans. They finished up with another barley-sugar each. George gave hers to Timmy who disposed of it with a crick-crack, swallow!

'Have we all got torches?' asked Julian. 'I know it will be bright moonlight tonight, but as we shall presumably be getting down – or up – dark caves, we shall want torches.'

Yes – they each had a torch. Wilfrid, for some reason, had two, rather small but quite efficient.

'What's the plan going to be, Ju?' asked George, and Timmy gave a little whine, as if to say 'Yes, tell us.' He sat by George, listening earnestly, with Wilfrid on the other side of him.

At times he sniffed at the baby hedgehog still in the boy's pocket, and apparently quite happy there. Wilfrid had been busy catching insects for it, much to Timmy's interest.

'I propose that we go to the cliffs – the Wailing Cliffs – as soon as it's twilight, and make our way down,' said Julian. 'There is probably some kind of pathway down, I should think – even if only a rabbit path. I'll lead the way down, of course. Anne and Wilfrid are to come between me and Dick, with George and Timmy behind.'

'Right!' said everyone.

'We are, of course, to make as little noise as possible,' said Julian. 'And do try not to send stones hurtling down the path or cliff, just in *case* anyone's about! When we get down to the rocks, we'll let Wilfrid go ahead, because he saw where the men went in and out earlier on.'

Wilfrid felt suddenly important – it was like planning an exploration! He suddenly remembered something – the wailing noise.

'I hope the girls won't be scared when they

hear the awful wailing noise,' he said. 'It's only the wind screaming in and out of the holes and corners of the great cliffs.'

George made a scornful noise. 'Who's scared of the wind!' she said.

'Timmy might be,' said Julian, smiling. 'We *know* what makes the wailing. He doesn't! You may have to hold him when it begins, George. He'll be a bit uneasy.'

'He won't!' said George. 'Timmy's not afraid of anything in the world!'

'Oh yes, he is,' said Dick, at once. 'I know something that scares him dreadfully – makes him put his tail down and flop his ears.'

'You do not!' said George, angrily.

'Well, haven't you seen him when you speak sharply to him?' said Dick, with a chuckle. 'He goes all shaky in the legs!'

Everyone laughed except George. 'He does not,' she said. 'Nothing scares Timmy, not even me. So shut up, Dick.'

'It may be that it would be best for only one or two of us to go right into the depths of the caves,' went on Julian. 'If so, the rest must wait in hiding. Just keep on the look-out for any signal from me. I don't expect we shall see a soul down there tonight, but you never know. If there is a way through the cliffs to that underground chamber where we saw the golden statues, we shall be in real luck. We shall then be absolutely certain how things can be taken in and out.'

'Taken *in*? But I thought they had been there for ages,' said Dick, 'and were probably only taken out to sell. *Smuggled* out.'

'Well, I think it may be more than that, said Julian. 'It might even be a central clearing-ground for a great gang of high-class thieves, who would hide valuable stolen goods there till it was safe to sell them. However, that's only guessing!'

'*I* think somebody's discovered the underground chamber, full of that rich old man's treasures, and is taking them out bit by bit,' said Dick. 'Anyway, whatever it is, it's awfully exciting. To think we know so much!'

'All because we went down the well to get some water!' said Anne.

'Put on your sweaters,' said Julian. 'It may be freezing cold in the wind that rages round those cliffs!'

'I'm longing to start!' said George. 'It's an adventure, this – do you hear that, Timmy? An adventure!'

'Anything more, Julian?' asked Anne. Julian always sounded so very grown-up when he gave them a plan of campaign. She felt very proud of him.

'That's the lot,' said Julian, 'except that we'll have some sort of a meal before we go this evening. Wilfrid will have to lead the way for us, as he's the only one who knows it – but when we come to the cliff, *I'll* lead you down. Can't have anyone missing a footstep and rolling headlong, frightening any robber or smuggler!'

'Do you hear that, Timmy?' said George, and Timmy whined, and put a paw on George's knee as if to say: 'It's a pity you haven't sure feet like mine, with rubber pads beneath, so that *your* footing is always sure!'

George patted his paw. 'Yes – you've fine sure feet, Tim. I wish I could buy some like them!'

The time seemed to go very, very slowly after that. Everyone was eager to start, and kept looking at their watches! The sun left a bright glow in the sky, so they would probably start more or less in daylight, which would, however, soon fade into twilight.

They had another meal, but strangely enough, nobody felt very hungry! 'We're too excited!' said Julian, giving Timmy a biscuit. Timmy was the only one who didn't seem at all excited. As for George, she fidgeted and fidgeted until everyone was quite tired of her!

At last they started off. Wilfrid led them at first, as he knew the way. Actually he found that he didn't really know it – it was the loud wind that guided him, just as it had done before. 'Awfully like far-off voices shouting to one another,' he said, and everyone at once agreed.

When they came near to the cliff, the sound gradually changed into the mournful wailing noise that gave the cliffs their name. 'EEE-ee-OOOOO-oo-EEEEEEEEAH-OOO!'

'Not very nice,' said Anne, shivering a little. 'It sounds as if someone is crying and sobbing and howling!'

'Good name for this place – Wailing Cliffs,' said Dick. 'Wow – what a wind up here! I'm glad my hair's my own! It would certainly be blown off if it weren't! Hang on to old Timmy, George – he's more blowable than we are – not so heavy!'

George put her hand on Timmy's collar at once. How DREADFUL if Timmy were to be blown over the cliff! He gave a grateful lick. He didn't like the wind here very much – it had a truly miserable voice!

They came to the edge of the cliff and looked down cautiously, in case anyone should be on the rocks below. But, except for some big gulls preening their feathers there, there was no sign of life.

'No boats about – no steamer – nothing,' said Dick. 'All clear, Julian!'

Julian had been looking for a good path down the cliff. There didn't seem to be a continuous one. 'We'll have to go so far – then climb down a bit – then walk along that ledgy bit, see – then climb down that slanting rock – the great big one – and get down on to the more level rocks. OK everyone?'

'I'll let Timmy go first,' said George. 'He is so sure-footed and will know the best way. Go on, Timmy – lead us down!'

Timmy understood at once and went in front of Julian. He took the first little path down the cliff, slid down the next bit, walked along the ledge that Julian had pointed out, and then stood and waited for everyone. He gave a little bark as if to say 'Come along. It's easy! Follow me!'

They all followed, some more carefully than others. George and Wilfrid were least careful, and poor Wilfrid lost his footing and slid quite a long way on his behind. He didn't like it at all, and looked quite scared!

'Watch your feet, now, Wilfrid,' said Julian. 'It's getting a bit dark, so don't try any funny tricks. You tried to *jump* over that big stone instead of stepping over carefully. I really don't want to send Timmy down to the bottom of the cliff to pick up your pieces!'

At last they were all down the cliff and on the rocks below. The tide was out, so that waves did not splash up and soak them. Anne suddenly slipped into a pool and made her shoes wet, but that didn't matter. They were only plastic ones.

'Now – exactly where did you see those men, Wilfrid?' asked Julian, stopping on a big flat rock. Wilfrid jumped beside him, and pointed.

'See the cliff over there? See that funny rock shaped rather like a bear? Well, that's where I saw the men. They went by that rock, and disappeared.'

'Right,' said Julian. 'Now, no more talking please – though this wailing sound would drown almost anything. Follow me!'

He went over the rocks towards the big bear-like one that Wilfrid had pointed to. The others followed, a little tide of excitement welling up inside them. Anne caught hold of Wilfrid's hand, and squeezed it. 'Exciting, isn't it?' she said, and Wilfrid nodded eagerly. He knew he would have been scared stiff by himself – but with the others it was an adventure – a really exciting adventure!

They came to the bear-like rock. Near it was a dark place in the cliff – a way in? 'That's where the men came out, Julian,' said Wilfrid, keeping his voice low. 'Do we go in there?'

'We do,' said Julian. 'I'm going in first and I'm going to stand quite still and listen, as soon as I get the sound of the wind and sea out of my ears. If I hear nothing I'll whistle, see? Then you can all come in too.'

'Right!' said everyone, thrilled. They watched as Julian went to the dark slit-like opening. He paused and looked inside. It was so dark that he knew they would all need their torches! He switched on his powerful one and shone it into the passage. He saw a channel that ran slanting upwards for some way, and on either side a rocky ledge, not too rough. Water ran down the rocky channel and bubbled out beside him, to join the sea over the rocks.

'I'm just going into the cliff tunnel a little way, to see if I can hear anything or anyone,' he said. 'Wait here.' He disappeared inside the dark opening and everyone waited in impatient excitement.

A gull suddenly swooped down close to their heads. 'Ee-ooo, ee-ooo, EEE-OOO!' it screeched, and made them all jump violently. Wilfrid almost fell off his rock, and clutched at George. Timmy growled, and looked up angrily at the seagull. Silly bird, frightening everyone like that!

There came a low whistle, and Julian appeared again, his torch switched on. 'All clear,' he said. 'I can't hear a sound inside the opening, and I've been some way along. It's not hard going. There's a funny little stream flowing down, and a ledge either side we can walk on. Very convenient! Now, no talking please

– and be careful even of your whispers – every sound seems to be magnified in here. Keep hold of Timmy, George, in the steepest places.'

Timmy gave a little whine of surprise when George took him inside the cliff. At once his whine was magnified all round them, and everyone jumped. Timmy didn't like it at all.

George took firm hold of Timmy's collar. 'You're to keep close by me,' she whispered, 'and you're not to make a sound. This is an adventure, Timmy – a big adventure – and you're in it as much as any of us. Come along!'

And there they go, all of them, climbing up the dark passage into the cliff! What will they find – what will they see? No wonder their hearts beat fast and loudly, no wonder Timmy keeps close to George. An adventure? He must be on guard then – *anything* might happen in an adventure!

[16]

A journey underground

It was very dark inside the cliff. The children's torches made bright streaks everywhere, and were very useful indeed for seeing the safest places to tread. As Julian had told the others, there was a curious little stream flowing down the middle of the steep passage, with uneven ledges on each side of it. It had worn this little channel for itself during the many, many years it had flowed down inside the cliff.

'It's probably water draining from the surface of the cliffs,' said Julian in a low voice, picking his way carefully. 'Be careful here – the ledges are *very* slippery!'

'Oooh!' said Wilfrid, treading on a slippery bit, and finding one of his feet in ice-cold water.

The echo took up the noise at once, 'OOOOH-OOOOOOH-OOOOOH!' Poor Wilfrid's little

'Oooh' echoed up and down and all round them! It was very weird indeed and nobody liked it. Anne pressed close to Julian, and he squeezed her arm comfortingly.

'Sorry about my "Oooh",' said Wilfrid, in a low voice. 'My oooh, oooh, oooh!' said the echo at once, and George simply couldn't *help* giving a giggle, which at once repeated itself a score of times!

'You really will have to be quiet now,' came Julian's voice, almost in a whisper. 'I have a feeling we're coming to some big opening. There's suddenly a great draught blowing down this steep passage – I can feel it round my head.'

The others felt it too, as they climbed higher up the steep passage, trying to avoid the tiny stream that splashed down its worn channel. It made a nice little noise – very cheerful, Anne thought – and gleamed brightly in the light of their torches.

Julian wondered how in the world anyone could take crates or boxes down such a steep dark passage! 'It's *wide* enough, I suppose,' he thought. 'But only just – and the bends in it must be very awkward for boxes to get round! I do hope we don't meet anyone round a bend, carrying a crate or two! Wow, the draught is quite a wind now! There *must* be an opening somewhere.'

'Ju – we've not only gone upwards, we've gone a good way forward too,' whispered Anne. 'Wasn't the old castle somewhere in this direction?'

'Yes – I suppose it would be,' answered Julian, stopping to think. 'Gosh – I wonder if this passage comes up in one of its cellars! An old castle like that would have huge cellars – and probably a dungeon or two for prisoners! Let me think – we must have left the cliff behind now – and yes – I think we *may* be heading for the castle. Why didn't I think of that before?'

'Well, then – the well wall must run down beside the castle foundations!' said Dick, in much too loud a voice. The echo made every-one jump violently, and Julian stopped climbing and hissed at Dick. 'Whisper, can't you, idiot! You nearly made me jump out of my skin!'

'Skin, skin, skin!' said the echo, in a peculiar whisper that made George want to laugh.

'Sorry!' whispered back Dick.

'I think you may be right about the well wall running down beside the foundations of the castle,' Julian said, whispering again. 'I never thought of that. The castle wasn't very far from the well. It would probably have enormous cellars spreading underground.'

'The wall in the well, that that funny little door was in, was terrifically thick,' said Dick. 'I bet I was looking into one of the castle cellars, when I peeped through it!'

This was all very interesting. Julian thought about it as they went on and on through the endless passage. It ran more or less level now, and was easy to walk through, for it was much wider.

'I think this part of the passage was man-made,' said Julian, stopping and facing the others, his face bright in the light of their torches. He went on in a loud whisper, 'Up through the cliff the passage was a natural one, awfully difficult to climb – but here it's quite different – look at these old bricks here – probably put there to strengthen the tunnel.'

'Yes – a secret way from the castle to the sea!' said Dick, almost forgetting to keep his voice down, in his excitement. 'Isn't it thrilling!'

Everyone began to feel even more excited – all except Timmy, who didn't much like dark, secret passages, and couldn't imagine why Julian was taking them for such a gloomy and peculiar walk. He had splashed solemnly through the stream the whole time, finding the stone ledges much too slippery for his paws.

The draught grew stronger and was very cold indeed. 'We're coming near to the opening where the draught comes from,' whispered Julian. 'All quiet, now, please!'

They were as quiet as possible, and Anne began to feel almost sick with excitement.

Where were they coming to? Then suddenly Julian gave a low exclamation.

'Here we are! An iron gate!'

They all tried to crowd round Julian to see. The gate was a big strong one, with criss-cross bars of iron. They could easily see between the bars, and they shivered in the draught that swept through the great gate.

Dick shone his torch through the bars, his hand shaking in excitement. The bright ray of light ran all round what looked like a stone room – quite small – with a stout, nail-studded door at the far end. This door was wide open, and it was through this that the steady draught blew.

'This is a cellar – or a dungeon, more likely!' said Julian. 'I wonder if the gate is locked.'

He shook it – and it swung open quite easily, as if it had been well-oiled! Julian stepped into the dungeon, flashing his torch all round the dark and dismal little place.

He shivered. 'It's cold as ice, even on this warm day!' he said. 'I wonder how many poor, miserable prisoners have been kept down here in the cold!'

'Look – here's a staple in the wall,' said Dick, standing beside him, examining the half-hoop of iron deeply embedded in the stone wall. 'I suppose the unhappy prisoner was tied up to this, to make his punishment even worse.'

Anne shivered. 'How could people be so cruel?' she said, her vivid imagination seeing wretched men here, with perhaps only crusts of bread to eat, water to drink, no warmth, no bed, only the stone floor!

'Perhaps some of them escaped out of the gate and went down the cliff passage,' she said, hopefully.

'No – it's much more likely that the passage was used to get *rid* of the prisoners,' said Dick. 'They could be dragged down to the sea and drowned – and nobody would ever know.'

'Don't tell me things like that,' said Anne. 'It makes me feel I shall hear groans and cries. I don't like this place. Let's go.'

'I hate it too,' said George. 'And Timmy's tail

is right down. I feel as if this horrid dungeon is full of miserable memories. Julian, *do* let's go.'

Julian walked over to the nail-studded door and went through the doorway. He looked out on to a stone-paved passage, with stone walls and ceiling. He could see other doors, iron-barred, along a dismal stone passage. He came back to the others.

'Yes – these *are* the castle dungeons,' he said. 'I expect the castle cellars are somewhere near too – where they stored wine and food and other things. Come on – let's explore. I can't hear a sound. I think this place is absolutely empty.'

They all followed Julian down the stone passage, looking in at each miserable dungeon as they passed. Horrible! Dirty, damp, cold, bare – poor, poor prisoners of long ago!

At the end of the passage was another iron-barred door, but that too was wide open. They went through it and came out into an enormous cellar. Old boxes were there, old worm-eaten chests, broken chairs, loose papers that rustled as their feet touched them – the kind of junk that can be found in a thousand cellars! It all smelt rather musty – though, as Julian said, the draught that blew everywhere took away some of the smell.

They came to some stone steps and went up them. At the top was another great door, with an enormous bolt on it. 'Fortunately the bolt is *our* side,' said Julian, and slid it out of its socket. He was surprised that it went so smoothly – he had expected it to be rusted and stiff. 'It's been oiled recently,' he said, shining his torch on it. 'Well, well – other people have been here not long ago, and used this door. We'd better go quietly in case they are *still* here!'

Anne's heart began to beat loudly again. She hoped there was no one waiting round a corner to jump out at them! 'Be careful, Julian,' she said. 'Somebody may have heard us! They may be waiting to ambush us. They . . .'

'All right, Anne – don't worry!' said Julian. 'Old Timmy would give us a warning growl if he heard a single footstep!'

And good gracious – at that VERY moment Timmy *did* give a growl – an angry, startled growl that made everyone jump, and then stand still, holding their breath.

Dick looked round at Timmy, who was growling again. His head was down and he was looking at something on the floor. What was it? Dick swung down his torch to see. Then he gave a small laugh. 'It's all right. We don't need to be scared yet. Look what Timmy's growling at!'

They all looked down – and saw a great fat toad, its brilliant eyes staring steadily up at them. As they exclaimed at it, it turned aside, and crawled slowly and clumsily to a little damp spot in the corner of the wall.

'I've never seen such a big toad in my life!' said Anne. 'It must be a hundred years old! Goodness, Timmy, you made me jump when you suddenly growled like that!'

The toad squatted down in its corner, facing them. It seemed to glare at poor Timmy. 'Come away, Tim,' said Dick. 'Toads can ooze out a very nasty-smelling, nasty-tasting stuff. Never bite a toad!'

Julian had now gone through the door at the top of the steps. He gave a loud exclamation – so loud that the others rushed to him in alarm, wondering what was exciting him.

'Look!' said Julian, shining his torch into the dark space beyond. 'See where we've come to! Did you ever see such a storehouse of wonders!'

In the treasure chamber

Julian's torch shone steadily into the vast room, which seemed to have no end! The others shone their torches too, and Timmy pressed between their legs to see what the excitement was.

What a sight! They were actually in the enormous chamber that the boys had seen through the opening in the well wall! What a place it was – absolutely *vast*, thought Anne, awed at the size, the height and the great silence.

'There are the golden statues!' said Dick, going over to a group of them. 'Wonderful! Strange faces they have, though – not like ours. And look how their slanting eyes gleam when we shine our torches on them. Makes them look as if they're almost alive, and looking at us.'

Anne suddenly gave a cry and rushed over to something. 'The golden bed!' she said. 'I *wished* I could lie on one – and now I shall!' And with that she climbed on to a vast four-poster bed with a great canopy, now rotting to pieces.

The bed gave a mournful creak, and the part that Anne was lying on suddenly subsided. The canopy collapsed and Anne disappeared in a cloud of dust. The bed had, quite literally, fallen to pieces! Poor Anne.

The others helped her up and Timmy looked at the clouds of dust in surprise. What was Anne doing, making such a dust! He sneezed loudly, and then sneezed again. Anne sneezed too. She scrambled quickly out of the collapsed bed and dusted herself down.

'It has a carved gold headpiece, and gold legs and end-piece,' said Dick, shining his torch on it. 'What a monster of a bed, though – I should think *six* people could sleep in it at once! What a pity it has been lost here so long – all the hangings fell to pieces as soon as Anne climbed on the bed part! *What* a dust!'

There was no doubt about it, there were priceless treasures in this vast underground cellar. The children could not find the sword with the jewelled handle, nor the necklace of rubies, which Julian thought were probably locked away in one of the chests. But they found many other wonderful things.

'Look in this chest – this beautiful carved chest!' called Anne. 'Gold cups and plates and dishes. Still bright and clean!'

'And look what's in here!' shouted George. 'Wrapped up in stuff that falls to pieces when I touch it!'

They crowded round a great enamelled box. In it was a set of animals carved out of some lovely green stone. They were absolutely perfect, and, when Anne tried to stand them up, each of them stood as proudly as once they did many years ago when little princes and princesses played with them.

'They're made of green jade,' said Julian. 'Beautiful! Goodness knows how much they're worth! They should be in some museum, not mouldering away in this cellar.'

'Why didn't those collectors take these – and the golden statues – and all the other things?' wondered Anne.

'Well, that's obvious,' said Julian. 'For one thing this is a secret cellar, I should think, and nobody would be able to get into it unless they knew the secret way to it. There's probably a sliding panel or hidden door that leads to it, somewhere in the castle above. It's very cold, and ruined in many parts – and some of the walls have fallen in – so I suppose it was pretty impossible to get to the cellars even if the secret way was known!'

'Yes – but what about the way *we* came up,' said Dick. 'From the sea – up the cliff passage!'

'Well – I don't know exactly why that hasn't been used before,' said Julian, 'though I could make a guess! Did you notice that great heap of fallen rocks near the entrance to the cliff passage? I should think that that part of the cliff fell at one time, and hid the passage completely –

blocked it up. Then maybe a storm came, and the sea shifted some of the rocks – and lo and behold, there was the secret passage – open again!'

'And somebody found it – somebody, perhaps, who had heard the old legends about the castle of Whispering Island!' said Anne.

'A collector of old things, do you think?' asked George. 'What about those two men on the island – the ones we saw in the courtyard – do you suppose *they* know of this entrance?'

'Yes, probably,' said Julian. 'And it's likely they were put on guard in case anyone else found it and came to rob the secret chamber. The things here are priceless! Those men are not there to guard the animals on the island, as they were in the old couple's day. They had *genuine* keepers, like that nice old man Lucas who told us about this island this morning.'

'You think these men are in somebody's pay then – somebody who knows about this great chamber under the castle, and wants to get the centuries-old treasures?' said Dick.

'Yes,' said Julian. 'And what's more I don't believe that the real owner of the island – the great-nephew of the old couple who owned it – even *knows* they're here, or that anyone is taking things from the island. For all we know he may live in America or Australia, and not care tuppence about his island!'

'How extraordinary!' said Anne. 'If *I* owned an island like this, I'd live here and never leave it. And all the animals and birds would be protected as they once were, and . . .'

'Dear Anne – what a pity it *isn't* yours!' said Julian, ruffling her hair. 'But now, the thing is – what are we going to *do* about this? We'll talk about it when we're back at the cottage. Hey, it's getting late! It will be pitch dark outside, unless the moon is up and the sky is clear of clouds!'

'Well, come on then, let's go,' said Dick, making for the great nail-studded door. Then, as Timmy suddenly gave a blood-curdling growl, he stopped in fright. They had *shut* the door – but now it was opening. Somebody was coming into the great underground chamber! Who *could* it be?

'Quick – hide!' said Julian, and he pushed the two girls behind a great chest. The others were near the golden bed and they crouched behind it at once, Dick's hand on Timmy's collar. He had managed to stop the dog from growling, but was afraid that Timmy would begin again at any moment!

A man came into the room – one of the two big fellows that the children had seen in the courtyard. He didn't seem to have heard Timmy growling, for he sauntered in, whistling lightly. He shone his torch all round, and then called loudly.

'Emilio! Emilio!'

There was no answer at all. The man yelled again, and then an answer came from beyond the door, and hurrying footsteps could be heard. Then in came the other big rough fellow, and looked round, shining his torch. He lighted an oil-lamp on a box, and switched off his torch.

'You're always sleeping, Emilio!' growled the first man. 'You are always late! You know the boat comes tonight to take the next batch of goods – have you got the list? We must wrap them up quickly and take them to the shore. That little statue has to go, I know!'

He went over to the statue of a boy whose eyes gleamed with emeralds. 'Well, boy,' said the man, 'you're going out into the world! How'll you like that after being in the dark so long? Don't glare at me like that, or I'll box your ears!'

Apparently the golden boy went on glaring, for the man gave his head a sharp smack. The other fellow came over and shifted a long, deep box over from the wall to the little golden statue. Then he began to wrap it up carefully, rolling material round and round it from head to foot while the golden boy stood patiently.

'What time is Lanyon coming for it?' asked Emilio. 'Have I time to wrap another?'

'Yes – that one over there,' said the first fellow, pointing. Emilio went whistling over to it, passing the chest behind which the girls were hiding. They crouched right to the floor, afraid of being seen. But Emilio was sharp-eyed, and thought he saw something move as he passed by the chest. He stopped. What was that poking out by the side of the chest – a foot! A FOOT!

Emilio rushed round the chest, his torch switched on again. He gave a loud shout. 'Carlo! There's someone here! Come quickly!'

Carlo, the second man, dropped what he was holding and raced round to Emilio, who had now pulled the girls roughly to their feet.

'What are you doing here? How did you get in?' shouted Emilio.

Julian shot out from his hiding place at once, followed by Dick and Wilfrid. George was doing all she could to hold back Timmy, who was now deafening everyone with his angry barks. He did his best to get away from George, but she was afraid he might fly at Emilio's throat. The two men were full of amazement to see the five children and Timmy!

'Keep that dog back or I'll shoot him,' said

Carlo, producing a gun. 'Who are you? What do you mean by coming into this place?'

'We came by boat – but the boat got washed out to sea,' said Julian. 'We've been camping on the island. We just – er – wandered into this place by mistake.'

'By mistake! Well, I can tell you that you've certainly made the biggest mistake in your life!' said Carlo. 'You'll have to stay here for quite a long time – till our job's done, at any rate!'

'What's your job?' asked Julian, bluntly.

'Wouldn't you like to know!' said Carlo. 'Well – one part of it is to guard the island, and keep off strangers! Now, we've jobs to do tonight and tomorrow, and I'm afraid you're going to have a miserable time! You'll stay down here in this old cellar till we come back again – and what will happen to you after that, I don't know, because I'll have to tell my employer you've been spying down here. I wouldn't be surprised if he doesn't hand you over to the police – or lock you up down here for a month, on bread and water!'

Timmy growled very fiercely indeed, and tugged hard to get away from George and fly at this hateful man. She hung on to him for all she was worth, though how she longed to let him leap at the man and get him on the ground!

'Better go, Carlo, or we'll miss that boat out there,' said Emilio, grumpily. 'We'll deal with these kids when we get back!' He shouldered the box into which he had put the wrapped statue, and started for the door. Carlo followed him, backing all the time to make sure that George did not set Timmy on to him. He shut the great door with a loud bang, and shot the bolt.

'Don't say anything for a minute in case they are listening outside the door,' said Julian. So they all stood in silence, Anne's knees trembling a little. Oh dear – how unlucky to be caught like this!

'Relax!' said Julian at last. 'You all look so stiff and tense!'

'Well, I should *think* so!' said Dick. 'I don't particularly want to stay shut up here till those men deign to come back and do a bit more stealing. Suppose they *never* come back! We'd be here for keeps!'

'No, Dick!' said Anne, and to everyone's surprise, she began to laugh. 'We can *easily* escape!'

'What – through that locked and bolted door?' said Dick. 'Not a hope!'

'But we *can* easily escape!' said Anne, and George suddenly brightened up and nodded her head, smiling. 'Oh yes – of course! Don't look so solemn, Dick! Look up there!'

Dick looked up to where Anne was pointing. 'What am I supposed to look at?' he said. 'The old stone wall?'

'No – just there – over the top of that tall chest,' said Anne.

Dick looked – and then a large smile came over his face. 'WHAT an idiot I am! That's the old iron door in the side of the old well wall, isn't it – the opening I looked through! It looks just like an ordinary ventilation hole from down here – and I don't really believe anyone would ever notice it except us, who know what it is. I see what you're getting at, Anne!'

'Good old Anne!' said George, realising what Anne had in mind. 'Of course – we've only got to climb up to that hole in the wall, open the door there, and then go up the well – and we're safe!'

'Yes. But it's easier said than done,' said Julian, soberly. 'We've got to get hold of the rope, and climb right up it to the top – *not* very easy!'

'Suppose the rope's at the top, with the bucket hanging on the hook,' said Anne. 'We'd never reach it then!'

'We'll think of something!' said Julian. 'Anyway, it's our only hope of escape. Now – we'll push that huge, high chest or wardrobe or whatever it is, right over against the wall, under that opening into the well – there's a sturdy little one over there. Come on! We'll be through that opening in no time, and up the well. What a shock for dear Emilio and Carlo, when they come back and find that the birds have flown!'

[18]

A most exciting time!

It was quite a job pushing the heavy chest over towards the stone wall of the castle. It took all of them shoving with all their might, to do it.

'We seem to be making an awful noise with the chest scraping over the floor,' panted Dick. 'I hope we're not heard!'

Timmy wished he could help. He kept jumping up and pressing his paws on the side of the chest, but Dick stopped him. 'You're getting in the way,' he said. 'You go and sit near the door and warn us if you hear those men coming.'

So Timmy ran to the door and sat there, his head cocked to one side listening, while the others went on shoving the heavy chest along. At last it was in position. Then came the job of hoisting a stout little wooden table on top. Julian climbed up to the top of the chest to take the table from Dick, but just couldn't manage it, it was so heavy and solid. So Wilfrid climbed up beside him, and between the two of them they pulled up the little oblong table, and set it firmly on top of the chest. Julian stood on it – and found he could easily reach the little iron door that led into the old well.

'Good,' he said, and he gave the door a hard shove. It shook a little but didn't budge. He gave it another hard push. 'What's up?' said Dick, climbing up beside Julian. 'It *must* open – the bolt's not there any more – it fell off into the well. I expect it's rusted a little again. We'll both shove it together.'

The girls watched the boys anxiously, dreading every moment to hear the two men returning. Together the boys pushed at the iron door – and it groaned and then gave way, swinging open inside the well wall! To the boys' delight, there was the rope, hanging near them!

'We've done it!' Dick called down softly to the girls. 'We'll come down and help you up to the table here – then we'll try our luck up the well.'

The girls were soon on the chest top. There wasn't room for everyone on the table, and the boys were debating what to do next.

'*You* go up the rope, Julian,' said Dick. 'You can climb up to the top and get out and look around and make sure there's no one about. Then Wilfrid can climb up – do you think you can, Wilfrid?'

'Of course,' said the boy. 'Then I can help Julian to wind up the girls!'

'Right!' said Dick. 'I'll stay here with the girls, and help each of them on to the rope, first Anne – and you two can wind the rope up, with her on it. Then George can go – and I'll follow last of all and shut the well door.'

'And when the men come they won't know how in the world we got out of the treasure chamber!' said Anne, grinning. 'What a shock for them!'

'When you've all gone up safely, I'll climb in myself and shut the door,' said Dick. 'Ready, Ju? I'll shine my torch for you!'

Julian nodded. He squeezed through the old

iron door, reached out for the rope, and swung on it for a moment. Then up he went, hand-over-hand, till he reached the top, a little out of breath, but delighted to be out in the open air and the bright moonlight. It seemed almost as light as day!

He called down the well. 'I'm at the top, Dick, and all's well. Moon's out, and all is quiet.'

'You next, Wilfrid,' said Dick. 'Can you get hold of the rope all right, do you think? For *pity's* sake don't fall into the water. My torch will give you plenty of light.'

'Don't worry about *me*! It's just like being on the ropes at gym in school,' said Wilfrid, scornfully. He swung his legs into the opening, leapt at the rope, hung on, and began to climb up just like a monkey.

Julian's voice came down the well again, echoing hollowly, sounding rather odd. 'Wilfrid's safely up. Now send Anne – we'll wind up the rope for her so that she doesn't need to climb, only to hang on.'

Through the opening went Anne, and sat on its ledge. 'Can you swing the rope a bit, Julian?' she called. 'It's rather far for me to jump.'

'Watch out! For goodness' sake be careful!' called Julian, in alarm. 'Tell Dick to help you.'

But the well wall opening was so small that Dick couldn't even look through it while Anne was sitting there. 'Don't jump till you've got firm hold of the rope, Anne,' he told his sister, anxiously. 'Is Ju swinging it to and fro? Can you see it clearly? It's so dark in the well, and my torch isn't too good now!'

'Yes. I can see it,' said Anne. 'It bumped against my legs then, and I just missed getting it. Here it comes again – I've got it! I'm going to hold on to it tightly and drop off the ledge. Here I go!'

She sounded very much braver than she felt. She let herself drop off the ledge, and there she swung on the thick rope, with the black water far below! 'Wind me up, Ju!' she called, and held on as the two boys at the top exerted all their strength. Dick saw her disappear up the well, and heaved a sigh of relief. Now for George.

He climbed down from the table and chest and looked for George and Timmy, shining his torch everywhere. To his utmost surprise he couldn't see them! He called softly, 'Timmy!'

A small stifled whine came from somewhere. Dick frowned. 'George – where are you? For goodness' sake buck up and come out from where you're hiding. Those men might come back at any time! Don't play the fool.'

A dark curly head poked out from behind a large box near the door, and George spoke in a very fierce voice. 'You *know* Timmy can't hang on to a rope! He'd fall and be drowned. I think you are all horrid to forget that he can't climb. I'm staying here with him. You go on up the well.'

'Certainly *not*!' said Dick at once. 'I shall stay here with you. I suppose it's no use asking you to let *me* stay with Tim, while you climb up?'

'Not the slightest use. He's *my* dog, and I'm jolly well sticking by him,' said George. 'He'd never desert *me*, I'm sure of that.'

Dick knew George only too well when she was in one of her determined moods. Nothing, absolutely nothing, would make her change her mind!

'All right, George – I expect I'd feel the same if Timmy was mine,' said Dick. 'I'm staying here with you, though!'

'No,' said George. 'We'll be all right, Tim and I.'

Dick ran to the chest and table that he had used to get up to the opening in the well wall, and climbed quickly to the top. He swung himself through, sat on the edge of the opening and called up the well.

'Julian? Are you there? Listen – George won't leave Timmy because he can't climb up the rope. So I'm staying with her!'

No sooner had he said these words than he heard someone unlocking the door of the room they were in! Timmy growled so fiercely that Dick's heart jumped in fear. Suppose Tim leapt at those men – and one of them had a gun!

George heard the noise and the key turning in

the door, and quick as lightning she went behind a pile of boxes with Timmy. 'Go for them, Timmy, just as soon as you can!' she said. 'Get them down before they can hurt you.'

'Woof,' said Timmy, understanding every word. He stood beside George, ears cocked, showing his teeth in a snarl. The door opened, and a man came in, carrying a lantern. 'I've brought you a light,' he began – and then Timmy leapt at him!

Crash! Down went the lantern and the light went out. Down went the man too, shouting in fear as the big dog leapt on his chest, his hairy face so close that the man could feel the dog's hot breath. The man's head struck against the edge of a chest, and he was suddenly still and silent.

'Knocked out, I do believe!' said Dick to himself, and very cautiously shone his torch round. Yes – there was the man on the floor, eyes closed, unmoving!

George was at the open door, looking out, Timmy by her side. 'Dick! I'm taking Timmy down the secret way through the cliffs. I'll be perfectly safe with him.'

'I must tell Julian,' said Dick. 'He's still at the top of the well, expecting you and Timmy. You go as quickly as you can – and be careful. Timmy will look after you.'

George disappeared at top speed, her shoes making no sound. She looked anxious but not afraid. 'She's so brave!' thought Dick, for the hundredth time. 'Doesn't turn a hair! Now I'd better get back to that opening in the well, and tell Julian that George and Timmy have gone down the secret way. That man is still knocked out, thank goodness!'

He was soon on top of the chest and table, and peering through the hole. He could see the light from Julian's torch far away at the top, the light flashing on and off as if signalling. Dick called up 'Julian!'

'Oh, so you're still there,' said Julian, sounding very relieved. 'Anything happened?'

'Yes,' said Dick. 'I'll tell you in a minute. Swing the rope a bit, Ju.'

The rope swung near Dick, and he caught it, and was just about to swing himself into the well when he heard a noise. He looked back into the vast room, which was now in darkness, for he had switched off his torch.

Someone came in hurriedly. 'What's happened? Why didn't you—' Then he stopped as the light from the lantern he carried picked out the figure of the man on the floor. He gave an exclamation and knelt down by him. Dick grinned to himself – what about a nice little shock for this fellow? He reached down to the sturdy little table, gave it a shove that sent it hurtling down to the floor, and then swung himself into the well on the rope. He was just in time to see the table fall with a crash by the man with the lantern, and to hear him shout in fear – and then Julian and Wilfrid hauled him up the well, still grinning to himself. 'Bit of a shock for those men!' he thought. 'George and Timmy disappeared – and the rest of us gone most mysteriously! Pull, Julian, pull! I've a nice little story to tell you!'

And soon he was up on the well wall, telling the others what had happened. They laughed in delight.

'Good old George! Good old Timmy!'

'George knows the way down the cliff passage all right – and if she didn't Timmy would take her safely,' said Julian. 'We'll go down on the rocks and meet her, I think. She should be all right because the moon's out now, and everything is as light as day!'

And off they all went through the wood, laughing when they thought how puzzled and mystified those men would be!

[19]

Anne is a tiger!

In the meantime, George was hurrying down the secret way through the cliffs. Timmy ran first in front and then behind, his ears pricked for any possible pursuer or danger. He could hear no one. Good! Both he and George were glad to hear the babbling of the funny little underground stream as it ran swiftly down towards the sea. 'It's a nice friendly sound, Tim,' said George. 'I like it.'

Once or twice they slipped from the wet ledges into the water, and George felt a bit afraid of falling and breaking her torch. 'It wouldn't be much fun if we had to go down this passage in the pitch dark!' she told Timmy, and he gave a little woof of agreement.

'What's that bright light?' said George, suddenly, stopping in the passage. 'Look, Tim –

*aw*fully bright. Is it someone coming with a lantern?'

Timmy gave a loud bark and rushed in front. *He* knew that lantern all right! It was the one that somebody sometimes hung in the sky, and that George called the moon. Didn't she know?

George soon did know, of course, and cried out in delight. 'Oh, it's the *moon*, of course, dear old moon. I'd forgotten it was a moonlit night tonight. I wonder where the others are, Timmy. You'll have to smell them out!'

Timmy already knew where they were! He had caught their scent on the wind. They weren't very far away! He barked joyously. Soon they would all be together again!

He and George came out of the tunnel in the cliff and found themselves on the rocks. The sea was splashing over them, and the waves gleamed brightly in the bright moonlight.

George saw something moving in the distance. She put her hand on Timmy's collar. 'Careful, Tim,' she said. 'Is that someone coming over there? Stay by me.'

But Timmy disobeyed for once! He leapt away and splashed through the pools, over seaweed, over slippery rocks, barking madly. 'Timmy!' called George, not recognising who was coming. 'TIMMY! COME BACK!'

And then she saw who were coming over the rocks in the bright moonlight, picking their way through the slippery seaweed. She waved and shouted joyfully.

'Here I am! I've escaped all right!'

What a joyful meeting that was! They all sat down on a convenient rock and talked nineteen to the dozen, telling each other what had happened. And then a big wave suddenly came up and splashed all over them!

'Blow!' said Julian. 'Tide's coming in, I suppose. Come on – let's get back to Whispering Wood.'

Anne gave a most enormous yawn. 'I don't know what the time is,' she said. 'And it's so bright everywhere that I'm not sure if it's day or night. All I know is that I'm suddenly most awfully SLEEPY.'

Julian glanced at his watch. 'It's very late,' he said. 'Long past our bedtime. What shall we do – risk sleeping here on the island – or find Wilfrid's boat and row across to the mainland – and have a nice, long, peaceful snooze in that dear little cottage?'

'Oh, don't let's stay on the island!' said Anne. 'I'd never go to sleep! I'd be afraid those men would find us.'

'Don't be silly, Anne,' said George, trying not to yawn. 'They wouldn't have the remotest idea where to look for us! I honestly don't fancy looking for Wilfrid's boat, rowing all the way to the mainland, and then climbing up that steep hill to the cottage!'

'Well – all right,' said Anne. 'But oughtn't somebody to be on guard – oughtn't we each to take a turn?'

'Why so fussy, Anne?' asked George. 'Timmy would hear anyone!'

'I suppose he would,' said Anne, giving way. 'We'll stay here then.'

They were all very tired. The boys pulled up

armfuls of old dry bracken and spread it on a sheltered patch of grass, where bushes surrounded them and sheltered them from the wind. It was not far from the cove where Wilfrid's boat lay. They snuggled into the bracken.

'Nice and cosy!' said George, yawning. 'Ohhh! I've never felt so sleepy in my life!' And in three seconds she was sound asleep! Wilfrid dropped off at once too, and Dick and Julian were soon giving little gentle snores.

Anne was still awake. She felt nervous. 'I'd dearly like to know if those men are safely underground,' she thought. 'I can't imagine that they are very pleased at us getting away – they'll know we'll go to the mainland as soon as we can and tell everyone what we have found! I should have thought they would try to stop us leaving. They must *know* we have a boat!'

She lay and worried, keeping her ears open for any strange sound. Timmy heard her tossing and turning and crept over to her very quietly, so as not to wake George. He lay down beside Anne, giving her a loving lick, as if to say 'Now, you go to sleep, and I'll keep watch!'

But still Anne didn't fall asleep. Still she kept her ears wide open for any unusual sound – and then, quite suddenly, she heard something. So did Timmy. He sat up, and gave a very small growl.

Anne strained her ears. Yes – it was certainly voices she could hear – low voices, that didn't want to be heard. It was the men coming to find Wilfrid's boat! Once they had that, the children couldn't get away from Whispering Island!

Timmy ran a little way from the bushes, and looked round at Anne as if to say 'Coming with me?'

Anne got up quietly and went to Timmy. He ran on in front, and she followed. She really *must* see what was happening, then if it was anything important, she could run back and rouse everyone. Timmy was taking her to the cove where Wilfrid had left his boat, hauled high up on the sand for fear of big waves.

They were both as quiet as they could be. Timmy growled a little when he heard the voices again, much nearer this time.

The men had come quietly round the island in their own boat, to set Wilfrid's boat adrift. Anne saw them pushing Wilfrid's boat down the sand towards the sea. Once it was adrift, she and the others would be prisoners on the island! She yelled at the top of her voice.

'You stop that! It's OUR boat!' And Timmy began to bark his head off, prancing round the men, and showing his big white teeth. The barking awoke all the others and they leapt up at once. 'That's Timmy!' shouted Julian. 'That's Timmy barking! Come on, quickly – but be careful!'

They ran at top speed to the cove. Timmy was still barking madly – and someone was yelling. It sounded like Anne. 'ANNE – no, no, it couldn't be quiet little *Anne*!' thought Julian.

But it was! For when the four arrived at the cove, there was Anne yelling to Timmy to bite the men, and dancing about in a rare old temper!

'How DARE you come and take our boat! I'll tell Timmy to bite you! And he will too! Get them, Tim, get them! How DARE you take our boat! *Bite* them, Timmy!'

Timmy had already bitten both the men, who were now rowing away in their own boat at top speed. Anne picked up a stone and sent it whizzing after them. It struck their boat and made them jump.

Anne jumped too when she turned and saw Julian, George, Wilfrid and Dick. 'I'm so glad you've come!' she said. 'I *think* Timmy and I have frightened them off. The beasts!'

'Frightened them off! You've scared them stiff!' said Julian, hugging his sister. 'You even scared *me*! Good gracious – the mouse has certainly turned into a fearsome tiger! I can almost see smoke coming out of your nostrils.'

'A tiger? Did I *really* sound like a tiger?' said Anne. 'I'm glad! I hated you all thinking I was a mouse. You'd better be careful now, I *might* turn into a tiger again!'

The men were now out of sight, and Timmy sent a volley of barks after their vanished boat. What chance had any men against a dog and a tiger? WOOF!

'Julian – why can't we row back to the mainland *now*?' demanded Anne. 'I'm so hungry and there's nothing to eat here now. And I wasn't really very comfortable in the brackeny bed. I'm longing to sleep in a *proper* bed. I've a good mind to take that boat of Wilfrid's and row myself back, if you don't want to come.'

Julian couldn't help laughing at this new fierce Anne. He put his arm round her.

'I believe it's dangerous to say no to a tiger,' he said. 'So you shall have your way, Anne. *I'm* awfully hungry too – and I bet the others are.'

And, in five minutes' time, the six of them were out on the sea, Julian taking one oar, and Dick the other. 'Swish-swash – swish-swash' went the oars, and the boat rocked as it sped along.

'I bet if those men spot us out on the sea in a boat, going across to the mainland, they will feel pretty uncomfortable!' said Julian. 'They'll know we'll be going to the police first thing tomorrow. This has been quite an adventure, hasn't it! I shall be glad of a little peace now!'

Well – you'll soon have it, Julian! That little cottage is waiting for you all, with its glorious view over the harbour and Whispering Island. You'll have quite a bit of excitement tomorrow, of course, when the police take you back to the island in their boat, and you show them the old well, the vast treasure chamber, the secret passage, and all the rest. You'll be there when all the men are rounded up, you'll watch them chugging off, prisoners, in the police boat, amazed that the Famous Five should have defeated them. What an adventure! And what a relief when all the excitement is over, and you lie peacefully on the hillside, with the little cottage just behind you.

'Now for a real lazy time!' said Anne, when the Five had seen the last of the police. 'Let's all go out on the hill in the sunshine, and have orangeade and biscuits and fruit salad – and Wilfrid shall play his magic pipe and bring his furred and feathered friends to see us.'

'Has he found his pipe then?' said Dick, pleased.

'Yes. He took the well bucket to get some water to drink – and lo and behold, the pipe was in the bottom of the bucket!' said Anne. 'He thinks it must have fallen there the last time he went to fetch water from the well – and nobody noticed it!'

'Oh *good*!' said George, thankfully. 'Wilfrid, what about playing a tune on your little pipe? I'm so glad it's found. I'd like to hear it again.'

Wilfrid was pleased. 'All right,' he said. 'I'll see if my friends here still remember me!'

He sat down on the hillside a little away from the others and began to blow down the pipe – and out came the strange little tune! At once the birds in the trees around turned their heads. In the bushes the lizards raised themselves, put their quaint heads on one side and listened.

Rabbits stopped their play. The big hare bounded up the hill, its great ears taking in every note. A magpie flew down to the boy's foot and sat there.

Wilfrid didn't stir. He just went on playing as the creatures came to listen. Timmy listened too, and went to the boy, pressing against him, licking his ear. Then he went back to George.

We'll leave them all there in the sunshine, quiet and peaceful, watching the little creatures that Wilfrid can always bring around him.

Julian is lying back, looking at the April sky, glad that their adventure ended so well. Dick is looking down at Whispering Island, set in the brilliant blue harbour. Anne is half asleep – quiet little Anne who *can* turn into a tiger if she has to!

And George, of course, is close to Timmy, her arm round his neck, very happy indeed. Good-bye, Five – it *was* fun sharing in your grand adventure!

Special note from Enid Blyton

My readers will want to know if Whispering Island is real, set in the great blue harbour in the story – and if the little cottage on the hills is there still – and the golf course in the story – and Lucas, who tells the children about the island. Yes, the island is real, and lies in the great harbour, still full of whispering trees. The little cottage on the hills is still there, with its magnificent view and its old well – and Lucas can be found on the golf course, nut-brown and bright-eyed, telling stories of the animals and birds he loves so much. I have taken them all and put them into this book for you – as well as the friends you know so well – The Famous Five.

FIVE ARE TOGETHER AGAIN

[1]

Back for the holidays

'George, can't you sit still for even a minute?' said Julian. 'It's bad enough to have the train rocking about all over the place, without you falling over my feet all the time, going to look out of first one window and then the other.'

'Well, we're nearly at Kirrin – almost home!' said George. 'I can't *help* feeling excited. I've missed old Timmy so *much* this term, and I just can't *wait* to see him! I love to look out of the window and see how much nearer we are to Kirrin. Do you think Timmy will be on the station to meet us, barking madly?'

'Don't be an idiot,' said Dick. 'He's a clever dog, but not clever enough to read railway timetables.'

'He doesn't need to,' said George. 'He *always* knows when I'm coming home.'

'I really believe he does,' said Anne, seriously. 'Your mother always says how excited he is on the day you are arriving home from school – can't keep still – keeps going to the front gate and looking down the road.'

'Dear, dear Timmy!' said George, falling over Julian's feet again, as she scrambled once more to the window. 'We're nearly there. Look, there's the signal-box, and the signal is down. HURRAH!'

Her three cousins looked at her in amusement. George was always like this on the way home from school. Her thoughts were full of very little else but her beloved Timmy all the way home. Julian thought how much she looked like a restless boy just then, with her short, curly hair, and her determined expression. George had always longed to be a boy, but as she wasn't, she made up for it by trying to speak and act like one, and would never answer to her full name of Georgina.

'We're coming into Kirrin station!' yelled George, almost falling out of the window. 'I can see Peter, the guard. Hey, we're back again. WE'RE BACK AGAIN!'

The train slid into Kirrin station, and Peter waved and grinned. He had known George since she was a baby. George opened the door and leapt out of the carriage.

'Home again! Back at Kirrin! Oh, I do hope Timmy will be at the station!' she said.

But there was no Timmy there. 'He must have forgotten you were coming,' said Dick, with a grin, and at once got a scowl from George. Peter came up, smiling all over his face, and gave them his usual welcome. Everyone in Kirrin village knew the Five – which, of course, included Timmy the dog.

Peter helped the children with their luggage, and wheeled it down the platform on his trolley. 'Had a good term?' he asked.

'Fantastic!' said Dick. 'But it seemed very long, as Easter is so late this year. Gosh – look at the primroses on the railway banks.'

But George had no eyes for anything just then. She was still looking out for Timmy.

Where was he? WHY hadn't he come to the station to meet them? He came last time and the time before! She turned a troubled face to Dick.

'Do you think he's ill? she asked. 'Or has he forgotten me? Or . . . ?'

'Oh, don't be silly, George,' said Dick. 'He is probably in the house somewhere and can't get out. Look out – the trolley nearly ran you over then.'

George skipped out of the way, glaring. WHERE was Timmy? She was sure he was ill – or had had an accident – or was tied up and couldn't get away. Perhaps Joanna, who helped her mother in the house, had forgotten to let him loose.

'I'm going to take a taxi home, if I've enough money,' she said, taking out her purse. 'You others can walk. I must see if anything's happened to Timmy – he's *never* missed meeting our train before.'

'But George, it's such a lovely walk to Kirrin Cottage!' said Anne. 'You know how you love to see your island – dear old Kirrin Island – as

we walk to your mother's house – and the bay –
and hear the waves crashing on the rocks.'

'I'm taking the station taxi,' said George,
obstinately, counting the money in her purse.
'If you'd like to come with me, you can. It's
Timmy I want to see, not islands and waves and
things! I'm SURE he's ill or has had an accident
or something!'

'All right, George, do as you please,' said
Julian. 'Hope you find dear old Timmy is
perfectly well – and has only forgotten the time
of the train. See you later.'

The two brothers and their sister Anne set off
together, looking forward to the walk to Kirrin
Cottage. How lovely to see Kirrin Bay again,
and George's island!

'Isn't she lucky to have a real island of her
very own!' said Anne. 'Fancy it belonging to her
family for years and years – and then one day
her mother suddenly gives it to George! I bet
she worried and worried dear Aunt Fanny until
she gave in to old George. I do so hope Timmy
is all right; we shan't enjoy our holidays with

George's mother if there's anything wrong with Timmy.'

'Oh, George will probably go and live in Timmy's kennel with him,' said Dick, with a chuckle. 'Ha – look! The sea – and Kirrin Bay – AND the little old island as lovely as ever!'

'With its gulls circling round, and mewing like cats,' said Julian. 'And the old ruined castle there, just exactly the same as usual. Not a single stone fallen out of it, as far as I can see.'

'You can't *possibly* see that at this distance,' said Anne, screwing up her eyes. 'Oh, isn't the first day of the hols heavenly? We seem to have all the time in the world in front of us!'

'Yes. But, after a few days, the holidays *rush* by,' said Julian. 'I wonder if George is home by now.'

'Well, her taxi passed us going at a tremendous pace!' said Dick. 'I bet old George was shouting at the driver to go as fast as possible!'

'Look – there's Kirrin Cottage – I can just see the chimneys in the distance,' said Dick. 'Smoke is coming from one of them.'

'Funny – why only one?' said Julian. 'They usually have the kitchen fire going, and a fire in Uncle Quentin's study. He's such a cold mortal when he's working out all his wonderful figures for his inventions.'

'Perhaps he's away,' said Anne, hopefully. She was rather afraid of George's hasty-tempered father. 'I should think Uncle Quentin could do with a holiday at times – he's always buried in rows and rows of figures.'

'Well, let's hope we don't disturb him too much,' said Julian. 'It's hard on Aunt Fanny if he keeps yelling at everyone. We'll try and be out of doors most of the time.'

They were nearly at Kirrin Cottage now. As they came near to the front gate, they saw George come running down the garden path. To Julian's horror, she was crying bitterly.

'I say – it does look as if something has happened to old Timmy,' he said. 'It's not like George to cry – she *never* cries! What *can* have happened?'

In great alarm they began to run, and Anne

shouted as she ran, 'George! George, what's the matter? Is something wrong with Timmy? What's happened?'

'We can't stay at home,' wept George. 'We've got to go away somewhere. Something awful's happened!'

'What is it? Tell us, you idiot!' said Dick, in alarm. 'For goodness' sake, what's happened? Is Timmy run over, or something?'

'No – it isn't Timmy,' said George, wiping her eyes with her hand, because, as usual, she had no handkerchief. 'It's Joanna – Joanna, our dear, darling Joanna!'

'What's the matter with her?' asked Julian, thinking of all kinds of dreadful things. 'GEORGE, will you please TELL US!'

'Joanna's got scarlet fever,' said George, sniffing dolefully. 'So we can't be at Kirrin Cottage.'

'Why not?' demanded Dick. 'Joanna will have to go to hospital – and we can all stay at Kirrin Cottage and help your mother. Poor old Joanna! But cheer up, George, scarlet fever isn't much of a thing to have nowadays. Come on – let's go in and see if we can comfort your mother. Poor old Aunt Fanny, she *will* be in a stew – with all of us four cousins at Kirrin Cottage too! Never mind, we can—'

'Stop jabbering, Dick,' said George, exasperated. 'We *can't* stay at Kirrin Cottage. Mother wouldn't even let me go in at the front door! She shooed me away, and said I was to wait in the garden, the doctor was coming in a minute or two.'

Someone called to them from a window of Kirrin Cottage. 'Are you all there, children? Julian, come here, will you?'

They all went into the garden, and saw their Aunt Fanny, George's mother, leaning out of a bedroom window.

'Listen, dears,' she said. 'Joanna has scarlet fever, and is waiting for an ambulance to take her to the hospital, and—'

'Aunt Fanny – don't worry. We'll all turn to and help,' called back Julian, cheerfully.

'Dear Julian – you still don't understand,'

said his aunt. 'You see, neither your uncle nor I have had scarlet fever – so we are in quarantine, and mustn't have anyone near us, in case we get it, and give it to them – and that might mean we'd give it to all you four.'

'Would Timmy get it?' asked George, still sniffing dolefully.

'No, of course not. Don't be silly, George,' said her mother. 'Did you ever hear of dogs getting measles or whooping-cough or any of *our* illnesses? Timmy isn't in quarantine. You can get him out of his kennel as soon as you like.'

George's face lit up immediately, and she shot round the back of the house, yelling Timmy's name. At once there came a volley of barks!

'Aunt Fanny – what do you want us to do?' asked Julian. 'We can't go to my home, because Mummy and Daddy are still in Germany. Should we go to a hotel?'

'No, dear, I'll think of somewhere you can all go,' said his aunt. 'Good gracious, what a row

Timmy is making! Poor Joanna – she has such a splitting headache.'

'Here's the ambulance,' cried Anne, as a big hospital van drew up outside the gate. Aunt Fanny disappeared from the window at once to tell Joanna. The ambulance man went up to the front door, his mate behind him, carrying a stretcher. The four children watched in surprise. 'He's gone to fetch dear old Joanna,' said Julian. And sure enough the stretcher was soon carried out with Joanna lying on it, wrapped round in blankets. She waved to the children as the men carried her out.

'Soon be back!' she said, in rather a croaky voice. 'Help Mrs Kirrin if you can. So sorry about this!'

'Poor Joanna,' said Anne, with tears in her eyes. 'Get better quickly, Joanna. We shall miss you so!'

The ambulance door closed and the van went off very smoothly and quietly.

'Whatever shall we do?' said Dick, turning to Julian. 'Can't go home – can't stay here! Oh, here's TIMMY! How are you, Tim, old thing? Thank goodness *you* can't get scarlet fever. Don't knock me over, old boy. Down! Gosh, what a licky dog you are!'

Timmy was the only one in high spirits. The others felt really down in the dumps. Oh dear – what was to be done? Where could they go? What a horrid beginning to a holiday! Down, Timmy, DOWN! What a dog! Anyone would think he had never even *heard* of scarlet fever! WILL you get down, Timmy!

[2]

Plans for the Five

George was still looking upset. What with her fears that Timmy might be ill or hurt, and now her distress at Joanna being carried off in the ambulance, she wasn't much help to anyone.

'Do stop sniffing, George,' said Anne. 'We've just got to be sensible and think of some way out of this.'

'I'm going to find Mother,' said George. 'I don't care if she's in quarantine or not.'

'Oh no you're not,' said Julian, taking her firmly by the arm. 'You jolly well know what quarantine means. When you had whooping-cough *you* weren't allowed to come near any of us, in case we caught it too. You were infectious, and that meant that you didn't have close contact with anybody for at least a few weeks. I think it's only two weeks for scarlet fever, so it won't be too bad.'

George went on sniffing, trying to pull away from Julian's hand. Julian winked at Dick, and said something that made George pull herself together at once.

'Well, REALLY, George!' he said. 'You're acting *just* like a weepy girl. Poor Georgina! Poor little old Georgina!'

George stopped sniffing immediately and glared at Julian in fury. If there was one thing she really hated it was to be told she was acting like a silly *girl*! And how *awful* to be called by her real name, Georgina! She gave Julian a hefty punch, and he grinned at her, warding her off.

'That's better,' he said. 'Cheer up! Just look at Timmy staring at you in amazement. He's hardly ever heard you crying before.'

'I'm NOT crying!' said George. 'I'm – well, I'm upset about Joanna. And it's awful to have nowhere to go.'

'I can hear Aunt Fanny telephoning,' said

Anne, who had very sharp ears. She fondled Timmy's head, and he licked her hand. He had already given everyone a wonderful welcome, whining with pleasure, and licking lavishly. He had been mad with joy to see George again, and was surprised and sad to find her looking so miserable now. Dear Timmy – he certainly belonged to the Five!

'Let's sit down and wait for Aunt Fanny,' said Julian, settling himself on the grass. 'We look a bit silly standing staring at Kirrin Cottage like this. Aunt Fanny will come to the window in a minute. She is sure to have thought of a good idea for us. TIMMY! I shan't stay sitting down for long if you keep licking my neck like that. I shall send you for a towel in a minute, so that I can wipe it dry!'

The little joke made everyone feel better. They were all sitting on the grass now, and Timmy went lovingly from one to the other. All his family back again – it was too good to be true! He settled down at last, his head on George's knee, George's hand caressing his ears.

'Aunt Fanny's put down the telephone,' said Anne. 'Now she'll come to the window.'

'You've got ears like a dog – just as good as Timmy's,' said Dick. '*I* couldn't hear a thing!'

'Here's Mother!' said George, and leapt to her feet as Aunt Fanny came to the window and leaned out.

'It's all right, dears,' she called. 'I've been able to arrange something for you. I have been telephoning the scientist that your father has been working with, George – Professor Hayling. He was coming here for a day or two, and when I told him he couldn't, because we're in quarantine, he at once said that *you* must all go *there* – and that Tinker, his son – you remember him, don't you – would be delighted to have your company!'

'Tinker! Goodness, yes, I shall never forget him – or his monkey either!' said Julian. 'He's the boy who owns that old lighthouse at Demon's Rocks, isn't he? We went to stay there with him, and had a marvellous time.'

'Well – you're not staying at the lighthouse,

I'm afraid,' said his aunt, from the window. 'Apparently a storm blew up one night and damaged it, and it's not safe to live in any more.'

Groans from all the Five, of course, Timmy joining in as usual! 'Where are we to go then? To Tinker's *home*?' said Dick.

'Yes. You can get a bus from here, at Little Hollow, that will take you almost to Big Hollow, where Professor Hayling lives,' said Aunt Fanny. 'You're to go today. I'm so very sorry about this, dears, but it's just one of those things we have to put up with. I'm sure you'll have a good time with Tinker, and that monkey of his. What was it called now?'

'Mischief,' said everyone together, and Anne smiled in delight to think of being with the naughty little creature, and watching its wicked ways.

'The bus will pass in ten minutes,' said her aunt. 'And have a good time, dears, and send me a card or two. I'll let you know how we get on – but I really don't think that either your uncle or I will catch scarlet fever, so don't worry. And I'll send you some money to spend. You'd better run for the bus now.'

'Right, Aunt Fanny, and thank you!' called Julian. 'I'll look after everyone and keep them in order – especially old George. Don't worry at all – and I do hope you or Uncle don't go down with the fever. Good-bye.'

They all went to the front gate where the luggage still stood. 'Anne, go out into the road and stop the bus when it comes,' ordered Julian. 'Then Dick and I will heave our bags aboard. Gosh, I wonder what it will be like with old Tinker at Big Hollow. I've a feeling it might be rather exciting!'

'*I* don't think so,' said George, mournfully. 'I like Tinker all right – he's funny – and that little monkey is a darling – such a *naughty* little thing too. But oh dear, don't you remember what it was like when Tinker's *father* came to stay with us? It was *awful*! He never remembered to come to meals, and was always losing his coat or his hanky or his money, and losing his temper too. I got very tired of him.'

'Well, he'll probably get very tired of *us*!' said Julian. 'He won't find it very funny to have four kids parked on him, especially if he's in the middle of difficult work – to say nothing of a rather large, licky dog leaping round the house as well.'

'Timmy isn't likely to lick *him*,' said George, at once, and put on one of her scowls. '*I* didn't like Tinker's father at all.'

'Well, don't look like a thunderstorm,' said Julian. 'I don't expect he'll like any of *us* either. But it's kind of him to let us come and stay at Big Hollow, and we're jolly well going to behave ourselves, see? There's to be no back-chat from *you*, George – even if he dares to disapprove of Timmy!'

'He'd better *not*,' said George. 'In fact, I've a good mind not to go. I think I'll live in the summer-house with Timmy, at the bottom of the garden!'

'You will NOT!' said Julian, taking firm hold

of her arm. 'You'll play fair, come with us, and behave properly! Listen, there's the bus. Come on, we'll all wave, and hope there are a few empty seats.'

Anne had already stopped the bus, and run round to ask the driver if he would help with the bags. He knew the children very well, and leapt down at once.

'You're going back to school pretty quick!' he said. 'I thought the schools had only just broken up.'

'They have,' said Julian, 'but we're off to stay at Big Hollow. The bus goes there, doesn't it?'

'Yes, we go right through the village of Big Hollow,' said the driver, carrying three bags at once, much to Julian's envy. 'Whereabouts are you staying there?'

'At Professor Hayling's house,' said Julian. 'I think that's called Big Hollow too, like the village.'

'Ah, we pass it,' said the driver. 'I'll stop the bus just outside and give you a hand with your things again. My word – you'll have to mind your ps and qs there – old Professor Hayling's a bit peculiar, you know. Goes off the handle properly if things don't go his way! Once a horse got into his garden and believe it or not he chased that horse for two miles, shouting at it all the way. And bless me, when he got back home, tired out, there was that horse, chewing up his garden again. The horse was cute – he'd taken a short cut back. Yes – you be careful how you behave at Big Hollow. The old man might get cross and pop you into one of his strange machines and grind you up into little pieces!'

The four children laughed. 'Oh, the old Professor is all right,' said Julian. 'A bit forgetful, like most people who work with their brains all the time. My brain goes fairly slowly – but my Uncle Quentin's goes about a hundred miles an hour, and I bet the Professor's does too! *We'll* be all right!'

Away went the bus, bumping over the road from Kirrin and Little Hollow, and on to Big Hollow. The four children gazed out of the windows as they passed alongside the shore, where the sea shone as blue as cornflowers, and once more saw Kirrin Island out in the big bay.

'Wish we were going *there*!' sighed George. 'We'll have to take a picnic meal there sometime, and enjoy ourselves. I'd like old Tinker to visit my island. He may have a lighthouse of his own, but having an island is MUCH *better*!'

'I think I agree with you,' said Julian. 'Tinker's lighthouse is certainly lovely and all on its own, and the view from it is amazing – but there's something about Kirrin Island that I *love*. Islands are quite different from anything else!'

'Yes. They are,' said Anne. '*I'd* like one too. A very little one, so that I could see all round it at one glance. And I'd like one little cave to sleep in – just big enough for *me*.'

'You'd soon be lonely, Anne,' said Dick, giving his sister a friendly pat. 'You love to have people round you, you like to be friendly!'

'So does Timmy!' said Julian, as Timmy left his place by George's knee and went to sniff at a string bag held by an old man, who at once fondled the big dog, and fumbled for a biscuit out of a paper bag. 'Timmy doesn't mind how many people there are around, so long as one or two of them have a biscuit or a bone to hand out!'

'Come to heel, Timmy,' said George. 'You're not to go round begging, telling people you are half-starved! I should think you eat more than any other dog in Kirrin. Who eats the cat's dinner whenever he can, I should like to know?'

Timmy gave George a loving lick and settled down beside her, his head on her toes. He got up politely every time someone entered or left the bus. The driver was most impressed.

'I wish all dogs were as good on my bus as yours,' he told George. 'You'd better get ready to jump out. Our next stop is supposed to be a little way beyond Big Hollow, but I'll stop for a moment, and you can get out.'

'Thanks a lot,' said Julian, gratefully, and when the bus stopped with a jerk a minute later, all the Five were ready to jump out.

The bus went on, and left them standing outside a large wooden gate. The drive from it led steeply downwards, and a large house could just be seen hidden in a hollow by great trees.

'Big Hollow!' said Julian. 'Well – here we are. What a strange place – sort of mysterious and brooding. Now to find old Tinker! I bet he'll be pleased to see us all, especially Timmy! Help me with the bags, Dick!'

Big Hollow – and Tinker and Mischief again!

The four children and Timmy went through the big heavy gate, which groaned loudly. Timmy was very startled to hear the mournful creak, and barked sharply.

'Sh!' said George. 'You'll get into trouble with the Professor, Timmy, if you raise your voice like that. I expect we'll have to talk in whispers, so as not to disturb the Professor – so just see if you can whisper too.'

Timmy gave a small whine. He knew he couldn't whisper! He trotted at George's heel as they all went down the steep drive to the house. It was a curious house, built sideways to the drive, and had astonishingly few windows.

'I expect Professor Hayling is afraid of people

peering in at his work,' said Anne. 'It's very, very secret, isn't it?'

'I know he uses miles and miles of figures,' said Dick. 'Tinker told me one day that his monkey Mischief once chewed up a page of figures when he was very small – and Professor Hayling chased him for a whole hour, hoping to catch him and find even a *few* bits of paper still in his mouth, so that he could rescue at least part of his figures. But Mischief fled down a rabbit hole and didn't come up for two days, so it wasn't any good.'

Everyone smiled at the thought of poor Mischief hiding down a rabbit hole. '*You* couldn't do that, Timmy old thing!' said Julian. 'So just be careful of any paper *you* eat.'

'He wouldn't be so silly,' said George, at once. 'He knows perfectly well what's eatable and what's not.'

'Ha! *Does* he!' said Anne. 'Well, I'd just like to know what kind of food he thought my blue slipper was that he chewed up last hols!'

'Don't tell tales on him,' said George. 'He only chewed it because someone shut him in your bedroom and he hadn't anything else to do.'

'Woof,' said Timmy, quite agreeing. He gave Anne's hand a little lick, as if to say, 'Very sorry, Anne – but I was so *bored*!'

'*Dear* Timmy! I wouldn't mind if you chewed up *all* my slippers!' said Anne. 'But it would be nice if you chose the very *oldest* ones!'

Timmy suddenly stopped and looked into the bushes. He gave a low growl! George put her hand on his collar at once. She was always afraid of snakes in the springtime.

'It might be an adder!' she said. 'The dog next door trod on one last year, so I heard, and his leg swelled up terribly, and he was in great pain. Come away now, Timmy – it's an adder, with poison in its fangs!'

But Timmy went on growling. Then he suddenly stood still and sniffed hard. He gave an excited whimper and pulled away from George, jumping into the bushes – and out came, not a snake, but Mischief, Tinker's bright-eyed little monkey!

He at once leapt on to the dog's broad back, put his little monkey fingers under Timmy's collar, and chattered in delight. Timmy nearly dislocated his neck to twist his head round to lick him!

'Mischief!' cried everyone at once, in real delight. 'You've come to welcome us!'

And the little monkey, jabbering away excitedly in monkey language, leapt first on to George's shoulder, and then on to Julian's. He pulled Julian's hair, twisted his right ear round, and then leapt from him to Dick, and on to Anne's shoulder. He cuddled into her neck, his eyes bright and brown, looking very happy.

'Oh! *Isn't* he pleased to see us again!' said Anne, delighted. 'Mischief, where's Tinker?'

Mischief jumped off Anne's shoulder and scampered down the drive as if he quite understood all that Anne had said. The children raced after him – and then a loud voice suddenly roared at them from one side of the drive.

'What are you doing here? Clear out! This is private ground. I'll fetch the police. Clear OUT!'

The Five stopped still in fright – and then Julian saw who it was – Professor Hayling! He stepped forward at once. 'Good-afternoon,' he said. 'I hope we didn't disturb you, but you did tell my aunt we could come here.'

'Your aunt? Who's your aunt? I don't know any aunt!' roared the Professor. 'You're sight-seers, that's what you are! Come to pry into my work, just because there was a piece about it in some silly paper! You're the third lot today. Clear out, I tell you – and take that dog too. How DARE you!'

'But – don't you *really* know us?' said Julian, very startled. 'You came to stay at our house, you know, and—'

'Stuff and nonsense! I haven't been away for years!' shouted the Professor. Mischief, the monkey, was so frightened that he leapt away into the bushes, making a funny little crying noise.

'I hope he fetches Tinker,' said Julian, in a low voice to Dick. 'The Professor has forgotten who we are, and why we've come. Let's retreat a bit.'

But as they went cautiously back up the steep path, followed by the angry Professor, a loud voice hailed them, and Tinker came racing up with Mischief on his shoulder, clinging to his hair. So the little monkey had gone to fetch him. 'Good for *him*!' thought Julian, pleased.

'Dad! Don't yell at our friends like that!' cried Tinker, dancing about in front of his angry father. 'You asked them here yourself, you know you did!'

'I DID NOT!' said the Professor. 'Who are they?'

'Well, George, that girl, is the daughter of Mr Kirrin, and the others are his niece and nephews. And that's their dog, Timmy. And you asked them all here because Mr and Mrs Kirrin are in quarantine for scarlet fever,' shouted Tinker, still dancing about in front of his father.

'Stop jigging about like that,' said the Professor, crossly. '*I* don't remember asking them. I would have told Jenny the housekeeper if I had.'

'You did tell her!' shouted Tinker, still jigging about, with Mischief the monkey jigging too in delight. 'She's angry because you left your breakfast and now it's almost dinner-time. She's cleared it away.'

'Bless us – so *that*'s why I feel so hungry and cross!' said Professor Hayling, and he began to laugh. He had a tremendous laugh, and the children couldn't help laughing too. What an odd fellow – so brainy, such a fine scientist – with the most enormous amount of knowledge in his head – and yet no memory for such ordinary things as breakfast and visitors and telephone calls.

'It was just a misunderstanding,' said Julian, politely. 'It was very, very kind of you to invite us here when we can't be at home because of the scarlet fever. We'll try not to be a nuisance, and if there's anything we can do to help you, please ask us. We'll make as little noise as possible, and keep out of your way, of course.'

'You hear that, Tinker?' said Professor Hayling, suddenly swinging round on the startled

Tinker. 'Why can't you do the same – make very little noise, and keep out of my way? You know I'm very busy now – on a MOST IMPORTANT project.' He turned to Julian. 'You'll be very welcome if you keep Tinker out of my way. And NOBODY – absolutely NOBODY – is to go up into that tower. Understand?'

They all looked up to where he was pointing, and saw a tall, slender tower rising up amid the trees. It had curious tentacle-like rods sticking out at the top, and these shook slightly in the breeze.

'And don't ask me questions about it,' went on the Professor, looking fiercely at George. 'Your father's the only other man who knows what it's for, and *he* knows how to keep his mouth shut.'

'None of us would *dream* of prying,' said Julian. 'It's very, very kind of you to offer to have us here, and do believe me when I say we shan't be any trouble to you at all – but a help if you'll allow us.'

'Ah well, you sound a sensible fellow, I must

say,' said the Professor, who had now calmed down, and looked quite peaceable. 'Well, I'll say good-bye for now and go and have my breakfast. I hope it's fried eggs and bacon. I'm very hungry.'

'Dad – Jenny's cleared your breakfast AWAY! I told you that before!' said Tinker in despair. 'It's almost dinner-time, now.'

'Ah good – good!' said the Professor. 'I'll come at once.'

And he led the way indoors, followed by the five children, with Timmy and Mischief, all looking rather worried. Really, nobody *ever* knew what the Professor was going to do or say next!

Jenny certainly had a good dinner for them all. There was a large and delicious stew with carrots, onions and peas swimming in the gravy, and plenty of potatoes. Everyone tucked in well, and Mischief, who loved the peas, took quite a few from Tinker's plate, his little paw creeping up, and neatly snatching a pea from the gravy.

The girls went out to help bring in the next course, which was a big steamed pudding with plenty of raisins in it. Mischief at once jigged up and down in delight, for he loved raisins. He leapt on to the table, and received a sharp smack from the Professor, who unfortunately smacked the pudding dish at the same time, making the pudding jump in the air.

'Good gracious, Dad – we nearly lost the pudding!' cried Tinker. 'And it's my favourite. Oh, don't give us such *small* pieces! Mischief, get off the table. You are NOT to put your paw into the sauce!'

So Mischief disappeared under the table, where he received quite a lot of raisins from various kindly hands, unseen by the Professor. Timmy felt rather left out. He was under the table too, having been rather scared by the Professor's angry voice, but as he didn't very much like raisins, he wasn't as lucky as Mischief.

'Ha – I enjoyed that!' said the Professor, having cleaned his plate thoroughly. 'Nothing like a good breakfast!'

'It was midday dinner, Dad!' said Tinker. 'You don't have pudding at breakfast.'

'Dear me, of course not – that was pudding!' said his father, and laughed his great laugh. 'Now you can all do exactly what you like, so long as you do NOT go into my study, or my workroom, or that tower. AND DON'T MEDDLE WITH ANYTHING! Mischief, get off the water jug, you'll upset it. Can't you teach that monkey some table manners, Tinker?'

And with that he marched out of the room, and disappeared into some mysterious passage that apparently led to his study or workroom. Everyone heaved a sigh of relief.

'We'll clear away and then I'll show you your rooms,' said Tinker. 'I do hope you won't find it too dull here.'

Dull, Tinker! You needn't worry! There is far too much excitement waiting for the Five – and you too! Just wait a bit, and see!

[4]

Jenny has a very good idea

Tinker raced out to the kitchen to fetch a tray or two. He made a most peculiar noise as he went, and for a moment Timmy looked extremely startled.

'Goodness – don't say that Tinker *still* has that awful habit of pretending to be some kind of car!' groaned Julian. 'How on earth does his father put up with it? What's he think he is now? A motorbike by the sound of it.'

There was a sudden crash and a loud yell. The Five raced down the kitchen passage to find out what had happened, Timmy at the front.

'Accident!' bellowed Tinker, scrambling up from the floor. 'I took the bend too quickly, and my front wheel skidded, and I went bang into a wall! I've bent my mudguard.'

'Tinker – do you mean to say you're *still*

being silly enough to pretend to be cars and motorbikes and tractors and lorries?' demanded Julian. 'You nearly drove us all mad, driving about all over the house, when you stayed with us. Have you *got* to be a machine of some sort?'

'Yes,' said Tinker, rubbing one of his arms. 'It sort of comes over me, and away I go. You should have heard me yesterday, being a lorry absolutely *loaded* with new cars for delivery. Dad *really* thought it was a great lorry and he rushed out into the drive to send it away. But it was only me. I hooted too – like this!'

And the sound of a loud and a deep hooter immediately filled the passage! Julian shoved Tinker into the kitchen and shut the door.

'I should have thought that your father would have been driven completely mad by now!' he said. 'Now, you just shut up. Can't you grow up a bit?'

'No,' said Tinker, sullenly. 'I don't want to grow up. I might be like my father and forget to eat my meals, and go out with one sock on and one off. And I'd hate to forget my meals. Just think how *awful* it would be! I'd always be hungry.'

Julian couldn't help laughing. 'Pick up your tray, and help to clear away!' he said. 'And if you simply can't HELP being a car sometimes, for goodness' sake go outside! It sounds terrible in the house. You're much too good at awful noises.'

'Oh, am I *really* good?' said Tinker, pleased. 'I suppose you wouldn't like to hear me being one of those new planes that go over here sometimes, making a funny droning noise?'

'No, I WOULD NOT!' said Julian, firmly. 'Now will you PLEASE get that tray, Tinker. And tell Mischief to get off my right foot. He seems to think it's a chair.'

But Mischief clung to Julian's ankle and refused to move. 'All right, all right,' said Julian. 'I shall just have to walk about all day with you riding on my foot.'

'If you *stamp* as you walk, he soon gets off,' remarked Tinker.

'Why didn't you tell me that just now?' asked Julian, and stamped a few steps round the room. Mischief leapt off his foot at once and sat on a table, making an angry noise.

'He sits on Dad's foot for ages, even when he walks about,' said Tinker. 'But Dad doesn't even notice him there! He even sat on Dad's head once, and Dad thought he was wearing his hat indoors and tried to take it off. But it was only Mischief there!'

That made everyone laugh. 'Now come on,' said Julian, briskly. 'We really must clear away the dinner things. We three boys will carry out the loaded trays and you girls can wash up. And DON'T let Mischief think he can carry teapots or milk jugs.'

Jenny was very pleased with their help. She was short and fat, and waddled rather than walked, but managed to get here and there remarkably quickly.

'I'll show your visitors their bedrooms after we've cleared,' she said. 'But, you know, Tinker, those mattresses we sent to be remade haven't come back yet. I've told your father a dozen times to telephone about them, but I'm sure he hasn't remembered.'

'Oh JENNY!' said Tinker, in dismay. 'That means that the two beds for visitors can't be slept in! What ever are we to do?'

'Well, your Dad will have to ring up for new mattresses to be sent today,' said Jenny. 'Maybe they would send them out by van.'

Tinker immediately became a furniture van and rushed down the passage, into the dining-room and back again, Mischief following him in delight. He made a noise exactly like a slow-moving van, and the children couldn't help laughing.

The Professor shot out of his study, his hands to his ears. 'TINKER! COME HERE!'

'No thanks,' said Tinker, warily. 'Sorry, Father. I was a van bringing the mattresses you forgot to order for the beds for visitors.'

But the Professor didn't seem to hear. He advanced on Tinker, who fled upstairs with Mischief leaping after him. Professor Hayling turned on Jenny.

'Can't you keep the children quiet? What do I pay you for?'

'Cleaning, cooking and washing,' she said, briskly. 'But I'm not a nurse for children. That Tinker of yours could do with half a dozen nurses, and he'd still be a nuisance to you while he was in the house. Why don't you let him take his tent and camp out in the field with his friends? It's hot weather and those new mattresses haven't come, and they'd all love it. I can cook for the children and take them out meals – or they could come and fetch them.'

The Professor looked as if he could give Jenny a big hug. The children waited eagerly to see what he would say. Camping out – that would be fun in this weather – and honestly, living in the same house as the Professor wasn't going to be much fun. Timmy gave a little whine as if to say 'Fine idea! Let's go at once!'

'Good idea, Jenny, VERY good idea!' said Professor Hayling. 'But that monkey's to camp out too. Then perhaps he won't jump in at my workroom window and fiddle about with my models!'

He marched back into his study and slammed the door so hard that the whole house shook. Timmy was startled and gave a yelp. Mischief the monkey leapt up the stairs again, howling in fright. Tinker began to dance round in joy, and very firmly Jenny took hold of him and propelled him into her big, clean kitchen.

'Wait, Jenny, I've remembered something. We've only one tent, and that's mine, a small one. I'll have to ask Dad if I can get two big ones!' And before anyone could stop him he was banging at the Professor's door, then flung it open, and shouted out his request.

'WE WANT TWO MORE TENTS, DAD. CAN I BUY THEM?'

'For goodness' sake, Tinker, clear out and leave me alone!' shouted his father. 'Buy SIX tents if you want them, but GET OUT!'

'Ooh, thanks, Dad!' said Tinker, and was just slipping out of the door when his father yelled again.

'But what on earth do you want TENTS for?'

Tinker slammed the door and grinned at the others. 'I'd better buy Dad a new memory. He's only *just* told us we can camp out, and he knows there's only my very small tent – almost a toy one.'

'I'm glad we shan't be in the house,' said Anne. 'I know what a nuisance it is to *George's* father to have us around, playing about. We'll be better out of the way.'

'Camping out again!' said George, very pleased. 'Let's catch the bus back home and get our own tents. I've got them all stored away in the garden shed. We can just ask Jim the carrier to take them in his van, when we've found them.'

'He's calling here today – I'll give him the message for you, if you like,' said Jenny. 'The sooner you get the tents, the better. It was a kind thought of the Professor's to ask you all here, but I just knew it wouldn't work! You'll be all right out in the field at the back of the house – he won't hear a thing, not even if you all yell together! So you get your tents and put them up, and I'll see what I can find in the way of ground-sheets and rugs.'

'Don't bother, Jenny,' said Julian. 'We've got all those things – we've often camped out before.'

'I only hope there aren't any cows in the field,' said Anne. 'Last time we camped, a cow put its head into my tent opening, and mooed. I woke up with such a jump, and I was too scared to move.'

'I don't think there are any cows,' said Jenny, laughing. 'Now I MUST get on with the washing-up, so will you bring out the dinner things please – but don't let that monkey carry anything breakable, for goodness' sake! He tried to balance the teapot on his head last week – and that was the end of the teapot!'

Soon everyone was hard at work, clearing away, and helping Jenny with the washing-up.

'I shall like camping out,' Anne told her. 'I'd be scared of staying here in the house. Professor Hayling is a bit like my Uncle Quentin, you know – forgetful, and quick-tempered and a bit shouty.'

'Oh, you don't want to be scared of him,' said Jenny, handing Anne a dish to dry. 'He's kind, for all his crossness when he's upset. Why, when my mother was ill, he paid for her to go into a really good nursing-home – and believe it or not, he gave me money to buy her fruit and flowers!'

'Oh goodness – that reminds me – we MUST send Joanna some flowers,' said George. 'She has scarlet fever, you know. That's why we're here.'

'Well, you go and telephone the florist,' said Jenny. 'I'll finish this job.'

But George was rather afraid that Professor Hayling might rush out to see who was using the telephone!

'I'm sure we can buy flowers in Kirrin village, and have them sent,' she said. 'We've got to go and get our things ready for Jim, and I can order the flowers then. We might as well come back on our bicycles – they'd be useful here.'

'Well, you'd better go now,' said Jenny, 'or

you won't be back in time for tea, and *then* there'd be trouble.'

'*I'll* bring back Anne's bicycle,' said Julian. 'I can easily manage it beside mine as I ride back.'

'Look, George,' said Dick, 'you needn't come. I'll order the flowers and I can bring your bike back too. So you stay with Anne.' Reluctantly George agreed.

Off went Julian and Dick, leaving Tinker and the girls to help Jenny. But Jenny soon sent Tinker off, afraid that he would drop things and break them.

'You go and be a nice, quiet, purring Rolls-Royce at the bottom of the garden,' she said. 'And when you think you've done thirty miles or so, come back for petrol.'

'Lemonade, you mean!' said Tinker, with a grin. 'All right. I haven't been a Rolls-Royce for a long time. Dad won't hear me right at the bottom of the garden!'

Off he went, and Jenny and the girls finished the washing-up. Mischief was a nuisance and went off with the teaspoons. He leapt to the top of a high cupboard, and dropped them there.

Tinker suddenly put his head in at the window. 'Come on out to the field where we're going to put up our tents,' he called to Anne and George. 'We'll choose a nice sheltered spot. Buck up! You must have finished washing-up by now. I'm tired of being a Rolls-Royce!'

'You go with him, Anne,' said George. 'I don't feel like it just now.'

So down the garden went the two children and out through a gate at the bottom into a big field.

'Good gracious!' said Tinker, staring. 'Look at all those caravans coming in at the gate at the other end of the field. I'll soon send them off. It's OUR field!' And away he marched to the gate in the distance.

'Come BACK, Tinker,' shouted Anne. 'You'll get into trouble if you interfere. COME BACK!'

But Tinker marched on, his head held high. Ha – he'd soon tell the caravan folk it was HIS field!

[5]

The travelling circus

Anne watched anxiously as Tinker went on and on over the field. There were now four caravans trundling in the far gate, and behind them, in the lane, were vans – enormous vans – all with enormously large words painted on them.

TAPPER'S TRAVELLING CIRCUS

'Hoo! I'll tell Mr Tapper what I think of him, coming into *my* field!' said Tinker to himself. Mischief the monkey was on his shoulder, jogging up and down as Tinker marched along, muttering furiously.

Four or five children from the caravans looked at him curiously as he marched along. One small boy rushed up to him, shouting in delight to see the monkey.

'A monkey, look, a monkey!' he cried. 'Much smaller than our chimp. What's he called, boy?'

'Mind your own business,' said Tinker. 'Where's Mr Tapper?'

'Mr Tapper? Oh, you mean our grandad!' said the boy. 'He's over there, look, beside that big van. Better not talk to him now. He's busy!'

Tinker walked over to the van and addressed the man there. He was rather fierce-looking and had a long, bushy beard, enormous eyebrows that hung down over his eyes, a rather small nose, and only one ear. He looked inquiringly down at Tinker, and put out his hand to Mischief.

'My monkey might bite you,' said Tinker, at once. 'He doesn't like strangers.'

'I'm no stranger to *any* monkey,' said the man, in a deep-down voice. 'There's isn't a monkey in the world, nor a chimp either, that wouldn't come to me if I called it. Nor a gorilla, see?'

'Well, *my* monkey won't come to you,' said Tinker, angrily. 'But what I've come to say is—'

Before he could finish his sentence, the man made a curious noise in his throat – rather like Mischief did when he was pleased about anything. Mischief looked at the man in surprised delight – and then leapt straight from Tinker's shoulder to his, nuzzling against his neck, making little crooning noises. Tinker was so amazed that he stared without saying a word.

'See?' said the man. 'He's my little friend already. Don't gawp so, little fellow. I've trained the monkey family all my life. You lend me this little chap and I'll teach him to ride a small tricycle in two days.'

'Come here, Mischief!' said Tinker, amazed and angry at the monkey's behaviour. But Mischief cuddled down still farther into the big man's neck. The man hauled him out and handed him to Tinker.

'There you are,' he said. 'Nice little fellow he is. What is it you wanted to say to me?'

'I've come to say that this field belongs to my father, Professor Hayling,' said Tinker. 'And you've no right to bring your caravans here. So please take them all out. My friends and I are planning to camp out here.'

'Well, I've no objection to that,' said the big man, good-temperedly. 'You choose your own corner, young man. If you don't interfere with us, we shan't interfere with you!'

A boy of about Tinker's age came sidling up, and looked at Tinker and Mischief with interest. 'Is he selling you that monkey, Grandad?' he asked.

'No I'm NOT!' almost shouted Tinker. 'I came to tell you and your caravans to clear out. This field belongs to my family.'

'Ah, but we've an old licence to come here every ten years, and show our circus,' said the bearded man. 'And believe it or not, there's been a Tapper's circus in this field every ten years since the year 1648. So you just run home and make no silly fuss, young man.'

'You're a fibber!' cried Tinker, losing his temper. 'I'll tell the police! I'll tell my father! I'll—'

'Don't you talk to my grandad like that!'

shouted the boy, standing beside the old man. 'I'll hit you if you do!'

'I'll say what I like!' shouted Tinker, his temper now quite lost. 'And just you shut up!'

The very next moment Tinker found himself flat on his back on the grass. The boy had shot out his fist and hit Tinker hard in the chest! He struggled to his feet, red in the face, quite furious.

The old man fended him away. 'Don't you be silly now, boy,' he said. 'This youngster is a Tapper, like me, and he'll never give in. You go home and be sensible. We're not going to take notice of a hot-headed little kid like you. Our circus is coming in this here field, just like it has for years and years!'

He turned and walked to the nearest car-avan. It was drawn by horses, and he clicked to them. They strained forward and the car-avan followed. Others behind began to move too. The circus boy put his tongue out at Tinker. 'Sucks to you!' he said. 'Nobody gets the better of my grandad – or of me either! Still

– it was plucky of you to go for him. I enjoyed it.'

'Shut up!' said Tinker, alarmed to find himself very near to tears. 'You just wait till my dad tells the police! You'll all go out much quicker than you came in – and one of these days I'll knock *you* down!'

He turned and ran back to the gate. He wondered what to do. He had so often heard his father say that the field behind their house belonged to him, and that he had let this or that farmer have the grazing rights for his horses and cattle. How DARE the travelling circus come into his father's field?

'I'll tell Dad,' he said to Anne, who was waiting at the gate. '*He* ought to turn them out! It's *our* field and I love it, especially just now when it's so green and beautiful, and the hedges are just going to be covered in white may. I'll tell Dad the boy knocked me down – shot out his fist just like *that* – and down I went. I'd like to do the same to *him*!'

He went into the house, followed by a puzzled Anne.

He looked into the sitting-room and saw George there.

'Tinker! That boy knocked you down!' said Anne, in a horrified voice. 'Why did he do that?'

'Oh – just because I told his grandad to take his caravans away,' said Tinker, feeling rather grand. 'He didn't hurt me at all – just punched me on the chest. Still – I said what I had gone to say.'

'But *will* they take the caravans away out of the field?' asked Anne.

'I told them I'd tell the police,' said Tinker. 'So I bet they'll skedaddle. They haven't any right to be there. It's *our* field!'

'*Are* you going to the police?' asked George, disbelievingly. 'I really don't see why you have to make such a fuss about it all, Tinker. They might make it difficult for *us* to go camping there.'

'But I tell you it's *my* field – Dad's always

said so!' said Tinker. 'He said it wasn't any use to him, so I could consider it my own. And I do. AND we're going to camp in it, whatever anyone says! It's a travelling circus that's coming there, so the old man said.'

'Oh TINKER! How marvellous to have a circus at the bottom of the garden!' said George, her eyes shining, and Anne nodded too. Tinker glared at them.

'JUST like girls to say a thing like that!' he said. 'Would *you* want people trespassing all over a field that belonged to you, with horses neighing and tigers and lions roaring, and bears grunting, and chimpanzees stealing things – and nasty circus boys being rude all the time, ready to knock you down?'

'Oh Tinker! You *do* make it sound so exciting!' said George. 'Will there really be lions and tigers? Suppose one escaped – what a thrill!'

'Well – *I* shouldn't like that,' said Anne, at once. 'I don't particularly want a lion peering in at my window, or a bear clomping round my bedroom!'

'Neither do I,' said Tinker, in a most decided voice. 'That's why I'm going to tell Dad about it. He's got the old document that sets out our rights to that field. He showed me it one day. I'll ask him about it, and if he'll let me see it, I'll take it straight to the police and let them turn out that rude old man and his horrible circus.'

'How do you *know* it's horrible?' asked George. 'It might be really good. I'm sure they'd let us camp in the corner nearest the garden, and we'd get a great view of what's going on all the time. Look – there's your father strolling down the path, smoking a pipe. He never does that if he's busy. It would be a good time to go and ask him about the document. He might even show it to us.'

'All right,' said Tinker, rather sulkily. 'But you'll see I'm right. Come on.'

However, Tinker proved to be quite, quite wrong! His father went to fetch the old, yellowed piece of parchment at once. 'Ha! Here it is!' he said. 'It's pretty valuable too, because it's so old. It dates back quite a few centuries.'

He undid the rather dirty piece of ribbon round it and unrolled it. Neither the girls nor Tinker could read the old-fashioned lettering.

'What does it all say?' asked Anne, with great interest.

'It says that the field known as "Cromwell's Corner" is to be held by the Hayling Family for always,' said Professor Hayling. 'It was given to them by Cromwell because our family allowed them to camp in that field when they sorely needed a rest after battle. It's been ours ever since.'

'So NOBODY else is allowed to camp in it, or use it for grazing or anything, unless we say so!' said Tinker, triumphantly.

'Quite right,' said his father. 'But wait a minute – I seem to remember an odd clause that said something about a travelling show – a show that had rights to camp in the field since about 1066. Not even Cromwell could alter that – it was in the original deeds, long before Cromwell battled in that district. Now let's see – that piece would come about the end, I expect.'

The two girls and Tinker waited while the Professor pored over the old and beautiful lettering. He jabbed his finger on to three lines towards the end.

'Yes. There it is. I'll quote it. Listen! "And let it be known that Ye Travelling Show so-named 'Tapper's Travelling Show', which has always had camping rights, shall still have the right to claim these once every ten years so long as the show travels the country ways – Given under my hand . . ." and so on and so on. Well – I don't expect that Tapper's Travelling Show is going now, all these years and years after the document was drawn up and signed in the year 1648. See – here's the date – if you can read the old figures!'

The children stared at the date, and then glanced up at Tinker. He looked angry and very red in the face. 'You might have told me all that before, Dad,' he said.

'Why?' asked his father, astonished. 'What possible interest can it have for you children?'

'Only that there's a circus called Tapper's

Travelling Circus in that field this very minute,' said Anne. 'And the old man with it is called Tapper – and he said it was his right to be there, and —'

'He was rude to me and I want you to turn out this circus this very day!' said Tinker. '*We* want to camp there.'

'I'm sure Mr Tapper would have no objection to you camping there,' said his father. 'Aren't you being rather silly, Tinker? *You* weren't rude to any of the circus folk, were you?'

Tinker went very red, turned his back and stalked out of the room, Mischief clinging to his neck. He rubbed his chest where the circus boy had punched him. 'Just you wait!' he said in a whisper. 'I'll punch *you* one day!'

'Anne, if you and the others want to camp in the field, I'll go and speak to Mr Tapper,' said the Professor, puzzled by Tinker's behaviour.

'Oh no – it's all right,' said Anne, hastily. 'He has already said that it didn't matter if we camped there. Oh – there are the boys back again. I'll just go and see if they have brought back all our bicycles safely. Thank you for showing us that marvellous old document, Professor!'

And away she went looking rather hot and bothered!

[6]

Getting ready for camping out

Dick and Julian were most interested to hear about Tinker and the travelling circus – and the old, old document.

'You made a bit of a fool of yourself,' said Julian, looking at Tinker. 'Still, there's no harm done, apparently. I vote we go and see where we can put up our tents. Personally, I shall be thrilled to see a bit of circus life so close to me! I wonder how they'll manage to put on a show. I suppose they've everything with them, and can put up a circus ring and a tent and anything else necessary.'

'There are a lot of big vans,' said Anne. 'I went down to have a look about half an hour ago. The field is almost full now, except for one corner near our hedge that I suppose they have left for our tents.'

'I saw the posters about the circus as we cycled back,' said Dick. 'Dead-Shot Dick – Chimpanzee that plays Cricket – the Boneless Man – Madelon and her Beautiful Horses – Monty and Winks, the Clowns – the Dancing Donkey – Mr Wooh, the Wonder Wizard – gosh, it sounded *quite* a circus. I'm glad we can camp in the same field – we shall really see behind the scenes, then.'

'Don't forget there was Charlie the Chimp, and the Bonzo Band,' said Julian. 'What fun if the chimp got loose and peeped in at the kitchen window!'

'It wouldn't be at *all* funny,' said Anne. 'Jenny would run for miles! So would Tinker's monkey!'

'What about putting up our own tents after tea?' said Dick. 'Jim said he'd have them here by tea-time. It's hotter than ever today. I don't feel I can do much at the moment. I just want to laze.'

'Woof,' said Timmy, who was lying down with his head on his paws, panting.

'You feel the same, old chap, don't you?' said Julian, poking him with his toe. 'You're tired out with your long run back from Kirrin, aren't you?'

'The roads were so *dusty*!' said Dick. 'He kept sneezing whenever a car passed us, because the dust got up his nose. Poor old Tim. You really are tired out with that long, long run!'

'Woof!' said Tim, suddenly sitting up straight and pawing vigorously at George. Everyone laughed.

'He says he's not at *all* tired, he wants a walk,' chuckled Dick.

'Well, if he's not tired, I *am*,' said Julian. 'It really was a job sorting out all our things at Kirrin – and cycling all the way back. NO, Timmy – I am NOT going to take you for a walk!'

Timmy whined, and at once Mischief the monkey leapt down from Tinker's shoulder and went to cuddle against the big dog, making small comforting noises. He even put his thin little arms round Timmy's neck!

'You're being just a *little* soppy, Mischief,' said Tinker, but Mischief didn't care. His big friend was sad about something, or he wouldn't have whined. Timmy put out a big red tongue and licked the little creature delicately on his nose. Then he suddenly pricked up his ears, and sat straight up. He had heard a noise from somewhere. So had all the others.

'It's music of some kind,' said Anne. 'Oh – I believe I know what it is!'

'What?' said the others.

'It must be Tapper's Travelling Circus Band practising for opening night,' said Anne.

'Well, that's tomorrow,' yawned George. 'Yes – it does sound like a band. Maybe we shall see the bandsmen after tea, when we put up our tents. I'd like to see the Boneless Man, wouldn't you?'

'NO!' said Anne. 'He'd be all limp and wriggly and horrid – like a worm or a jellyfish! I shan't go and see him. But I'd love to see the horses and the Dancing Donkey. Does he dance to the band, do you think?'

'We'll find out when we go,' said Dick, 'as it opens tomorrow. If Mr Tapper isn't annoyed about Tinker trying to turn them out, he might let us wander round.'

'I don't think I want to come,' said Tinker. 'Mr Tapper was rude – and that boy knocked me flat.'

'Well, I expect I'd do the same if I thought you were being rude to *my* grandad,' said Julian, lazily. 'Now – it's settled, is it, that we go down with our things to the field after tea, and see if we can put up our tents in some sheltered corner?'

'Yes,' said everyone. Dick idly tickled Mischief's nose with a thin blade of grass. The monkey sneezed at once, and then again. He rubbed his little paw across his nose and stared disapprovingly at Dick. Then he sneezed once more.

'Borrow a hanky, old thing,' said Julian. And, to everyone's intense amusement, Mischief leapt across to Dick and neatly pulled his handkerchief out of his pocket! Then he pretended to blow his nose.

Everyone roared with laughter, and Mischief was delighted. 'You'll be stolen to act in a circus one day, if you behave like that!' said Dick, snatching back his hanky. 'The Pickpocket Monkey!'

'He'd be very good in a circus,' said Julian.

'I'd *never* let him join a circus!' said Tinker at once. 'He might have a dreadful life.'

'No. I don't think he would,' said Julian. 'Circus folk love their animals and are proud of them. And after all, if they treated them unkindly, the animals wouldn't be happy or healthy, and couldn't enjoy their acts. *Most* circus people treat their animals like one of the family.'

'What! Even a chimpanzee!' said Anne, in horror.

'They're nice creatures – and very clever,' said Julian. 'Mischief, do *not* remove my handkerchief, please. It was funny the first time, but *not* a second time. Look at him now, trying to undo Timmy's collar.'

'Come and sit quietly by me, Mischief,' ordered Tinker, and the little creature obediently went to him and cuddled on to his knee, making a soft, crooning noise.

'You're a humbug,' said Tinker, fondling him. 'You be careful I don't give you away to the circus, and get an elephant in exchange!'

'Idiot!' said Dick, and everyone laughed at the thought of Tinker and an elephant. What in the world would he do with it?

A voice called from the house. 'Tinker! Jim's here with all the camping things. He's put them in the hall, *just* where your father will fall over them. You'd better come and see to them now.'

'In a few minutes, Jenny!' called back Tinker. 'We're busy.'

'You're a real fibber, Tinker,' said Dick. 'We are *not* busy. You could easily go to find out where the things are, and see if they're all there. There are quite a lot.'

'We'll go in twenty minutes or so,' said Anne, yawning. 'I bet Tinker's father is asleep this hot afternoon. He won't stir out of his study.'

But she was wrong. Professor Hayling was wide awake, and when he had finished his work, he wanted a drink of very cold water. He threw open his study door, strode out towards the kitchen – and fell over a pile of all kinds of camping gear, bringing them down with a tremendous noise.

Jenny rushed out of the kitchen with loud screams of fright, and the Professor bellowed in anger as he took a ground-sheet off his head, and a tent-pole off his back. 'WHAT ARE THESE THINGS? I WILL NOT HAVE THEM IN THE HALL! JENNY! JENNY! Take them down to the bonfire and burn the lot!'

'Our camping things!' cried George, listening in horror. 'Quick! We must get them! Oh, I do hope Tinker's father hasn't hurt himself. Bother, bother, bother!'

While Julian and Dick deftly removed everything that had fallen on to the angry Professor and took it all down the garden, Anne and George comforted him, and made such a fuss of him that he began to feel decidedly less angry. He sat down in a chair and wiped his forehead. 'I hope you've taken all those things down to the bottom of the garden,' he said after a while.

'Yes,' said Tinker, truthfully. 'Er – they're all by the bonfire, but it's not lit yet.'

'I light it myself tomorrow,' said his father, and Tinker heaved a sigh of relief. His father would forget, of course – and anyhow, everything was going to be taken into the camping field after tea.

'Have a cup of nice hot tea,' said Jenny, appearing with a tray of tea things. 'Sit down and drink this. It's newly made. Best thing to have after a fall and a shock.'

She turned and whispered crossly to Tinker, 'Didn't I call to you and tell you the Professor would trip over those things, the poor man? Now you just get your own tea, while I take him into the dining-room and comfort him with a nice hot scone, and a cup of tea!'

'I'll get *our* tea,' said Anne. 'Then we'll set up the tents down in the field, and enjoy ourselves.

And Tinker, don't you get into any more trouble with the circus folk.'

'I'll see he doesn't,' said George, firmly. 'Come on – let's go down to the field while Anne gets the tea. I could do with a bun or two!'

Between them, Dick and Julian had lugged all the things down the garden – two tents, ground-sheets, blankets, tent-pegs and all the rest. Timmy ran with them in excitement, wondering what all the fuss was about. Mischief, of course, leapt to the top of whatever was being carried, and chattered excitedly all the way down the garden.

He got into trouble when he ran off with a tent-peg, but Timmy managed to catch him and make him drop it. Then, very solemnly, Timmy carried the tent-peg to Julian.

'Good dog!' said Julian. 'Just keep an eye on that wicked little monkey, Tim, will you? There are all sorts of things he might run off with!'

So Timmy kept an eye on Mischief, nosing him away whenever he thought the monkey was going to pick up something he shouldn't. Finally Mischief became tired of Timmy's nose and leapt on his back, where, clinging to the dog's collar, he rode just as if he were on horseback. 'Only it's dogback, not horseback,' said George, with a laugh.

'They would make quite a good pair for the circus,' said Dick. 'I bet Mischief could hold on to reins, if Timmy had any!'

'Well, he's not *going* to have any,' said George. 'The next thing would be a whip! Whew! What a lot of things we've got – is that the lot?'

It was, thank goodness. A bell rang out from the house at that moment, and everyone heaved a sigh of relief.

'Tea at last!' said Dick. 'I could drink a whole potful. Come on – we've finished piling up all the things. We'll get busy after tea with them. I can't do a thing more. Don't you agree, Timmy?'

'WOOF!' said Timmy, heartily, and galloped up the garden path at top speed, with Mischief scampering after him.

'Talk about a circus!' said Dick. 'We've a ready-made one here! All right, Anne – we're coming! We're coming!'

[7]

In the circus field

Nobody wanted to spend a long time over tea. They all longed to go down to the field and set up their little camp.

'We shall have a wonderful look-in at what goes on in a circus camp,' said Dick. 'We shall be living so near the circus folk! I do hope Mischief won't get too friendly with the people there. They might take him away with them when they leave.'

'*Indeed* they won't!' said Tinker, fiercely. 'What a thing to say! As if Mischief would go with them, anyhow! I don't expect he'll mix with the circus crowd at all.'

'You wait and see!' grinned Dick. 'Now buck up with your tea – I'm longing to go and set our camp in the field, and see what's going on there.'

It wasn't long before they were ready. They were soon down by the fence, and gazed over it in amazement. Great vans were in the field, all with Mr Tapper's name on and all painted in bright colours. There were caravans too, much smaller than the great vans, and these had windows, each with neat lace curtains. The circus folk lived in the caravans, of course, and George found herself wishing that she herself could go about in one, instead of living in a house that couldn't move anywhere!

'Look at the horses!' cried Dick, as a bunch of them appeared with tossing heads and beautiful long thick tails. The boy who had knocked Tinker down was with them, whistling. They were all coming from a big horse-van, and were delighted to be in a field with lush green grass.

'Is that gate properly shut?' yelled an enormous voice, and the boy yelled back, 'Yes, Grandad. I shut it. There's nowhere the horses can get out. Don't they like this grass!'

Then he saw Julian and the others all looking

over the fence, and waved to them. 'See our horses? Aren't they a great lot?'

And, just to show off a little, he leapt on to the back of the nearest one, and went all round the edge of the field with it. George watched him enviously. If only *she* could have a horse like that!

'Well, let's take our camp things into the field,' said Tinker. 'The nearer we are to the circus the better. We ought to have some fun.'

He climbed over the fence and Dick followed. 'I'll hand everything over,' said Julian. 'George can help me – she's a strong old thing!'

George grinned. She loved to hear anyone say that! It was quite a job getting some of the things over the fence. The tents, neatly wrapped though they were, were heavy, awkward things to handle, but at last everything was safely over, lying on the grass.

Then Julian, Anne and George climbed over the fence too, and stood in the field, looking round for a good corner to set up their things.

'What about near those bushes over there?'

said Julian. 'There's that big tree behind as well to protect us from the wind – and we aren't *too* near the circus folk – they might not like us right on top of them – and yet we're near enough to see what's going on.'

'Oh, it's going to be FUN!' said Anne, her eyes shining.

'I think I'd better go and find the old grandad – Mr Tapper,' said Julian. 'Just to tell him we're here, in case he thinks we're intruders and have no right to be here.'

'You haven't got to ask his permission for us to be in MY field!' said Tinker, at once.

'Now don't keep flying off the handle like that, Tinker,' said Julian. 'This is merely a question of good manners – something you don't seem to know much about! How do we know that the circus folk won't resent us camping so near them? Much better to show ourselves friendly from the start.'

'All right, all right,' said Tinker, sulkily. 'But it is *my* field, after all! You'll be telling me to be friends with that nasty circus boy next!'

'Well, you'd better be – else he might knock you flat again!' said George. 'Anyway, be sensible, Tinker – it's not often people have a circus just at the bottom of their garden, and can pop over the fence and mix with the circus folk.'

Julian walked over to the nearest caravan. It was empty – no one answered his knock.

'What you want, mister?' called a high little voice, and a small girl with tangled, untidy hair came running up.

'Where's Mr Tapper?' asked Julian, smiling at the bright-eyed little thing.

'He's with one of the horses,' said the small girl. 'Who are you?'

'We're your neighbours,' said Julian. 'Will you take us to Mr Tapper?'

'Old Grandad's this way,' said the child, and slipped a dirty little hand into Julian's. 'I'll show you. I like you.'

She led the children to the middle of the camp. A mournful howl came from somewhere behind them and George stopped suddenly.

'That's Timmy! He must have found out that we've got out of the garden. I'll go back for him.'

'Better not,' said Julian. 'There might be ructions if he met the chimpanzee. A big chimp would make mincemeat of him!'

'It *wouldn't*!' said George, but all the same she didn't go back to fetch Timmy. Julian hoped that the dog wouldn't jump over the fence and come to find them.

'There's old Grandad Tapper on those steps,' said the little girl, smiling up at Julian, whose hand she still held. 'I like you, mister.' Then she shouted loudly to the old fellow sitting on the steps of a nearby caravan. 'Grandad! Here's folks to see you!'

Grandad was looking at a beautiful chestnut-brown horse, tethered close to him. He had one of the horse's hooves in his hand. The children stood and gazed at him – black beard, frowning eyebrows – and, oh dear! thought Anne, only one ear, poor man. What *could* have happened to the missing one?

'GRANDAD!' called the girl again. 'SOME FOLKS TO SEE YOU!'

Mr Tapper looked round, his eyes very bright under his black eyebrows. He set the horse's hoof down, and gave the lovely creature a pat. 'You don't need to limp any more, my beauty,' he said. 'I've taken out the stone that was in your hoof. You can dance again!'

The horse lifted up its magnificent head and neighed as if it were saying thank you. Tinker almost jumped out of his skin, and Mischief slipped from his shoulder and cuddled under his arm in terror.

'Now, now, little monkey, don't you know a horse's voice when you hear one?' said Grandad, and Mischief poked his head out from under Tinker's arm to listen.

'Does that horse *really* dance?' said Anne, longing to stroke its long, smooth nose.

'Dance! It's one of the finest dancing horses in the world!' said Grandad, and began to whistle a lively little tune. The horse pricked up its ears, gazed at Grandad, and then began to dance! The children watched in astonishment.

There it went, round and round, nodding its head to the tune, its feet tapping the grass in perfect time to Grandad's whistling.

'Oh, the lovely thing!' said George. 'Do *all* your horses dance as well as this one?'

'Yes. Some a good deal better,' said Grandad. 'This one has a fair ear for music, but not as good an ear as some. You wait till you see them dressed up, with feathery plumes nodding on their heads. Horses – there's nothing in the world as beautiful as a good horse.'

'Mr Tapper – we come from the house over the fence there,' said Julian, feeling that it was time to explain their visit. 'As you probably know, Tinker's father owns this field, and—'

'Yes, yes – but we have an old right to come every so often,' said the old man, raising his voice. 'Now don't you start arg—'

'I haven't come to argue with you,' said Julian, politely. 'I've only just come to say that we – that is my friends here and I – would like to come and camp in this field, but we shouldn't annoy you in any way, and . . .'

'Oh well – if that's what you want, you're more than welcome!' said the old man. 'More than welcome! I thought maybe you'd think you could turn us out – like that youngster there would like to do!' And he nodded at Tinker.

Tinker went red and said nothing. The old man laughed. 'Ha! My grandson didn't think much of that idea, did he, youngster? He hit out, and down you went on your back. He's got a temper, he has, young Jeremy. But another time maybe he'll find himself on *his* back, eh?'

'Yes. He will,' said Tinker, at once.

'Right. Well, you'll be even with one another then, and you can shake hands like gentlemen,' said the old man, his eyes twinkling. 'Now – what about you bringing your gear right into the field, and setting up your tents? I'll get old Charlie the Chimp to help you. He's as strong as ten men!'

'The *chimpanzee*! Is he tame enough to help

us to put up our *tents*?' said Anne, disbelievingly.

'Old Charlie is cleverer than all of you put
together, and as tame as you are!' said Grandad. 'And he could beat you three boys at cricket
any day! You bring your bat along one morning and watch him. I'll call him to help you.
CHARLIE! CHARLIE! Where are you? Snoozing I
suppose!'

But no Charlie came. 'You go and fetch him,'
said the old man, pointing to a corner of the
field where stood a big, strong cage, with a
tarpaulin roof to keep out the rain. 'He'll do
anything you want him to do, so long as you
give him a word of praise now and again!'

'Let's get him, Ju,' said Dick, eagerly. 'Fancy
having a chimpanzee to help us!'

And off they all went to the great cage.
CHARLIE! CHARLIE! Wake up, you're wanted!
CHARLIE!

[8]

Charlie the Chimp is a help!

Tinker came to the big cage first. He peered
inside. Charlie the Chimp was there all right,
sitting at the back of his cage, his brown eyes
looking at the children with curiosity. He got
up and went over to where Tinker was peering
in and pressed his nose against the strong wire,
almost against Tinker's. Then he blew hard and
Tinker backed away, surprised and cross.

'He *blew* at me!' he said to the others, who
were laughing at Tinker's disgust. The chimp
made a funny noise that Mischief the monkey
immediately tried to imitate. The chimpanzee
stared at Mischief, then he grew very excited.
He rattled his cage, jumped up and down, and
made some very odd noises indeed.

A boy came running up at once. It was the
boy who had knocked Tinker down. 'Hey –

what are you doing to the chimp?' he called. 'Oh – aren't you the boy who shouted at my grandad – the one I knocked down?'

'Yes. And don't you dare try that on again, or you'll be sorry!' said Tinker in a fierce voice.

'Shut up, Tinker,' said Julian. He turned to the boy. 'Your name's Jeremy, isn't it?' he said. 'Well, we've just been talking to your grandad over there, and he said we could get the chimpanzee to help us with our camping gear. It's all right for him to come out of his cage, isn't it?'

'Oh yes – I take him out two or three times a day,' said Jeremy. 'He gets bored in his cage. He'd love to help put up your tents – he's always helping us with things like that. He's as strong as a lion.'

'Is he – er – is he safe?' asked Dick, eyeing the big animal doubtfully.

'Safe? What do you mean – safe?' asked Jeremy, surprised. 'He's as safe as I am! Charlie, come on out! Go on, you can undo your cage perfectly well, you know you can!'

The chimpanzee made a funny little chuckling noise, put his hand through the wire, reached the bolt, pulled it, took his hand back – and pushed open the cage door.

'See! Easy, isn't it?' said Jeremy, grinning. 'Charlie boy, come along. Your help's wanted!'

Charlie lumbered out of his cage, and went with the children to where they had left their tents and ground-sheets and the rest. He walked with his fists on the ground in a most inelegant manner, making a funny little groaning noise all the time. Mischief was rather afraid of him, and kept well to the back – but the chimpanzee suddenly turned round, caught hold of Mischief, and sat him up on his shoulder! Mischief held on, not knowing whether to be scared or jubilant!

'I wish I had my camera here,' said Anne to George. 'Just look at them – Mischief is as pleased as can be!'

They arrived at the pile of camping gear. 'Carry this, Charlie, and follow us,' ordered Jeremy. The chimp grabbed at this, that and the other, and, with his great arms full, followed the children to where they thought they could camp, with the great tree to shelter them from the wind.

'Drop those things, Charlie,' said Jeremy, 'and go back for the rest. Buck up. Don't stand there staring! You've got work to do!'

But Charlie still crouched there, staring straight at Mischief. 'Oh! He wants Mischief the monkey to go with him!' cried George. 'Go on, Mischief, have a ride again!'

Mischief leapt up on to the chimpanzee's shoulders. Charlie put up a great paw to steady him and then lumbered off to fetch the rest of the things. One of the ground-sheets came undone and slithered over his head like a tent, so that he couldn't see where he was going. In a rage he leapt on it and began to jump up and down, up and down, growling most terrifyingly. The children felt rather scared.

'Charlie, don't be silly!' said Jeremy, and pulled it away from him, rolling it up swiftly. The chimpanzee could manage it then, and his good temper immediately came back again.

Everything was soon piled up in one place, and Julian and Dick began to put up the tents. Charlie watched them with the greatest interest, and helped most intelligently when he saw that he could.

'He's a good sort, isn't he?' said Jeremy, proud that his friend the chimpanzee could show off like this. 'Did you see him put that tent-pole in exactly the right place? And you ought to see him fetch the pails of water for the horses each day. He carries a full pail in each hand!'

'He ought to get wages,' said Tinker.

'He does!' said Jeremy. 'He gets eight bananas a day and as many oranges as he likes. And he LOVES sweets!'

'Oh! I think I've got some!' said Tinker and delved into one of his pockets. He brought up a peculiar mixture of things, among which was a screwed-up sweet bag. Inside was a mass of half-melted boiled sweets.

'You can't give him *those*!' said Anne. 'They're old and sticky and messy!'

But Charlie thought differently. He took the paper bag straight out of Tinker's hand, sniffed it – and then put the whole thing into his mouth at once!

'He'll choke!' said Julian.

'Not Charlie!' said Jeremy. 'Let him be. He'll go straight back to his cage, get in, shoot the bolt and sit there sucking sweets till they're gone. He'll be as happy as can be.'

'Well – he certainly deserved a reward,' said George. 'He did all the heavy work! Come on, let's finish putting everything straight. Hey – won't it be fun sleeping out in tents tonight! We'd better have supper first.'

'You can come and join *us*, if you like,' said Jeremy. 'We don't have posh food like you, of course – but it's good food, all the same. Old Grandma cooks it in her pot. She's two hundred years old.'

The children laughed in disbelief. 'Two hundred! Nobody lives as long as that!' said George.

'Well, that's what she tells everyone,' said

Jeremy. 'And she looks it, too! But her eyes are as sharp as needles still! Shall I tell her you'll be here to supper?'

'Well – would there be enough for so many extra?' said Julian. 'We meant to bring our own meal. Should we bring that and share everything with you? We've more than enough. Jenny said she would have it all ready for us to bring down tonight – a meat-pie, cold sausages, and apples and bananas.'

'Sh! Don't say bananas in front of Charlie,' said Jeremy. 'He'll worry you for them all the time. All right – you bring your food and we'll share with you round our camp fire. I'll tell old Grandma. We're having a sing-song tonight, and Fred the Fiddler's playing his fiddle. Ah, that fiddle! Its tunes get into your feet and away you go!'

This all sounded very exciting. Julian thought they ought to go back home before anyone began to be worried about their complete disappearance, and pack up the food for supper that night.

'We'll be back as soon as we can,' said he. 'And thanks a lot for all your help. Come on, Mischief. Say good-bye to Charlie for the moment, and don't look so gloomy. We're coming back here tonight!'

They all went back over the fence, feeling a little tired now, but full of their plans for the evening. 'It's almost like *belonging* to the circus, going back to sit round a camp fire and eat supper from that old black stewpot on the fire,' said Tinker. 'I bet the supper will taste delicious. I hope Dad won't mind us popping off to the circus camp.'

'I don't expect he'll even notice that we've gone,' said George. 'My father never notices things like that. Sometimes he doesn't even notice when people are there, in front of his nose!'

'Well, that must be useful at times if they're people he doesn't like,' said Tinker. 'Now – let's see what Jenny's got that we can take back with us.'

Jenny listened wide-eyed to all they had to

say. 'Well, well, well!' she said. 'Camping out with the circus folk! Whatever next? I'd like to know what your parents would think of *that*!'

'We'll ask them, next time we see them,' said Julian, with a grin. 'What do you have for our supper? We're taking it down to our camp.'

'I thought maybe you'd do that,' said Jenny. 'It's all cold. A meat-pie, cold sausages, a cucumber and lettuce hearts and tomatoes, rolls, and apples and bananas. Will that be enough?'

'Gosh, yes,' said Tinker, thrilled. 'What about something to drink?'

'You can take lemonade or orangeade with you, whichever you like,' said Jenny. 'But listen now – don't go bursting into your father's workroom. He's worked hard all day, and he's tired.'

'And cross, I expect,' said Tinker. 'People are always cross when they're tired. Except you, dear, dear Jenny.'

'Ha! You want something else out of my cupboard, calling me your dear, dear Jenny,' she said with a twinkle.

'Could we have some sugar lumps?' asked Tinker. 'Oh, Jenny, there are the loveliest horses you ever saw down in the circus field. I want to give them a sugar lump each.'

'And yourself a few as well!' said Jenny. 'All right. I'll pack up everything for you, and give you a few enamel plates and mugs and knives. What about Timmy? Doesn't he want a meal too?'

'Wuff!' said Timmy, glad that someone had remembered him. Jenny patted his big head. 'It's all ready in the larder for you,' she said. 'George, you go and get it. He must be hungry.'

George fetched a plate of meat and biscuits from the larder and Timmy fell on it with happy little barks. Yes – he was very, VERY hungry!

At last all the food was ready, packed to take down the garden to the field. What a lot there seemed! Well, they would certainly have plenty to spare for their circus friends. They said good night to Jenny, and set off down the garden again. They thought they had better not disturb Professor Hayling.

'He might be cross and forbid us to go and eat with the circus folk,' said Tinker. 'Mischief, come off that basket, and don't pretend you weren't fishing in it for a banana. And please put on your best table manners tonight, or Charlie the Chimp will be ashamed of you!'

It was fun going back down the garden and over the fence into the field again. The sun was sinking fast and soon the shadows would fall. How lovely to sit round a fire and eat supper with the kindly circus folk – and perhaps to sing old songs with them – and hear Fred the Fiddler fiddle his old, old tunes! What fun to creep into a tent, and sleep with the cries of owls around, and stars shining in at the tent opening!

There they go, over the fence, handing the food one to another. Take your paw out of that basket, Mischief! That's right, Timmy, nibble his ear if he's as mischievous as his name! You're all going to have some fun tonight!

[9]

A wonderful evening

As soon as Jeremy saw the visitors climbing over the fence, he ran to help them. He was very excited at the thought of having guests. He took them over to old Grandad first, to be welcomed.

'Now I expect your friends will like to see round a bit,' said Grandad. 'Charlie the Chimp can go with you. We've a rehearsal on tonight, so the ring has been set up. You can watch some of the show.'

This was great news. The children saw that curved pieces of painted wood had been set together to make a great ring in the field, and as they went across the grass, the Musical Horses began to troop into the ring, the leading one ridden by Madelon, a lovely girl dressed in shimmering gold.

'How beautiful they are!' thought Anne, as she watched. 'Look at their great feathery plumes, nodding on their magnificent heads.'

The Bonzo Band struck up just then, and the horses at once trotted in perfect time to the music. The band looked a little peculiar as the bandsmen had not put on their smart uniforms. They were saving those for the opening night!

The horses trotted prettily out of the ring after two or three rounds, the beautiful Madelon on the leading horse. Then in came Fred the Fiddler and played his violin for a few minutes. First the music was slow and solemn, then Fred began to play quickly, and the children found themselves jigging about, up and down and round about. 'I can't keep still!' panted Anne. 'The tune's got into my feet.'

Charlie the Chimp came up just then, walking on hind legs, and looking unexpectedly tall. He usually walked on all fours. He began to jig about too, looking very funny. He ran right into the ring and put his arms round Fred the Fiddler's legs. 'He loves Fred,' said Jeremy.

'Now he's going to rehearse his cricket act. I must go and bowl to him.'

And off went Jeremy into the ring. The chimpanzee rushed over to him and hugged him. A bat was thrown into the ring, and Charlie picked it up and made a few swipes into the air with it, making delighted noises all the time.

Then a cricket ball was thrown to Jeremy, who caught it deftly. A small girl appeared from somewhere and set up three stumps for a wicket. 'Can't find the bails, Jeremy!' she called. 'Have you got them in your pocket?'

'No,' said Jeremy. 'Never mind, I'll knock the stumps right over!'

But that wasn't so easy with Charlie the Chimp at the wicket! He took a terrific swipe at the ball and it went right over Jeremy's head, too high to catch. The chimp lost his balance and sat down on the wicket, knocking the stumps out of the ground.

'OUT!' yelled Jeremy, but the chimp wasn't having that. He carefully put up the stumps again, and then set himself in front once more, waggling the bat.

It was the funniest cricket that the children had ever seen! The chimpanzee was very, very clever with the bat, and sent poor Jeremy running all over the place. Then he chased the boy all round the ring with the bat, making curious chortling noises. The children didn't know if he was amused or angry! Finally he threw the bat at Jeremy and walked off, scratching himself under one arm.

The children roared with laughter at him. 'He's as good as any clown!' said Dick. 'Jeremy, does he do this cricket act every night when the circus is open?'

'Oh yes – and sometimes he hits the ball into the audience,' said Jeremy. 'There's great excitement then. Sometimes, for a treat, we let one of the boys in the audience come down and bowl to Charlie. One bowled him right out once, and Charlie was so cross that he chased him all round the ring three times – just as he chased *me* just now. The boy didn't like it much!'

Charlie came up to Jeremy and put his great arms round him, trying to swing him off the ground. 'Stop that, Charlie,' said Jeremy, wriggling free. 'Look out – here comes the Dancing Donkey! Better get out of the ring – goodness knows what antics *he'll* be up to!'

In came the Dancing Donkey. He was dark grey, and tossed his head as he came galloping in. He stood and looked round at everyone. Then he sat down, lifted up a leg and scratched his nose. The children stared in astonishment. They had never in their lives seen a donkey do *that* before! Then, when the band suddenly began to play, the donkey stood up and listened, flapping his ears first one way and then another, and nodding his head in time to the music.

The band changed its tune to a march. The donkey listened again, and then began to march round the ring in perfect time – clip-clop-clip-clop-clip-clop. Then it apparently felt tired, and sat down heavily on its back legs. The children couldn't help laughing. The donkey got up, and somehow its back legs became entangled with its front ones and it fell down, looking most ridiculous.

'Has it hurt itself?' asked Anne, anxiously. 'Oh dear – it will break one of its legs if it goes on like this. Look, it can't untangle them, Jeremy.'

The donkey gave a mournful bray, tried to get up, and flopped down again. The band changed its tune, and the donkey leapt up at once, and began to do a kind of tap dance – clickety-click, clickety-click, clickety-click – it was marvellous!

'I shouldn't have thought that a donkey could possibly have been taught to tap dance,' said George.

Soon the donkey seemed to feel tired again. It stopped dancing, but the band still went on playing. The donkey ran towards it and stamped a foot.

A weird voice suddenly came from it. 'Too fast! TOO FAST!' But the band took no notice and went on playing. The donkey bent down, wriggled hard – and its head fell off on to the grass in the ring! Anne gave a shriek of fright.

'Don't be an idiot, Anne,' said Dick. 'You didn't think the donkey was a *real* one, did you?'

'*Isn't* it?' said Anne, relieved. 'It looks *just* like that donkey that used to give rides to children on Kirrin beach.'

The donkey now split in half and a small man climbed out of each half, both taking their legs carefully out of the donkey's legs. The donkey-skin fell to the ground and lay there, flat and collapsed.

'Wish *I* had a donkey-skin like that,' said Tinker. 'I've got a friend at school who could be the back legs and I'd be the front legs. The things we'd do!'

'Well, I must say you'd make a first-class donkey, the way you behave sometimes,' said George. 'Look, this must be Dead-Shot Dick coming on.'

But before Dead-Shot Dick could do any of his shooting tricks, the two donkey-men had run to the band and begun a loud argument with them.

'Why play so fast? You *know* we can't do our tricks at top speed. Are you trying to mess up our turn?'

The bandleader shouted something back. It must have been rude, because one of the donkey-men shook his fist and began to run towards the band.

A loud voice crashed in on the argument and made everyone jump. It was Mr Tapper, old Grandad, giving his orders in an enormous voice.

'ENOUGH! You, Pat, and you, Jim, get out of the ring. I give the orders, not you. ENOUGH, I SAY!'

The two donkey-men glared at him, but did not dare to say a word more. They stalked out of the ring, taking the donkey-skin with them.

Dead-Shot Dick looked very ordinary, dressed in a rather untidy flannel suit. 'He's not going to go all through his act,' said Jeremy. 'You'll see him another night, when the show's on for the public – he shoots at all kinds of things – even a five-pence piece dangling on a long string from the roof – and never misses! He's got a smashing rig-out too – sequins sewn all over his trousers and jersey – and his little horse is a wonder – goes round and round the ring and never turns a hair when Dead-Shot Dick fires his gun! Look – there he is, peeping in to see if Dick's coming back to him.'

A small white horse was looking anxiously at the ring, its eyes fixed on Dead-Shot Dick. It pawed the ground as if to say 'Buck up! I'm waiting for you! Am I to come on or not?'

'All right, Dick – you can go off now,' shouted Grandad. 'I hear your horse has hurt a foot – give him a good rest tonight. We'll want him on tomorrow.'

'Right, sir!' said Dead-Shot Dick. He saluted smartly, and ran off to his little horse.

'What's next, Jeremy?' asked George, who was enjoying everything very much.

'Don't know. Let's see – there's the acrobats – but the trapeze-swings aren't put up yet, so they won't come on tonight. And there's the Boneless Man – look, there he is. Good old Boney! I like him. He's free with his money, he is, not like some of the other folk!'

The Boneless Man looked very peculiar. He was remarkably thin, and remarkably tall. He walked in, looking quite extraordinary. 'He can't be boneless!' said Dick. 'He couldn't walk if he was!'

But the Boneless Man soon began to seem absolutely boneless. His legs gave way at the knees, and his ankles turned over so that he sank down to the ground, unable to walk. He could bend his arms all kinds of different ways, and turned his head almost completely round on his neck. He did a few peculiar things with his apparently boneless body, and finally wriggled along the ground exactly like a snake!

'He'll be dressed in a sort of snake-skin when he does his act properly,' said Jeremy. 'Funny, isn't he?'

'How on earth does he do it?' wondered Julian, amazed. 'He bends his arms and legs all the wrong ways! Mine would break if I did that!'

'Oh, it's easy for *him*!' said Jeremy. 'It's just that he's completely double-jointed – he can bend his arms both ways, and his legs both ways, and make them seem so loose that it looks as if he really *is* boneless. He's a nice chap. You'd like him.'

Anne felt a bit doubtful. What strange people made up a circus! It was a world of its own. She jumped suddenly as there came the sound of a trumpet blowing loudly.

'That's for supper,' said Jeremy, gleefully. 'Come on – let's go to old Grandma and her pot! Buck up, all of you!'

[10]

Round the camp fire

Jeremy led the way out of the circus ring. It had been well-lit, and the night seemed very dark outside the ring. They went over the field to where a large fire was burning, cleverly set about with stones. An enormous cooking pot was hung over it, and a very, very nice smell came to their noses as they went near.

Old Grandma was there, of course, and she began stirring the pot when she saw them. 'You've been a long time in the ring,' she grumbled to Grandad. 'Anything gone wrong?'

'No,' said Grandad, and sniffed the air. 'I'm hungry. That smells good. Jeremy, help your grandma.'

'Yes, Grandad,' said Jeremy, and took a pile of plates to the old lady, who at once began ladling out pieces of meat and potatoes and vegetables from the steaming pot. Old Grandad turned to Julian.

'Well – did you like our little rehearsal?' he asked.

'Oh *yes*!' said Julian. 'I'm only sorry you didn't rehearse *all* the turns. I badly wanted to see the acrobats and the clowns. Are they here? I can't see them.'

'Oh yes – there's one clown over there – look – with Madelon, who had the horses,' said Grandad.

The children looked – and were very disappointed. 'Is he a *clown*?' said Dick, disbelievingly. 'He doesn't look a bit funny. He looks miserable.'

'That's Monty all right,' said Grandad. 'He always looks like that out of the ring. He'll make you double up with laughter when the circus is on, he's a born clown – but a lot of clowns are like Monty when they're not performing – not much to say for themselves, and looking miserable. Winks is a bit livelier – that's him, pulling Madelon's hair. He'll get a smacked face in a minute, he's a real tease. There – I knew he'd get a clip on the ear!'

Winks went howling over to the children, boo-hooing most realistically. 'She smacked me!' he said. 'And she's got such p-p-p-pretty hair!'

The children couldn't help laughing. Mischief ran to the clown, jumped up on his shoulder and chattered comforting monkey words into his ear. Charlie the Chimp let himself out of his cage, and came to put his great paw into Winks' hand. They both thought that Winks really was hurt.

'That's enough, Winks,' said Grandad. 'You'll have the horses comforting you next! You do that in the ring tomorrow when we open, and you'll bring the house down. Sit down and have your supper.'

'Mr Tapper,' said Julian. 'There's another member of your circus we didn't see at the rehearsal – and that's Mr Wooh, the Wonder Magician. Why wasn't he there?'

'Oh, he never rehearses,' said Mr Tapper.

'He keeps himself to himself, does Mr Wooh. He may come and join us for supper, and he may not. As we're opening the circus tomorrow night, maybe he'll turn up tonight. I'm a bit scared of him, to tell you the truth.'

'But he's not a *real* wizard, is he?' asked Tinker.

'Well, when I talk to Mr Wooh I feel as if he is,' said Mr Tapper. 'There isn't a thing he doesn't know about figures, there isn't a thing he can't do with them. Ask him to multiply any number by any other number, running into dozens of figures, and he'll tell you in a second. He shouldn't be in a circus. He should be an inventor of some sort – an inventor whose invention needs pages and pages of figures. He'd be happy then.'

'He sounds a bit like my father,' said Tinker. '*He's* an inventor, you know, and sometimes when I creep into his study I see papers FULL of millions of tiny figures and plans and diagrams with tiny figures all over them too.'

'Very interesting,' said Grandad. 'Your

father and Mr Wooh ought to meet. They would probably talk figures all day long! My word – what's that you're handing round, young lady?'

'Some of the food *we* brought,' said Anne. 'Have a sausage or two, Mr Tapper – and a roll – and a tomato.'

'Well, thanks,' said Mr Tapper, pleased. 'Very kind of you. Nice to have met you all. You might be able to teach Jeremy a few manners!'

'Grandad – here's Mr Wooh!' said Jeremy, suddenly, and got up. Everyone turned round. *So this* was Mr Wooh, the Wonder Magician. Well, he certainly looked the part.

He stood there, with a half-smile on his face, tall, commanding and handsome. His hair was thick and black as soot, his eyes gleamed in the firelight, half hidden by great eyebrows, and he wore a thin, pointed beard. He had a curiously deep voice, and spoke with a foreign accent.

'So we have visitors this night?' he said, and showed a row of gleaming white teeth in a quick smile. 'May I join you?'

'Oh do, Mr Wooh,' said Anne, delighted to have the chance of talking to a Wonder Magician. 'We've brought plenty of food. Do you like cold sausage – and tomato – and a roll?'

'Most deelicious!' said the magician, and sat down cross-legged to join the group.

'We were disappointed not to see you at the rehearsal,' said Dick. 'I'd have liked to hear you doing all kinds of wizard sums in your head, as quick as lightning!'

'My father can do that too,' said Tinker proudly. 'He's a wizard at figures as well. He's an inventor.'

'Ha! An inventor? And what does he invent?' asked Mr Wooh, eating his roll.

That was enough to set Tinker describing at once how wonderful his father was. 'He can invent *any*thing he's asked for,' said the boy, proudly. 'He invented a wonderful thing for keeping aeroplanes dead straight in the right direction – better than any idea before. He invented the sko-wheel, if you know what that is – and the electric trosymon, if you've ever heard of that. I don't suppose you have, though. They're too—'

'Wait, boy!' said Mr Wooh, sounding most interested. 'These things I have heard of, yes. I do not know them, but I have certainly heard of them. Your father must be a very, very clever man, with a most unusual brain.'

Tinker swelled with pride. 'Something got into the papers about his inventions a little while ago,' he said, 'and reporters came down to see Dad, and his name was in the papers – but Dad was awfully cross about it. You see, he's in the middle of the biggest idea he's ever thought of and it messed up his work to have people coming to interview him – some of them even peered through the window, and went to see his wonderful tower, with its—'

'Tower? He has a tower?' said Mr Wooh, full of surprise. Before Tinker could answer, he received a hard poke from Julian's finger. He turned crossly, to see Julian frowning fiercely at him. So was George. He went suddenly red in the face. Of course – he had been told never to talk about his father's work. It was secret work, very secret.

He pretended to choke over a piece of meat, hoping that Julian would take the chance of changing the subject – and Julian did, of course!

'Mr Wooh, could you do a bit of magic reckoning with figures?' he asked. 'I've heard that you can give the answers to any sum as quick as lightning.'

'That is true,' said Mr Wooh. 'There is nothing that I cannot do with figures. Ask me anything you like, and I will give you the answer at once!'

'Well, Mr Wooh, answer this then,' cried Tinker. 'Multiply sixty-three thousand, three hundred and forty-two by eighty thousand, nine hundred and fifty-three! Ha – you can't do that in a hurry!'

'The answer is, in figures, 5127724926,' said Mr Wooh at once, with a slight bow. 'That is an easy question, my boy.'

'Crumbs!' said Tinker, astounded. He turned to Julian. 'Is that right, Ju?'

Julian worked out the sum on paper. 'Yes. Absolutely correct. Whew!' he said. 'You said that as quick as lightning!'

'Let *me* give him a sum to do!' cried George. 'What do you get if you multiply 602491 by 352, Mr Magician?'

'I get the figures 2–1–2–0–7–6–8–3–2,' said Mr Wooh, immediately. And once more Julian worked out the sum on paper. He raised his head and grinned. 'Yes – correct. How do you do it so quickly?'

'Magic – just a little elementary magic!' answered Mr Wooh. 'Try it sometime yourself. I am sure that this boy's father would be as quick as I am!' He looked at Tinker. 'I should much like to meet your clever father, my boy,' he said in his deep voice. 'We would have much, so much to talk about. I have heard about his wonderful tower. A monument to his genius! Ah, you see, even we foreigners know of your father's great work. Surely he is afraid of having his secrets stolen?'

'Oh, I don't think so,' said Tinker. 'The

tower is a pretty good hiding place, and—' He stopped suddenly, and went red again as he received an even harder kick from Julian. How *could* he be so stupid as to give away the fact that his father's secret plans and models were hidden in the tower!

Julian thought it was time to take Tinker firmly away from Mr Wooh and give him a good lecture on keeping his mouth shut. He looked at his watch, and pretended to be horrified at the time. 'Look. Do you know what the time is? Jenny will be ringing up the police if we don't get back straight away. Come on, Tinker, and you others, we *must* go. Thanks a lot, Grandad, for letting us share your supper.'

'But we haven't yet finished!' said Grandad. 'You haven't had enough to eat.'

'We really couldn't eat any more,' said Dick, following Julian's determined lead. 'See you tomorrow, Grandad. Good night, Grandma. Thanks very much indeed.'

'We've still got bananas and apples to eat,' said Tinker, feeling obstinate.

'Oh, we brought those for Charlie the Chimp,' said Dick, not quite truthfully. He could have boxed Tinker's ears! Silly little idiot, couldn't he realise that Julian wanted to get him away from this cunning Mr Wooh? Wait till he got Tinker by himself!

Tinker found himself hustled on all sides, and felt a bit scared. Julian sounded rather fierce, he thought. Old Grandad was most astonished at the sudden departure of his guests – but Charlie the Chimp didn't mind! The guests had left behind a generous supply of fruit!

Over the fence they all went, with Julian hustling Tinker in front of him. Once over the fence and out of Mr Wooh's hearing, Julian and George rounded on the boy angrily.

'Are you mad, Tinker?' demanded Julian. 'Didn't you guess that that man was trying to pump you about your father's hush-hush job?'

'He wasn't,' said Tinker, almost in tears. 'You're just exaggerating!'

'Well, I hope *I* never try to give away *my*

father's secret work!' said George, in a tone of such disgust that Tinker could have howled.

'I don't like him and I don't trust him,' said Julian, sounding suddenly very grown up. 'But there you sat lapping up everything he said, ready to pour out all he wanted to know. I'm ashamed of you. You'd get a jolly good thrashing if your father had heard you. I only hope you haven't already said too much. You know how angry your father was when a report of his latest ideas got into the papers, and swarms of people came prying round the house—'

Tinker could stand it no longer. He gave a forlorn howl that made Mischief jump, and fled up the garden to the house, the little monkey running swiftly behind him. He wanted to comfort Tinker. What was the matter? Poor little Mischief felt bewildered, and tried his best to catch up with the sobbing Tinker. He caught him up at last, leapt to the boy's shoulder and put his little furry arms round Tinker's neck, making a funny comforting noise.

'Oh Mischief,' said Tinker. 'I'm glad *you're*

still my friend. The others won't be now, I know. Aren't I an *idiot*, Mischief? But I was only being proud of my father, I was, really!'

Mischief clung to Tinker, puzzled and upset. Tinker stopped outside the tall tower. There was a light at the top. His father must still be working there. A faint humming noise came to his ears. He wondered if it was those strange, spindly tentacles right at the very top of the tower that made the noise.

Suddenly the light at the top of the tower went out.

'Dad must have finished his work for to-night,' thought Tinker. 'He'll be coming to the house. I'd better go. He might wonder why I'm all upset. Gosh, I never heard Julian be so angry before. He sounded as if he absolutely *despised* me!'

He crept up the path that led to the house, and in at the garden door. Better not go and see Jenny. She might worm everything out of him, and be as disgusted with him as Julian was. She would wonder why he wasn't camping out with them! He'd go upstairs and sleep in his own bed tonight!

'Come on, Mischief,' he said, in a mournful voice. 'We'll go to bed, and you can cuddle down with me. You'd never be mean to me, would you? You'd always be my friend.'

Mischief jabbered away, and the funny little monkey voice comforted Tinker all the time he undressed. He flung himself into bed, and Mischief lay at the bottom, on his feet. 'I shall never be able to get to sleep tonight,' said Tinker, still miserable. 'Never!'

But he fell asleep at once – which was a great pity, really. He might have shared in quite a bit of excitement, if he hadn't slept so soundly! Poor Tinker!

[11]

In the dark of the night

Julian and the others made no attempt to follow Tinker. 'Let him go, the little idiot!' said Julian. 'Come into one of the tents and have a low pow-wow before we get undressed and go to sleep.'

'I'm sorry poor old Tinker isn't going to camp out with us, our first night in the field,' said Anne. 'I don't think he *meant* to give anything away.'

'That's no excuse, Anne,' said George. 'He can be really stupid at times, and he's got to learn not to be. Let's go to our tent. I feel quite tired. Come along, Timmy!'

She yawned and Dick yawned too. Then Julian found himself yawning. 'Awfully catching, this yawning business!' he said. 'Well, it's turned out to be a lovely night as regards weather – warm and dry – and there's a nice little half-moon to look at. Good night, girls, sleep tight! And don't scream if a spider wakes you, because I warn you, I am NOT going to get up to deal with a harmless spider!'

'You wait till one runs all over *your* face!' said Anne, 'and starts making a web from your nose to your chin and catches flies in it!'

'Don't, Anne,' said George. 'I'm not a bit scared of spiders, but that's a horrible idea of yours! Timmy, please watch out for spiders, and give me warning of them!'

Everyone laughed. 'Well, good night, girls,' said Dick. 'Pity about young Tinker. Still, he's got to learn a few things, and keeping his mouth shut is one of them.'

They were all quite tired, and it wasn't long before everyone's torch was out, and peace and quiet descended on the little camp. Much farther up the field the circus was also peaceful and quiet, though there were still lights here and there in the tents. Someone belonging to the circus band was strumming a banjo, but not loudly, and the sound was pleasant to hear – strum-a-strum – strum-a-strum – strummmm . . .

A few clouds blew up and slid across the moon. One by one the lights went out in the circus tents. The wind blew softly through the trees, and an owl hooted.

Anne was still awake. She lay listening to the wind, and to the owl's 'Too-whoo-too-whit', and then she, too, fell asleep. Nobody heard someone stirring in the circus camp. Nobody saw a shadowy figure creep out when the moon was safely behind a cloud. It was late, very late, and the two camps were lost in dreams.

Timmy was fast asleep too – but in his sleep he heard a faint sound, and at once he was awake. He didn't move, except for his ears which switched themselves to listen. He gave a little growl, but not enough to wake George. So long as the person who was moving about in the circus camp did not come near to George's tent, or the boys' tent, Timmy did not mean to bark. He heard a tiny grunt and recognised it at once. Charlie the Chimp! Well, that was all right! Timmy fell asleep again.

Tinker, too, was fast asleep in his bed up at the house, Mischief at his feet. He had thought he would be too miserable to sleep, but found himself half-dreaming in no time. He didn't hear a small noise outside, a very small noise indeed – a little scrape, as if someone's foot had caught against a stone. Then there came other very small noises – and a whisper of a voice – and more noises again.

Nobody heard anything at all until Jenny woke up thirsty, and stretched out her hand to get a glass of water from her bed table. She didn't switch her light on, and was about to lie down again when her quick ears caught a little sound.

She sat up. 'That can't be the children,' she thought. 'They're camping down in the field. Oh my goodness me, I hope it's not a burglar – or someone trying to steal the Professor's secrets. He's got papers all over the place. Thank goodness he keeps most of them in that tower of his!'

She listened, and then lay down again. But soon she heard another little noise, and sat up, scared. 'It sounds as if it comes from the tower,' she thought, and got out of bed. No – there was no light in the tower – no light anywhere, that she could see. The moon was behind a cloud. She'd just wait till it slid out and lit up the courtyard below, and the tower. There! That was another little noise. Could it be the wind? No, it couldn't. And now, what was *that*? It sounded just like someone whispering down there in the court-yard. Jenny felt really frightened, and began to shake. She must go and wake the Professor! Suppose it was someone after his precious pa-pers? Or his wonderful new invention!

The moon swung out from behind the cloud and Jenny peered cautiously out of the window again. She gave a loud scream, and staggered back into her room, still screaming. 'There's a man! Help! Help! He's climbing up the wall of the tower! Professor! PROFESSOR HAYLING! Come quickly! Thieves, robbers, help, help! Get the police!'

There came a long slithering sound, and before Jenny dared to look out again, the moon had gone behind another cloud, and she could not see a thing in the sudden darkness. There was a deep silence after the slithering noise, and Jenny couldn't bear it. She rushed out of her bedroom, yelling at the top of her voice. 'THIEVES! ROBBERS! COME QUICKLY!'

The Professor woke with a jump, threw off his bedclothes and rushed out into the passage, almost colliding with Jenny. He clutched at her, thinking she was the thief, and she screamed again, sure that one of the intruders had got hold of her. They struggled together, and then the Professor realised that he wasn't holding a thief, he was holding poor, plump Jenny!

'JENNY! What on earth are you doing, waking up the whole household!' said the Professor, switching on the passage light. 'Have you had a bad dream – a nightmare?'

'No, no,' panted Jenny, out of breath with her struggle. 'There's robbers about. I saw one climbing up the tower wall – and there must have been others below. I heard them whispering. Oh, I'm scared! What shall we do? Can you telephone for the police?'

'Well,' said the Professor, doubtfully. 'Are you quite sure, Jenny, that you didn't have a nightmare? I mean – if there really *are* robbers, I'll certainly telephone – but it's rather a long way for the police to come out here, and—'

'Oh – then won't you just take a torch and look round the place?' begged Jenny. 'You know there's your precious papers in that tower. And isn't there that new invention of yours? Oh yes, I know I'm not supposed to know anything about it, but I do dust your rooms thoroughly, you know, and I see quite a lot, though I keep my mouth shut, and—'

'Yes, yes, Jenny, I know,' said poor Professor Hayling, trying to stop Jenny's stream of talk. 'But honestly, everything seems quiet now. I've looked out into the courtyard. There's no one there. And you know as well as I do that nobody can get into my tower. It has three different keys – one to unlock the bottom door

– one for the middle door, halfway up – and one for the top door. Jenny, be sensible. Nobody could have used my three keys. Look, there they are on my dressing-table.'

Jenny began to calm down, but she still wasn't satisfied. 'I *did* hear whispering, and I *did* see someone halfway up the wall of the tower. Please do come down with me, and let's look around. I daren't go on my own. But I shan't sleep again tonight till I know nobody's forced the tower door, or taken a ladder to go up the tower.'

'All right, Jenny,' said the Professor, with a sigh. 'Put on your dressing gown, and I'll put mine on too – we'll try the doors, and we'll look for a ladder – though, mind you, it would have to be an absolutely colossal one to reach the top of that tower. Nobody could possibly bring one that size and length into our small courtyard! All right, all right – we'll go.'

And so, a few minutes later, Jenny and the Professor were down in the courtyard. There was no sign of any ladder at all – no sign of

anyone climbing up the wall – and the downstairs tower door was safely locked! 'You unlock the door, and go up to the top room and
see if that door's locked too,' begged Jenny.

'I think you're being rather silly now, Jenny,'
said the Professor impatiently. 'Here, take the
keys yourself. This one's locked, of course –
and if the middle door is still locked, you'll
know nobody could have got into my top
room. Hurry, Jenny.'

So Jenny, still trembling, slid a key into the
bottom lock, opened the door, and began to
climb the spiral stair that led upwards. Halfway
was another door, also safely locked. She unlocked this too. She began to feel rather silly.
Nobody could have gone through locked
doors. And there now – the top one was well
and truly locked also! She gave a sigh of relief
and ran down the spiral stairway, locking the
middle door, and then the bottom one. She gave
the keys to the Professor, who by now was
feeling rather chilly!

'All locked,' said Jenny. 'But I'm still sure

someone was about. I could have sworn I saw someone up that tower wall, and heard somebody else whispering below.'

'I expect you were so scared that you imagined things, Jenny,' said the Professor, yawning. 'I think you'll agree with me that the wall is far too steep for anyone to climb – and I'm pretty certain I'd have heard it if a ladder had been dragged about the courtyard!'

'Well, I'm sure I'm very sorry,' said poor Jenny. 'It's a good thing we didn't wake Tinker – though I'm surprised Mischief didn't hear something and come running down the stairs.'

'But Mischief is surely with Tinker, camping out in the field!' said the Professor in surprise.

'No – Tinker and Mischief are back. I found them asleep in bed – but not the others!' said Jenny. 'Maybe Tinker had quarrelled with them. Funny that Mischief didn't come running out to see what was up – he must have heard us!'

'Mischief is clever – but not clever enough to open Tinker's bedroom door,' said the Professor, yawning again. 'Good night, Jenny. Don't worry. You'll feel all right in the morning, and that will be that!'

The Professor went sleepily to his room. He looked out of the window down into the courtyard and then across at the tower, and smiled. Dear Jenny! She did rather let her imagination run away with her! As if anyone in the world could get up into that tower room without a ladder! And HOW could a long, long ladder be brought into that small courtyard without either being seen or heard? The Professor yawned once more and climbed into bed.

But someone *had* been in the tower room! Someone very clever, someone very light-fingered! What a shock for poor Professor Hayling next morning when he crossed the courtyard, unlocked the bottom door of the tower – walked up the spiral stairway – unlocked the middle door, and went on up the stairway again – and finally unlocked the top door and opened it wide.

He stood and stared in horror. The place was

upside down! All his papers were scattered everywhere. He crouched down at once to see if any were missing. Yes – quite a lot! But they seemed to have been taken quite haphazardly – a few pages from this notebook – a few pages from that – some letters he had written and left on his desk to post – and good gracious, the ink was spilt all over the place – and the little clock was gone from the mantelpiece. So Jenny was right – a thief *had* been about last night. A thief that could apparently get through three locked doors – or else could climb up a long, long ladder that he had put outside without being seen – and taken away again!

'I'll have to ring the police,' he thought. 'But I must say it's a mystery! I wonder if Tinker heard anything in the night? No, he couldn't have, or he would have run to fetch me. It's a mystery – a real puzzle of a MYSTERY!'

[12]

A shock for Tinker

Tinker was horrified when Jenny told him the next morning what had happened. 'Your father's in a rare old state,' she said. 'He came down early this morning because he wanted to finish some work up in the tower – and as soon as he unlocked the top door into the tower room, he saw the whole room upside down and some of his precious papers gone, and—'

'JENNY! How awful!' said Tinker. 'Dad kept his most precious papers there – with all the figures for that new electric thing of his. It's a wonderful thing, too marvellous for words, Jenny, it's for—'

'Now don't you give away any of your father's plans, not even to *me*,' said Jenny. 'You've been told that before. Maybe you've been talking too much already, and somebody's ears took it all in!'

Tinker suddenly felt sick. *Was* it because of something he had been silly enough to say in public? In the bus, perhaps? Or in the circus field? What would the others say – especially Julian – when they heard that someone had come in the night and stolen precious papers containing figures and diagrams for some of his father's inventions? Julian would be sure to say that it was *his* fault for not keeping his mouth shut! Oh dear – would *this* be in the papers – and would hordes of people come visiting the place again, staring and whispering and ex-claiming in awe at his father's curious tower with its waving tentacles?

He dressed quickly and ran downstairs. Jen-ny had told him that she was sure she had heard whispering down in the courtyard the night before, and had seen someone climbing up the tower. 'Your father says nobody could have brought a long ladder into that courtyard,' she said. 'Not without us seeing it, anyway, or hearing some kind of noise when it was dragged in. But it might have been a sliding ladder, mightn't it? That would be a smallish thing, with ropes to pull out the sliding part.'

'Yes. Like the window cleaner uses,' said Tinker. 'It couldn't have been the window cleaner, could it?'

'No. He's a really decent fellow,' said Jenny. 'I've known him for twenty years. So put *that* out of your head. But the ladder could certainly have been the sort that window cleaners use. We'll go out into the courtyard as soon as I've finished washing-up, and see if we can find the marks where the ladder was dragged over the courtyard. Though I must say I didn't hear any *dragging* noises. I heard whispering – and a kind of slithery noise – but that's all.'

'The slithery noise *might* have been made by the ladder when it was dragged along!' said Tinker. 'Hey – look at old Mischief. He's listening as if he understood every word. Mischief, why didn't you wake me up last night when all this was going on? You usually wake if anything unusual happens, or you hear a strange noise.'

Mischief leapt into Tinker's arms and cuddled there. He didn't like it when Tinker was upset about anything; he knew by the boy's voice that he was worried. He made small comforting noises, and rubbed his monkey nose against the boy's chin.

'You'd better go to your father,' said Jenny. 'You might be able to comfort him a little. He's very upset indeed. He's up in the tower room, trying to sort out his papers. My word, they were left in a state – scattered all over the room!'

Tinker stood up to go, and was astonished to find that he was shaky at the knees. Would his father ask him if he had been talking about the work he was doing? Oh dear – he had even boasted about it just the day before, and talked about his father's sko-wheel, and the wonderful new machine, the electric trosymon! Tinker's knees became shakier than ever.

But, fortunately, his father was far too upset

about his muddled room and missing papers to worry about anything Tinker had said or done. He was up in the tower room, trying to discover which of his papers were missing.

'Ah, Tinker,' he said, when the boy came into the tower room. 'Just give me a hand, will you? The thief who came last night must have knocked the whole bunch of papers off the table, down on the floor – and fortunately he seems not to have seen some that went under the table. So I doubt very much if the papers he *did* take away with him will be of any use. He'd need to be quite a scientist to understand them, without having the ones he left behind.'

'Will he come back for the others, then?' asked Tinker.

'Probably,' said his father. 'But I shall hide them somewhere. Can you think of a good hiding place, Tinker?'

'Dad – don't *you* hide them,' begged Tinker. 'Not unless you tell *me* where they are! You know how you forget things! You might forget where you'd put this bunch of papers, and then you wouldn't be able to go on with your inventions. Have you copies of the stolen sheets of figures and diagrams?'

'No. But they're all in my head as well as on paper,' said his father. 'It will take me a bit of time to work them all out again, but it can be done. It's a nuisance – especially as I'm working to a date. Now run along, Tinker, please. I've work to do.'

Tinker went down the spiral staircase of the tower. He'd have to make sure that his father *did* hide away those papers very carefully indeed – in some really good place. 'Oh dear – I hope he won't do what he did with the last lot of papers he wanted to hide,' he thought. 'He stuffed them up the chimney – and they nearly went up in flames because Jenny thought she'd light the fire the next night, it was unexpectedly so cold. Good thing they fell down when she laid the fire and she rescued them before they got burnt! Why are brainy people like Dad so silly about ordinary things! I BET he'll either forget where he puts them – or go and hide them in some easy place where anyone could find them!'

He went to talk to Jenny. 'Jenny – Dad says that the thief only took *some* of his papers – and that he can't make much use of the ones he took, unless he has the whole lot. And Dad says he thinks that when the thief finds this out, he'll try to steal the rest of the papers.'

'Well, let him try!' said Jenny. '*I* could hide them in a place where no thief would find them – if your Dad would let *me* have them. I shan't tell you where!'

'*I'm* afraid he might hide them up a chimney again, or some silly place like that,' said Tinker, looking so worried that Jenny felt really worried too! 'They've got to be hidden somewhere NOBODY would think of looking. And if Dad finds a place like that he'll promptly forget all about it, and never be able to find them again! But a thief might find them – he'd know ALL the places to look in.'

'Let's go up to the tower room and clear up the mess that the spilt ink made, and see if your father has taken his precious papers and hidden them somewhere there,' said Jenny. 'It would be just like him to hide them in the very room that the thief went to last night! Up the ladder, in at the window – left wide open, I've no doubt – snatched up every paper he could see, the rogue, and then raced down the ladder again!'

'Come on up to the tower, then,' said Tinker. 'I only hope Dad isn't there!'

'He's just crossing the courtyard, look,' said Jenny, leaning out of the window. 'See, there he is – carrying something under his arm.'

'His morning newspapers,' said Tinker. 'It looks as if he's going to have a jolly good read, doesn't it? Oh dear, I do hope all this won't be printed in the newspapers – it would bring hordes of people down here again. Do you remember how awful it was last time, Jenny – people even walked over the flower-beds!'

'Hoo – some people like to poke their noses into everything!' said Jenny. 'I don't mind telling you that I emptied my dirty washing water out of the window on to a few of them – quite by mistake, of course – how was *I* to know they were out there, staring up and down?'

Tinker gave a shout of laughter. 'I wish I'd seen that!' he said. 'Oh Jenny – if people come poking their noses into Dad's business again, DO let's empty water on their silly heads! Come on, Jenny – let's go up to the tower room now Dad's out of the way. Quick!'

They were soon out in the courtyard and, as they crossed it, Jenny stopped and looked hard at the ground.

'What are you looking for?' asked Tinker.

'Just to see if there are any marks that might have been made by someone dragging a ladder across,' said Jenny. 'I heard a funny slithering sound, you know but it didn't *sound* like a ladder being dragged across.'

The two of them looked all over the courtyard, but could see no marks there that could possibly have been made by a ladder.

'Funny,' said Jenny. 'It worries me, that slithery sound.' She looked up at the tall, steep wall of the tower. It was made of flint-stones of all shapes and sizes, the kind found in the countryside round about Kirrin and Big Hollow.

'Well, I suppose a *cat* might climb up,' said Jenny, doubtfully. 'But not a *man*. He'd slip sooner or later. It would be far too dangerous. I doubt if even a cat would get far.'

'And yet you say you thought you saw someone up the tower wall!' said Tinker. 'Go on, Jenny – it must have been the shadow of a passing cloud that you saw! Look up this wall – now can you imagine ANYONE climbing up it at night, when it was dark?'

Jenny stared up. 'No – you're right. Only a madman would even try. Well, my eyes must have played me up, then, when I looked out last night – but I really *did* think I saw a dark shadow climbing up the tower wall. Still, it's easy to be mistaken at night. And I don't believe there was a ladder, either! There *would* be marks on the paving-stones of the courtyard if there had been a ladder. Oh well – let's hurry on up to the tower room before your Dad decides to go back to it again!'

They went up the spiral stairway. All the doors were unlocked, as it was plain that the Professor was going to come back again after he had read his papers.

'All the same – he shouldn't leave the doors unlocked, even for a minute!' said Jenny. 'Well, here we are – just look at the ink splashes everywhere – and that dear little clock that kept such good time is gone. Now what would the thief want with a clock, I'd like to know?'

'It would be small and neat enough to pop into his pocket,' said Tinker. 'If he was dishonest enough to steal Dad's papers, he would certainly not say no to a nice little clock like that! He's probably taken other things too!'

They went right into the room, and Jenny at once gave a loud exclamation. 'LOOK! Aren't those some of the papers your father was working on – on the table there? All covered with tiny figures?'

Tinker looked closely at them. 'Yes – they're his very latest papers. He showed me them the other day. I remember this diagram. Jenny –

how COULD he leave them on the table with the door unlocked this morning – when only last night the thief was here! How could he? He *said* he was going to hide them away so carefully, because, if the thief found them, he could use them with the other papers that were stolen – but as long as the thief only had half of them, they wouldn't be much use – and now he's forgotten all about hiding them, after all!'

'Look now, Tinker – let's hide them away ourselves,' said Jenny, 'and not tell him where they are. These thieves will have another try for them, no doubt about that. Let's think of some place where they'd be absolutely safe.'

'*I* know!' said Tinker. 'We could hide them on Kirrin Island! Somewhere in the old ruined castle! NOBODY would guess they were there.'

'Now that's a *fine* idea!' said Jenny. 'I'd be glad to think they were out of the house.' She gathered up the papers quickly. 'Here you are. You'd better tell Julian and the others, and go across to the island with them as soon as you can. My, what a relief to think they'll be well away from here. I'll be able to sleep soundly in my bed at nights then!'

Tinker stuffed the precious papers under his jersey, and he and Jenny ran at top speed down the spiral stairway. They saw the Professor not far off, and he turned and hailed them. 'Tinker! Jenny! I know what you're going to ask me! You want to know where I've hidden those papers of mine. Come here and I'll whisper!'

Not knowing quite what to say, the two went rather guiltily over to Tinker's father. He whispered loudly, 'I've wrapped them up, and put them under the coal at the back of the coal-cellar – right at the *very* back!'

'And a fine mess you've made of your trousers,' said Jenny, disgusted. 'And good gracious – you must have sat down in the coal yourself! You look a right mess. Come along and let me brush you down. Not indoors, though, or the place will be thick with coal-dust!'

'Don't you think it was a good hiding place, Jenny?' asked the Professor. 'Ha – you thought I'd forget to hide them, didn't you?'

He went off, looking very pleased with himself. Jenny chuckled in delight. 'Dear old Professor! He's hidden all his *newspapers* there, but not a single one of his own precious papers. And now whatever shall we tell him when he wants the morning papers? Tinker, you cycle out to the paper shop and get another lot. My goodness – what it is to have a brainy man in the house! Whatever will he do next?'

[13]

Quite a lot of plans!

After Tinker had fetched a new supply of morning papers, he decided to go down to the camp in the field and tell the others all that had happened that morning. He still felt angry about being ticked off by Julian the night before – but he simply couldn't wait to tell the others about the robbery – and about the grand idea he, Tinker, had of hiding the rest of his father's papers on Kirrin Island.

So off he went, with Mischief happily on his shoulder, holding tightly to his hair. The others were all there in the field. They had just come back from a shopping expedition, and Tinker's eyes gleamed when he saw the various tinned meats and tinned fruits, fresh rolls, tomatoes and apples and bananas that had been brought back from the shops at Big Hollow.

Julian was glad to see that Tinker looked bright and cheerful. He was afraid that the boy might have sulked, and that would have spoilt things for the others.

'Hi!' said Tinker. 'I've got news!' And he proceeded to tell the others all about the happenings of the night before, ending up with his father solemnly going off to hide his morning newspapers under the coal at the back of the coal-cellar, under the impression that he was hiding the rest of his precious papers.

'But why on earth didn't you tell him he had left his valuable papers behind and hidden his newspapers?' asked George.

'Because, if he knew that, he'd go and hide the *precious* papers somewhere, and forget where he'd put them – and they might be lost for ever!' said Tinker.

'Well, what are *you* going to do with them?' asked Dick.

'I've had rather a brainwave,' said Tinker, as modestly as he could. 'Er – I thought that *we'd* hide them away ourselves, where nobody could *possibly* find them.'

'And where is this wonderful hiding place?' asked Dick.

'On Kirrin Island!' said Tinker, triumphantly. 'Who'd think of looking *there*? And as we shall *all* know the hiding place, we can't possibly forget it. The papers will be absolutely safe. Dad can get on with the rest of his ideas without worrying about anything?'

'Have you told him all this?' asked Julian.

'Well, no,' said Tinker. 'Jenny thought we'd better just keep it to ourselves. She's pretty certain the thieves will try their hand at breaking in to get the rest of the papers, though.'

'Ha! Well, I vote we scribble some papers ourselves,' said Dick. 'Complete with wonderful diagrams, and all kinds of peculiar figurings and numberings. I feel I could do that very well! And we'd leave them up in the tower room for the thieves to take – they'd think they were the ones they'd missed!'

Everyone chuckled. 'Idiot!' said Julian. 'Still

– it's not a bad idea to leave something behind for the thieves that isn't worth a moment's look – and hide the genuine figures where they'd never dream of finding them – on Kirrin Island!'

'When shall we go?' asked George. 'It's ages since I've visited my island – and will you believe it, last time I rowed over *trippers* had been there and left their beastly mess everywhere! Paper bags, broken glass, lettuce leaves, orange peel, ugh!'

'Why DO people do that?' asked Anne. 'They'd hate to have to sit in the midst of *other* people's mess – so why in the world can't they clear up their own?'

'Oh, they're probably just like that in their own homes,' said Dick. 'All mess and litter – and yet it takes so little time to clear up a picnic mess, and leave the place decent for the next comers.'

'What did you do with all the mess left on Kirrin Island?' asked Julian.

'I buried it deep in the sand at the back of one of the beaches,' said George. 'Where the tide can't turn it all up again. And with every dig of my spade I said "Blow you, you awful trippers without manners, blow you – and next time you go anywhere, may you find someone else's litter to make you feel sick. Blow you!"'

George looked and sounded so very fierce that everyone burst out laughing. Timmy sat there with his tongue lolling out, looking as if he were laughing too, and Mischief made a funny little noise rather like a giggle.

'Good old George. She always says straight out what she thinks!' said Julian.

They sat and talked over their plans for some time. 'Dick and Julian had better make the fake plans and figures,' said George. 'They'd be better at that kind of thing than anyone else. And Tinker can plant them somewhere in his father's tower room for the thief to take if he goes there again – and I bet he will. He found it easy enough last night!'

'And George could take Tinker's father's papers with the *correct* figures and plans over to Kirrin Island,' said Anne.

'Not till night time, though,' said Dick. 'If anyone were on the watch, and saw George rowing over there, they might guess she was taking something important to hide. They might be watching her father too. By the way – where *are* these papers? You did not leave them behind at home, did you, Tinker?'

'I didn't dare to,' said Tinker. 'I felt as if there might be eyes peeping at me, watching and hoping I'd go out and leave the papers behind. I've got them under my jersey, just here!' And he patted the top of his stomach.

'Oh – so *that*'s why you look as if you've had too much breakfast!' said George. 'Well – what shall our plans be?'

'We'd better make out the false papers straight away, with figures and diagrams,' said Julian. 'Just in case thieves come sooner than we think. Tinker, we'd better go into *your* house to do those. If we go to George's her father might spot us and wonder what on earth we were doing. We'd probably be sent off, anyway, because of the scarlet fever business.'

'Well, what about *my* father?' said Tinker. '*He* might spot us too. Anyway, he's not keen on my having anyone there this week, because he's so busy with his new invention. It's awfully good, and—'

'*Tinker* – don't start spilling beans again!' said Julian, warningly. 'I say it would be best to go to your house.'

'What about *me* going indoors and bringing out Dad's big drawing-board, and some of his paper, and his mapping pens and ink, and doing the diagrams and things out here in the tent?' said Tinker. 'Honestly, I never know when Dad is going to come into my room. He'd wonder what on *earth* we were doing if he found us all there! We can have a good look at the papers I've got under my jersey, and do a whole lot in the same style – not the *same* figures, naturally – and we could do some diagrams too.'

'All right,' said Julian, giving way, as he saw that Tinker was genuinely afraid that his father might see them making the false papers. 'Go and get the drawing-board and come back with it, and anything else we'll need. You go with him, George.'

'Right,' said George, and she and Tinker went up Tinker's garden to the house. Tinker scouted round to see if his father was anywhere about, but couldn't see him. He found a large drawing-board, some big sheets of paper used by his father for working out his figures, and a book of odd but easy-to-copy diagrams. He also brought mapping pens, Indian ink and blotting-paper, and even remembered drawing-pins to pin the sheets of paper to the board. George carried half the things, and kept a sharp lookout for Tinker's father.

'It's all right. He's asleep somewhere – can't you hear that noise?' asked Tinker; and sure enough George could – a gentle snoring from some room not far off!

They went back down the garden and over the fence, handing everything to the others before they climbed over. 'Good!' said Julian. 'Now we can produce some beautiful charts of figures that mean absolutely nothing at all – and diagrams that will look perfect and not mean a thing either!'

'Better come into the tent,' said George. 'If anyone wanders down from the circus camp, they might ask us what we're doing.'

So they all went into the boys' tent, which was the bigger one, Timmy too, and Mischief, who was delighted to be with the big dog. Julian soon set to work, though he found the space rather cramped. They were all watching him in admiration as he set out rows of beautiful, meaningless, figures when Timmy suddenly gave a deep growl, and all his hackles rose up on his neck.

Julian turned the drawing-board over at once, and sat on it. The canvas doorway of the tent was pulled aside and in poked the grinning face of Charlie the Chimp!

'Oh, it's *you*, Charlie!' said Julian. 'Well, well, well, and how are you today?'

The chimpanzee grinned even more widely, and held out his hand. Julian shook it solemnly, and the chimpanzee went carefully all round the tent, shaking hands with everyone.

'Sit down, Charlie,' said Dick. 'I suppose you've let yourself out of your cage as usual, and come to see what we've got for our dinner. Well, you'll be glad to hear we've got enough for you as well as ourselves.'

Charlie squashed himself between Timmy and Tinker, and with much interest watched Julian at work with his pen and ink. 'I bet that chimp could draw, if you gave him a piece of paper and a pencil,' said Anne.

So, to keep him quiet, he was given a pencil, and a notebook. He at once began to scribble in it very earnestly.

'Goodness – he's doing a whole lot of funny figures!' said Anne. 'He's trying to copy *you*, Ju!'

'If he's not careful, I'll hand the whole job over to him!' said Julian, with a chuckle. 'George, let's talk about your plans for tonight. I think, if you are going over to Kirrin Island to hide those papers, you must take Timmy with you.'

'Oh, I will!' said George. 'Not that there will be a single soul on the island, but I'd like old Tim just for company. I'll take the papers straight to the island, land, and hide them.'

'Where?' asked Julian.

'Oh, I'll decide that when I'm there,' said George. 'Somewhere cunning! I know my own little island from top to bottom. And there those papers will stay until all danger is past. We'll let Professor Hayling think he has hidden them somewhere himself, and forgotten where! It will be fun to row across to my island at night, with Timmy.'

'The thieves can make do with *my* figures and diagrams if they come to the tower room again,' said Julian. 'Don't they look professional?'

They certainly did! Everyone looked at the neat figures and carefully drawn diagrams with admiration.

Timmy suddenly sat up and gave a deep growl again. Charlie the Chimp patted him as if to say 'What's wrong, old boy?' but

Timmy took no notice and went on growling. He suddenly shot out of the tent, and there was a shout from someone outside. 'Get off! Get down! GET DOWN!'

George swung back the tent opening. Mr Wooh was there, looking extremely frightened as Timmy growled menacingly round his ankles. Charlie the Chimp ran up to him on all fours and, angry because Timmy was snarling at his friend, showed his teeth suddenly at the big dog. George was terrified. 'Don't let them fight!' she cried, afraid that Timmy would get decidedly the worst of it. Charlie was jumping up and down in a most alarming way.

'Charleee!' said Mr Wooh in his deep voice. 'Charleee!'

And Charlie stopped jumping up and down and making horrible noises, and leapt straight on to Mr Wooh's back, putting his arms round his neck.

Mr Wooh bowed courteously to them all. 'I trust I have not disturbed you, my friends,' he said, with his strong accent. 'I'll now take a little walk with my friend Charleee. You come again to see our show, I hope. Yes? No?'

'Probably,' said Dick, noticing that the magician had taken a quick and interested look at Julian's figures and diagrams. Julian covered them up immediately, as if he didn't want the magician to see them. He had seen something in the man's eyes that puzzled him. Could Mr Wooh possibly have had anything to do with the theft of the papers the night before? After all, he was a wizard at figures himself – he might be able to read the Professor's figures and diagrams and understand them perfectly. Well – he wouldn't gather much from the ones Julian was now doing – they were more or less nonsense made up by Julian himself to deceive anyone interested in the real ones.

'I interrupt you? Pardon me!' said Mr Wooh, and bowed himself politely away from the group in the tent. Charlie the Chimp followed him, hoping that Mischief would too, so that they could have a game. But Mischief didn't want to. He didn't like Mr Wooh.

'Well, I didn't realise that anyone from the circus would walk down the field so quietly, and be able to hear what we were saying inside the tent,' said Julian, worried. 'I didn't like the look in his eyes. Dick – you don't suppose he heard anything we were saying, do you?'

'Would it matter?' said Dick.

'It might,' said Julian. 'Do you think he heard what George said about going over to Kirrin Island with the other papers – the valuable ones that the thieves didn't see in the tower room last night? I wouldn't let George go if I thought he had heard. In fact, I think she'd better *not* go. She might run into danger.'

'Don't be silly, Ju,' said George. 'I *am* going. And Timmy will be with me.'

'You heard what I said, George. You are *not* to go!' said Julian. '*I'll* take the papers and hide them on the island. I'll get them when it's dark, fairly late. I'll cycle over to Kirrin and untie the boat you keep there, and row over to the island.'

'All right, Julian,' said George, astonishingly

meekly. 'Shall we have a meal now? We've only to open the tins, and empty the tomatoes and lettuces out of the basket there. And the drinks are in that cool corner over there.'

'Right,' said Julian, glad that George had given way to him so easily. *He* would go across in George's boat and find a good hiding place. If danger was about, he reckoned he could deal with it better than George could.

Yes, Julian, you may be right. But don't be too sure about tonight!

[14]
Ladders – and a lot of fun!

The children stared after Mr Wooh and the chimpanzee. They saw Charlie pick up two empty buckets, one in each strong paw, and race off to the right with them.

'Where's he going?' said Anne, astonished at the rate he was running along.

'I bet he's going to get some water from the stream in those pails, and take them to whoever washes down the horses,' said George. She was right! Charlie soon came back again, walking this time, holding a heavy pail of water in each hand!

'Well, I must say that chimpanzee is jolly useful!' said Dick. 'Look – there's Madelon who trains those beautiful horses that paraded round the ring last night – she's wearing old trousers this morning, she looks quite different.

There – Charlie has set the pails of water down beside her. I bet that as soon as she wants any more water, he'll be off again to the stream!'

'I rather like old Charlie,' said Anne. 'I didn't at first – but now I do. I wish he didn't belong to Mr Wooh.'

Julian stood up, looking down at the paper on which he had so carefully written lines of small figures and drawn many peculiar diagrams. 'I somehow feel this isn't much good now,' he said. 'I think Mr Wooh must have guessed it was all a make-up as soon as he saw it. He gave himself away a bit, though – I saw him looking at the paper in a rather startled way, as if he'd seen something very like it very recently indeed!'

'So he had, the wretch, if he'd sent someone up to get my dad's papers out of the tower room!' said Tinker. 'Hey! What about having a look round the circus to see if we can spot a ladder anywhere – one tall enough to reach the tower room!'

'Good idea!' said Dick. 'Come on – we'll go

now. Chuck that drawing-board and diagram paper over our fence, Ju. I hardly think it's worth your while to finish it.'

The Five, with Tinker and Mischief, wandered down the field to where the circus was encamped. Dick spotted a ladder lying in the grass, and nudged Julian.

'Julian! See that? Would it reach the tower?' Julian walked over to it. It certainly was very, very long – but *would* it be long enough? No – he didn't think it would. Still – he might as well find out who owned it. At that moment up came the Boneless Man, walking perfectly. He grinned at the children – and then suddenly put all his double-joints to work, bent his knees into peculiar positions, twisted his head round so that he was looking over his own back, and then bent his double-jointed arms the wrong way, so that he looked very odd indeed!

'Don't! I don't like it!' said Anne. 'You look so peculiar and strange! Why are you called the *Boneless* Man? You aren't boneless – you just make yourself *look* as if you were, with all those funny double-joints of yours!'

The Boneless Man seemed suddenly to lose all his bones, and crumpled up on the grass in a funny heap. The children couldn't help laughing. He didn't look as if he had any bones at all then!

'Er – can you climb ladders if you're double-jointed?' asked Julian, suddenly.

'Of course!' said the Boneless Man. 'Run up them backwards, forwards, sideways – any way you like.'

'Is that *your* ladder, then?' asked Dick, nodding his head towards the ladder in the grass.

'Well – I use it, but so does everyone else!' said the Boneless Man, turning his head the wrong way round, so that it seemed as if it was put on back to front. It was odd to speak to someone whose head did that – one minute they were talking to his face, the next to the back of his head!

'I *wish* you wouldn't do that,' said Anne. 'It makes me feel giddy.'

'Do you use that ladder to put the flag on the top of the circus tent?' asked Dick. 'It doesn't look long enough for that.'

'It isn't,' said the Boneless Man, turning his head the right way round, much to Anne's relief. 'There's a much longer one over there – it takes three men to carry it, it's so heavy – but the centre circus pole is very tall, as you see. One man couldn't *possibly* carry the long ladder.'

The children looked at one another. That ruled out the very long ladder too, then. If it needed three men to carry it, Jenny would certainly have heard a lot more noise last night!

'Are there any more ladders in the circus camp?'

'No – just the two. Why? Thinking of buying one?' said the Boneless Man. 'I must go. The Boss is beckoning to me.' Off he went, walking in a most peculiar fashion, using his double-joints for all he was worth!

'What about the acrobats?' said Julian. '*They* must be used to climbing and clambering everywhere. I wonder if any of *them* could have climbed the wall?'

'I don't think so,' said Tinker. 'I had a good look at it this morning – and although there *is* a kind of creeper climbing up the wall, it stops halfway – and above that there's just the stone wall. Even an acrobat would have to have some help up the tower wall!'

'Could the *clowns* have found a way?' said George. 'No – I suppose they're not as good even as the acrobats at climbing. I don't believe the thief *could* have been anyone from the circus after all. Look – what's that on the ground over there – outside that tent?'

They all went over to see. It looked like a pile of dark-grey fur. George touched it with her toe. 'Oh – *I* know what it is – the donkey-skin!'

'Golly – so it is!' cried Tinker in delight, and picked it up – or tried to. It was much too heavy for him to hold up all of it.

In a trice Dick and George were inside that donkey-skin! Dick had the head, and found that he *could* see quite well where he was going,

for the donkey neck had neat eye-holes in it –
the head itself was stuffed with paper. George
was the back legs, and kicked up her feet and
made the donkey look extremely lively. The
others roared with laughter.

Someone shouted loudly. 'Hey – you leave
that donkey-skin alone!'

It was Jeremy. He came running up, looking
furious. He had a stick in his hand, and hit out
at the donkey's hind parts, giving poor George
a good old whack, and making her yell.

'Hey! Stop that, it hurt!'

Tinker looked furiously at Jeremy. 'How
dare you do that?' he shouted. 'Dick and
George are in the donkey-skin. Put down that
stick!'

But Jeremy gave the donkey's hind legs another whack and George yelled again. Tinker
gave a shout too, and flung himself on Jeremy,
trying to get the stick out of his hand. The boy
struggled, holding on to the stick, but Tinker
gave him a straight blow on the chest, and
down he went!

'Ha! I *said* I'd knock you down sometime, and I have!' yelled Tinker. 'Get up and fight. *I'll* teach you not to hit animals!'

'Now stop it, Tinker,' said Julian. 'Come out of the skin, you two idiots, before old Grandad comes up. He looks as if he's on his way now!'

Jeremy was up now, and danced round Tinker with doubled fists. Before either boy could exchange a blow, Grandad's great voice came to them.

'NOW THEN! STOP IT!'

Jeremy swung his fist at Tinker, who dodged, and then in his turn hit out at Jeremy, who ran back – straight into old Grandad, who at once clutched him.

By this time George and Dick were out of the donkey-skin, looking rather ashamed of themselves. Old Grandad grinned at them, still holding on to the furious Jeremy. 'Fight's off,' said Grandad to Tinker and Jeremy. 'If you want to go on, either of you, you can fight *me*, not each other.'

However, neither of the boys wanted to take

on old Grandad. He might be old, but he could still give some mighty slaps, as Jeremy very well knew. They stood staring at one another, looking rather sheepish.

'Go on – shake hands and be friends,' said Grandad. 'Quick, now, or I'll do a little fighting myself!'

Tinker held out his hand just as Jeremy held out his. They shook, grinning at one another. 'That's right!' said old Grandad. 'No harm done. No bones broken. You're quits now, so no more knocking each other about.'

'Right, Grandad,' said Jeremy, giving him a friendly punch. The old man turned to Dick and George. 'And if *you* want to borrow that donkey-skin, you're welcome,' said old Grandad. 'But it's manners to ask the owner's permission first.'

'Yes. Sorry,' said Dick, grinning. He wondered what Professor Hayling and Jenny would say if he and George did borrow it, and galloped into Hollow House at top speed. But no – he decided reluctantly that Jenny might be scared stiff and give notice, and that would never do. She wouldn't at all like being chased by an apparently mad donkey, nor would Professor Hayling.

Grandad went off, and Julian spoke to Jeremy, who wasn't quite sure whether to go or to stay. 'We saw old Charlie carrying pails of water for the horses,' he said. 'Isn't he strong!'

Jeremy grinned, glad to be friends again, and to be able to stay with the Five and Tinker. They wandered all round the field together, looking at the magnificent horses and at Dead-Shot Dick doing a little practising at shooting and then watched one small acrobat practising amazing jumps and somersaults.

Mischief the monkey came with them. He was absolutely at home with everyone in the circus now, man, woman or animal. He leapt on to the horses' backs, and they didn't mind! He pretended to help Charlie the Chimp to carry one of the pails of water – he ran off with Dead-Shot Dick's cap. He went into the chimp's cage and cuddled up in the straw with him, scrabbling about as if the cage belonged to him. He even went into Grandad's tent and came out with a small bottle of lemonade! He couldn't get the top off, and took it to Charlie, who was watching nearby! Charlie promptly forced it off with his strong front paws – and then, to Mischief's disgust, tipped up the bottle and drank the lot!

Mischief was very angry indeed. He ran to Charlie's cage, which was open, and sent the straw flying everywhere. Charlie sat outside his cage and enjoyed the fun, grinning happily.

'Come out, Mischief!' called Tinker. 'You're making a nuisance of yourself!'

'Let him be,' said one of the acrobats, who was standing nearby. 'Old Charlie enjoys a bit of temper – when it's someone else's! Look at him sitting grinning there.'

They watched for a few seconds more, to make sure that Mischief wasn't annoying the big chimpanzee, and then turned to watch Monty and Winks, the clowns, having an argument, which ended in Monty throwing water over Winks, and Winks emptying a basket of rubbish over Monty. What a pair!

When they turned to see if Mischief was still annoying Charlie, they saw that the little monkey had left the cage, and was tearing down the field to the fence. He leapt up, and over, and disappeared.

'He must think it's dinner-time,' said Tinker, looking at his watch. 'And gosh, so it is. Come on everyone, Jenny will be in a fine old fury if we're really late – it's hot dinner today.'

Away they all went in a hurry. Hot dinner! Over the fence, then, and up the garden at top speed. They mustn't keep a hot dinner waiting – or Jenny either!

[15]

A happy day – and a shock for Julian

Tinker and the Five were two minutes late for their dinner. Jenny was just taking it in, looking a little grim, as she had not been able to find the children anywhere. 'Ah – here you are at last!' she said. 'I looked down the garden but you were nowhere to be seen. It's a good thing you came in when you did – five minutes more and I'd have taken the dinner back again.'

'*Dear* Jenny, you know you wouldn't,' said Tinker, giving her a sudden squeeze that made her squeal. 'Oh, how good it smells! Mmmmm-mmmmm!'

'You and your mmmmms!' said Jenny, pushing Tinker away. 'And I've told you before, that I don't mind a gentle hug, but those *squeezes* of yours take all my breath away. *No*, Tinker, keep away from me – another squeeze like that and I'll feel like a lemon!'

Everyone laughed at that. Jenny did say the most amusing things. Anne felt sorry that she hadn't offered to stay and help her with the dinner. Oh dear – the time went so quickly, once they were all out together.

The talk at dinner-time was very lively. So was Mischief the monkey! He took bits from everyone's plate and handed some of them down to Timmy, who was lying under the table as usual. Timmy appreciated these titbits very much!

'Well! *I* didn't see a single ladder in the circus camp that was tall enough to reach up to the tower room,' said George.

'No. If there was one, it was jolly well hidden,' said Dick. 'Pass the mustard, someone!'

'In front of you, idiot,' said Julian. 'You know I'm beginning to wonder if Mr Wooh had anything to do with the stealing of your father's papers, Tinker. I can't somehow see him climbing high ladders – he's so – so . . .'

'Polite and proper,' said Anne. 'Actually, I can't think of *any*one in the circus who would either *want* the papers, or is nasty enough to steal them. They're all so nice.'

'I still think Mr Wooh is the most *likely* one,' said Julian. 'He's interested in complicated figures and clever inventions. But all the same, I'm beginning to think I'm wrong. He could NOT have got up to the tower room as there is no ladder long enough – and I really doubt if he'd *dare* to take a ladder into the courtyard and risk putting it up to the tower. He might so easily be caught.'

'Right. We'll rule him out,' said Tinker. 'But if nobody went up the spiral stairway, because all doors were locked, and nobody used a ladder, I don't see HOW those papers disappeared.'

'Wind took them out of the window, perhaps?' suggested Anne. 'Would that be possible?'

'No. For two reasons,' said Julian. 'One is that the window wasn't wide enough open for the wind to blow in with enough strength to blow papers *out*. And secondly, we'd have been sure to have found some of them down in the courtyard if they'd been blown out. But we didn't find a single one there.'

'Well – if nobody got through the three locked doors, and nobody got through the window, HOW did those papers get stolen?' demanded George. 'It would have been a miracle for those papers to have hopped away by themselves – and I don't believe in that kind of miracle!'

There was a long silence. What a mystery it was! 'I suppose Tinker's father couldn't *possibly* have gone walking in his sleep, and taken them, could he?' asked Anne.

'Well – I don't know if a sleep-walker can unlock doors with the right keys, and steal his own papers, leaving some on the floor, and then walk carefully down the spiral stairway still fast asleep, locking all the doors behind him, and then go to his own bedroom, get into bed, and then wake up in the morning without remembering a single moment of the whole thing!' said Julian.

'No. It can't be possible,' said Dick. 'Have you ever known your father to walk in his sleep, Tinker?'

Tinker considered. 'No, I can't say I have,' he said. 'He's a very light sleeper, usually. No. I don't believe Dad did all that in his sleep. It was somebody else.'

'It must have been some sort of miracle man, then,' said George. 'No *ordinary* person could do it. And whoever planned it wanted those papers very, very badly, or he would never have risked getting them against so many odds.'

'And if he wanted them so VERY badly, he'll certainly make an effort to get the ones he left behind under the table,' said Julian. 'Good thing we've got those! He will probably try to get up into the tower the same way as he did before – but goodness knows what it was!'

'Well – those papers will be safely out of his way, tonight!' said George. 'On my island!'

'Yes,' said Julian. 'I'll find a most unlikely

hiding place – somewhere about the ruined castle, I think. By the way – I hope you haven't *still* got them under your jersey, Tinker. No – you don't look fat any more. What have you done with them?'

'George said I'd better give them to her to keep, in case they slipped out of my jersey,' said Tinker. 'You took them, didn't you, George?'

'Yes,' said George. 'Don't let's talk about it any more.'

'Why not? The thief's not here. He can't be listening to us!' said Tinker. 'I believe you're cross, George, because Julian won't let you take the papers yourself!'

'Oh, do shut up, Tinker,' said George. 'I shall be jolly cross with *you* in a minute, if you let Mischief upset your glass of lemonade again, all over my bread. Take him off the table! His manners are getting worse!'

'They aren't – but your temper is!' said Tinker and promptly received a kick under the table from Julian. He was about to kick back but thought better of it. Julian could kick very much harder than he could! He decided to take Mischief off the table in case George smacked him. He put the little monkey under the table where Timmy was sitting quietly. Mischief immediately cuddled up to him, putting his little furry arms round the big dog's neck. Timmy sniffed him all over, and then gave him two or three licks. He was very fond of the naughty little monkey.

'What shall we do this afternoon?' asked Dick, when they had all helped Jenny to clear away and wash up. 'What about a swim in the sea? Is it warm enough?'

'Not really. But that doesn't matter, we always feel warm when we come out of the water and run about and then rub ourselves down,' said Anne. 'Jenny – do *you* feel like a swim?'

'Good gracious, no!' said Jenny, shivering at the thought. 'I'm a cold mortal, I am. The thought of going into that cold sea makes me shudder. If you want your towels, they are all in the airing cupboard. And don't you be late for tea, if you want any, because I've a lot of ironing to do afterwards.'

'Right, Jenny,' said Tinker, about to give her one of his 'squeezes' but thinking better of it when he saw her warning look. 'Julian, may I come with you to Kirrin Island tonight? I'd like a bit of fun.'

'You may not,' said Julian. 'Anyway, there won't be any fun.'

'There might be if Mr Wooh did hear George say she was taking those papers over,' said Tinker. 'He'd be waiting on the island – and you might be glad to have me with you!'

'I should *not* be glad to have you with me,' said Julian. 'You'd just be in the way. It would be much easier to look after myself than to see what *you* were up to all the time. I am going by myself. Please don't scowl at me like that, George.'

He got up from the table and went to look out of the window. 'Wind's died down a bit,' he said. 'I think I'll have a swim in an hour's time. If any of you others want to come, we'll go down together.'

They all went down to the beach after a while and swum, except Mischief, who put one small paw into the water, gave a howl and scampered back up the beach as fast as ever he could, afraid that Tinker might catch him and make him go in! Timmy went in, of course. He swam marvellously, and even gave Tinker a ride on his back, diving down when the boy felt heavy, so that Tinker suddenly found himself sprawling in the water! 'You wretch, Timmy!' yelled the boy. 'The water's gone up my nose. Wait till I catch you! I'll put *you* under!'

But he couldn't possibly catch old Timmy, who really enjoyed the joke. The big dog gave a joyful bark, and swam after George. How he loved being with them all!

The rest of the day went quickly. Jenny had a fine tea for them, with slices of ham, and salad, and fruit to end with, and said afterwards that she had time to play a game of Scrabble with them if they liked. Mischief sat on the table to watch.

'I don't mind you *watching*,' said Anne. 'But

you are NOT to scrabble, Mischief. You sent all my little ivory tiles on the floor last time we played, and I lost the game.'

Timmy watched gravely, sitting on a chair beside George. He simply could NOT understand what made the children play games like this when they could go for a nice long walk with him. They took pity on him when the game was over and went out for a two-mile walk along by the sea. How Timmy loved that!

'I shall cycle to Kirrin Village as soon as it's dark,' announced Julian. 'I suppose your boat is tied up in the usual place, George? I'm sorry I can't take you with me, but there *might* be a bit of danger, as we said. However I won't run into any if I can help it. I shan't feel comfortable until those secret papers are safely out of the way! You can give them to me just before I go, George.'

Anne suddenly yawned. 'Don't start too late or I shall fall asleep!' she said. 'It's getting dark already. All that swimming has made me feel tired!'

Dick yawned too. 'I'm jolly sleepy as well,' he said. 'I shall bed down in our tent as soon as you've gone, Ju. I'll see you off safely first, papers and all! You'd better go to your tent, too, girls – you look tired.'

'Right!' said Anne. 'You coming, George?'

'We'll all go,' said George. 'Come on, Tinker. Bet you I get over the fence and down to our tents first! Good night, Jenny. We're off!'

She and Anne and Tinker, with Timmy running behind, went off down the darkening garden. Dick and Julian helped Jenny to tidy up, and to draw all the curtains. 'Well, good night, Jenny,' said Dick. 'All you have to do is to lock the door behind us and go safely up to bed. We'll go down to our tents now. Sleep well!'

'Oh, I always do,' said Jenny. 'Look after yourselves now and don't get into any mischief! Hide those papers well, where nobody can find them!'

Julian and Dick went off down the garden, having heard Jenny carefully locking the door behind them.

Tinker and the girls were already over the fence, Mischief on Tinker's shoulder. Anne spoke anxiously to George. 'I do hope Julian will be all right going over to Kirrin Island,' she said. 'I wish he'd take Dick with him.'

'If he took anyone it should be *me*!' burst out George. 'It's *my* island!'

'Oh, don't be silly, George. The papers would be much safer with Julian,' said Anne. 'It would be an awful business for you, cycling by yourself to Kirrin, getting your boat into the water, and rowing over in the dark!'

'It would not!' said George. 'If Julian can do it, then so could I. You go into our tent, Anne, and get ready for bed. I'll come in a minute, after I've taken Timmy for a run.'

She waited till Anne had disappeared through the tent opening. Then she went quietly off by herself in the dark, Timmy trotting beside her, rather surprised.

Soon there came the sound of voices, as Julian and Dick reached the fence and leapt over it. They went to their tent and found

Tinker there, yawning and getting ready for bed.

Soon the three boys were all rolled up in their rugs, Mischief cuddled up to Tinker. After some time Julian sat up and looked at his watch, and then peeped out of the tent opening. 'Quite dark!' he said. 'But the moon's coming up, I see. I think I'll get the papers from George now, and set off on my bicycle to Kirrin. I can easily get it out of the shed.'

'You know where George keeps her boat,' said Dick. 'You won't have any difficulty in finding it. Got your torch, Ju?'

'Yes – and a new battery,' said Julian. 'Look!'

He switched on his torch. It gave a good, powerful beam. 'Shan't miss the island if I put *this* on!' he said. 'Now – I'll get those papers. Hey, George – I'm coming to your tent for the papers!'

He went over to the girls' tent. Anne was there, only half-awake. She blinked as Julian's torch shone into her eyes.

'George!' said Julian. 'Give me those papers

now, please – hallo – *Hey*, Anne – where is George?'

Anne started looking all round the tent. George's rugs were there, piled in an untidy heap; but there was no George – and no Timmy either!

'Oh, Ju! Do you know what George has done – she's slipped out with the precious papers – and taken Timmy too! She must have gone to fetch her bike, and ridden off to Kirrin to get her boat – and row over to Kirrin Island! Julian, whatever will happen if she rows over and finds somebody waiting to grab those papers from her?' Poor Anne was very near to tears.

'I could *shake* her!' said Julian, very angry indeed. 'Going off alone like that in the dark – cycling to Kirrin – rowing over to the island – and back! She must be mad! Suppose Mr Wooh and his friends are waiting there for her! The – silly – little – idiot!'

'Oh, Julian, quick! You and Dick get your cycles and try to catch her,' begged Anne. 'Oh please do! Anything might happen to her! Dear, silly old George! Thank goodness Timmy's gone with her.'

'Well, that's a blessing, anyway,' said Julian, still angry. 'He'll look after her as much as he can. Oh, I could shake George till her teeth rattled! I *thought* she was rather quiet tonight. Thinking out this plan, I suppose!'

He went up to the house with Dick and Tinker to tell Jenny about George, and then he and Dick at once went to get their bicycles. This was serious. George had no right to be out alone at night like this – and go rowing over to Kirrin Island – ESPECIALLY if there was any chance of someone lying in wait for her!

Jenny was very worried indeed. She watched the two boys cycling off in the dark. Tinker begged her to let him go too, but she wouldn't. 'You and Mischief would just be nuisances,' she said. 'Oh, won't I shake that rascal of a George when she gets back. What a girl! Well, well – thank goodness Timmy's with her. That dog's as good as half a dozen policemen!'

[16]

Night on Kirrin Island

It was certainly very dark when the half-moon
went behind the clouds. George was glad that
her bicycle lamp shone so brightly. The shadows in the hedges were deep and mysterious –
'as if they hid people ready to jump out at us,'
she said to Timmy. 'But you'd go for them at
once, wouldn't you, Timmy?'

Timmy was too much out of breath to bark
an answer. George was going pretty fast, and he
didn't mean to let her get out of sight. He was
sure she shouldn't be out by herself on a dark
night like this. He couldn't *imagine* why she
had suddenly taken it into her head to go for a
long night ride! He raced along, panting.

They met cars with dazzling headlamps, and
George had to keep pulling to the side. She was
terribly afraid that Timmy might be hit by one

of the cars. 'Oh dear – I'd never, never forgive myself if anything happened to Timmy,' she thought. 'I half wish I hadn't set out now. But I'm NOT going to let Julian hide anything on *my* island. That's my job, not his.' 'Timmy darling, PLEASE keep on my left side. You'll be safe then.'

So Timmy kept on her left, still mystified by this sudden journey out into the night. They came at last to Kirrin village, where windows were still lit here and there. Through the village and on to Kirrin Bay – ah, there was the bay! The half-moon slid out from behind a cloud and George saw the dark sea, shining here and there as the moonlight caught the crests of the waves.

'There's my island, look, Timmy,' said George, feeling a swelling of pride as she looked over the dark heaving sea to a darker stretch, which she knew was Kirrin Island. 'My very *own* island. Waiting for me tonight!'

'Woof,' said Timmy, rather quietly, because he really hadn't any breath to waste. *Now* what was George going to do? Why had she come out on this lonely ride without the others? Timmy was puzzled.

They came to the stretch of beach where boats were kept. George rode down a ramp to the beach, jumped off her bicycle, and put it by a bathing-hut in the deep shadows. No one would see it there. Then she went to stare over the sea at her island.

She had only looked for a moment or two when she clutched Timmy's collar, and gave an exclamation.

'TIMMY! There's a *light* on my island! Look, to the right there. Can you see it? Timmy, there's somebody camping there. How DARE they? It's *my* island and I don't allow *any*one on it unless they have my permission.'

Timmy looked – and yes, he could see the light too. Was it made by a camp fire – or a lantern? He couldn't tell. All he knew was that he didn't want George to go over there now. He pawed at her, trying to make her understand that he wanted her to go back home with him.

'No, Timmy. I'm *not* going back till I've found out who's there!' she said. 'It would be cowardly to turn back now. And if it's somebody waiting for me to turn up with the papers, they can think again. Look – I'm hiding them here under the tarpaulin in this boat. It would be idiotic to try and hide them on the island if there's someone there who *might* rob me of anything I've got – it might be one of the thieves who climbed into the tower room, and left some of the papers behind. If *he*'s waiting for me, he won't get any papers!'

George stuffed the parcel of papers under the tarpaulin as she spoke. 'It's Fisherman Connell's boat, called *Gypsy*,' she said, reading the name on the boat by the light of her torch. '*He* won't mind me hiding something in it!'

She covered up the papers with the tarpaulin, and then looked over to the island again. Yes – that light was still there. Anger welled up in George again, and she went to look for her own boat, which should be somewhere near where they were.

'Here it is,' she said to Timmy, who leapt in at once. She ordered him out for she had to pull the boat down to the water. Fortunately it was a small, light boat and as the tide was almost fully in, she didn't have very far to drag it. Timmy took hold of the rope with his teeth and helped too. At last it was on the water, bobbing gently about in the dim light of the half-moon. Timmy leapt in, and soon George was in too, though with very wet feet!

She took the oars and began to pull away from the shore. 'Tide's almost on the turn,' she told Timmy. 'It won't be too hard a row. Now we can find those campers and tell them what we think of them. You're to bark your very loudest and scare them, Timmy – in fact, you can chase them to their boat, if you like.'

Timmy answered with a small bark. He knew quite well that George didn't want him to make much noise. He thought it was odd that she was going over to her island tonight, all by herself. Why hadn't she taken the others? He was sure that Julian would be very cross!

'Now don't bark or whine, Timmy,' she said, in a whisper. 'We're almost at my landing place – but I'm going under those trees there, not landing here. I want to hide my boat.'

She guided the boat towards some trees whose branches overhung a tiny creek that ran a little way inland. She leapt out, and flung the mooring rope round the trunk of the nearest tree, and made it fast.

'There, little boat,' she said. 'You'll be safe there. No one will see you. Come on, Tim – we'll tackle those campers now.'

She turned to go, and then stopped. 'I wonder where *their* boat is,' she said. 'Let's have a look round, Timmy. It must be here somewhere.'

She soon found the boat lying on the sands, its rope thrown round a nearby rock. The tide was almost up to it. She grinned to herself. 'Timmy!' she whispered. 'I'm going to untie this boat and set it loose on the tide. It will soon be far away. Ha – what will those awful campers say?'

And, to Timmy's amazement, she undid the rope from the rock, rolled it up, and threw the coil inside the boat. Then she gave the boat a push – but it was still embedded in the wet sand.

'Never mind,' she said. 'Another ten minutes and the tide will be right under it – and then it will turn and take the boat with it!'

She began to make her way up the beach, Timmy close to her side. 'Now let's go after those campers, whoever they are,' she said. 'Where's their light gone? I can't see it now.'

But in a minute or two she saw it again. 'It's not from a camp fire – it's from a lantern of some sort,' she whispered to Timmy. 'We'll have to be careful now. Let's see if we can creep up behind them.'

The two of them made their way silently towards the middle of the little island. Here there was an old ruined castle – and there, in the courtyard of the castle, sitting in the midst of thick, overgrown weeds, were two men. George had her hand on Timmy's collar, and tugged it gently. He knew that meant, 'No barking, no growling, Tim,' and he stood perfectly still, the hackles on his neck rising fast.

The two men were playing cards by the light of a fairly powerful lantern, which they had set on a ruined stone wall. Timmy couldn't help giving a surprised growl when he saw one of them, but George hushed him at once.

Mr Wooh, the magician from the circus, was there, dealing out the cards! The other man she didn't know. He was well-dressed, and seemed bored. He flung down his cards as Timmy and George watched from a dark corner of the old castle, and spoke to his companion in an irritated voice.

'Well, whoever it is you said was bringing the rest of those papers here to the island doesn't seem to be turning up. The papers you've given me are good – very good – but of no use without the others. This scientist fellow you've stolen them from is a genius. If we get the complete set of papers, they will be worth a tremendous sum of money, which I can get for you – but without the other papers, there will be no money for you – the first set would be useless!'

'I tell you, someone will be here with them. I heard them say so,' said Mr Wooh in his stately voice.

'Who stole them – you?' asked the other man, shuffling the cards quickly.

'No. I did not steal them,' said Mr Wooh. 'Me, I keep my hands clean – I do not steal.'

The second man laughed. 'No. You let other people do your dirty work for you, don't you! Mr Wooh, the World's Most Wonderful Magician, does not soil his hands! He merely uses the hands of others – and charges enormous prices for the goods they steal. You're a cunning one, Mr Wooh. I wouldn't like you for an enemy! How did you manage to get the papers?'

'By using my eyes and my ears and my cunning,' answered Mr Wooh. 'They are better than most people's. So many people are stupid, my good friend.'

'I'm not your good friend,' said the other man. 'I've *got* to do business with you, Mr Wooh, but I wouldn't like to have you for a friend. I'd rather have that chimpanzee of yours! I don't even like playing cards with you! WHY doesn't this fellow come?'

George put her mouth to one of Timmy's ears. 'Timmy, I'm going to tell them to clear off my island,' she whispered furiously to the listening dog. 'Fancy fellows like *that* daring to set foot here – rascals and rogues! Don't come with me – wait till I call you, then if you have to rescue me, come at once!'

Leaving a most unwilling Timmy standing beside part of the old castle wall, she suddenly appeared before the two astonished men by the light of their lantern.

They leapt to their feet at once. 'It's the girl who's come – I shouldn't have thought that the boys would have let her,' said Mr Wooh, astonished. 'I am—'

'WHAT ARE YOU DOING ON MY ISLAND?' demanded George, angrily. 'It belongs to *me*.

I saw your light and came over with my dog. Be careful of him – he's big and strong and fierce. Clear off at once, or I'll report you to the police!'

'Easy, easy, now!' said Mr Wooh, standing very straight and looking immensely tall. 'So the boys sent *you* to hide the papers instead of daring to come themselves. How cowardly of them! Where are the papers? Give them to me.'

'I've hidden them,' said George. 'They're not very far away. You didn't think I'd be silly enough to come along to you with them in my hands when I saw your light and knew that people were here, did you? No – I've hidden them somewhere on the shore – where *you* won't find them. Now you just clear off, both of you!'

'A very brave and determined young lady!' said Mr Wooh, bowing solemnly to George.

'Do you mean to tell me that's a *girl*!' said the other man, amazed. 'Well! She's a plucky kid, I must say! Look here, kid, if you've got those papers, hand them over, and I'll give you a

whole lot of money which you can give to
Professor Hayling with my best wishes.'

'Come and get them,' said George, turning as
if to go. The two men looked at one another,
eyebrows raised. Mr Wooh nodded, and then
winked. If George had seen his face she would
have known what that wink meant. It meant
'let's humour this silly kid, follow her – see the
hiding place, snatch the papers and clear off in
our boat without paying a penny! But LOOK
OUT for the dog!'

George led the way, Timmy walking between
her and the two men. He was growling all the
time, deep down in his throat, as if to say 'Just
you lay a finger on George and I'll bite it off!'
The men took care not to go too near him! They
shone the lantern on him all the time, making
sure that he was not going to leap at them.

George led them to the shore, to the place
where they had left their boat. Mr Wooh gave a
cry. 'Where's our boat? It was tied to that rock!'

'Is this it over this ridge?' called George,
climbing up a steep bank that overhung the

water, which was now quite deep with the surging tide.

The men went to look – and then George gave them the surprise of their lives! She ran at Mr Wooh and gave him such a push that he fell right over the high bank into the sea below, landing with a yell and a terrific splash. George shouted a command to Timmy, who was now very excited, and the big dog did the same to the other man, leaping at him and pushing him over. He, too, shot over the ridge and fell into the sea with a splash. Timmy stood on the little cliff and barked madly, as excited as George.

'You'll have to swim to the shore of the mainland if you want to escape!' yelled George. 'The tide has taken away your boat – I set it loose! You'd better not get back on my island yet – Timmy's on the watch for you – and he'll fly at either of you if you try to set a foot on it again!'

Both men could swim, though not very well, and both were exceedingly angry and very frightened. They were sure they could never swim to the mainland – but how to get on the island to safety, they didn't know. That great, fierce dog was there, barking as if he wanted to bite them into small bits. Their boat had been set loose, there was no way to escape. They swam round in circles, not knowing what to do!

'I'm going back to the mainland now!' yelled George, climbing into her boat. 'I'll send the police to rescue you in the morning. You can get on my island now – but you're in for a VERY cold night! Good-bye!'

And off went George in her boat, with Timmy standing at the back, watching to make sure those men didn't swim after them. He gave George an admiring lick. She wasn't afraid of ANYTHING! He'd rather belong to *her* than to anyone else in the world. WOOF, WOOF, W-O-O-F!

[17]

And at last the mystery is solved!

George couldn't help singing loudly as she rowed back to the shore in her boat. Timmy joined in with a bark now and again. He was glad that George was so happy. He stood in the prow of the boat, wishing it was not night-time, so that he could see clearly where he was going. The moon clouded over, and the sea looked endless in the dark. Very few lights showed on the mainland at that time of night – just one or two from houses where people were still up.

Wait, though – what was that bright light suddenly shining out from the mainland? Was it someone trying to pick out their boat? Timmy barked at the light, and George, who, of course, was rowing with her back to the shore, shipped her oars for a moment and looked round.

'It's someone on the quay,' she said. 'Maybe a late fisherman. Good! He'll be able to help me drag my boat up out of the way of the tide!'

But it wasn't a fisherman. It was Julian and Dick. They had arrived about five minutes ago, and had looked at once for George's boat and hadn't found it. 'Bother! We're too late to stop her, then. She's gone over to the island!' said Julian and began to examine all the other tied-up boats to see if he could find one that he could borrow, belonging to a friend. *Somehow* they must get over to Kirrin Island, and rescue George. He felt sure she would be in danger of some kind.

Then suddenly the two boys heard the sounds of oars splashing not far out to sea. Well, if that was a fisherman coming home, maybe Julian could ask *him* to lend him his boat to go to Kirrin Island in. He could tell him that he was afraid his cousin might be in need of help.

Timmy, in George's boat, suddenly recognised the two boys when the moon swam out

from a cloud, and gave a delighted volley of
barks. George, wondering if it *was* Julian and
Dick, rowed as quickly as she could. She came
into shore, jumped out and began to drag in her
boat. The boys were beside her at once, and the
boat was soon in its usual place, carefully made
safe in case the tide was a high one.

'George!' said Julian, so overjoyed to see his
cousin safe and sound that he couldn't help
giving her a bear hug. 'You wicked girl! You
went to the island – just what I said you *weren't*
to do. You might have found the thieves on the
island, and *then* you would have been in trouble!'

'I *did* find them – but it's *they* who are in
trouble, not me!' said George. 'I saw a light
over there, took my boat and went over to the
island – and there they were – Mr Wooh the
Magician and another man – ON MY ISLAND!
Did you ever hear such cheek? They asked me
for the papers at once!'

'Oh, George – did you give them to the men?'
asked Dick.

'Of *course* not! I'd already hidden them where those men couldn't possibly find them. I wasn't idiotic enough to take them over to hide on the *island* when I saw somebody was there – probably waiting for me – *and* for the papers!' said George.

'But, George – if you knew somebody was there, why on *earth* did you risk going over to Kirrin Island then?' asked Julian, puzzled. 'It was a very dangerous thing to do.'

'I wanted to turn off whoever it was, of course,' said George. 'As if I'd allow just *any-one* on my island! It's mine, my very own, and I only allow people on it that I like. You know that.'

'I just NEVER know what you'll do next, George,' said Julian, patting Timmy on the head. 'How did you *dare* to go and tackle those men? Oh, I know Timmy was with you, but even so . . . why in the world didn't the men row after you, and ram your boat?'

'Well, you see, they couldn't,' said George. 'I found their boat, untied it, and set it adrift on the tide. It's probably half a mile away by now!'

The boys were so astonished that they couldn't even laugh at first. But then, when they thought of the two men marooned on Kirrin Island, their boat gone goodness knows where, they laughed till tears came into their eyes!

'George, I don't know how you can *think* of doing such things!' said Julian. 'Weren't the men furious?'

'I don't know,' said George. 'I didn't tell them about their boat. I pretended that I'd take them to where I'd hidden the papers – and then when we got on to a nice high ridge overlooking the sea, they looked over it to see if their boat was all right, and I gave Mr Wooh a jolly good push, and Timmy leapt at the man with him – and in they went – SPLASH! SPLASH!'

Julian really *had* to sit down and have another bout of laughing till the stitch in his side grew so bad that he was forced to get up and walk about. George suddenly saw the funny side of it all too, and she began to laugh as heartily as Julian. Dick joined in as well, and Timmy barked madly, enjoying the fun.

'Oh dear!' said Julian, feeling weak with laughter, 'and then I suppose you said a polite farewell and left them to their fate?'

'Well, actually I yelled out to tell them I'd send the police to rescue them in the morning,' said George. 'I'm afraid they'll both spend a very uncomfortable night – they were soaking wet, you see!'

'George – I'm beginning to think it was a good thing *you* went with the papers to the island, and not me, after all,' said Julian, 'I should *never* have thought of doing all the things you did – pushing the men into the sea – really, how *could* you and Timmy dare to do such things? And setting their boat loose! What on earth will the police say when we tell them?'

'I don't think we'd better tell them, had we?' said George. 'I mean – they might think I'd gone too far. Anyway, why not let the two men kick their heels on the island all night, and we'll decide what to do about the police in the morning. It's funny – I suddenly feel awfully tired.'

'I bet you do!' said Dick. 'Come on, let's get our bikes. Oh, and those precious papers – where are they?'

'Under the tarpaulin in Fisherman Connell's boat,' said George, and suddenly gave the most enormous yawn. 'I hid them there.'

'I'll get them,' said Julian. 'Then off we go back to Big Hollow House. The others will be getting awfully worried by now!'

He found the papers in the fishing boat and then the three of them rode off quickly along the road from Kirrin to Big Hollow, Timmy running behind them. Julian kept laughing to himself. George was amazing! Fancy tackling those two fellows like that – pushing them into the water, and setting their boat adrift. Julian was sure he would never have thought of doing such daring things himself.

At last they were back at the tents, and the

others crowded round them to hear what had
happened. Anne looked very white. Jenny was
with her, comforting her – she had *just* made up
her mind to telephone the police, and was *most*
relieved to see George again.

'We'll tell you all the details in the morning,'
said Julian. 'But all I'll say now is that the
papers are safe all right, here in my pocket –
the thieves were probably Mr Wooh and another man. They were on the island tonight,
waiting for George. They *had* overheard what
she said in the tent! However, George and
Timmy pushed them both into the water and
set their boat adrift, so things are settling down
nicely! They will have to spend the night on the
island, cold and wet through!'

'*George* did all that!' said Jenny, amazed.
'*Well!* I never knew she was so *dangerous!*
Good gracious! I feel right-down scared of
her! Settle down to sleep in your tent, dear –
you look tired out!'

George was glad to flop down on her rugs.
Now that the excitement was all over she felt

too sleepy for words! She fell asleep at once – but Julian and Dick didn't. They lay awake for some time, chuckling over George's deeds of daring. What a cousin to have!

When they were up at the house at breakfast next morning, Jeremy came up the garden and put his head in at the dining-room window.

'Hey!' he said. 'Mr Wooh's not in his tent this morning! He's disappeared! And poor old Charlie the Chimp is too miserable for words.'

'Ah – we can tell you *exactly* where Mr Wooh is,' said Julian. 'But – wait a bit, Tinker, where are you going? You haven't finished your—'

But Tinker had gone off with Jeremy at top speed! He was very fond of Charlie. Oh dear, would the chimpanzee weep for his master and refuse to take his food? Tinker called Mischief and they both ran down to the fence with Jeremy and climbed over it. Tinker went straight to Charlie's cage. The chimpanzee sat with his head in his hands, rocking himself to and fro, making sad, crying noises.

'Let's get into the cage with him,' said Tinker.

'He'll like to be comforted. He must be missing Mr Wooh very, very much.'

They crawled into the cage and sat down in the straw, each putting an arm round the sad chimpanzee. Old Grandad was very surprised to see them both there.

'Don't know what's happened to Mr Wooh,' he said. 'Didn't come home last night! Here, Jeremy, you come on out. I can't spare you to cry over Charlie all morning. He'll soon perk up. *You* can stay with him, Tinker, if you like.'

Jeremy crawled out of the cage and went off crossly. Tinker sat with his arm round Charlie, wishing he didn't look so terribly sad. As he sat there, he heard a funny little noise going on all the time. 'Tick-tick-tick-ticka-ticka-tick-tick-tick-tick-ticka-ticka-tick. 'Sounds like a watch or something,' said Tinker, and scrabbled about in the straw. Perhaps Mr Wooh's big gold watch had fallen into Charlie's cage? His hand felt something small and round and smooth at the bottom of the cage. He riffled away the thick straw, and drew out the object underneath it. He stared and stared at it in the utmost surprise. Charlie saw him looking at it, snatched it away and hid it in the straw again. He made a few growly noises as if he were angry.

'Charlie, *where* did you get that little clock?' said Tinker. 'Oh, CHARLIE! Well, as you're so sad this morning, I'll give it to you for your very own. Just to cheer you up. But oh, Charlie, I *am* surprised at you!'

He slid out of the cage and went back over the fence and into his own garden. Up the path he ran and burst into the dining-room, where the others were still finishing their breakfast.

'What's up?' said Dick.

'Listen! I know who the thief was who climbed in at the tower window . . . I KNOW WHO HE WAS!' cried Tinker, almost shouting in his excitement.

'WHO?' said everyone, in amazement.

'It was CHARLIE THE CHIMP!' said Tinker. 'Why didn't we think of him before? He can climb anything! It would be quite easy for him to swing himself up that rough-stoned wall, hanging on to the bits of creeper here and there – and to the uneven stones – and climb through the window into the tower room, collect all the papers he could hold – and climb down again – *slither* down again, probably . . .'

'THAT must have been the slithering sound I heard!' said Jenny. 'I *told* you I heard a queer slithering noise!'

'And the whispering you heard must have been Mr Wooh trying to make him go up the tower wall and into the window!' said Julian. 'Gosh – I bet poor old Charlie's been taught to get into all sorts of windows and take whatever he sees. Mr Wooh must have known Tinker's father worked out all his ideas up in the tower.'

'Wooh could easily teach him to take papers,' said Julian. 'But there were, of course, too many for old Charlie in the tower room. He wouldn't be able to carry them *all* in his front paws, for he needed *all* his paws to climb down that steep wall – so he must have crammed as many as he could into his mouth – and dropped the rest under the table! Charlie the Chimp – well! Who would have thought *he* could be the thief!'

'Wait a bit – how on earth do you know it was Charlie?' said Dick. 'Nobody saw him. It was at night.'

'Well, I *do* know it was Charlie,' said Tinker. 'You remember that dear little clock on the tower room mantelpiece? Well, it disappeared on the night when those papers were stolen – and *I* found it hidden in the straw in Charlie's cage this morning! He snatched it away from me, and almost cried – so I let him keep it! It was ticking loudly just like it always did. It was the loud ticking that told me it was there in the cage!'

'Who wound it up at nights, to keep it going?' said Julian, at once, most astonished.

'Charlie, I suppose,' said Tinker. 'He's very clever with his paws! The clock was quite safe, hidden in his cage. Nobody would be likely to get into the chimp's cage and sit there with him – but *I* did this morning, and that's how I found it. I heard it ticking, you see. I bet old Charlie was clever enough to pop his precious clock into his mouth when he saw any of the men coming to clean out his cage!'

'Well, I'm blessed!' said Jenny. 'How was it that Mr Wooh never saw him bringing it along with the papers that night, when he stole them?'

'Well, as Tinker told you – my guess is that old Charlie must have put the little clock in his mouth then, along with the papers,' said Dick. 'He needed all his four paws, climbing – or rather *slithering* down that wall – and he's got a jolly big mouth! You should see what a lot of food he can stuff into it!'

'Yes. And Mr Wooh would take the papers, of course – Charlie would just take them from his mouth and hand them to him – but he'd be crafty enough to keep his precious new toy hidden in his mouth! Poor old Charlie! Can't you see him listening to the clock, and cuddling it – like a child with a new toy!' said George.

'He sounded exactly as if he were crying this morning,' said Tinker. 'I couldn't bear it. Poor old Charlie! He couldn't understand *why* Mr Wooh didn't go and see him today. He was *so* miserable!'

'I think we'll *have* to get the police along now,' said Julian. 'Not only to catch Mr Wooh and his friend, left so conveniently marooned by George on her island – but also because Mr Wooh should be charged with stealing your father's irreplaceable charts and diagrams, Tinker. Goodness knows what else he has taught poor old Charlie to steal. I bet he's sent the chimp into a lot of houses, and up many walls, and into many windows.'

'Yes. There's probably been a trail of robberies wherever the circus went,' said Jenny. 'And many innocent people must have been suspected.'

'What a shame!' said Anne. 'But, oh dear – if Mr Wooh goes to prison, whatever will become of poor old Charlie the Chimp?'

'I bet Jeremy will take him,' said Tinker. 'He loves him, and old Charlie adores Jeremy! He'll be all right with Jeremy and old Grandad!'

'Well, Tinker, I think you'd better go and tell your father all this,' said Jenny. 'I know he's busy – he always is – but this is a thing *he* ought to deal with and nobody else. If you'd like to fetch him, George could tell him the whole story – and then I rather guess *he'll* ring up the police – and Mr Wooh will find himself in a whole lot of trouble.'

So there goes Tinker, with Mischief on his shoulder, to find his father, down the hall – up the stairs – along the landing – into his father's bedroom . . . R-r-r-r-r-r-r-r-r! Tinker, you sound like a motor-scooter going up a steep hill! PARP-PARP! *Don't* hoot like that, you'll make your father so angry that he won't listen to a word you say!

But the Professor *did* listen – and soon Jenny heard him telephoning the police. They're coming straight away, and that means that Mr Wooh the Magician is in for a most unpleasant time, and his magic won't help him at all! He'll have to give back the papers that he made Charlie steal – and plenty of other things,

too! There he is, marooned on the island, quite
unable to escape, waiting fearfully with his
companion, for the police!'

'Another adventure over?' said George, with
a regretful sigh. 'And a jolly exciting one too!
I'm glad you solved the mystery, Tinker – it was
clever of you to find the little tower room clock.
I bet Mr Wooh wouldn't have let Charlie keep
it, if he'd known he'd taken it from the tower
room! Poor old Charlie the Chimp!'

'I'm just wondering if Dad would let me keep
Charlie here, while Mr Wooh is in prison,'
began Tinker, and stopped as Jenny gave a
horrified shriek.

'*Tinker!* If you so much as *mention* that idea
to your father, I'll walk straight out of this
house and NEVER COME BACK!' said Jenny.
'That chimp would be in my kitchen all day
long – oh yes, he would – and things would be
disappearing out of my larder, and my cupboards, and my drawers, and he'd dance up
and down and scream at me if I so much as said
a word, and . . .'

'All right, dear, dear Jenny, I won't ask for Charlie, honest I won't,' said Tinker. 'I do love you a *bit* more than I'd love a chimp – but think what a companion he would be for Mischief!'

'I'm not thinking anything of the sort!' said Jenny. 'And what about you taking a bit of notice of that monkey of yours – bless us all if he hasn't helped himself to half that jar of jam – just *look* at his sticky face! Oh, what a week this has been, what with chimps and monkeys and children and robberies, and George disappearing, and all!'

'Dear old Jenny,' said George, laughing as she went off into the kitchen. 'What an exciting time we've had! I really did enjoy every minute of it!'

So did we, George. Hurry up and fall into another adventure. We are longing to hear what you and the others will be up to next. How we wish we could join you! Good-bye for now – and take care of yourselves, Five. Good luck!